T0248240

ANIMALS OF THE ALPINE FRONT

Also by Don Zancanella

Western Electric
Concord
A Storm in the Stars

ANIMALS OF THE ALPINE FRONT

A Novel

Don Zancanella

Delphinium Books

ANIMALS OF THE ALPINE FRONT

Printed in the United States of America

For information, address DELPHINIUM BOOKS, INC.,
1250 4th Street Suite 5th Floor
Santa Monica, California 90401

Library of Congress Cataloguing-in-Publication Data is
available on request.
ISBN 978-1-953002-40-2
$PrintCode

Jacket and interior design by Colin Dockrill, AIGA

For Paul and Jean

PART I

1913: Ulfano

In a village northeast of Trento, a man in a green hat was going from house to house. When Teresa saw him, she was feeding the chickens. At first she thought he was a peddler. Then she noticed the insignia on his coat and ran inside.

"We're next," she told her mother as she concealed herself behind the cupboard. They weren't used to being called on by officials, but her mother wasn't alarmed. With her usual forthrightness, she threw open the door before the man could knock.

"Good day," he said. "I'm conducting a census. Only a few questions, I promise to be brief."

"A census? For what purpose?" Teresa's mother asked.

"To gather information about those who live in this sector. It's a necessity if the government is to serve its citizens well."

"Which government? Vienna or Rome?"

"Neither. I represent la Provincia. Do you wish to see my badge?" He sounded irritated, as though he'd been asked to explain himself too many times before. But since their little village sat precisely on the border between Italy and the empire of Austria-Hungary, civil servants had to tolerate such queries. Indeed, it had become a kind of game.

"I don't care about your badge," her mother said. "Just ask your questions and be on your way." From her hiding place

Teresa was unable to see them; nonetheless, she knew two things: The man wanted to come inside, and her mother was blocking the door. It wasn't that her mother felt threatened; it was that she didn't like having her day disrupted, especially by someone who showed up unannounced. In her mother's view, the farther into the house the man came, the more he could inconvenience her. As expected, she won the battle, and he had no choice but to continue from where he stood.

"Question one: What is your name?"

"Anna Miori."

"Question two: Who else lives in this house and what are their names?"

"Only my daughter, Teresa Miori."

"Question three: Which languages are spoken in the house?"

"What do you think? The language that is presently coming out of my mouth."

"I shall mark Italian," he said.

"Question four: How are you employed?"

"Look around you. Even an idiota can see." And so it went.

After the man had departed, Teresa's mother said, "You can come out now. I don't know why you're hiding." A moment later, she added, "It doesn't matter where he's from. We're so far up in the mountains, no one cares about us. But I suppose the poor fellow has to do his job."

Since Teresa had never been more than a few kilometers from Ulfano, she found it difficult to comprehend how remote their village actually was, much less what it meant to be governed by Vienna or Rome. However, some Ulfano residents worked in Trento and returned with stories. From these she had constructed a picture of the outside world: carts and wagons and motorcars crowding the streets; countless shops, some of which existed to sell only a single item such as shoes or sweets or clocks; houses as large as castles; and a train station from which one could embark upon a journey to anywhere in the world. Not that she had much interest in taking a train to some distant place. She didn't mind an occasional walk to another village, but she wasn't the sort of person who dreamed of travel, who felt the need to wander and explore. Even if she had been, there was the problem of the ticket—buying one would take money, which she did not have. With thoughts like these in her head, she went out to milk Gilda, who was waiting patiently in her stall.

That evening an early autumn snowstorm swept across the Dolomites. As night descended, she and her mother banked the fire, ate a supper of polenta and hot milk, and climbed into the bed they shared. The wind struck the house with such force, its timbers groaned. During a pause between gusts, Teresa spoke.

"When the man asked you how many people live here, why did you say two?"

"What a ridiculous question. I said two because your father is never coming back."

Teresa rolled over to face the wall. Though she'd known what her mother's reply would be, she wanted to hear it anyway. She disliked uncertainty and preferred to be told the truth, even if it meant having her fears confirmed. When her father left, she was twelve years old; now she was fifteen. Did three years equal never coming back? Yes, it probably did.

"Tell me a story about when you were a girl."

"Not now. Say a prayer instead."

Sometimes she wanted to pinch her mother. Pinch her and say, "Listen to me. I say things for a reason." But the two of them got along well enough, and why start something, especially when it was time to sleep.

In the morning, they opened the shutters and looked out

upon the snow. Such a change it was from the day before, when everything had been green. Teresa got up and dressed in her warmest clothes. As she had no proper boots, she pulled an old pair of her father's wool socks right over her shoes. Then once again she went out to care for Gilda. She resented that theirs was one of the few dwellings in the village without an attached barn. Yet if she understood one thing, it was that no matter the weather, no matter how she felt, the cow must be fed and milked. From the cow she went to the chickens, checking to make sure they were safe inside the pollaio. Finding their water frozen, she broke the ice and scooped out the floating shards.

By the time she was done, the snow had stopped falling but the wind still swirled it about. White plumes rose, white swells tumbled, and as she made her way back to the house, there were moments when she could see nothing at all. Then, from the corner of her eye, she spied something moving, something dark and low to the ground. Curious and a bit fearful, she stopped and waited for the clouds of snow to part.

Il Cane

As soon as Teresa was back inside, she said, "Mama, I saw a wolf."

Glancing up from her mending, her mother shook her head. "There haven't been wolves in these mountains for years. Surely it was a dog."

"If it's a dog, it must be hungry. I should put out some food."

Her mother frowned. "We don't need a stray around here. Best to leave it alone."

But Teresa was seldom easily dissuaded. She wanted what she wanted and, in this matter as in many others, refused to

4

give up. She had once asked her father to build her a small wagon like one that belonged to a boy in the village. At first he said yes, but each day thereafter he had an excuse—*I don't have enough wood. Girls don't pull wagons. What would I use for wheels?* Still, she refused to stop asking, and one morning he got out his tools and set to work. So she wasn't surprised when her mother wearied of being pestered about the dog. "Do as you please," she said. "There's still a little meat from Sunday's supper. If the beast bites you, don't expect me to salve your wounds."

With no further discussion, Teresa prepared the food and opened the door. Taking five quick steps, she set the plate on the ground and scurried back inside. Chased by the frigid wind.

"Is it still there?" her mother asked, her tone of voice betraying more interest than had been suggested by their earlier exchange.

"I'm not sure. It's getting dark. I think I saw its eyes."

"That fellow who lives by the mill has dogs. It could belong to him."

"Severino? I don't think so. He keeps them locked in a pen."

Her mother was chopping vegetables for soup. Teresa, never one to stand idle, fetched the broom and began to sweep. Soon, her mother spoke again.

"You're planning to catch it?"

"Maybe."

"You probably scared it off."

No, she had not; in the morning the plate was clean.

She continued to put out food for the next several days, and every bit disappeared. Late at night, when she was in bed, she could picture the dog crouched outside, awaiting its next meal. Teresa herself had never faced real hunger, but there had been times when she'd been able to tell from her mother's tone of voice that once she was done with the potato she was eating, she shouldn't ask for more.

Then the weather turned, the snow began to melt, and she expected her feeding of the dog to come to an end. But the following morning there it stood, with neither darkness nor snow to obscure her view. It obviously wasn't a wolf—its muzzle was square rather than tapered, its ears were folded, and its rough coat consisted of patches of brown and white with only a hint of wolfish gray. She thought it might be the kind of herding dog known as a cane di oropa, although this one wouldn't be much good for herding—its left eye was clouded and it had a crooked leg. That evening, she watched from the cowshed as the dog bolted its supper. Then she went back inside.

"You're not still feeding that thing, are you?" her mother said.

"You told me I could. It hasn't done any harm."

When Teresa and her mother argued, they seldom raised their voices. In fact, it was the opposite, their remarks diminishing in volume until they were hissing at each other like a pair of indignant snakes. A result, perhaps, of living in such a small house. Her father had been gone so long, she had difficulty remembering if things had been different when he was there. Was her mother more short-tempered now, or had she actually become more agreeable? If her father had stayed, would her mother be arguing with him while Teresa stood back and observed?

Her mother said, "You'd better stop giving that animal a reason to visit or it will never go away."

Teresa didn't follow her mother's advice. Instead, she began testing how close she could get to the dog. When it seemed to have lost all fear, she approached and stroked its fur. She could feel its ribs and hip bones. If she hadn't started feeding the poor thing, it wouldn't have survived. Since the dog was male, she decided to name it Allucio, after Allucio of Campigliano, a saint the village priest, Don Tomasi, admired. If Teresa remembered correctly, St. Allucio was a shepherd who built shelters on mountain passes. He was known as a liberator of captives and helped end a war between two city-states. She considered Don Tomasi a pompous fool, but there was no reason she couldn't name the dog after his favorite saint.

Teresa had always been fond of animals, domestic as well as wild. When she was very young, she would visit the cow even after it had been milked. Although they no longer owned a horse, she knew the location of every one in the vicinity and was never bashful about asking if she could ride. And while most children in the village considered the killing of a pig an occasion for celebration, she absented herself from such events, claiming illness if anyone inquired. She could think of nothing worse than seeing an animal in pain. Why she had such feelings, she wasn't sure. For most people, riding a horse was a way to get from one place to another. For her, it was being in the company of the horse that mattered. She knew animals were kept because they were useful, but was it too much to ask that they be treated well?

In an effort to placate her mother, she said, "I will teach the dog to guard our house." But she had no intention of doing so. Why bother? Ulfano was free of crime.

Then one day, when her mother was out in the garden, Teresa invited Allucio inside. After inspecting the premises briefly, he turned around, turned around again, and curled up near the hearth. When her mother came back, she saw the dog, glanced at Teresa, and went about her work. Teresa wasn't foolish enough to think she'd somehow outflanked her mother. If the dog caused any trouble, he'd be sleeping outdoors again.

But he didn't, and soon Teresa and Allucio had become fast friends. She liked how he followed her as she went about doing her chores. She also liked taking the dog with her when she walked through the village—even though her mother's friend Oriana said, "No young man will want a girl with a dog. It makes you seem eccentric."

"Do you consider me eccentric?" Teresa asked.

Oriana thought for a moment. "Not necessarily, but to woo a man, you must make a good first impression. Show off your hair—it's your best feature. The dog should stay at home. Why put your prospects at risk?"

Teresa considered saying, "Wooing a man is the furthest thing from my mind." Instead she offered a proverb: *Chi ama me, ama il mio cane.* Whoever loves me, loves my dog.

If nothing else, the dog gave Teresa and her mother something to talk about. After her father went away, the house had fallen silent. But now they could discuss the amusing way Allucio stretched when he got up from a nap and what he might be thinking as he observed them from his rug by the hearth. Her father ran off with a widow from the next village over. It was rumored they'd gone to Rome.

Carlo

On the other side of the world, in a mining camp in the Colorado mountains, Carlo Coltura worked in his brothers' saloon. His father, a stone mason, had laid the saloon's foundation, using limestone he quarried himself, while his brothers had gone all the way to Omaha to buy a zinc-topped bar. Upon its completion, the Coltura Brothers Saloon was considered one of the few buildings that might endure in a mining camp made mostly from sheets of canvas and unpainted wood.

Since Joe and Salvatore were more than ten years older than Carlo, they seemed less like brothers than uncles—that is, like grown men. What people noticed about them first was their size. Joe towered over nearly every fellow in the camp, while Salvatore reminded people of a grizzly bear, even to his shambling walk.

Carlo was no grizzly bear and probably never would be. Joe compared him to a sapling: taller by the day but still more stick than tree. He admired his brothers and thought perhaps he'd be invited to help run the saloon when he was older. For now, however, he did as he was told.

His chores included wiping tables, sweeping the floor, and disposing of the foul contents of a brass cuspidor that sat at the end of the bar. If he was lucky enough to finish early, he went fishing or scavenged around the mouths of abandoned mine shafts. Occasionally, he found something of value, a long piece of chain or a serviceable shovel, which he then tried to sell. They were never worth much money, but it seemed a shame to let good tools sit out in the weather and rust.

Today, when he was done working, he said goodbye to his brothers and proceeded up the street and into the nearby hills. Walking at a brisk pace, he went past the boiler works, past the ore-crushing machine known as the slow-drop stamper, and through the scattering of miner's shacks on the west side of the valley. As he left the camp behind, an elderly mule in a small corral caught sight of him and brayed. "Same to you," Carlo said.

A little farther on, he crossed a dry gulch where some Cornishmen were endeavoring, in violation of common practice, to tunnel straight into solid rock. His father had warned him to avoid them, not because there was anything wrong with Cornishmen but because it was foolhardy to attempt such a difficult and dangerous method of mining gold.

From inside the shaft came the sound of digging, the tinks and thunks of hammers on chisels, the scraping of shovels, some words in Cornish and some in English, followed by a burst of laughter that turned into a cough. A moment later, two of the Cornishmen emerged pushing a cart filled with fragments of stone, what miners called muck. One of them scowled at him and the other just looked tired. When they were done emptying the cart onto the pile of rubble beside the entrance, the scowling one said, "What are you looking at?"

"You need some help? I work for two-bits an hour." Despite his father's warning, he didn't think it could hurt to assist them for an afternoon. They'd been digging for weeks, and as far as Carlo knew, there had been no mishaps. The fact was his father couldn't resist criticizing methods different from his own, whether or not those methods were flawed.

But the tired one said, "If I can do the job myself, why would I pay you?"

Unable to refute such logic, Carlo shrugged and continued on his way. A few yards down the dusty path, he heard a low rumble and felt the ground convulse beneath his feet. By the time he turned, the rumble had become a roar and a cloud of dust was pouring from the mine. The shaft was collapsing. Though he'd been told about such disasters, he had never expected to be present when one occurred.

A second roar followed, louder than the first, and the two men he'd seen earlier came stumbling out. Carlo stepped toward them but they waved him off and pointed in the direction of the camp. He understood. There were others still trapped inside and they wanted him to sound the alarm. He ran as fast as he could, shouting for help as he went. When he reached the saloon, he called for his brothers, then crossed the road to ring the emergency bell that hung from an iron stanchion in front of the union hall.

Minutes later he was following his brothers and six other men back to the Cornishmen's mine, where they began removing debris. Soon more men came, and they all started digging, digging, digging without pause until darkness came. Then lanterns were lit and a few of the wives brought sandwiches and water so they could work through the night. But it was to no avail. Three lifeless bodies were retrieved, their crushed and mutilated faces causing Carlo to turn away. Two others were buried beneath so much rock that a difficult decision was made: The mine shaft would be their grave.

Although Carlo wasn't allowed inside the shaft to help dig, he did what he could to assist. When tools broke, he brought new ones; when the rubble at the entrance began to impede the work, he helped haul it away, and during the night he built a fire in an empty coal oil tin so the men could warm their hands.

His father didn't participate in the rescue because he was off prospecting for gold in the hills to the south. Therefore, when Carlo got home, the cabin was empty. He had no mother, not since he was four years old. He seldom thought about her death but, given the day's events, did so now. That spring she had gone searching for mushrooms, intent on finding some like the ones she knew from her girlhood in the mountains of Italy. Also, sorrel and wild chives. When she returned, she cooked the mushrooms, along with chives and a silver dollar, which she'd always been told would turn black if the mushrooms weren't safe to eat. Just as she hoped, the dollar remained silver, but within an hour she was having cramps and vomiting, and two days later she was dead. She said she'd taken only two bites of the mushrooms to see if they needed salt. Carlo had been too young to understand what had happened. One day he had a mother and the next day she was gone.

He wondered if any of the dead Cornishmen had children and, if they did, who was left to care for them at home. After his mother died, he still had a father, but his father was distant and ill-tempered. At least he had his brothers. They weren't an adequate substitute for his mother, but when death visited your family, you had to make do with whatever remained.

Casting these mournful thoughts aside, Carlo left the cabin and stepped out into the darkness. In the distance, the old mule brayed, dogs barked in reply, and as he counted his blessings—suppose the Cornishmen had hired him and he'd followed them underground?—he returned to the saloon.

Trento

Teresa hadn't been completely surprised by her father's betrayal. He'd always been a layabout, a philanderer, occasionally even a drunk. As she got older, she grew to understand how much his behavior hurt her mother. It was one thing to avoid work but quite another to make the lives of those close to you more difficult. He took as few jobs as possible, most often seasonal ones such as cutting wood or picking apples, and usually quit after a few weeks. Then he would spend his time in the village bar reading the newspaper and flirting with whatever girl was working there that day. If they were lucky, he went hunting with a borrowed gun and came home with a hare. He never made much money, but as she learned after he left, not much was better than none. She wondered how long they would be able to get by with only a garden, some chickens, and a cow.

Her mother must have been having similar thoughts because one spring morning she told Teresa she wanted her to go to work in Trento, a day's walk away. At first Teresa found the idea appealing. She would get to live in a city and she wasn't opposed to that. Yet the more she considered it, the more she was filled with apprehension. Would she be lonely? Would her employer treat her well?

"Do I have to?" she said. She was beginning to realize they weren't discussing some small matter. She was being asked to leave her home. Her mother explained that she wasn't thinking only about the money Teresa would earn.

"If you stay here, you'll marry a boy from the village. Is there one you have your eye on perhaps?"

"No!" she said, vigorously shaking her head.

"Of course not. And it's to your credit. Most of them are useless louts, as my own experience shows."

Teresa knew exactly the kind of men her mother was talking about and couldn't help but laugh.

So the arrangements were made. Letters traveled back and forth between her mother and a woman who served as an agent for the employment of girls like her. At a certain point it occurred to Teresa that Allucio couldn't come along. Her living quarters were to be in her new employer's house and it wasn't even worth asking if she could bring a dog. To be separated from him would be terrible for them both. Allucio would wonder what had become of her and it would be impossible to explain. But she had no choice. She must go.

"You can return home often," her mother said. "Trento isn't far."

She began to cry. Peering into Allucio's one good eye, she saw a look of concern. "I'm so sorry," she sobbed. Then she gathered in her emotions and began pretending all would be well. That was what you did to protect those in your care.

Her mother found her a ride to Trento with a man who was going there to sell his cheese. Their goodbyes were unsentimental. "After all," said her mother, "you're not going to Egypt." Her mother sometimes treated serious matters in a lighthearted manner. Only recently had Teresa begun to see how wise it could be to approach life that way.

"If I don't like it, I'll quit and come home."

"Of course. You always end up doing as you please."

When the man arrived, she climbed into his wagon, fixed her gaze on the horns of his ox, and never once looked back. "You'll find I'm easy to travel with because I never complain," he told her as they set out. Then, for the next three hours, he complained about how much it cost him to produce his cheese, how little his customers were willing to pay, his crooked competitors, and the ache in his back that came from all the stirring and pouring and lifting and carrying the making of cheese required. "Everyone thinks cheesemakers have it easy," he said. "Not so, not so at all."

When at last they arrived in Trento, she discovered it was just as she had imagined, just as everyone said: The houses were large and the streets wide and paved with stones. Every shop had an attractive sign explaining what was sold inside. Delivery boys dashed about as if they were running a race. Motorized vehicles nearly outnumbered the horse-drawn ones and had engines that growled like beasts. And at the center of the city was the great duomo, as imposing as the mountains she'd left behind, but made by the hands of men.

She took a special interest in what the ladies wore. Their dresses were sleek and colorful, while their hats, adorned with feathers and flowers, were clearly made to be admired rather than to protect the wearer from the sun. As for Teresa, she wore a simple woolen dress, an apron with pockets, a headscarf, ankle socks, and sturdy black shoes. No one would admire her.

Her job was to be the cook's helper in the home of the

Benedetti family. A villa of some distinction, it had three stories, a large veranda, and electrified lamps throughout. Surrounding the villa were extensive grounds, with a garden behind an iron fence, and stables where Signor Benedetti kept not only horses but, she was told, a shiny new motorcar. It occurred to Teresa that her mother would consider such a machine an extravagance while her father would believe owning it to be a sign of good character. How two such different people ended up together was a mystery she doubted she'd ever solve.

To her surprise, she was given her own room, with a bed, a chair, a washstand, and a built-in shelf. Although she wasn't sure how she'd use the shelf, she liked being able to do with it as she pleased. Across from the bed was a window that looked out on a corner of the garden, as well as a row of hooks on which to hang her clothes. By the time she was done unpacking her bag, a feeling of independence had descended upon her. Here she was, with a paying position and a private room to sleep in.

She expected the kitchen to have a large staff but soon discovered it was just herself and Frau Merz, a stout, round-faced woman who, when Teresa told her she had no experience working in a kitchen except that of helping her own mother, said, "I have modest expectations. The ways your mother taught you should be adequate. And if not, I'll show you how we do it here." Other employees included a sullen girl named Silvia, who cleaned the rooms upstairs, a stable boy, and a gardener who cared for the villa's extensive grounds.

One thing Trento had in common with Ulfano was that it seemed uncertain of its identity. It was ruled by Austria-Hungary yet most people spoke Italian. The signs on buildings and streets were in German or Italian or both. No doubt some newcomers found this disconcerting, but Teresa was used to such an arrangement. What did it matter if the Italians called it Trento while the Austrians called it Trent?

Some Luck

On a blustery day in March, Carlo returned from an afternoon of scavenging and hiking in the nearby hills to find his father waiting for him at home.

"Run and get your brothers," he snapped. "I need to talk to them." Carlo was taken aback. Although his father often gave him sharply worded orders, asking his brothers to leave the saloon unattended was an exceptional request.

"Right now?"

"Yes, go!" he said, raising his hand in a motion that meant, *I don't want to hit you, but if you test me, I will.*

With no further hesitation, Carlo hurried down the hill to the saloon, went in the back door, and found Joe behind the bar.

"Papa wants to see you," he said. "Sal, too."

"About what?"

"I don't know. I tried to tell him you're busy. He said it couldn't wait."

Joe shook his head and then asked one of the customers if he'd watch the place for a while. Sal emerged from the storeroom and the three of them strode toward home.

"How did he look?" Sal asked.

"What do you mean? Like he always does." He pictured his father: his furrowed brow, his black mustache, and beneath it, his perpetual frown.

"Did something bad happen?"

"I don't know. He just told me to bring you home."

When they entered the cabin, their father was pacing and his mouth was moving as if he'd been talking to himself. Now he stopped in the middle of the room. Joe said, "So here we are. What did you want us for?" Carlo was afraid of his father but wasn't sure if his brothers feared him or simply tolerated his bad temper because it was the way he'd always been. While the days when his father could physically intimidate Joe and Sal were long past, he still ruled the house.

"I found a seam. A good one. One that's going to pay." He opened his hand to reveal a chunk of reddish quartz, the kind indicative of gold.

Joe and Sal glanced at each other. "Where is it?" asked Sal. The ceiling of the cabin seemed especially low when his brothers were present. If Joe was an inch taller, he'd have hit his head on the beams.

"I can't tell you. You'll open your big mouths and some guy will jump the claim and say he found it first."

"We wouldn't do that," Joe said.

His father shoved the quartz in his pocket and thrust out his chin. "I'll show it to you after I've filed the papers. Then you can help me dig. Or I'll sell it to a syndicate. We can take the money and go home."

Carlo had never heard any of them talk about going home. His father sometimes mentioned the place where he'd grown up but only to say the work there was hard, the food scarce or poor in quality, and he'd been glad to leave it behind. Of course he'd probably describe this mining camp in a similar way if anyone asked.

Sal was nodding, thinking it through. "You say it's a good seam. How much do you think it'll yield?"

"I don't know yet," his father said. "A hell of a lot, I hope."

They opened a bottle of wine and drank a toast. His father and brothers looked stunned. Despite having come to Colorado to find gold, they'd long ago stopped hoping their dream would come true. Carlo, on the other hand, had been born here, had grown up here, and hadn't come in search of anything. It was where he was from. If he got any of this gold, it would be an accident of birth. It was also possible that the new claim would fail to produce as much as his father seemed to be expecting. He liked to talk big and this could be one of those times.

Early the next morning Carlo went to the little school on the hillside above the camp to inform his old teacher, Miss Donovan, about his father's good fortune. Although he'd stopped attending last year, he visited Miss Donovan often and could tell her things he couldn't tell anyone else. When he arrived, she was kneeling in front of the stove, starting the morning fire.

"*Mio padre*—my father—he's had some luck," he said.

She stopped what she was doing, turned, and smiled. "Oh, Carlo, hello. He did? What sort of luck?"

"He made a strike."

"Well, that is good news. Please offer him my congratulations." As she spoke, she glanced back at the stove. Seeing a satisfactory blaze, she shut and latched the door. "Will you keep helping your brothers, or do you plan to work in your father's mine?"

"I'm not sure. My father says—" he began and then stopped midsentence when two girls arrived. He'd been about to tell Miss Donovan that they might be returning to the place his father sometimes called "the old country," but the girls were laughing and talking and Miss Donovan was trying to get ready for class. Instead, he told her he needed to get to work and slipped back out the door.

Although Carlo had liked school, when he became the oldest boy in class, he couldn't bring himself to continue. And Miss Donovan hadn't tried very hard to change his mind. Perhaps her wish that he remain in school was outweighed by her knowledge of how things worked in a mining camp and the fact that rather than a passionate student he was merely a boy who enjoyed her company and considered school a pleasant place.

That night, he shared with his father Miss Donovan's congratulations. As soon as he began, he knew he'd made a mistake. It hadn't occurred to him that his father's warning about not telling anyone might include her. She was a teacher and, in Carlo's mind, entirely above reproach. Apparently, his father didn't share that view.

"Who? Who congratulates me?"

"Miss Donovan. My teacher."

"Your teacher?"

He nodded. "Yes. You know the one. Up at the school."

"What did I tell you? I said say nothing to nobody. Why does she need to know?"

Before Carlo could reply, his father grabbed him by the shirt and struck him, first with the back of his hand and then with his palm. Smack, smack, hard and fast. He didn't use his fists, but he didn't need to—like all miners, his hands were as hard as stone.

The instant Carlo was released, he fled out into the night. He touched his face and discovered his nose was bleeding. To make it stop, he pinched his nostrils shut. He understood the importance of keeping a gold strike secret, especially before a claim had been filed. Others might try to steal it, by trickery or by force. Miss Donovan, however, would do nothing of the kind.

He should have known how his father would react. His anger wasn't only about keeping the gold strike secret. He had never liked being told what others thought about him or anything he did. Even to say congratulations was to judge him in some fashion. In his father's view, Miss Donovan was suggesting he'd been lucky. If she was going to say anything, she should have said the gold strike was what he deserved.

Still dripping blood, Carlo walked to the saloon and found Joe. "What the hell happened to you?" his brother asked.

"Papa hit me," he said and told him the rest of the story.

Joe shook his head and brought a towel out from under the bar. "Nobody's gonna jump his claim. Definitely not your teacher. Tilt your head back, you need to get that stopped."

Carlo resented his father's accusations. He admired Miss Donovan and wished he were still in school. She sometimes took them up on the ridge to teach them about the trees. "Gather 'round," she'd say. "This is a white pine. It has tenacious roots and loves to grow on cliffs. You can identify it by its needles—they always come in pairs." From where they were standing, they could see the entire valley—the dusty gray sage, the ochre hills, and the blue mountains beyond. "Now I want you to look at the clouds," she'd add. "See how low they are? That means in the morning we'll probably wake up to snow."

Gaetano

Teresa wrote to her mother often. She told her about grinding walnuts and kneading dough and Frau Merz's imposing demeanor and scrubbing the kitchen floor. None of it was unusual or of much consequence, but what else could she say?—it was how she spent her time. Occasionally, she was able to describe errands she'd been sent on, to the butcher or the greengrocer or the pescivendolo, whose stall was always so busy, she had to stand in a queue. She also said she was attending mass regularly. Although her mother didn't always answer her letters, when she did, she mentioned Allucio. This pleased Teresa while also making her sad.

There were four Benedetti children, two younger than

Teresa and two, Cristian and Lia, about her age. The younger ones were seldom in evidence as they were under the care of a nanny in rooms upstairs. But Cristian and Lia, she saw nearly every day. Whenever they were about, she scrutinized their clothes, their hair, their manners, yet they didn't bother to look at her. She understood. No doubt other kitchen maids had come and gone, so why take an interest in this one? They were the first well-to-do young people she'd ever had a chance to observe. She wished she had brothers and sisters. She wished her father wasn't in Rome with a woman not her mother. However, she did have a dog, while the Benedetti family, to their distinct misfortune, did not.

The first weeks passed quickly. Teresa worked hard, did as Frau Merz instructed, and felt herself becoming accustomed to her new job. But she hadn't forgotten what her mother had said about coming home, so after a month in Trento she decided it was time.

She had only Sunday free and it took her six hours to walk up the mountain and down into the valley, which hung like a green bowl between two rocky peaks. That meant she could spend just two hours with her mother and Allucio before she had to return—barely enough time to describe Frau Merz's method of making gnocchi and eat a bowl of soup. So what her mother had said about coming home wasn't true. At best she'd be able to make the trip a few times a year. When she got back to Trento, she went to her room and cried. She didn't blame her mother. Perhaps her mother thought her capable of walking faster than she actually could. In any event, the separation from her village, from her mother, from her dog, from her childhood, suddenly seemed quite complete.

Cristian and Lia had a friend named Gaetano. While Teresa searched for pebbles in a bowl of peas, she could see the three of them outside enjoying the garden after they came

21

home from school. Cristian and Lia were lively and as fair as Austrians, while Gaetano was solemn and dark. Most days they sat at a table beneath a vine-covered trellis playing scopa while they talked. Teresa didn't know how to play scopa and didn't want to learn. No, it was what they were discussing that interested her. They might be talking about their studies, or about their teachers, but most likely they were gossiping about other young people they knew. Some boy was in trouble with his parents or some girl was in love with some boy. Frustratingly, she didn't know enough to imagine anything more specific. Silvia, the housemaid, said, "I don't know why you care about them. They don't care about you." The venom in her tone, Teresa thought, was directed less at Cristian and Lia than at how the world worked.

Occasionally, Cristian, Lia, and Gaetano would burst into the kitchen in search of food. Frau Merz disapproved but seldom chased them away. Like Cristian and Lia, Gaetano took little interest in the help, yet on two occasions he acknowledged Teresa's presence. The first was when he took a piece of cake and said, "Did you make this? It's very good." The second occurred one evening when she'd gone outside to fetch a bucket of coal and failed to notice him seated on a bench, in the shadows beneath the trees.

"Buonasera," he said.

She jumped and nearly dropped the bucket. "*Caspita!* What are you doing here?"

He smiled, amused by her expression of surprise. "I'm waiting for Cristian. That looks heavy. May I help you carry it inside?"

"I can manage. You gave me a start. There's never anyone out here at night."

"I find it peaceful, like being in the country. A short time ago I heard a thrush. Such a lovely song."

"I grew up in the country, and I can tell you, it's not always peaceful there." She felt awkward. Instead of disagreeing with him, she should have said something about the thrush.

"Where exactly are you from?" he asked.

"A village in the mountains. One you wouldn't have heard of."

"Why did you leave and come here?"

She considered saying, *What does it look like? To carry buckets of coal.* Instead, she said, "To make a little money to send home." She shifted from one foot to the other and back again. The handle of the bucket was digging into her palms.

"The mountains are beautiful, but the winters there are harsh." He motioned to the space beside him. "Put the coal down and sit."

"No, I'm sorry. I need to return to the kitchen. Frau Merz is waiting for me." Her mind was a jumble. She hoped her unease hadn't been too obvious. If only she hadn't been carrying a bucket. She should have said something about the thrush when she had the chance.

After that evening, Teresa watched Gaetano even more intently than before. Failing to sit with him might have been the biggest mistake of her life. She disliked it when he conversed with Lia. She especially disliked it when Lia laughed. She kept hoping to find him on the bench again, but what were the chances of that?

Then relief arrived, from an unexpected source. Signora Benedetti asked her to accompany her to Rome. Although the Signora had seldom spoken to her, she now pulled her aside and explained that for her journey she needed a companion—a girl to help her dress and care for her things. Immediately, Teresa agreed. Though she'd found Trento interesting and a welcome change from her mountain village, everyone said Rome was more magnificent by far. She stopped thinking about Gaetano. For now anyway. Presumably, he'd still be here when she returned.

She told Frau Merz about the invitation. "Why me and not Silvia?" she asked.

"Silvia's a sourpuss. She does her job well enough, but can you imagine traveling with her? The Signora made the right choice." Teresa was pleased with Frau Merz's assessment—far better to be deemed the *right choice* than a sourpuss. Still, she had to pause for a moment to consider how much simpler her existence had been in Ulfano. No one there had ever chosen her to do anything, and she'd had no encounters in gardens with young men. And then she reminded herself that she intended to stop thinking about Gaetano and would not resume until she'd come back from Rome.

Teresa wrote to her mother about the trip. Her mother had never been anywhere distant or important and suddenly Teresa felt sorry for her. When her mother first told her she was sending her to work in Trento, she had been a bit resentful—or perhaps a better word was anxious. Now she could see more clearly what had been in her mother's mind. Not only the extra money coming home, but the enriching of her daughter's life.

They departed the following week. The purpose of the trip was to allow Signora Benedetti to visit her sister, for an entire month. Before they left, a great many goodbyes had to be said. All four children embraced their mother; then her bespectacled husband did likewise while Teresa stood back and observed. She wondered how it felt to have so many people care about your welfare, and know they'd be awaiting your return.

"Is It Not Beautiful?"

A week after Carlo's father announced his strike, he burst through the door and began waving his arms and dancing across the room.

"The assay came back," he said. "It's better than I expected. I'll be selling the claim to the highest bidder. And then we can go home."

Carlo didn't know what to think. Once again this talk of home. Could he be serious? He wondered about his brothers. They'd spent their childhood in Italy; maybe they'd be pleased.

"Do Joe and Sal know?"

"Yes. I stopped by the saloon."

"And what did they say?"

"They'll think about it." But his eyes shifted and Carlo knew he wasn't telling the truth. Not the whole truth anyway.

"I want to talk to them myself."

"Then go," he said and began opening a bottle of wine.

When Carlo got to the saloon, Joe said, "I didn't tell him we'd think about it. I said neither of us would be going." He gestured toward the tables, the bar, the walls, and said, "We can't leave all this behind."

Carlo was stunned. Would it really be only him and his father returning to a country he knew little about? He looked at his brother in despair.

"You'll be all right," Joe said. "It's a beautiful place. The mountains are greener than the ones around here and there are lots of rivers and lakes. At least that's how I remember it. The name of the village is Ulfano. When we left, I was just a kid."

"I should stay here," Carlo said.

Joe shook his head slowly. "No, he wants you to go with him. And Sal and I, well, we think that's a good idea."

"I wouldn't be any trouble . . ."

Again, he shook his head. "Papa has plenty of money now. He'll take good care of you."

It sounded to Carlo as if his fate had already been determined. He couldn't blame his brothers for not wanting to be responsible for him. And although his father could be endlessly disagreeable, he often said that Carlo's proper upbringing was the most important thing he owed to his dear departed wife. An upbringing his father thought should include the occasional bloody nose.

The next day, Carlo got up early and was at the school when Miss Donovan arrived.

"We're going back," he said bluntly.

"To Italy?"

"Trentino. That's the name my father uses."

"Yes, in the north."

"But I don't want to!" Carlo said, unable to contain his dismay. "My brothers are staying here. I'll be all alone."

"I'm sorry. I can see why you'd be upset." He appreciated her honesty. She didn't insist change would be easy or that the company of his father would be enough.

"I can barely speak the language . . ."

"You'll learn. It will take some time, but if everyone around you is speaking Italian, you'll have no choice."

Since Joe and Sal would continue to live in the cabin, preparations to leave were simple. He and his father needed only to pack their clothes and a few personal items. The rest of their belongings could be left behind. No doubt Joe and Sal would be glad to have more room. And they wouldn't miss their father's bad temper—of that, Carlo had no doubt.

When they were ready to depart, Joe took them by wagon to Denver, where they were to board the train. As they waited at the station, Joe gave Carlo a package from Miss Donovan.

"She dropped this off last night," he explained, "after you were asleep."

Carlo removed the brown paper and discovered it was a book about trees. He thrust it back at Joe. The book made him feel even worse about leaving. "I don't want it," he said. He knew it was a childish response. Also a superstitious one, as it seemed to him that accepting the book would mean he was never coming back.

"Keep it. If I try to return it, she'll say I didn't do my job."

His father pointed a finger at Carlo. "Shut up and put it in your bag."

Minutes later the train arrived and their journey began.

From Denver they crossed dry plains and verdant farmland and stared out the window at the fantastic arrays of lights when they passed through cities after dark. There were dense forests and rivers so large, he was left wondering at the skill it must have taken to build bridges across. Occasionally, the train stopped and they had barely enough time to get off and stretch their legs in a high-ceilinged depot or on the streets of a town he'd never see again. His father was uncommonly talkative with the other passengers. He told them about Joe and Sal and their saloon in Colorado. He said he was going home to Italy, where he planned to fix up his house and buy some land. Carlo was surprised to learn his father still owned a house in Trentino. Had he been planning to return all along?

After six days and nights they reached New Jersey, where they were to board a ship. Carlo knew almost nothing about what to expect. How large would the ship be, what would their quarters be like, what would the food be like, how many other passengers would be onboard, and if he got seasick, how miserable would he actually feel? Not to mention the most important question: When they arrived in Italy, what sort of life would he have? So much uncertainty, stretching so far ahead.

The night before their scheduled departure, they walked along the docks. "Look there. Can you see it?" his father said, pointing across the gray water.

"See what? That barge?"

"Italy. Trentino." He put his hand on the back of Carlo's neck and roughly directed his gaze. "Open your eyes, it's right there."

Carlo reached up and pushed the hand away. "You're hurting me," he said.

"Stop complaining. I'm making a joke. It's time for you to grow up."

He stood staring at the ocean. When his father and brothers had crossed it from east to west, they had done so with a sense of adventure and a hopefulness about the future that was nothing like what Carlo now felt. It was as if he was traveling into the past, one he himself hadn't experienced. Going backward, going to a darker place, a place of uncertainty rather than one of promise. His father, aging as he was, seemed to see it as a return toward good memories and the familiarity of his ancestral home. That he neither knew nor cared what Carlo thought wasn't surprising. It was how he'd always behaved.

Crossing the Atlantic took two weeks. Carlo got only mildly seasick and enjoyed roaming about the ship. He was befriended by members of the crew, many of whom were Italian. Yet, when he told them the name of the village that was his destination, they said they'd never heard of it. One even went so far as to insist there was no such place: "At school I won a prize for geography. I would know if it exists." Carlo was made uneasy by the sailor's declaration. Maybe Ulfano wasn't well known because it was so small. But what if the sailor was right? Well, he would find out soon enough.

When at last they reached the port of Genoa and disembarked, Carlo looked in amazement at the harbor. Dozens of ships beside dozens of quais and then row upon row of receiving houses and warehouses, all built nearly on top of each other, a dense and tangled jumble of salt-stained wood and smoke-blackened brick.

They entered the city and walked up the narrow streets, Carlo clinging more closely to his father than he had since he was a child. Shopkeepers shouted at each other from open doors, heaps of fish were being transported in handcarts, and fires burned in barrels and pits for purposes he couldn't comprehend. The smells alone were overwhelming, some enticing and some so foul, he had to hold his nose. After asking numerous people for directions to the transport office, his father purchased seats in a diligenza, and they began their journey northward on poorly maintained roads. Again, Carlo was overcome by the feeling they were moving backward, into the past, into the old country, a place that seemed antique and mysterious rather than fresh and new.

After two days in the coach, the time came for them to proceed on foot. They asked the driver to stop, waited for their bags to be unloaded, and watched the coach disappear over a nearby hill. As Carlo stood in the middle of the road, he considered how very far they'd come. Across America, across the ocean, and now up into these unfamiliar mountains, farther and farther from Joe and Sal and Miss Donovan. It seemed entirely possible he'd never see them again.

The path they now followed was steep. Each of them carried two pasteboard suitcases, one in either hand. These mountains were more precipitous than the ones in Colorado. And, as Joe had told him, more lushly green. *What will it be like to live here?* he wondered. The closer they got to their destination, the more curious he became. The more apprehensive he became.

In midafternoon the road emerged from the woods and Carlo saw before him a cluster of buildings clinging to the mountainside ahead. There, under an enormous azure sky, his father dropped to his knees and began to sob. "I didn't think I'd come back. The place of my birth, my home. Look, Carlo. Is it not beautiful?"

Carlo nodded, but for the moment he was more interested in his father's emotion than in the village itself. Never had he seen him like this. Had he really been longing for home all the years he lived in Colorado, all the years of Carlo's life? He found it hard to believe that this was some special place, some mountain paradise. At least their journey was over and they had arrived. He thought about the skeptical Italian sailor and wished he could speak to him now. *See, you were wrong*, he'd say. *Ulfano does exist.*

Rome

Teresa had never been on a train before. The trees and houses passed so quickly, she had to turn away from the windows to keep from becoming ill. It wasn't merely the speed she found noteworthy. The passengers were well dressed, the employees were polite, the seats were upholstered in blue velvet, and the fixtures were polished brass.

Late in the afternoon they reached Tiburtina Station. As they stepped down onto the platform, the mass of people was so great, Teresa was afraid she'd get separated from Signora Benedetti and then what would she do? But suddenly a man sent by the Signora's sister appeared and led them to a carriage, so her fears were allayed. *I am in Rome*, she thought and tried to fix the moment in her mind so she'd be able to remember it whenever she chose to, in a few years or in fifty years, should she live so long.

As they traveled through the city, the Signora directed her attention toward some remarkable sites. "Look, the Basilica di San Clemente," and "You must have heard of the Circo Massimo. We're about to pass it on the left." It was as if the Signora was speaking to a friend. Teresa hadn't expected her to be so kind. Yet she also wondered briefly if having wealth made it easier to be congenial. Why be ill-humored if you have lots of money? Why be disagreeable if all your needs are met?

When she'd first learned she was going to Rome, it had occurred to her she might cross paths with her father. Now that she saw how immense the city was, any hope of such an encounter disappeared. Perhaps it was for the best. If she ran into him, what would she say? *Come back to the mountains and resume the life you lived before?* Or, more likely, *Don't you owe us an apology? You didn't even say goodbye.* She recalled the day her mother told her he'd left—the day she said, "I know there are nights he doesn't come home, but this time he won't be back." Yet even after several weeks had passed, she believed, in her child's mind, that he'd gone away for some good reason and would eventually return. Precisely when she finally accepted his absence as a fact, she couldn't say. Maybe the process wasn't complete. Would there come a time when she simply didn't care?

They reached the Signora's sister's villa as the sun was setting. Its façade shone golden, the graceful stone pines in the garden were like black lace shawls against a violet sky, and from the windows came flashes of reflected light.

Although Teresa wasn't sure what would be asked of her, she soon discovered she had little difficulty doing the Signora's bidding. She helped her dress, accompanied her when she and her sister made social calls, and, at night, helped her take down her hair and prepare for bed. Teresa couldn't avoid comparing her employer's life to that of her mother's. While Signora Benedetti could sip tea for the better part of an afternoon, her mother spent her days washing clothes at the village basin, digging potatoes, and gathering wood.

The Signora's sister was married to a banker named Giorgio Moretti, who had many influential friends. Nearly every evening at least four or five men in black evening dress and an equal number of wives in fashionable gowns arrived for supper and afterward stayed to talk, discussing Italian politics and international events well into the night.

Teresa wasn't always able to follow their conversations. What did she know of prime ministers and military expenditures and corrupt officials and treaties with foreign powers? They seemed especially concerned about Italy's role in Europe—if France and Germany went to war, how should the government respond?

Still, she felt privileged to be allowed to listen, and on occasion, they spoke about issues she could understand. For example, there was the time they discussed the Pope's recent criticism of the tango. "It's not that the dance is too exotic," said one man, "it's that it's not *Roman*." Another said, "The Holy Father thinks it leads women to be unfaithful." And a third, "If he tried it, he might like it." Everyone turned to look at him. "*The dance*," he exclaimed, "I'm talking about *the dance*!" and they all threw back their heads and laughed.

One evening, a banker's wife opened the newspaper and read aloud an item about an Englishman who had been protesting the mistreatment of donkeys in Naples. "He thinks there ought to be a law preventing them from being whipped," she explained.

"What business is it of his?" said a man with an extravagant mustache. "They're only donkeys."

"You forget that the great Garibaldi was opposed to the mistreatment of animals," another man said. "I stand with Garibaldi on matters great and small."

"Why would an Englishman care about Italian donkeys?" said the woman who read the article. "Surely there are donkeys in need of his attention in London . . ."

A fourth man interrupted: "My father had a donkey who could bark like a dog," and a fifth man said, "The internal combustion engine is already replacing the donkey. In a few years even the poorest peddler will own a motorized cart."

They soon moved on to other topics, but the following morning, Teresa rescued the newspaper from the rubbish heap, tore out the article about the Englishman and the donkeys, and tucked it away. The subject interested her and she wanted to examine it again. For all the disparaging things she said about Don Tomasi, he had done an adequate job of teaching her—and her mother and father before her—how to read.

In the days that followed, she fretted about returning to the kitchen in Trento. She'd done her best to be of value to Signora Benedetti. Maybe when they were back at the villa, she'd be invited to continue in her current role. She even imagined herself becoming a sort of trusted assistant, the kind the Signora could depend upon and in whom she would confide.

Then one evening the Signora and her sister made plans to see a play. Teresa accompanied them in the coach and was looking forward to the performance. She'd never been inside a theater and began to get excited, so much so that she laughed too loudly when the Signora's sister made a joke. But as soon as the coach came to a halt, the two women got out and, with no further thought, shut the door in Teresa's face. She gasped, then quickly collected herself. Going to the theater with them had been a fantasy. They hadn't intended to be cruel, she'd merely misunderstood her place.

When the visit to Rome finally came to an end, Teresa reflected on the experiences she'd had there. It seemed to her they were of opposing types. Some had made her feel more capable and more aware of what lay beyond the tiny village of her birth. Others had pressed her inward, causing her to conclude she was fit only for the life of a peasant; at most, an assistant to the cook.

Back at the Villa Benedetti, Teresa again found herself observing Cristian and Lia, but now her perspective had changed. When she'd begun working there, she'd been naive enough to think they might somehow become friends. Now, having seen more of the world they inhabited, she knew that was just a dream. As for Gaetano, he scarcely even glanced at her.

On a more positive note, Frau Merz seemed pleased to have her back. Not only did she seem less exasperated when Teresa made a mistake, she sometimes invited her to conclude the day by remaining in the kitchen to chat.

"Have you any brothers and sisters?" Frau Merz asked. She crossed her large pink arms on the table in front of her, like a farmer in from the fields.

"No. There's just me."

"Consider yourself lucky. I have three brothers, Matthias, Noah, and Jan. As I was the youngest, you'd think I'd have been cosseted; instead I was ignored. I once stayed with the neighbors for a week, and no one noticed I was gone. Although I return to Austria every year to visit them, Trento is now my home."

Teresa then described Ulfano, its peculiar residents and

some amusing aspects of rural life: "Sometimes in winter the snow is so deep, we make tunnels between the kitchen and the cowshed. We have a shoemaker who thinks he's an opera singer and a priest who thinks he's a bishop. Everyone mocks him behind his back." After making such comments, she wondered if she was becoming a "city girl." Growing up in Ulfano, she'd heard such creatures spoken of with a combination of admiration and disapproval. The label could be applied to a girl from the mountains who had turned her back on her people but also to a girl who had successfully taken advantage of what the city had to offer. She hoped the latter applied to her.

Occasionally, they were joined by the stable boy Luca, the ancient gardener Rodolfo, and even the disagreeable upstairs maid Silvia. Then Frau Merz would produce a bottle of grappa and pour out tiny glasses, which they sipped as they conversed. Their tongues thus loosened, they would turn their attention to topics not unlike those Signor Moretti and his friends debated in Rome. But being who they were, they spoke with the understanding that whatever occurred—elections, the passing of laws, perhaps even war—their only choice would be to make the best of the situation. Unlike the bankers and their wives, they didn't expect the world to bend to their will.

If Frau Merz was too tired to talk, Teresa went walking along the river. She liked how the sunlight glanced off the water and how the town seemed at peace as the day came to an end. She used the time to think about any number of things— Silvia's sour temperament, the fine clothes the Signora's sister wore, the Englishman who liked donkeys, and what Gaetano actually thought of her. No, not the last item, she shouldn't waste her time on that. Frau Merz said it wasn't seemly for her to go walking along the river by herself, but old Rodolfo, who expressed his opinions bluntly, said, "What's wrong with walking by the river? Leave the girl alone."

An Important Man

Carlo surveyed the village as they approached. They passed a cluster of three houses, white with russet shutters, a barn with a collapsing wall, and then two more houses and a herd of goats grazing beneath some trees. The houses were arranged in a haphazard manner, stacked against the mountainside, gripping the steep slope with all their might. At the bottom of the town, a tavern that brought to mind his brothers' saloon stood by the road. From behind it, a woman carrying a rake appeared. Upon seeing them, she stopped, leaned forward, and squinted. "Is that you, Angelo Coltura?"

"It is," his father said.

"And who is this with you?"

"My boy Carlo."

"And where is your wife?"

He glanced at her, shook his head, and marched onward. Others looked down from windows and peered over stone walls. "Angelo!" an old man shouted yet none of them succeeded in bringing his father to a halt.

Carlo looked from side to side, trying to take everything in. The most obvious difference from the mining camp in Colorado was that the houses they were passing looked far more permanent, as if they'd been there for a hundred years. And he could see actual gardens, not merely the odd patch of turnips, as well as whole herds of goats. So maybe this place really was better than where they'd come from. Even if that turned out to be true, he'd never admit it to his father. And it couldn't be true because it wasn't just the quality of the houses that mattered. It was who lived here, which didn't include his brothers or anyone else he knew.

At last they turned off the main road and went up a steep street with walls close on either side. Before long, the street became an alley and the alley a flight of stone steps. At the top of the steps was a blue door. From his pocket his father produced an iron key and put it in the lock. Carlo wondered where he'd kept the key during all the years of his absence. The lock turned and with a firm push his father opened the door. It took a moment for Carlo's eyes to adjust, yet soon he could see before him a large, high-ceilinged room. The walls were stone and the air felt damp and cool.

"I thought some squatter would have moved in," his father said. "But it's exactly as I left it. Come in and look around."

Carlo walked through the house slowly. On the ground floor was one large room and three smaller ones; on the floor above, he found a kitchen, a pantry lined with empty shelves, and a room in which a mural depicting a castle had been painted on the wall.

"Well, what do you think?" his father asked.

"It's okay."

"Is that all?"

"Did you build it yourself?"

"My father did."

"It's larger than our house in Colorado."

"Of course it is. What did you expect?"

For a moment Carlo wanted to lash out at him, to say, *I didn't expect anything. I didn't know this place existed until a few weeks ago.* Then he softened. Maybe his father knew what he was doing. Maybe coming here really would be good for them both. He only wished the old man wasn't always so arrogant, so certain he was right.

Their first days in the village were filled with celebration.

His father had many old friends who were happy to see him again. Yet some seemed to take his return as evidence that going to America had been a mistake. They, too, celebrated, less because his father had returned than because they'd been wise enough to stay put. "I don't know why you left in the first place," said one. "You're lucky you held on to your house," said another. "That made it easy to come back."

As it turned out, the house wasn't enough. His father soon began spending the money he brought with him, the proceeds from the sale of the claim. In a period of a few days, he bought the small house next door, a matched team of white horses with a stylish red trap for them to pull, and a walking stick with a handle made from mother of pearl and gold. He also hired a housekeeper, a woman named Flavia Sala, who acted as though Carlo didn't exist and had a habit of muttering to herself.

With evidence of his wealth suddenly on display, his father's old friends became even friendlier and those who had found satisfaction in his apparent inability to thrive in America altered their opinions overnight. "What a success!" they said. "I think I'll go to America, too. I've heard gold there is as common as sheep shit. You must scrape it off your boots before you come inside."

Now Carlo understood. His father hadn't returned for the beauty of the valley or because he owned a spacious house. He'd returned because he knew that if he brought his money to this poor village, all his old friends would envy him and he would be transformed—immediately, almost magically—from an insignificant stone cutter into *un uomo importante*—an important man. Carlo wondered what his brothers would say if they were here. He could picture himself listening as Joe and Sal commented on their father's behavior. They were old enough to express their own opinions, old enough to tell their father he wasn't as important as he thought. Of course, they'd do so gently—there were lines even they wouldn't cross.

At the tavern his father stood drinks for everyone and told stories about America, stories Carlo knew were untrue. Their money seemed to be worth five times more here than in Colorado. A few lira bought them an enormous meal. When a traveling tailor passed through the village, his father ordered two new suits.

Then, in a further and quite unexpected expression of his newfound wealth, his father informed him that he intended to become mayor. When Carlo asked him who the current mayor was, his father said, "There isn't one. There never has been. They need a man like me to show them how to get things done."

Carlo was incredulous. "What sort of things?"

"For one, that fool Zito needs to stop letting his pigs roam free. And someone should tell Don Tomasi to silence the bells after sunset. Haven't you noticed? He has someone ring them every hour of the night."

"You think he'll listen to you?"

"I don't care if he listens—when I'm mayor, I can force him to stop."

"What will I do?" asked Carlo. They'd never discussed where he might work, and he couldn't picture himself being part of his father's outrageous scheme.

"Do? I'm sure you can find a job. Or you can go back to school. There's a boarding school attached to the cathedral in Trento. If I pay your fees, you can enroll there."

Carlo didn't know what to think. Perhaps having an educated son was part of being an important man. Or he simply wanted him out of the way. Then he remembered his enjoyable days with Miss Donovan, and before his father could change his mind, he said, "School, yes. I'd like that. I'll start as soon as I can."

And so, before Carlo had become accustomed to Ulfano, he prepared to leave it behind. It occurred to him that attending school in Trento might mark the beginning of his future even more definitively than crossing the ocean. He would be away from his father and, for the first time, on his own.

A week later he departed, carrying the same pasteboard suitcases he'd brought all the way from Colorado. His father didn't offer to walk with him, but he did give him one of the suits he had discarded when the new ones arrived. Threadbare and olive green, it fit, but poorly, for Carlo was now as tall as Sal, with arms like sticks and ankles that continued past his cuffs for several inches before his big feet jutted out.

Miss Donovan would be pleased that he was returning to school, even if it was as an escape. For the first time since leaving Colorado, Carlo had a sense of purpose, one he felt good about, one that wasn't being forced on him by his father. He didn't think his father would miss him—although he wondered if he'd be lonely, living in such a large house with only the housekeeper creeping about.

He expected to have difficulty finding the cathedral, but it turned out to be so large, he could see it long before he reached the edge of town. Surprisingly, it was not a single building but a group of structures huddled around a massive church—a church with so many towers and cupolas and balustrades, it was difficult to take it all in. He located the school and presented himself there, prepared to make a case for his admission. But he needn't have worried—the wad of lire he offered when the question of fees arose proved more than adequate and he was enrolled on the spot.

Unfortunately, being a newcomer at the school wasn't

easy. The boys there had been together since they were seven or eight, and he made a convenient target. Before long, his bedding was tied in knots, his shoes were thrown out the window, and his food was adulterated with salt. He complained to his Latin teacher, Brother Toscano, and was told that, like Jesus, he needed to have a thick skin. But after Carlo's mother had died, they'd stopped going to church, so he knew nothing of Jesus's skin.

Another problem was his poor Italian. Since the teachers were willing to make few allowances, his written work received terrible marks. Worse yet, when the bullies mocked him, he was easily flustered. One of them would say something to him, and before he could decipher it, laughter would erupt on all sides.

Just as he was about to give up and accept the humiliation he would face upon going back to live with his father, he made friends with a curly-haired boy named Vitale, who told the others to leave him alone. "He's from America, you idiots," he said. "That's where they make the best movies. Give him some respect." A year older than Carlo, Vitale was among the school's ruling class. Without his new friend's intervention, Carlo wouldn't have made it through the first month.

From then on, school was satisfactory, though he didn't like how the brothers pressured the students to enter the priesthood. Unsure of how to respond, he asked Vitale if he planned to be ordained.

Vitale laughed. "Me? Are you joking? I can't think of anything worse." He caught himself and glanced around to make sure no one was listening. "I want to be a soldier. I want to fire a gun."

"How about you?" Vitale continued. "To what do you aspire?"

"I don't know. Not the priesthood. I'm sure of that." Carlo

wouldn't have had the courage to be so forthright if Vitale hadn't spoken first.

Vitale shrugged. "I suppose you can do as you please. Brother Enoch says your father's rich."

"I don't have any money of my own, if that's what you're thinking. It's true that my father struck gold in America, but he's spending it as fast as he can." Carlo hoped he wouldn't ask for examples. While he didn't mind criticizing his father in the privacy of his own mind, he preferred to avoid saying things that would paint his father as a buffoon.

"The main reason to have money is that girls like it," Vitale said. "They pretend otherwise, but I have older sisters and I've heard how they talk about men. Their clothing, their occupation, the cut of their hair and manner of speech, all are merely ways to assess their worth. Their worth in lire, that is, not their true worth as men."

Safe Travels, My Little One

The first time Teresa heard old Rodolfo talk about his pigeons, she assumed they were for eating; but no, they were homing pigeons, which he sometimes entered in races. Signor Benedetti allowed him to keep them behind the stables. Currently, he had fourteen.

"I'd like to see them," she said.

He looked surprised. "If you wish. I'll warn you, they're only pigeons. They look no different from any others you've seen."

She could tell he didn't mean it, that he considered his pigeons exceptional. "Tomorrow then," she said.

They met in the garden behind the villa and she followed him toward the stables. Whether or not his birds were truly special, she felt asking to see them was the polite thing to do.

It seemed to Teresa that in villages such as Ulfano, old men like Rodolfo were valued for their wisdom (as long as they weren't drunks). They knew the local secrets and could tell interesting stories about days gone by. That didn't appear to be the case here in the city, where they worked at rather menial jobs and tended to remain out of sight.

She had visited the stables only once before, a few days after her arrival. Since then, she'd had no reason to go there and wasn't even sure she was allowed. If Signor Benedetti found her where she didn't belong, she might be given a scolding or, worse, get sent home.

As they approached, she heard someone singing. For a moment she considered running back to the house. But it was just Luca, cleaning out a stall.

"So you've come to see his children," Luca said.

"Please ignore the blockhead," Rodolfo replied. Teresa knew better than to take their banter seriously. It was always playful and, as far as she could tell, didn't do any harm.

In the stable were five horses, and in the stall at the end, the Signor's motorcar, which she'd learned from eavesdropping was his pride and joy. As yellow as the sun and as pointed as an arrow, it looked as though it could leave the surface of the earth and take flight. But Rodolfo didn't approve. "It frightens the animals," he said.

Beyond the end of the stable they followed a path through some dense greenery and into a clearing. Although they were in the city of Trento, they might as well have been deep in the forest, surrounded as they were by towering trees. At the edge of the clearing was a small structure made of wire and wood.

She could hear the birds before she saw them, cooing in their distinctive manner. The sound reminded her of bubbles rising from a pond. Rodolfo remained quiet as she inspected the cages. They had been crafted as carefully as an armoire, the planks sanded smooth, the wire mesh stretched tight, the joints fitted with care. As for the pigeons, she was struck by their coloring—fawn and rust, cobalt and slate. All quite handsome and no two alike.

Rodolfo took one out and insisted she hold it. "Be firm," he said. "They're stronger than they look." And so they were. Even though she had the bird's wings pinned tightly against its body, with every part of its being it strained toward the sky.

"If you release them, they come back. Is that correct?"

"Yes. Always." After a moment he added, "Unless they get killed by a hawk."

As he fed them, he told her about each one. "Aurora is crafty," he said, pointing to a gray bird with an ivory head. "I had to wire the latch because she could open it herself. Greta here is a peacemaker. If a fight breaks out, she intervenes." She asked him about the one she was holding. "Pietro is like me," he said. "Old but strong. Did you know that news of Napoleon's defeat at the Battle of Waterloo was carried to England by a pigeon? Four hundred kilometers means nothing to a bird in flight." The old fellow's pride in his birds was touching. He clearly spent a good deal of time and effort learning about them and keeping them healthy. It made her wish she had a pigeon or two herself.

Teresa would have liked to stay longer, but it was time to return to work. She thanked Rodolfo, acknowledged Luca as she passed the stable, and hurried back to the house. Still, she wasn't quick enough; as she entered the kitchen, Frau Merz said, "You're late. Where have you been?"

"Rodolfo was showing me his pigeons."

Frau Merz shook her head.

"He's very fond of them," Teresa added.

"That's the problem. He spends too much time with those creatures."

Teresa thought she was going to say more, but she returned to her work, something to do with a joint of beef. A few minutes later, Frau Merz disappeared into the pantry. When she came back, she stopped in the middle of the kitchen: "Many years ago his wife and four children died of cholera. I shouldn't blame him for wanting to care for some birds."

The more Teresa was around Frau Merz, the more she could see how she looked upon the villa as her home and the other members of the staff as her family. Even grumpy Silvia. Didn't every family have a Silvia, the person no one liked but whom they nonetheless accepted?

Not long thereafter, Rodolfo sought Teresa out and asked for her help.

"Remember I told you how I train the young ones?"

She nodded. "You take them away and let them fly back. A short distance at first and then a little farther each time."

"Yes," he said, looking pleased that she'd listened so carefully. "When you go to the shops for Frau Merz today, may I send one with you? You can keep it in your pocket and release it before you return."

Her first thought was to say no, to avoid trouble with Frau Merz. But it was unlikely she'd find out, and if she did, Rodolfo would defend her. He'd been there longer than anyone and was the one person Frau Merz never ordered about.

"Where should I do it?" she asked. "I'm only going to the butcher. Is that far enough?"

"It will do. Or you could go a little farther. Hold it in both hands like I showed you," he said. "And toss it into the air."

She put on her shawl and departed with the list of things Frau Merz wanted from the butcher in one pocket of her apron and the bird in the other. She intended to release it first, not wanting to risk taking it into the shop.

As she made her way toward the center of town, she kept

her hand on the bird, feeling it breathe. Though it was smaller than an adult pigeon, Rodolfo had assured her this wouldn't be its first flight. She felt as if she was doing something improper, something better done in secret, and then admonished herself for having such ridiculous thoughts.

When she was beyond the most well-trafficked quarter, she turned down a deserted street. The breeze today was mild, but surely there would be another spell of cold before summer arrived. At last she came upon a secluded piazza. She'd had this place in mind the entire time but hadn't been certain she could find it. There were a few mulberry trees and a bank of shrubs coming into flower behind a protective hedge. Some distance away was the cathedral and three smaller buildings of gray stone. She glanced around to make sure no one was watching. Taking the bird from her pocket, she held it away from her body. "Safe travels, my little one," she whispered, setting it free exactly as Rodolfo had demonstrated, with a gentle toss. It rose sharply, wheeled left, overtopped the nearest building, and disappeared from sight.

Unexpectedly, her eyes filled with tears. It was going home, so why cry? Perhaps because she could imagine, it being so young, the uncertainty it must feel. Then again, maybe it had no fear. It was, after all, a homing pigeon and that's what they were made for. She laughed at herself for having such complex feelings about a bird.

As she turned to go back toward the butcher shop and complete her errand, she found a tall, thin boy standing in her way.

"May I help you?" she asked.

He stared at her for a moment, furrowed his brow, and spoke. "A bird. You threw it into the air."

"So I did. And it flew away." He sounded like a foreigner.

She wondered where he'd come from. She'd hoped to release the bird without letting anyone see.

"But why?"

"It's a pigeon. The kind that always flies home." She gestured upward, as if by "home," she meant the sky.

"I've heard of such a thing. Will it have far to go?"

"Not very far. I work in the kitchen at the Benedetti villa, on Via—" She stopped midsentence. He didn't need to know where she lived.

"Is it carrying a message?"

"No." She paused. "I suppose it could."

Peering down at her, he asked if she had other birds.

"So many questions. Yes, there are others. I wouldn't want the poor thing to go home to a hollow house."

He looked puzzled and she realized the phrase she'd used was an idiom of the mountains that wasn't common here. Before she could explain, he said, "I'm from Colorado. Mi chiamo Carlo Coltura."

"Colorado?"

"In America."

"Then what are you doing here?" She hadn't meant to sound accusing, but that was the way it came out. Was she fated to adopt her mother's blunt manner of speech? She hoped not. As this thought was passing through her mind, the boy blinked and stepped back.

"I . . . I attend the cathedral school."

"And you came all the way from America?"

"No. Yes. I can't talk anymore. I should be on my way."

She almost called him back to apologize for her abruptness; however, that might make things worse. As she turned to go up the street, it occurred to her that yet another way in which the city was different from her village was that in her village one rarely encountered a stranger. And if a stranger did happen to pass through, someone warned you, so you could prepare yourself to meet them or find a place to hide.

At the butcher shop, she obtained the items on her list—sausages, coda di bue for soup, a shoulder of pork—and returned to Villa Benedetti, where she showed Frau Merz her purchases and began working on the evening meal. The next time Rodolfo visited the kitchen, she nodded in his direction to show things had gone as planned.

Before the Bird Comes Out to Sing

The dormitory windows faced east, toward the morning sun. With the arrival of spring, Carlo was waking up earlier every day. He still wasn't fully accustomed to the school and its routines, but thanks to Vitale's intervention, he was no longer teased as much.

His room, which housed twelve boys, was on the third floor, and from there he could see a corner of the market and the road leading into the mountains to the north. The shrubs and trees were coming to life, bursting with pastel flowers and tiny leaves. Some mornings, if the others were still sleeping, he liked to get dressed, go outside, and make a circuit of the cathedral square. As he walked, he watched the shops opening up and wondered what it would be like to work in one, even own one, as his brothers owned the saloon.

One day, when he was about to turn back toward the dormitory, he caught sight of a figure standing at the edge of a garden in the direction of Via Calepina—a girl who appeared to be holding something in her hands. After a moment of stillness, she made a sort of lunge and threw her possession into the air. Which, instead of falling to the ground, fluttered briefly before soaring across the sky. Filled with curiosity and overcoming his shyness, he approached and asked her to explain what she'd just done. She told him she had released a homing pigeon but seemed reluctant to say more. He continued asking her questions until she turned the tables and started questioning him. The most important thing he learned was that she worked for the Benedetti family. While he wasn't as obsessed with girls as some boys were, he found this one appealing and wondered if Vitale would have some idea about where that particular family lived. Not that he'd know what to do with such information. Perhaps send her a note asking if the pigeon had returned. He was surprised he'd had the nerve to speak to her. If he'd given the matter more thought, he wouldn't have opened his mouth.

Later that same morning Brother Enoch brought him a letter, the first Carlo had received since he'd been at the school. It appeared to be from his father but then he opened it and discovered it was a letter his brother Joe had sent to them both. Apparently his father had read it and forwarded it on to him.

Dear Papa and Carlo, it began.

I hope you are doing well and that Trentino is still as beautiful as I remember. I write to tell you that Sal has gotten married. I told him he needed to send a letter to the two of you, but I know he never did. So it falls to me. Her name is Inez. She is the daughter of Thomas Butler, who owns the dry goods store (where Inez works as a clerk).

I know it may seem sudden as this will be the first time you've heard her name. Someday you will meet her, at least that is Sal's hope. I've always said he has no manners. Maybe marriage will straighten him out.

We're having some bad weather but the miners haven't stopped drinking, so our business does all right ...

A few additional remarks about the saloon followed, yet it was clear he'd written them only to fill the page. Sal married! That was certainly unexpected. Joe always seemed to have a girl on his arm, but not Sal. Would he ever get to meet Inez? Or would his brothers become little more than infrequent correspondents who, over the years, reported briefly on marriages, births, and deaths? Carlo realized then that the letter had made vivid an uncomfortable fact: The people and places he left behind in Colorado weren't going to remain the same. Yes, there would be marriages, births, and deaths. New people would arrive and others would move away. As for the camp itself, there was even the possibility that when the gold ran out, the entire town would die.

Several days later, Vitale came to him with a peculiar look on his face. "I'm here to bid you farewell," he said. "I have enlisted in the Italian military and will be leaving tomorrow afternoon."

Carlo was surprised and disappointed. He hadn't expected Vitale to act on his ambitions so soon. Frowning, he said, "Shouldn't you finish the term?"

"Why bother? My father has agreed to give me three horses so I can join the cavalry. I'll be going south to Ascoli Piceno for training. I have a letter of introduction to give to the comandante there."

They talked then about how a war might be coming. For the past several weeks, rumors had been circulating among the boys, prompted by letters from their fathers and older brothers, as well as by provocative articles that were appearing in the newspapers almost every day. France wanted Germany to return Alsace, Germany refused and wanted to exert more influence in the east, and Italy wanted Austria-Hungary to give up Trento and Trieste. Therefore, the armies of all those countries seemed poised to act. When Carlo first arrived in

Italy, he'd been unable to determine if Trento was Austrian or Italian. Now he understood that while the great majority of residents considered themselves Italian, they lived under the Austro-Hungarian flag. Serbia, too, was growing in power and no one was happy about that.

"I wouldn't mind a *small* war," Vitale said. "I should like to test myself, although I'd prefer it didn't last too long."

"I doubt my father would give me even one horse. Certainly not three. My only choice would be the infantry. I don't mind walking but not with a pack on my back." In truth he knew little about the military, the cavalry, or the infantry or whatever other types there were. His remark about walking with a pack was merely a guess, based on something he'd read.

After supper Vitale filled his valise as Carlo watched. "I wonder what sort of gun you'll be given?" he asked. Vitale, his thoughts already elsewhere, said, "Now, where did I leave my cap?"

The next day they embraced, and Vitale, in an uncharacteristically formal manner, said, "I give you my word and bond: We will meet again."

"I suppose I'll still be here," Carlo said. He'd begun to feel a little sorry for himself. Vitale was about to have an adventure and he was being left behind. He wondered if any of the other boys would be leaving or if Vitale was uncommonly brave. For a moment he pictured himself in an empty school, the only student in his classes, alone in the dining hall eating the evening meal.

In the days after his friend's departure, Carlo rededicated himself to his schoolwork. He'd discovered he was especially good at mathematics and could lose himself in the solving of problems for hours at a time. It helped that mathematics required almost no Italian—or English, for that matter. Only numbers and signs. But even mathematics couldn't prevent him from thinking about Joe and Sal, Miss Donovan, his loneliness, and the circumstances that had put him in this place. If he were a homing pigeon, back to Colorado he'd fly.

One day, hoping he might once again meet the girl with the bird, he returned to where he'd first seen her. He thought about what he might say. Of course, he could ask after the pigeon and there was always the weather; it looked as though it might rain. If he had enough courage, he could ask where she was going and pretend to have some reason to follow the same route.

But she wasn't there, so he continued walking, lost in thought, until he'd passed the last row of houses and gone beyond the city's edge. Then, suddenly, he heard a peculiar sound. It was a whirring noise, smoothly metallic, the sound a cuckoo clock makes before the bird comes out to sing. Yet what rounded the corner ahead was not a mechanical bird; it was a cadre of men on bicycles. He withdrew into the shadows beneath the trees and watched as they swept past. From the rifles slung over their backs, he knew them to be soldiers but their uniforms, with capes billowing out behind and wide-brimmed hats with black feather plumes, were unlike any he'd seen. More like infernal specters escaped from a nightmare, or ravens turned into men. He recalled Vitale talking about a unit of the Italian armed forces known as Bersaglieri. He said you couldn't join; you had to be chosen. He said they rode their *biciclette* like demons. He said they'd never been defeated in battle, and their uniforms alone were enough to make women swoon. At the time he'd assumed Vitale was exaggerating, but no, they were exactly as he said.

PART II

Disruption in the Street

On a sunny day near the end of June, Luca, the stable boy, burst into the kitchen and said, "Have you heard? The archduke has been assassinated."

"The archduke?" said Frau Merz.

"Yes, Franz Ferdinand, heir to the Austro-Hungarian throne. People are saying this may lead to war." Teresa had never seen Luca so agitated. He seemed truly alarmed.

That evening, the servants gathered and discussed the event. "The Austrians may attack the Serbs," said Frau Merz. "And if that happens, the Germans will surely join in. The important question is what will the English and Russians do? If they mind their own business, the whole thing could fall flat."

"What about Italy?" Teresa asked. She hadn't expected Frau Merz to be so well informed.

"As usual, the prime minister will be indecisive. Or maybe I should say cautious. In truth, it's not a bad trait."

Next, Rodolfo spoke: "If we do join the war, we can put four million men in uniform. Italy, you may be interested to learn, has artillery pieces more accurate than the fabled French 75s." Everyone looked surprised at the old gardener's martial enthusiasm. In response, he became sheepish: "Although in general, war is sinful. It makes men forget themselves."

Teresa wasn't sure what he meant. Forget themselves? She supposed it had to do with men becoming so caught up in the war, they made poor decisions. She was about to ask him to explain when Frau Merz stood and said, "Enough of this for now, it's time we go to bed."

For several days thereafter, it looked as if they'd been wrong. War did not break out. The ministers and ambassadors gave speeches and the generals held their fire. But one morning as Teresa was coming down the stairs to begin her day of work, she encountered Signora Benedetti, already fully dressed despite the early hour. "Terrible news," she exclaimed. "Austria-Hungary has declared war on Serbia, and the Germans and Russians are said to be mobilizing." So it *had* happened, just as Frau Merz predicted. "It's not safe for us to remain in Trento," the Signora continued. "We're preparing to go south. My husband has already departed. We received a warning that he might be arrested for his political activities, so he left for Milano in the middle of the night."

Teresa spent the rest of the morning helping the Signora pack. Heaps of clothing were crammed into suitcases and seemingly random household items were selected by the Signora as she scurried about the house. "That lamp, we must take that lamp," and "the picture of the Blessed Virgin but not the one of my mother—I've never liked that rendering and don't mind leaving it behind." Everything they intended to take with them was deposited in the entryway in preparation for their departure. And all the while Frau Merz was bringing hampers of food up from the kitchen—Teresa counted five.

"What should we do when you're gone?" Teresa asked the Signora.

She looked bewildered, as if the question made no sense. Perhaps she thought the servants would simply evaporate if the family wasn't there. At last she said, "You'll have to ask

Frau Merz. Maybe you and the others could remain here and care for the house. You'll continue to be paid. With luck we won't be away too long." She cast a distraught glance around the room. "As you can see, I'm very upset."

Teresa was at once surprised and unsurprised by this turn of events. No matter how frequently people had mentioned the possibility of conflict, they would always conclude by saying, "Then again, nothing may happen." Even now, as it appeared half of Europe was about to go to war, it was difficult to know what to expect. It seemed obvious that Trento, an Austrian city filled with Italians, could not remain the same.

At one point Silvia, who seldom spoke to Teresa, said, "I've heard that ten thousand Austrian troops will be here by the end of the week with another five thousand in Rovereto. Italy might choose to remain neutral, but any politician or civil servant of Italian heritage in Trento will be thrown into prison or deported."

Teresa didn't know where Silvia got such information; still, it rang true. She could see the girl was frightened and felt sorry for her. Teresa herself was not particularly worried, at least not yet. She was of no importance to anyone, and as for her heritage, she'd just say, "I'm from Ulfano," and let them try to figure it out.

Signor Benedetti had taken the motorcar at his wife's urging, so now she and her children were left with only a horse-drawn coach. Teresa helped them load up and then watched as the Signora, Cristian, Lia, and the two little ones climbed in. The coach was being driven by a colleague of Signor Benedetti who also wanted to leave. As they disappeared up the street, she felt relief that they had escaped mixed with anxiety about being left behind. She thought about the ten thousand soldiers Silvia said were coming. Such a large number! Where would they live? Why were they being placed in Trento? It was all quite difficult to comprehend.

That evening there was great commotion in the streets. People shouted, church bells rang, and the trams were filled with young men, some saying *Viva Italia* and others waving Habsburg flags. "Ignore them," Frau Merz said. "They'll use any opportunity to get themselves drunk." But Teresa was too curious to remain inside. She walked to a nearby piazza and listened to the talk. Everyone had something to say about what would happen next: Italy would join the war on the side of the Austro-Hungarians. Italy would join the war on the side of the French. All of Italy would be annexed by the Germans. Trento would be attacked by the British and the French. As she listened, she felt someone approach from behind. It was Gaetano. "What do you think of all this?" he said.

"I'm not sure. It's confusing. Did you know the Benedettis have gone south?"

"Yes. It would have been dangerous for them to stay. Anyone connected to the Italian government will be at risk."

"Italy hasn't declared war."

"Even so, the Austrians will want Trento entirely under their control."

Once again, she was being told that Austrian soldiers would soon be descending upon the city. She was beginning to get frightened. "Are you leaving as well?" she asked.

"In the morning. I may join the Benedetti family. Or I may enlist. Italy will need men in uniform no matter what path they choose to take."

"I'll miss you," she whispered, and immediately felt it was too bold a thing to say.

"Come with me," he said, and she followed him into the shadows beneath some poplars. She was sure he was going to kiss her, and although she knew she shouldn't allow it, she had no intention of telling him to stop. When they reached a place where they couldn't be seen, he pulled her to him and held her in a firm embrace. Was he intending to do more than kiss her? What should she do if he tried? As he put his mouth on hers, she thought she might not resist.

However, he did not put his hands where they didn't belong or push her to the ground. He simply kissed her a second time and said goodbye. In return she spoke not a word—they had kissed and he was leaving and there was nothing more to be said or done.

With the Benedetti family gone, Frau Merz called the members of the household staff to the kitchen. "Although the family is absent," she told them, "we will carry on as usual, to the best of our abilities, and as conditions require. Our main objective is to make sure their home is as they left it when they return."

Teresa was relieved to see Frau Merz in control. So they were to be caretakers of the property. That made sense to her. And the Signora had promised they'd still be paid.

Then Silvia said, "I'm not staying. I'm off to live with my sister in Siena." They all looked at her. Perhaps she expected them to beg her to remain, but no one did. She simply wasn't pleasant to be around.

"I fear I'll be forced into the Austrian army," Luca said.

Rodolfo was peeling an apple with a folding knife. Without looking up, he said. "You have nothing to worry about. They won't want a fellow with a limp."

"I can take on some of Silvia's duties," Teresa said. "I don't suppose the kitchen will be very busy since the family won't have to be fed." As she spoke, she noticed Silvia rolling her eyes—she didn't believe Teresa could do her job.

They then discussed the various rumors they'd heard: The price of flour was already rising in anticipation of shortages; to board a train was going to require some special identification; the renowned German diplomat Prince von Bülow was now in Rome attempting to convince Italy to join the German cause. Only Luca had news that wasn't purely speculation: "You know how the signs on streets and buildings in our city have always been a mix of German and Italian? Well, the Italian ones are coming down."

The Imperial Army

While it seemed possible that Italy would remain neutral and Trento peaceful, the boys at the cathedral school could talk of nothing but war. Although Carlo didn't feel knowledgeable enough to contribute much, he was deeply curious about what the others had to say. He kept reminding himself that this conflict was really about the French and the Germans—or so he understood. Also that Germany and Austria-Hungary called themselves the Central Powers; England, France, and Russia called themselves the Allies; and Italy was still figuring out what to do—or so he understood. While he considered Miss Donavan an excellent teacher, what he'd learned in school about the geography and history of Europe wouldn't fill a page. Who were the Habsburgs anyway? How was it that Trento could float like an Austro-Hungarian island in the middle of the Italian state?

He sometimes thought about Vitale. If the Italians decided to enter the war, his friend would get his chance to fight. Carlo pictured him on horseback, galloping into battle, his saber flashing in the sun. He also thought about the brown-haired girl he'd met in the quiet garden behind the cathedral. One of the other boys had been able to tell him where the Benedetti family lived, and Carlo was now trying to work up the courage to go there and seek her out.

Then one morning he awoke to the sound of booted footsteps coming down the hall. By the time his eyes were fully open, they'd arrived at the door: six Austrian soldiers in blue-gray uniforms. After a brief pause, they entered the room and coolly surveyed the rows of beds in the early morning light. From where he lay, he could see four of his classmates, all of them emerging from sleep and wearing expressions of alarm. He tried to think of a reason for the Austrian soldiers' presence—a prank of some kind or a misunderstanding about the nature of the school. But no, he could tell already that the soldiers had come to take them away.

The soldiers were speaking German, so Carlo couldn't understand. He tried instead to guess their meaning by watching how the other boys behaved. Everyone was grabbing their clothes, clumsily putting a leg into a pair of trousers, searching for their shoes. Then an idea came to him. Still without his shirt on, he went to the small box where he kept his valuables. From it, he removed the documents showing him to be an American citizen and thrust them toward the nearest soldier. The man read the papers, ripped them in half and tossed them on the floor.

Suddenly, one of their teachers, Brother Leonardo, appeared, his eyes bright with panic. "You can't do this," he shouted. "They are students and not even Austrian. They want no part of your war."

The soldiers ignored him and shoved the boys—eleven including Carlo—toward the stairs. But Brother Leonardo wasn't ready to give up. He rushed at one of the soldiers and grabbed him by the arm. The soldiers glanced at each other as if to determine how to manage this inconvenience. Suddenly, one of them drew his pistol and struck Brother Leonardo on the side of the head. He moaned and fell to his knees, blood streaming down his face. The boys looked on in horror; their scholarly, soft-spoken teacher appeared to be badly hurt. Yet Brother Leonardo got to his feet again and stumbled toward the man who'd hit him. As he lurched forward, another soldier leveled his rifle and shot him dead. It happened so quickly. The sound was deafening. Everyone stopped moving and held their breaths. Carlo's mouth went dry and a stab of pain passed through his head. He shut his eyes briefly; when he opened them, nothing had changed.

At last one boy spoke. "You didn't have to do that." The soldier holding the gun replied in words of German even Carlo could understand: "Yes, I think I did." Never had Carlo been so terrified. He feared the boy's remark would be considered impertinent and that it would lead to further violence. But the soldier with the pistol said, "Let us proceed. We have a long way to go."

Outside, four more bewildered students huddled together. A woman who worked in the school's kitchen stood beside them and protested, asking the soldiers to explain on whose authority they were acting.

"An order of general mobilization has been issued," one of the soldiers told her. "It's all quite legal and no further explanation is required."

Minutes later all fifteen boys were loaded into the back of an open lorry idling on a nearby street. They were still settling onto the rough plank seats when the lorry pulled away. On the faces of the others, Carlo could see his own feelings reflected. All of them were stunned and frightened, confused and robbed of speech. One boy pounded his fists against his temples and another was looking in Carlo's direction. Or not looking: His eyes were unfocused, as though he was in a trance.

Traveling north, they left the city and began climbing into the foothills. The lorry ahead of them, which carried the soldiers, bathed Carlo and his schoolmates in a cloud of dust. Eventually, some of the boys began talking, their voices quavering with distress. One began sobbing about Brother Leonardo and another spoke indignantly about this injustice—which his father would *do something about.* Carlo wondered about his own father. How would he find out he'd been taken from the school? But rather than share his concern aloud, he remained silent, studied the landscape, and kept his thoughts to himself.

They passed a wagon filled with firewood being drawn by a mule and then a tinsmith pushing a heavy cart. They passed fields of yellow flowers and a cemetery enclosed by a low stone wall on which three girls sat drying their hair in the sun. He wondered what would happen if he were to jump out and flee. Despite his lack of knowledge about the military, he was certain that any soldier anywhere who deserted was treated harshly. He was now under their control.

At a farming village six more boys—or rather men, they appeared to be at least twenty-five—were gathered up. Surprisingly, they didn't seem very frightened. Maybe farm boys were hardier than schoolboys. Or they'd heard this was coming and had been able to prepare.

Late in the afternoon the trucks stopped and they were allowed a meager supper and a chance to piss. They talked more freely, and when Carlo explained where he was originally from, everyone laughed. Of the entire group, his situation—an American recently arrived in Italy and now suddenly an Austrian conscript—was considered the most absurd. One boy mentioned Brother Leonardo. This time no one cried, and Carlo was left with the disturbing feeling that he wouldn't be mentioned again.

As they continued, darkness began to fall. Carlo thought they might travel all night, but eventually they stopped. Each of them was given one thin blanket and told to sleep on the ground. They were guarded as if they were prisoners, the sentries visible in the moonlight every time he opened his eyes. Again, he thought about the girl with the brown curls, the one who threw the pigeon into the sky. He wished he'd gone looking for her when he had the chance. He'd assumed there was no hurry. But perhaps this was better. He didn't have to experience the disappointment and embarrassment that would come when she told him she scarcely remembered him and wished he'd go away.

The conditions were so cold and uncomfortable, he was relieved when sunrise came and they climbed into the lorry again. He spent the morning drowsing and finally fell fast asleep, wedged between two other boys. When he awoke, they were entering a broad valley that had been cleared of trees. In the center of the valley stood several rows of buildings, all of them long and narrow and made of unpainted wood. The trucks came to a stop and the soldiers clambered out.

"This is where you will undergo your training," shouted a man Carlo took to be an officer. "At the end of six weeks you will be prepared to fight with honor in the emperor's army."

He went on to explain that tomorrow they would be formally inducted and issued a uniform and boots, but now it was time to sleep. "Don't even think about sneaking off," he growled—at least that was Carlo's interpretation, based on the man's expression and the motions he made with his hands. But his next few words were beyond Carlo's ability to comprehend.

"What was that?" he whispered to the fellow on his left.

"If you do," the fellow whispered back, "I'll stick a poker up your ass and make you dance a jig."

Someone down the line said, "Go fuck yourself." Within seconds, three soldiers descended upon the man who had been foolish enough to speak and began beating him with the butts of their rifles and kicking him with their boots. When the man was mutilated and unconscious, they dragged him away. For a brief moment Carlo pictured the Cornishmen who had died in the mine collapse. He hadn't thought he'd see another blood-soaked body so soon.

The officer in charge said, "What do you suppose he expected?" and then led them toward the barracks where they were to spend the night.

At the entrance they were given two blankets and instructed to find an empty cot. Two blankets and a cot! Already things were improving, and Carlo wondered if last night had been a test. Many of the cots were occupied, and as Carlo walked down the long row, heads rose briefly and fell back again, their curiosity satisfied. When at last he found a bed to claim, he removed his shoes, covered himself, and fell instantly asleep.

He was awakened by someone pounding on his leg. "Get up, get up. The last one outside will be punished. Didn't you hear the bell?"

No, he had not. So it was only with luck that three others were still behind him when he burst out the door and into the cold morning air. There, on a broad expanse of hard-packed dirt, fifty men were hurriedly forming themselves into rows, while the officers called zugsführers shouted at them from both sides. Finding a spot between two men who seemed to know what they were doing, he glanced nervously about. For two days the lorry had carried them northward. Now they were in a place of rolling hills with mountains all around. He assumed they were somewhere in Austria but wouldn't have been surprised to learn they were in Switzerland or Germany. Or Timbuktu.

By the end of the morning, they had marched from one end of the compound to the other at least a dozen times;

been given tunics, breeches, nailed boots, and caps; and watched a demonstration of the proper way to carry a rifle. However, there weren't enough rifles to go around, so for now they could only hold their hands just so and pretend. He wondered what Vitale was doing. Surely nothing so mindless as this. Unlike Vitale, Carlo had never had any interest in the military. Yet here he was. At one point, with no warning, one of the zugsführers drew his pistol and began shooting over their heads. As they all dove to the ground, he laughed and said, "I was only testing you. It appears you all survived. Next time don't be so slow."

Thus began Carlo's period of training in the Imperial Army of the Empire of Austria-Hungary, which, for reasons he hadn't been told and suspected he might never be told, needed his help to fight their war.

Going to See Dante

In the days that followed, Teresa felt an atmosphere of unease descend upon the villa. It was partly because it was empty—where before there had been talk and laughter, there was now, at least on the upper floors, only motionless air. Outside, things were changing as well. Soldiers in Austrian uniforms and vehicles bearing the insignia of the Austro-Hungarian Empire—a black eagle with two heads beneath a single crown—had begun streaming into Trento. Luca, who spent more time than the rest of them roaming the streets, said, "You ought to see how many there are by the Duomo. They've made the piazza into a military camp. There must be a thousand men."

One morning they began hearing the sounds of explosions, some so close as to be alarming and some quite far off, like thunder from an impending storm. "They're blowing up bridges," Luca said.

At first Teresa was frightened. She hadn't expected the violence to begin so soon. For now it was only bridges, but what might come next? Eventually, she got used to it, the explosions as well as the gossip about what was being destroyed. And then she decided she wanted to see for herself how the city was being transformed. She asked Frau Merz if there were any errands that needed to be done.

"By yourself?" she replied, sounding even more uneasy than usual about her going out alone.

"I'll take Luca."

"You know what they can do to you—to women?"

"Yes. I know." She may have grown up in a tiny village, but the old women there knew a good deal about men and what they were capable of, and Teresa had heard them talk. In the short time she had lived in Trento, she had come to realize that city dwellers believed people from the mountains were naive. That belief was wrong.

Frau Merz thought for a moment and said, "Get me some dried figs. No tarrying. I'll expect you back by noon."

She found Luca and they walked toward the center of town. His head reached only to her shoulder, but despite his limp, it was Teresa who struggled to keep up. She didn't know much about him. He'd been injured in an accident, was friends with Rodolfo, and was one of the Benedetti family's most steadfast employees. All those things she'd learned from Frau Merz; for the most part he kept to himself.

The outlying districts were unusually empty. She had assumed the departure of the Benedetti family was exceptional, due to Signor Benedetti's stature in governmental affairs, but perhaps a larger number of people than she realized had gone south. Then again, maybe everyone was staying inside, peering out from behind their curtains, afraid of what might come.

They bought the figs Frau Merz wanted and continued toward the railway station, where soldiers began to appear. First in twos and threes and then in groups of a dozen or more, some strolling casually and some marching in ordered ranks. The square where an enormous statue of Dante Alighieri stood was filled with Austrian soldiers, the irony of which escaped her until Luca explained that the statue had been erected to show that Trento would remain truly Italian no matter where national borders were drawn.

They stood in a recessed doorway and watched the soldiers pass. A few civilians remained visible. All were elderly, the kind of stooped, slow-moving creatures who went out for their daily loaf of bread even in the driving rain. Just then they heard the sound of another explosion. It came from a different direction than those they'd heard earlier in the day. An old man pushing a cart filled with cabbages stopped beside them.

"You know what they're doing, don't you?" he said, his voice tight with suppressed rage. "They're destroying buildings on the edge of town to make room for fortifications. If something is in their way, they don't hesitate to knock it down."

"Fortifications?" Teresa said. "Who do they hope to keep out?"

"The French, the English. The wolves from the mountains."

"Not the Italians?"

"If by *the Italians* you mean the Italian government, they will dither until we all die." Then he shrugged and plodded onward, the sounds of the wheels of his cart on the cobblestones receding as he disappeared from sight.

"I think we ought to go home," Luca said. "You've seen what you wanted to see." Before she could respond, a soldier appeared. Teresa said, "Oh my!" and Luca placed himself in front of her to block the man's approach. When the soldier spoke, it was in a language that was unfamiliar to her. However, Luca was able to translate.

"He wants to know what we're doing. He says it's not illegal for us to be here but recommends against it."

"Ask him why," she said. "Is there something we should fear?"

Luca's eyebrows went up. She could tell he didn't want to relay her message—it might be taken as insolence. Nonetheless, he spoke again, and again she couldn't understand.

To her surprise, the soldier laughed, made another brief remark, and walked off shaking his head.

"What happened?" Teresa said. "What did you tell him?"

"I said you were an unschooled girl from the mountains who wanted to see Dante. That you were under the impression he was still alive."

"Very amusing," she said and gave him a playful shove. A few steps farther on, she asked Luca what language he and the soldier had been speaking. Some rare dialect of German perhaps?

"Hungarian."

Teresa gave him a look that meant *I need an explanation*.

"I learned it from my grandmother," he said, and they continued up the street.

Back at the Villa Benedetti, they told the others what they'd seen. Frau Merz said, "I know how to deal with them. If any of those fellows give you trouble, come to me. I suppose you forgot my figs."

"Of course not," Luca said. "When I'm sent on a mission, I always complete it."

Rodolfo cocked an eye in Frau Merz's direction. "She likes

to think she's fearsome. All that's fearsome about her is her cooking."

Later that week, they heard someone knocking at the door. As Silvia was no longer employed there, it fell to Teresa to hurry upstairs and see who it was. Only strangers used the main entrance, so she released the latch with some anxiety. There on the stoop stood two soldiers. To her surprise, their manner was relaxed rather than threatening. One of them tipped his gray kepi and the other merely touched the brim.

They introduced themselves by reciting the name of their unit, words that were meaningless to her. One of them said, "Have you any livestock? We have orders to confiscate all horses and mules. You can keep your cows for now."

For a moment she considered lying. Then she noticed two other men were at that moment disappearing around the corner of the house. They'd find what they were looking for no matter what she told them. "I'll fetch the groom," she said.

It was all done in a businesslike manner. There were three horses remaining—those that hadn't been used to pull the carriage that took the Benedetti family south. Teresa and Luca watched as the soldiers, who were stern but not combative, led them away. She couldn't tell what Luca was thinking. His face was expressionless and he said scarcely a word. Maybe he thought it was for the best. No one had been riding them and now they wouldn't have to be fed. Yet when she and Luca returned to the kitchen and told Frau Merz what had transpired, Luca began to sob.

"What will I tell Signor Benedetti?" he moaned. "I'm responsible for his horses. We'll never get them back."

"You had no choice," said Frau Merz.

"That was my job! What am I to do now?"

"There is still the cow, the chickens, and the rabbits. And if you have time left over, you can help Rodolfo with the garden and the upkeep of the house."

But the next day the same men returned and took the cow, the chickens, and the rabbits. As soon as they were gone, Luca cried again. Teresa assumed they'd failed to confiscate Rodolfo's pigeons only because they were on the far side of the trees, out of sight. Once again Luca asked what he was supposed to do now that the animals were gone, and once again Frau Mertz dismissed his concerns: "You can start by washing the windows in the conservatory," she said. "After that you can polish the silver. It hasn't been done in weeks."

In the aftermath of these events, Teresa sat down to write to her mother. This time there was no shortage of things to tell her—the soldiers, the demolition of bridges and buildings, and the removal of the livestock, to name only a few. But when she completed the letter and put it out, the *postino* didn't take it. There was no *postino*—the mails had been stopped.

Training Camp

For the first few days at the training camp, all his attention was on learning how the military worked. Carlo supposed his feelings were like those of an animal, a dog for example, that has been taken by humans to a new place: Where do I get food, where do I sleep, how can I avoid being punished, and what will happen next? One thing he wasn't sure about was if he should keep to himself. It might be best to form an alliance, but only if he could find others in whom he could place his trust.

He wondered again if his father knew he was no longer in Trento. Carlo couldn't imagine him trying very hard to find him. He'd seemed relieved when he went away to school. It was as though he had considered it his sacred duty to take his youngest son back to Italy—a way, perhaps, of keeping his promises to his dead wife—but after the task had been completed, he lost interest. No, his father wouldn't spend much time finding out what had become of him.

The training itself wasn't bad. They were taught to respond to commands, to march in formation, wheel right, wheel left, and after a truckload of Mausers arrived (still without cartridges), to strip and clean their rifles and deploy bayonets. The food was adequate, and because it was early summer, the weather neither too cold nor too hot. At first no one seemed to know where they'd be going when their training ended; then word arrived that they were being sent to the Russian front. This Carlo found concerning—not because he knew anything about the Russian front but because it sounded so far away. Once again his poor knowledge of geography troubled him. All he knew was that Russia was enormous, spreading all the way to the Pacific, and Germany was somewhere off to the north. England was an island, and Italy, well, at least Miss Donovan had made sure he could identify the boot.

The number of conscripts in the camp—and they were all conscripts—had been increasing by the day. In addition to Italians, there were Bosnians, Magyars, Slovenes, and Czechs. Far fewer Austrians than he'd expected; perhaps they were being trained somewhere else. The officers in charge continued to speak German, aided by hand signals, emphatic tones of voice, and easily understood words such as "Schnell!" and "Halt!"

One morning an oberleutnant, noticing how poorly Carlo spoke Italian, asked him where he was from. When he said, "Colorado," the officer laughed. "I myself lived in Pennsylvania," he replied. For a few minutes then they shared memories of America—the food, the various kinds of entertainment, especially the sport of baseball, and a little information about where each of them had lived. The officer said he'd just opened a dry goods store in Scranton when his aging parents in Amstetten called him home. It was wonderful to meet a fellow with whom he had a few things in common—although since the Pennsylvanian was an officer, they could never be friends.

"What about you, why did you come here?" the officer asked.

"My father wanted me to. He insisted."

"Ah yes, the father," he said and shook his head. "A condition we have in common, one we cannot escape."

Thereafter, that particular officer seemed to give him special treatment—some lapse in attention that would earn another man a reprimand was overlooked for him. Still, he felt quite alone. The Italians he'd arrived with, including those who'd been his classmates at the school in Trento, banded together as a group. So, too, did the other nationalities, eating together, conversing, and playing the card games they grew up with during the hour between supper and sleep. As the only American (save for the officer), Carlo was a group of one. He wished he had a book to occupy himself. He'd seen no reading matter of any kind except manuals of military procedure and the German Bibles he noticed a few men reading before bed. He'd left the book about trees Miss Donovan had given him back at the cathedral school.

He remained uncertain of their location. He entertained fantasies of escape, of making his way back to Trento, but he'd probably end up lost. He was also dissuaded by the image of that poker up his ass—although he suspected that in reality deserters were simply shot. Were his feelings shared by others? Did they consider themselves prisoners rather than patriots preparing to fight for a noble cause? It was difficult to tell since all he ever heard anyone talk about was food and sleep.

One afternoon they were marched to the top of a distant hill carrying fully loaded packs. If they slowed their pace at all, their commanders called them donkeys and jabbed them with batons. The sun went down and still they marched, reaching their destination halfway through the night. Able to rest at last, they dropped their packs, gulped what water they had left, and threw themselves to the ground. Before he could shut his eyes, the man next to him pointed to a cluster of lights far in the distance and said, *Venezia, Venezia!* So now at least he knew that much. After less than an hour's rest, they began the return trip, arriving at the camp at dawn. His shoulders hurt from the pack, his feet hurt from the walking, and he pictured Vitale on horseback, riding through some village and waving at all the girls.

Some days were arduous and others just dull, but what all of them seemed to care about most was that the end of their training was coming and they were about to be sent somewhere else. One fellow told him his brother had gone through military training before the war and it lasted ten weeks instead of six. "Is this true?" they asked the zugsführer. "Indeed it is," he replied. "We've shortened it because you are all so intelligent." Then he looked at the sky and laughed.

The talk about Russia and the Eastern Front increased. The officers told them things had been going well there and the Russian girls were charming. And that they spread their legs for any man in uniform, especially one from the Imperial Army, or so it had been reported. However, just as their departure seemed imminent, Carlo was told he'd be remaining behind. He didn't understand why, even after the order had been translated into Italian, so he sought out the officer from Pennsylvania and asked him to explain.

"You said you were a miner," the officer replied. "There is a need for men with your skills in the mountains. You and a few others are being sent to the Südtirol. You'll be most useful there."

"I was never a miner. I lived in a mining camp and sometimes helped my father but—"

"It's too late to change the order. Besides, you should be thankful you're not going east. Fighting the Russians won't be easy. I predict the plains will be drenched in blood."

Despite the officer's remark, Carlo was disconcerted. He didn't want to be left behind. Was he fated to spend his days in uniform digging iron or coal or some other mineral necessary to the war effort and never fire a gun? Vitale would be outraged to be given such an assignment. But Carlo lacked Vitale's patriotic fervor. If the South Tyrol was going to remain peaceful, perhaps, as the officer said, he should be pleased he was being sent there.

Carlo wasn't the only one with questions. Some of the other Italians had begun speaking out about the fact that Italy was still neutral. Didn't that mean they could remain neutral as well?

In response, the zugsführer—who they'd begun calling "the Camel" for the hump on his back—ordered the Italian conscripts to assemble. He said he needed to clarify their status since some of them seemed confused:

"Although Italy is thus far neutral, you yourselves are not. You are members of the Imperial Army. If Italy declares war on Austria-Hungary, you will fight against your countrymen. If you refuse to do so, we will not treat you as Italians and grant you the status of prisoners of war. We will treat you as traitors and execute you at once. If, on the other hand, Italy makes the wiser choice and joins with us to fight the Allied Powers, then all Italians and all Austrians and all Hungarians and, yes, all Germans will be brothers in arms. Which will be excellent, don't you agree?"

How strange, Carlo thought, to be a member of "the Imperial Army." While it sounded grand, when he looked around at his fellow conscripts, it was difficult to put much faith in their ability to fight. The boy on his left had a blank look on his face and Carlo could tell he hadn't been listening; the boy on his right couldn't stop scratching the seeping crimson rash on his arms and neck.

After the Camel's speech, none of them asked about neutrality. Or rather all but one didn't. A man who had been a paperhanger in Trento continued to insist he be allowed to return home. The next morning when they got out of bed and reported for duty, he was gone.

"Back to Trento?" some fool asked.

"Where else?" the Camel replied.

Rosa

Being unable to write to her mother was upsetting; being unable to write to Gaetano was heartbreaking. She'd been about to begin her first letter to him when the mail between Trento and the Italian territories was stopped. Suppose he hadn't heard about that. He might assume she didn't care.

"He probably received a commission and is now drinking brandy in a garden in Florence with some other officers," Frau Merz said. Then she added, "It's not healthy for you to think about him so much."

"How do you know how much I think about him?"

"You mention him at every opportunity."

"I don't."

"Ask Luca. You do."

It was true. She meditated on him every day. Next time she saw him, *she'd* be the one to lead them into the woods. Thinking about what they'd do when they got there made her feel faint. She worried that he'd forget her. He was older, more worldly, and no doubt already meeting new girls, so what was to secure her place in his heart?

She looked out the window at the trees. "Maybe he just went to visit the Benedetti family. If so, he'll be back soon."

"I told you to stop it," Frau Merz said.

Then one day in May the news they'd been waiting for arrived. Italy was entering the war. To the surprise of many, they were joining the Allies—the French, the British, and the Russians. On the other side, the Central Powers: the Germans, Austro-Hungarians, and Turks.

Overnight, the city of Trento became an Austrian fortress, surrounded no longer by a country unable to make up its mind but by enemy territory. In response, more of those with Italian citizenship and Italian sympathies chose to leave. Or were evacuated by force. Not only prominent politicians like Signor Benedetti but professionals, civil servants, and those whose families had some status in the Italian state. Teresa watched from an upstairs window as carriages, motorcars, and people on foot streamed southward out of town in anticipation of the exits being sealed. While some servants appeared to be accompanying the families they worked for, Teresa gave no thought to leaving. Frau Merz said that after the Signora and the children were settled, they might send for the villa's staff. But it was easy to see that little consideration was being given to those employed in the kitchens or gardens or stables. They would continue to work in much the same way as before.

Even so, Teresa wondered about her safety. If, as people said, Trento was coveted by both sides, wouldn't there come a time when the city would be attacked? In truth, she had so little knowledge about war, she wasn't sure what to worry about. Except, of course, for Gaetano. She would worry about his fate, and about the possibility she'd never see him again.

In the days that followed, she noticed that several of the houses on their road had been abandoned. The signs weren't always obvious—an unswept walk, draperies no longer being drawn. But not everyone had disappeared. Across the way, a girl about her age was coming and going at various times of the day. When, one morning, Teresa saw her locking the front door and preparing to leave, she ran outside and called to her.

"Hello. I see you, too, have remained behind."

The girl turned, a look of alarm on her face. She was petite, pretty, with dark hair and tired eyes suggesting it had been a while since she'd slept.

Teresa walked briskly across the road to meet her, continuing to speak as she went: "I didn't mean to startle you. I was only wondering—so many people have gone away."

The girl nervously fingered the key to the house. Realizing what she was doing, she dropped it in her pocket and said, "I woke up one morning and discovered I was all alone. The family I work for left halfway through the night."

"They didn't tell you? How impolite. Were the other servants treated as poorly?"

She shook her head. "They went away with the family. So now I am by myself."

Teresa wondered what the girl did to deserve such treatment. Maybe they just forgot her. It was possible such a thing could have happened in the confusion and rush. "I'm sorry," she said. "Are you planning to stay? Even though everyone else is gone?" She couldn't imagine being placed in such a position—abandoned without any instructions and left to fend for yourself.

"I haven't any choice. I came a long way to work for them and don't know where I'd go."

They talked for a few minutes about how the city had changed. Her name was Rosa and Teresa could see that, despite her situation, she was doing her best to act brave. Before they parted, she invited her to come to the Benedetti house for the evening meal. Teresa felt somehow responsible for the girl, or at least that the two of them, being in similar situations, would be wise to lean on each other for support.

"There are four of us," she explained. "You'll enjoy having someone to talk to."

"You're very considerate," Rosa said.

Back at the house she told Frau Merz that she'd taken the liberty of inviting someone to supper.

"Tonight? Who?"

"A girl from up the street. She was left behind by her employer and now she's in the house alone."

"The poor thing. I'll prepare something special," she said.

Teresa left Frau Merz and went upstairs. Since the departure of the family, she had been spending less time in the kitchen. With such a small number to feed and no formalities attending meal services, Frau Merz preferred to cook alone. Instead, Teresa cleaned and did laundry and helped Rodolfo in the garden. She liked working outdoors, even when the weather was bad. Rodolfo seemed to enjoy her company; at least that was how she interpreted his tendency to work alongside her rather than sending her off to do some task by herself.

That evening, Rosa arrived and they gathered in the kitchen to eat. When Frau Merz asked her to tell them about herself, she did so without hesitation. She'd obviously been starved for company and relished the chance to speak.

"I come from a village near the town of Brunico," she began. "My father died of consumption. My mother died while giving birth to my sister, who died as well, God rest their souls." She paused while they all exclaimed and offered their sympathy for her parents' and sister's deaths. "Therefore,

I was raised by my aunt," she continued. "When I was fifteen, a boy said he wanted to marry me but that we must first go to Gorizia to make peace with his father. Yet when we got there, his father wouldn't hear of it and I was abandoned on the streets. Fortunately, a priest took pity on me. He helped me come here to Trento and find work."

Several questions followed. Frau Merz wanted to know what her position was in the house across the road, while Rodolfo was curious about the name of the helpful priest. "Perhaps I know him," he said.

Next, the others told their stories, none of which Teresa had heard before, at least not in such detail. Rodolfo was once a soldier, Luca had a twin brother who died in the same railroad accident that left him with a limp, and Frau Merz had never married but still had numerous family members in the Austrian village where she was born. She went to visit them every year. Teresa told her story last and felt it was the least interesting. She grew up in the mountains. Her father ran away. Her family now consisted of her mother and her dog.

Rodolfo didn't mention the wife and children who died of cholera. Teresa wasn't surprised he chose not to bring that up. She couldn't imagine experiencing such a loss.

Rosa returned nightly for the next few days. The five of them got on well, and although the explosions continued and the number of soldiers and gray vehicles in Trento steadily increased, the evenings around the table were pleasantly serene. But Teresa was not so naive as to think it could last forever or even very long, and so it did not. On a rainy afternoon, four soldiers, one of whom introduced himself as Hauptmann Schneider, arrived at the door and told her the house was to be requisitioned for military use. Unlike the previous men who had confiscated the livestock, Hauptmann Schneider wore the kind of beribboned uniform that designated high rank.

"May I ask what that will consist of?" It was Frau Merz. Teresa hadn't realized she was standing behind her. She must have heard the heavy footsteps in the ingresso and come to see who it was.

"I intend to live here," Hauptmann Schneider explained. "Myself and a few others who comprise my staff." He motioned to the men accompanying him. "Nothing more than that."

"And will you need to be fed?" Frau Merz asked.

"Of course. You'll be well provisioned. Simply cook as you would if the previous occupants were still here. Also, you'll do our laundry. We will arrive in two days." Teresa hoped that when he said, "Myself and a few others," he meant it and didn't show up with fifty men. Ten might be all right.

That night at supper they discussed the soldiers. Naturally, they would have to be accommodating; were there things they could do to prepare?

"No special preparations are necessary," Frau Merz said. "We will treat them as we would any other guests."

"What shall I do if soldiers come to my door?" Rosa asked.

"They didn't seem dangerous," Teresa said. "They had good manners and spoke with respect." Then she reminded herself that Rosa was all alone. "What if you were to come and live with us?" she said, glancing at Frau Merz to be sure she hadn't overstepped. Frau Merz nodded and said, "Yes, you ought to move here. Provided you're willing to work."

Rosa didn't hesitate to accept. "Thank you. I'll go back tonight and gather my things."

Teresa, pleased by Frau Merz's response, said she would help.

Visiting the house across the road was eye-opening. Rosa's quarters were little more than a closet, and while the Benedettis had left many of their belongings behind, here only a few pieces of furniture remained.

"I'm surprised you didn't hear them packing."

"I guess I'm a sound sleeper," Rosa said.

They passed a room that contained only a single chair and paused to look inside. The emptiness made Teresa uncomfortable. She wasn't sure she wanted to live in a house filled with soldiers, but it would be worse to be in one devoid of life.

Rosa turned to her. "Do you think my employer will be angry that I didn't stay?"

Teresa, gesturing toward the empty room, said, "I don't think they're coming back."

The Bosnian

Italy's declaration of war did not cause Carlo's orders to be revised. He was still being sent into the mountains to do some sort of mining. He watched the others march off 120 at a time to board a train to the Eastern Front and continued to wonder if he was being treated unfairly or spared a terrible fate.

When the camp was nearly empty, he was allowed to sleep late and wander about. At first he enjoyed the freedom, but it quickly wore thin. The one remaining cook stopped preparing meals and his evenings were filled with boredom. He'd have liked to go walking into the surrounding countryside. Unfortunately, he wasn't allowed to go beyond the fence.

He went to the Camel and said, "Tell me to do something. Give me a job." He was directed to shovel out the latrines. Two other men who'd been caught stealing cigarettes were ordered to assist. They had to tie handkerchiefs saturated with camphor over their noses and mouths to block the stench. It took them five days to finish and he didn't ask for work again.

As far as Carlo could tell, the Austrians didn't fear the Italians. All their efforts seemed to be directed against the

Russians and the French. Yet he was also aware of how little he knew—it was entirely possible that fighting had commenced on the border between Italy and Austria already. One thing he'd learned about being in the military was that no effort whatsoever was spent on keeping ordinary conscripts informed.

After two weeks of waiting, he and three others were given a Puch touring car and sent toward the Dolomites. Two were Austrians from the Tyrol, members of the Jäger Battalion. The other was a stout Bosnian with thick black eyebrows who wore the uniform of his country's army, including a reddish-brown fez. In a low, gravelly voice he said his name was Alexi.

One Austrian drove, the other sat beside him, and Carlo and the Bosnian rode in back. Carlo was becoming more confident that he had stumbled into some good fortune. If most of the men he'd trained with were in an uncomfortable, slow-moving train en route to Russia, wasn't it better to be traveling briskly through the mountains by car? The road was not always the best but the weather was delightful. With the top of the car down, he could feel the warm sun, see the deep, velvety green forest on either side, and gaze up at a cloudless sky. It reminded him of Colorado, and for the first time since leaving Trento, he felt more free than oppressed. But he didn't expect that feeling to last.

Carlo asked Alexi, in the mixed language they had both learned to use in the training camp, if he, too, came from a family of miners.

"Sì, carbone," the Bosnian said.

"You mined coal?"

"Yes. And my father before me."

"Di dove sei?"

"Dove?"

"Where. Where are you from?"

"Ah, Tuzla. It's a very beautiful city. And you?"

"Not from a city. Hardly a villaggio. We called it a mining camp. I don't know what they'd call it here."

"One's home is beautiful because it is one's home, don't you agree?" After pausing for a moment, Alexi added, "We won't speak of the fact that it was a Bosnian who assassinated the archduke and started this infernal war." Then he shrugged in a way that Carlo found so amusing, he couldn't help but laugh.

Eventually the mountains began to close in around them, sheer rock faces streaked with ice and snow. The trees became smaller and clung to the steep slopes with partially exposed roots. As the sun disappeared behind a distant ridge and the air grew colder by the mile, they took blankets from their kit and wrapped themselves against the wind. At times the road seemed narrower than the width of the car, with a steep cliff face on one side and a terrifying precipice dropping into pure darkness on the other. Thus, Carlo was relieved when, rather than continuing to drive by the weak carbide headlamps, the Austrians elected to stop for the night. They slept in their seats, not for comfort but for warmth. For the past several weeks Carlo hadn't been dreaming; here that changed. He was at sea again, standing on the deck of the ship, when someone approached him out of the fog. He expected it to be his father, but instead, it was the sailor who had told him Ulfano did not exist. However, this time he seemed to be saying that it was his home in Colorado that didn't exist. Before he could protest, he heard the voices of his companions in the car. They were all awake, it was morning and time to motor on.

Near noon on their second day of travel, they emerged from a narrow pass into a valley and saw laid out before them a large encampment, twice the size of the place they'd trained. There were rows upon rows of tents, dozens of wagons and lorries, a paddock holding hundreds of horses and mules, and an entire cow pasture filled with artillery pieces of different sizes, some with barrels so huge, Carlo thought it must take five men to load a single shell.

They presented themselves to the quartermaster, who assigned places to sleep. Then they made their way to the mess tent, where they were served plates of stew so boiled down and thick, it was like glue, and black bread as heavy as rock. Carlo gobbled it up and left not a scrap behind. Afterward, he sat outside on a tree stump as more men arrived and lorries were unloaded and mules were outfitted with panniers and led toward the perimeter of the camp in preparation to depart. Just as he was becoming immersed in a reverie about a day spent fishing with his brother Joe, the Bosnian appeared.

"So this is war," he said, lowering his haunches onto a second stump nearby.

"Not yet. I think this is where we wait to go to war," Carlo replied.

From off in the mountains there came the sound of several explosions, five or six, each seemingly closer than the one before. Alexi took no note of them. Instead, he said, "I would like to visit Italy. Especially Florence and Rome."

"I haven't been to either one."

Alexi looked surprised. "You have been to America. That's even better."

"I guess so," he said, wishing he could explain that America was so expansive that to generalize about it was nearly meaningless. But it was too complicated a topic for his vocabulary, so he didn't try.

"Also Naples," the Bosnian added.

"Maybe after this is over," Carlo said tentatively. He didn't like talking about the future in terms that were too specific—it seemed like tempting fate. Alexi, though, had no such fears:

"I'd like to visit the volcano there—what's it called? And

of course Pompeii. Also Sicily. Then across the Mediterranean to Egypt. The Nile, the Great Pyramid of Giza. Who wouldn't want to see that?"

Carlo admired his enthusiasm and thought perhaps he, too, should be imagining journeys to far-off places. To do so wasn't exactly to plan a future, but it was to think beyond their current situation, beyond whatever this war held for them in the months to come. For a time they sat in silence. The moon rose, remaining visible at the horizon for only a few minutes before disappearing behind heavy clouds.

As they were about to go off to their beds, Alexi held his hand out, palm upward.

"Snieg," he said.

Carlo looked up and saw the crystals, glistening as they fell.

"Yes, snieg. In May."

Snow fell through the night and by morning was knee-deep. As Carlo and Alexi followed the flow of men toward the mess tent for breakfast, Carlo began worrying about the quality of the boots he'd been issued. If there was one thing he despised, it was cold feet. Although his father had always made sure he had clothing to wear, it was never more than adequate, and he'd spent whole winters walking through the snows of Colorado wearing the cheapest of shoes. Which was to say he knew about cold feet.

They sat at a long table made of rough planks, drinking coffee turned gray by a splash of tinned milk and eating the usual black bread. Alexi began his meal with a prayer, and Carlo, out of respect, waited until he was finished before taking his first bite. He noticed how damaged Alexi's hands were—on one, he was missing the ends of two fingers, and on the other, half his thumb. The clasped hands of a man who had spent years working in mines.

Upon returning to the barracks, they were ordered by the barracks chief to stand at the foot of their cots and await their assignment for the day. The tent was full of recent arrivals, and as far as Carlo could tell, none of them knew what to expect.

Soon an unteroffizier and a korporal entered and began working their way down the line. Some men were given verbal instructions, usually about doing menial work around camp, while others were handed slips of paper, which they read with great interest, anxious to know what they'd be doing next. When the unteroffizier reached Carlo, he presented him with one of the papers and waited for him to read it. Carlo looked down. As expected, it was in German so he could only shake his head.

"Italienisch?" said the unteroffizier.

"Sì." He'd have tried to explain that he was actually American, but that would have made him a novelty and he preferred not to attract attention.

The korporal snatched the paper from his hand and translated. Or rather attempted to translate, because he did such a poor job, Carlo was left to do much of the deciphering himself. The gist of it seemed to be that he should wait to be visited by Oberleutnant Haas, who oversaw the miners and engineers.

He remained standing until the process of giving orders was complete. Although most of the men went directly outside to begin work, a few returned to their cots and gathered their belongings, as if they were being sent elsewhere. Soon only he, Alexi, and one other fellow remained. This third man was an Austrian with a slender face and straw-colored hair who said his name was Florian.

"So we are to wait for the oberleutnant," Carlo said.

Florian's expression was one of undisguised contempt. "I despise it here. I want to go home." Carlo was taken aback by his outspokenness. Even though there was no one of authority present to hear him, he didn't think it was worth taking chances. He'd seen what could happen to a conscript who said too much.

Half an hour passed and then an hour. Carlo and Alexi discussed the weather and the kinds of food they wished they'd be served, while Florian paced uneasily about the room. When they ran out of things to talk about, they sat on their respective cots and stared blankly at the floor. Carlo wondered what was happening in Colorado at this precise moment. How was business at the saloon? Was Miss Donovan at the school? What was the weather like? He'd seen it snow in May there as well.

At last Oberleutnant Haas arrived. He was broad shouldered, with a pockmarked face and hair as red as a fox.

"So you are my miners," he said.

Once again Carlo had the urge to explain that he was no miner, merely the son of one, but he kept his mouth shut. If they decided they'd made an error, there was no telling where he'd be sent.

"You know how to use explosives, nicht ist dach recht?" the oberleutnant asked. They glanced at each other uneasily. Before any of them could answer, he laughed and said, "Don't look so alarmed. Setting a charge is less dangerous than being shot at, I promise you that." Carlo could only hope that if explosives were involved, Alexi and Florian had enough experience to keep them from being blown to bits.

The oberleutnant explained they would be going southeast into the mountains, where they would be put to work digging tunnels and constructing gun placements and bunkers. These would create a barrier the Italian forces would be unable to breach. Not mining exactly, but making large holes in the rock.

"When do we leave?" Carlo asked.

"Next summer," Oberleutnant Haas said, laughing again. And then, "Tomorrow, of course."

The Horse

The soldiers moved in the following day. Teresa was relieved to see only Hauptmann Schneider and eight others—more than had visited the previous afternoon but better than the dozens she had feared. She hoped they wouldn't break the crystal or pocket the silver or treat old Rodolfo with disrespect. She hoped they would keep their hands to themselves.

The first thing they did was take possession of various rooms, without asking which ones they should or shouldn't use. Then they assembled in the dining room and began ordering food as if they were at an inn. Frau Merz prepared the meal with Teresa's help, and she and Rosa served, trembling as they did so while also observing with watchful eyes. What a disaster it would be to ladle soup into some korporal's lap. Save for the officer in charge, all the soldiers were quite young, closer to schoolboys—she noticed their thin wrists and smooth cheeks—than grown men.

Since Ulfano was near the border, Teresa knew a bit of German, but Rosa, coming from farther north, understood every word. When they returned to the kitchen between the canederli and the rabbit stew, Teresa tugged on Rosa's apron and asked what they'd been saying.

"They're talking about how lucky they were to find this place and how comfortable they'll be. Also some remarks on military matters, the orders they've been given and the stupidity of the commanders higher up." But a little later she took Teresa aside and whispered in her ear: "One of them said we're both rather comely and asked me to tell him your name." Teresa blanched and pushed Rosa away.

The following morning their new lodgers left early and didn't return until dark. This pattern repeated itself for the next several days, which was a relief. It would have been awkward to have them spend their time roaming about the house. Still, they expected to be fed morning and night, so the kitchen was once again busy, almost like before.

At the end of the week, perhaps because he was beginning to feel more at home, Hauptmann Schneider explained that his job was to oversee logistics and transportation within the city and the others comprised his staff. That explained why they had taken over Signor Benedetti's library, covering the desk with maps and charts that they perused after supper and sometimes well into the night.

Teresa was pleased that Rosa had moved in. In the kitchen they often worked side by side, finishing each job with such care and efficiency, Frau Merz said that after the war was over, the two of them should open a trattoria. Since Silvia was gone, they shared the task of cleaning the soldiers' rooms. Fortunately, Hauptmann Schneider was strict with his subordinates and they maintained their quarters well.

One day Luca informed them that wounded men had begun arriving in Trento. He said a building previously used for some aspects of city government had been transformed into a hospital, with stretcher after stretcher being unloaded from ambulances arriving from the front.

Rosa began to cry—"To think of all those poor boys"— but Frau Merz said, "That means the Austro-Hungarian forces are suffering for their aggression, which they deserve." Although Frau Merz had explained why she was sympathetic to the Italians, Teresa still found it surprising that she could have such firm opinions when the alliances and grounds for dispute among the various nations seemed to change by the day.

She wondered again about Gaetano. Was he in danger? She'd like to see him in uniform. He was probably an officer, with ribbons on his pockets and gold epaulets. She wondered as well about her mother's health and safety but continued to believe that the worst that could happen was a passing army would take the vegetables from her garden. She couldn't imagine soldiers occupying their small house in Ulfano as the Austrians were doing here. And then she thought about Allucio. Did he ever think about her? How the minds of dogs worked would always be something of a mystery. She hoped he hadn't forgotten her but couldn't blame him if he had.

The next morning, after the soldiers had finished their breakfast and departed, they heard something outside, a strange buzzing sound. Luca burst into the kitchen shouting, "Aeroplanes! Aeroplanes! Come look!" They followed him outside, lifting their faces to the sky, and saw not one, not two, but five biplanes, the sounds of their engines reminding Teresa of enormous bees. After flying over the city, they banked toward the river and circled back.

"Who do they belong to?" she asked.

"See the red and green markings? Italiano!" Luca replied.

"Maybe they're going to drop bombs on us," Rosa said, even as she waved. Suddenly, up the street, some Austrian soldiers appeared and began shooting their rifles into the sky. Teresa was paralyzed—not by the danger but by the spectacle of it all. Although she knew she ought to run back inside, she was too fascinated to leave.

When the flying machines were gone and the shooting had stopped, Luca pulled Teresa aside. "Yesterday I saw one of Signor Benedetti's horses. A very fine animal. One of those they took away."

She could see he was pained by this discovery. He'd cared for the horses every day for years, forming a deep attachment to them, only to have them so abruptly removed.

"He's gone lame," he continued. "If he doesn't recover quickly, they'll send him to the butcher and carve him into chops."

"I'm very sorry. Is there anything to be done?"

"We could find the officer in charge and you could speak to him," he said. "Tell him I can care for the animal if they'll let me take it back."

Teresa had merely been trying to be kind and was surprised by his request. Why had he chosen her to ask for help? Perhaps because Rodolfo was old, Frau Merz wanted them to keep to themselves, and he didn't know Rosa well. Still, she was only a girl. She said, "Oh, Luca, I'm sure they wouldn't listen to me."

She thought about the horse for the rest of the day. Suppose she were to approach Hauptmann Schneider. What good was a lame horse to the army? Maybe he could intervene. She'd never spoken to him about anything important, not beyond asking if he wanted another helping of potatoes.

She went to Frau Merz and said, "Would you talk to the Austrians for Luca? He happened to see one of the horses they took from here and noticed it was lame. He'd like to have it returned to his care."

"That would be foolish," she said. "They'd consider it meddling—if they considered it at all."

"Maybe you could make it sound as if he'd be helping them, rather than the reverse. He's good with horses and knows what to do when one is hurt."

Frau Merz shook her head. "No. You must listen to me. Asking questions about the horse would be a mistake."

She understood Frau Merz's reasoning. Although they

were polite enough, the Austrians were enemy occupiers. Best to speak only when spoken to, best to keep their mouths shut.

Teresa found Luca and told him the bad news. Instead of looking crestfallen and giving up, he said, "There are other ways."

It took her a moment to figure out what he was proposing, but when she did, she responded as forcefully as she could: "Most definitely not. Imagine how they'd deal with you! They'll throw you in jail. They might even stand you up before a firing squad."

"You haven't been to where the horses and mules are being kept. It's all very disorganized. They'll never know it's gone."

"And what about the men staying here?"

"They have no reason to go out to the stable. They think it's empty. If by chance they notice the horse, I'll say it's been here the whole time. That it was left behind because it's lame."

She could see he'd given the matter a good deal of thought—and that he was intent on taking action, no matter the risks.

"I want to go with you," she said.

"I don't need any help." Although he was an unassuming young man, she'd noticed a certain fierceness—perhaps the result of his injury—emerging from time to time.

"Please. I promise not to interfere." She still thought she could talk him out of it. Or if not, help him avoid getting caught.

At eleven o'clock that night they met by the back door. Before they set off, Luca lifted his tunic to show her the halter and lead rope he had wrapped around his waist.

"Can you tell it's there?" he asked.

She raised an eyebrow. "It's a good thing it's dark."

They slipped out of the house and hurried up the street. Luca had spent his entire life in Trento and knew all the shortcuts, the narrowest passageways, the most secluded lanes. The city was supposedly under curfew but it wasn't being rigorously enforced. Luca said he'd been out at night on several occasions without encountering any difficulty. "We'll avoid the places where the feldgendarmerie—the military police—congregate," he explained.

Despite the fact that the city was now entirely under military rule, at that time of day, in the neighborhoods they were traversing, there had been little visible change. The side streets were dark, not because of the curfew but because the good citizens of Trento—the ones remaining—had already gone to bed.

Luca led them to a blacksmith shop adjacent to a small, fenced enclosure. "There he is," he whispered, using a discreet nod to guide her gaze toward a corner of the pen.

"How did you find him?" she asked and shivered, more from nervousness than cold.

"I suppose you could call it an accident, but I have a good eye for horses. I knew it was him at once, even from a long way off."

Teresa waited in the shadows as Luca coaxed the horse to him. First it seemed wary, then it snorted in recognition. At the far end of the street she could see a well-lighted taverna with soldiers going in and out. And hear their voices, their laughter, some of which sounded overloud and forced. She kept one eye on the taverna and the other on Luca. If any of the soldiers came in their direction, she'd whisper a warning before they were close enough to pose a threat.

As Luca steadied the horse and began slipping the halter over its head, she glanced back the way they had come. For a moment she thought she saw movement in the darkness. But no, the way remained clear.

She held the gate for Luca and the horse as they stepped

out onto the street. "Quickly," she said, wincing as the latch, despite her best efforts, shut with a resonant click. Then up the road they went, moving more slowly than she would have preferred, to keep from causing the animal pain. Soon they passed beneath a gaslight and for the first time she could see for herself how the horse's gait was off.

"Does he have a name?" Teresa asked, when she felt it was safe to talk.

"You'll think it's silly," Luca said. "Signor Benedetti calls him Il Conte because he prefers names that are grand. But look at his face. He is no count. And he has a taste for carrots, so to me he is Coniglio, my gentle rabbit friend."

Teresa was surprised rescuing the horse had gone so smoothly. The rest of the way wouldn't be dangerous, along back streets and alleys, all of them dark.

"You were right," she said. "You didn't need my help."

"A man and a woman together are less suspicious than a man alone. No one stopped us, so what we did was right."

They arrived home at half-past midnight. As usual, Luca would sleep in the stable. "Thank you for helping," he said before she returned to the house. "If anyone asks, I'll say I never saw you tonight." But Teresa wasn't worried. Who was going to care about one animal of questionable value in a city turned upside down?

A Great Mouth

The following morning, they joined a large column of men, mules, and machinery trudging into the mountains toward Italy. Toward the front. Florian called their attention to an enormous artillery piece being pulled by a tractor. "Look, a Skoda 305," he exclaimed.

"You seem to know all the names," Alexi said. "How is that?"

"They interest me."

"What about you?" Alexi asked Carlo. "Are you fond of artillery pieces?"

Florian scowled. "I didn't say I was *fond* of them. I simply know their names."

"Now, if you were to ask me about *my* interests, I would say food and wine and tobacco—" Alexi began, but Florian interrupted.

"The Skoda is one of the largest guns in use. It suggests to me that the days ahead will be unpleasant. It suggests there will be a major attack."

Carlo glanced at Alexi, who appeared chastened, his habit of making light of things brought to a temporary halt.

By noon much of the snow was gone, replaced by deep mud. A pack mule slipped sideways, fell, and brayed in agony. Its driver, after examining the animal briefly, shot it in the head. Carlo scarcely had time to realize what was happening before the gun was fired. He, Alexi, and Florian were walking together. As instructed by Oberleutnant Haas, they were to remain with the column until they reached the foot of a massif known as the Nave di Ferro, where they would join a company of engineers.

Carlo felt as though he'd become a leaf in a river, carried along without his consent. He supposed this was true of the other men as well—most of being a soldier was just doing what you were told. It would have been easier if the army had been one toward which he felt some allegiance. He was going to be toiling in the mountains on behalf of an empire he cared nothing about. In service of a cause he scarcely understood. As they walked along, he realized he didn't know what day of the week it was. He considered asking someone but was afraid he'd sound foolish. Besides, it didn't matter anymore.

Carlo enjoyed Alexi's company, but the Austrian, Florian, was insufferable, opening his mouth only to complain. Apparently, he'd been denied entry into the elite Kaiserjäger, the Emperor's Hunters, and had thereafter decided to be satisfied with nothing less.

"I find this unjust," he said after rations had been distributed at midday. "They give us only enough for a rat. How are we to march on such meager fare?" He held up a scrap of sausage and gave it a vigorous shake. "I intend to protest." Carlo looked at Alexi. It required little intelligence to know that any protest from a common soldat would be ignored, even considered insubordination.

"Protest if you must," Alexi said. "And then prepare to get a riding crop across the face."

The mud was so difficult to walk in that they were relieved to reach a higher altitude, where the ground was frozen and the snow had yet to melt. But not Florian, who said, "Now I am getting cold." Carlo and Alexi looked at him and shook their heads. For the next hour they tramped on without saying a word.

At last they reached the Nave di Ferro, or rather the encampment in the valley beneath its great rock face. This cluster of tents was far smaller than the one they'd left behind. Everything was snow-covered except for the towering cliffs, which were slate gray and streaked with ice. High up, a pair of chamois leaped from pinnacle to pinnacle, oblivious to the humans below. Oberleutnant Haas stopped, stood in his stirrups, and looked back.

"We have arrived," he shouted. "Prepare to bivouac. The horses and mules eat first."

Before their departure, they had been issued heavy

ordnance capes and canvas tarps in which to wrap themselves, should they be required to sleep out. Although they'd be inside a tent, Carlo could tell he would need the cape, the tarp, his blanket, and every piece of clothing in his kit if he hoped to keep warm tonight. He began feeling miserable and then told himself to stop; he was certain there were more days like this to come.

Some hardy soul, one for whom music was more important than rest, began playing his ocarina. "You'd think he'd offer something uplifting," Alexi said, "but no, he plays a melancholy tune."

As the sun disappeared over the peaks, Oberleutnant Haas made his way through the camp, stopping here and there to check on his men.

"Is this where we will be working?" Florian asked.

"Ah, the miners," he replied. "No, I'm afraid not. We have farther to go."

And so, after a frigid night, they set out again. This time there were just fourteen of them, four groups of three men on foot, Haas on horseback, and a muleteer leading six mules laden with supplies. Higher and higher they went, following a narrow trail cut into the rock. They passed a small unoccupied dwelling, perhaps a shepherd's hut, which Carlo suspected would be the last evidence of human life they'd see. Gusts of wind blew great clouds of snow down upon them. Spirals of snow danced atop the peaks. The roar of the wind encompassed everything, occasionally sounding to Carlo like a ghostly moan. They pulled their capes tight and kept their eyes on the trail. In the valleys the snow was thigh deep. On the ridges, nothing but ice. After stopping to rope themselves together, they joked that if a man fell into a crevasse it would be a race to see who could get his knife out quickest to cut the bastard loose. There were blasts of wind so powerful, they had to stop in their tracks. Only after it abated could they trudge slowly on.

When night fell, they tried to erect tents, but the wind made doing so impossible. Instead, they dug snow caves in great wind-blown drifts and prepared for a long cold night. At last Florian broke his silence:

"They are trying to kill us," he said. "They want to see how long men can survive under the worst of conditions. When we perish, they'll say, 'Now we know.'"

Alexi laughed. The relationship between the gruff Bosnian miner and the perpetually dissatisfied young Austrian was a peculiar one. No one could make Alexi laugh like Florian and yet no one could silence Florian as readily as Alexi. For all their outward differences, they shared some inscrutable bond.

As exhausted as Carlo was, he had difficulty falling asleep. He thought about his brothers and the stories he could tell them about this journey if he ever returned to Colorado and could sit in their saloon. Although Colorado had blizzards, he remembered none as fierce as this. He also thought about his father and wondered if he'd successfully made himself mayor. He was a difficult old man and Carlo could picture him forcing himself on the villagers. He doubted they'd put up with him for long. Then, as he continued thinking about the people who'd been part of his former existence, it occurred to him that no one knew where he was—not his brothers, not his father, not Miss Donovan or the bird girl or the other boys at school. He had vanished into the army, into the mountains, into the war.

Overnight the weather changed. The wind diminished, the clouds dispersed, and they emerged from their caves into a sunlit alpine day. By the time they rolled their bedding and ate the rations they were supposed to eat last night and the ones meant for the morning as well, it was almost hot.

They removed their capes and coats and even their tunics and noticed how their tendons, tightened for hours against the cold, began at last to unclench.

"Maybe it won't be so bad to spend the summer here," Florian said. "Provided they send enough food."

He was slim and muscular, and Carlo had begun to realize that he complained about food not because he was a glutton but because he could consume twice as much as everyone else and still not feel full.

"You're aware that inside a mine, seasons don't exist?" Alexi said.

Carlo nudged him with his elbow. "Let him be optimistic. He'll learn the truth soon enough."

Florian threw up his hands. "I already told you, I'm no miner. I come from a farm near Linz. They wouldn't allow me in the Kaiserjäger because I was a poor marksman. To my endless misfortune, I was sent here instead."

So, thought Carlo, of the three of us, one is a genuine miner, one has a father who was more prospector than hardrock miner, and one grew up on a farm and knows nothing of mining at all.

Even though the sun was out, today's travel was no easier than yesterday's. The trail remained treacherously icy and soon the wind picked up again, nearly blowing them off their feet. Each time it seemed they had gone as far as they could go, that they'd reached the very top of the world, they would surmount a ridge and see another row of peaks higher than the ones before. A man ahead of them lost his footing and tumbled off the trail. Carlo lunged to catch him and managed to snag his coat sleeve but the sleeve slipped from his grasp. While the man didn't fall far, he broke his leg and cracked his head on a rock. A second man collapsed from exhaustion and couldn't be revived. Both men were tied to the backs of mules, the injured one upright with a bandage on his head and his leg in a makeshift splint; the dead one crosswise, like an oddly shaped sack of oats. Once they were adequately secured, the caravan moved on. Or perhaps not so adequately secured—before they'd gone very far, the dead man's hand slipped free and began flailing about, as though signaling for attention. The plan was to bury the poor fellow as best they could when they stopped for the night.

Carlo tried to make the time pass more quickly by attempting to recall the Italian word for everything in sight: Cliff was *scogliera*, boulder was *masso* or possibly *roccia*, and stumble was *inciampare*, which, as he'd gotten increasingly weary, he did every few yards. In the end he discovered that the best way to keep himself going was to make his mind utterly blank, as blank and featureless as an unbroken expanse of snow. It was a kind of waking sleep, a mental void into which time disappeared. But his mind wouldn't remain entirely blank because one thought kept forcing itself in: *My feet are very cold.*

At last, late in the afternoon, they arrived at a camp perched on a saddle between two jagged limestone peaks. Even smaller than the camp they'd left two days before, it consisted of a few crude wooden structures and no more than a dozen tents. As Carlo gazed off toward the horizon, so tired he could scarcely think, Alexi thrust out his arm and pointed upward. There, within an enormous stone cirque, was a large black opening, a gaping mouth.

"How terrifying! It looks as though the mountain is screaming," Florian said.

Carlo, more fatigued than frightened, chose to think of it as a giant yawn.

The Language of the Enemy

In the morning Teresa and Luca revealed to Frau Merz what they'd done. She might disapprove but she could be trusted with the truth.

"You put us all at risk," she said, her fierce stare forcing them both to cower.

"If they come looking for the horse, I'll admit my guilt," Luca replied. "I'll say it was me alone."

Teresa threw him a reassuring look. "I don't believe you'll be accused of anything. If the police discover the horse, they'll just take it back." Frau Merz, whose use of sarcasm wasn't always gentle, turned to Teresa and said, "How did you become so knowledgeable about the military police?" She considered responding: *Why would they want to punish someone for such a minor offense?* However, Frau Merz was right—she knew nothing about the military police and how they might behave.

In the days that followed, Teresa visited the stable numerous times. Since she'd assisted in the rescue, she couldn't help but take an interest in the horse's welfare. She wasn't worried about their Austrian tenants—they came and went by the front entrance, cared little about the garden, and not at all about the more removed parts of the estate. This wasn't surprising. Why pay attention to the stable boy or the outbuildings as long as there were clean beds to sleep in and enough food to eat?

According to Luca, the horse was in a bad way, but he knew how to treat it. He'd begun rubbing its leg with liniment every day and had wrapped the offending joint in a poultice impregnated with pitch.

"What'll you do when it's fully recovered?" she asked.

"I don't know. Put a saddle on him and ride away. Or perhaps the war will end, Signor Benedetti will return, and everything will be as before."

She didn't think that was likely. The last time Frau Merz went to the market, she came home looking worried and told them what she'd heard: Great battles were now being waged from the Brenner Pass all the way to Gorizia and the Carso Plateau, some far up in the mountains and others on the eastern plains. If Teresa knew little about the military police, she knew even less about battles—what they looked like, who the participants were, and how they were fought. She wanted to understand, but it was as if Frau Merz were telling her about the weather in Portugal.

Trento itself was not without violence. Only last week two men considered to be agents of the Italians had been arrested, tried, and hanged. The execution had been conducted at the Castello del Buonconsiglio. Luca reported that he had seen the bodies with his own eyes before they'd been cut down: "It was horrible. The birds had pecked so much flesh off their faces, I could see the bones beneath."

"They must have done *something*," Rosa said. "They wouldn't have been hanged based on suspicion alone."

Lately Rosa had been defending the Austrians. It was true that the ones living with them treated them well, yet as Rodolfo pointed out, they could treat them however they pleased because they had all the power.

"If those men did *something*, as you say, surely it was on behalf of their country," Teresa replied. Maybe it hadn't been such a good idea to invite Rosa to move in.

"I'm thinking of volunteering to help the wounded," Rosa said. "It doesn't matter which uniform they wear. They all deserve care. You should come along."

Teresa wasn't sure what to say. She couldn't disagree with her reasoning, and surely, given the extraordinary circumstances, Frau Merz would permit them to be absent for a few hours a week.

"Yes," she said, feeling cornered. "We should offer our help."

The following morning they walked to where the large civic hall had been converted into a hospital. In the building's forecourt, tents had been erected, and it appeared the incoming wounded were being held there for preliminary treatment or until a bed was available inside. When they came upon a nurse walking briskly between two of the tents, Rosa stopped her and explained that they wished to volunteer.

The nurse, clearly preoccupied with other matters, took a moment to collect her thoughts. "You'll have to speak to the doctor in charge," she said.

"Where can we find him?" Rosa asked.

"Follow me."

She led them into one of the tents and they proceeded down a central aisle, each side flanked by rows of the wounded in cots. Teresa alternated between gazing in stark horror and averting her eyes. It was simply too much to take in: bloody bandages, bodies shaking in pain, faces with only the mouth and nostrils left visible, unbandaged wounds that looked like freshly chopped meat. And flies everywhere. Some of the men were silent, while others moaned like injured beasts or sobbed in their sleep. One poor boy called for his mother and another said *shut up*. When they emerged from the tent, Teresa had to gasp for air.

"The smells," she said.

"Carbolic," replied the nurse. "And also gangrene."

As Teresa regained her composure, they entered a makeshift office space, with trestle tables and cabinets to hold files. The nurse left them there with a short, red-faced man whose expression suggested he, like the nurse, had little time to spare. Rosa began speaking at once, in German, and the man responded in kind. Rosa followed with a question and he nodded approvingly, waving his hands in a manner that made Teresa think he was explaining how overwhelmed they were. Then both of them turned toward her.

"He wants to know what language you speak—your mother tongue," Rosa said.

"Italian. You know that."

"Yes. So you cannot work here."

"I know a little German. I can get along."

"That's not the reason. They've been told not to employ anyone whose first language is Italian. It belongs to the enemy."

The enemy's tongue—what an outrageous thought. Teresa began to protest, but the doctor broke in, using Italian himself: "I'm sure you are a good girl. However, we have been ordered to consider all Italian speakers potential saboteurs and spies."

"There are Austrian officers living in the house where she's employed," Rosa said. "She cleans up after them and prepares their—"

Again, the doctor interrupted: "I cannot speak for the men living in your house. I only know what the regulations say."

As they made their way home, Rosa complained on Teresa's behalf: "That's a ridiculous rule. You're no spy. Still, I'm glad they'll allow me to help. Did you see those poor men?"

"How could I avoid it?" Teresa said, unable to contain her annoyance. Before visiting the hospital, she'd been uncertain about volunteering; now she felt rejected and demeaned. She wanted to go back to the doctor and insist he change his mind.

A little farther along Rosa spoke again: "Let me ask you, do you consider yourself loyal to the Italian cause? Because I do not. I probably shouldn't say this, but my sympathies are with Austria-Hungary and Germany. I hope the Central Powers prevail."

Teresa looked at her. What an unexpected remark! It was one thing to have such feelings and leave them unspoken, quite another to say them aloud. Even so, she was impressed by how confident Rosa was in her opinions. Rather than get into an argument about the Allies and Central Powers, she decided to opt for simple honesty:

"I consider myself loyal to my mother and my dog. They are my family. Besides, my thoughts about the war don't matter. The generals and politicians will do as they please."

In the days that followed, additional evidence of the Austrians' fear of spies and saboteurs emerged. An article in the newspaper said that the churches of Trento were now prohibited from ringing their bells because they might be used to signal an uprising. Leaflets were distributed telling residents to hand over all guns to the authorities, as well as any pigeons, as they might be employed to send messages across enemy lines. There was even a rumor that a woman had been taken into custody because she was sending information to aeroplanes by arranging her linens in certain meaningful patterns when she hung them out to dry.

As soon as Teresa saw the leaflet about pigeons, she found Rodolfo and asked him if he was concerned. He was in the garden pruning rosebushes, moving in the same deliberate manner as her mother often did—a manner that allowed one to accomplish a great deal while giving the appearance of scarcely moving at all.

"Can something be done to protect them?" Teresa asked.

Without looking up he said, "I've placed them out of harm's way."

A few weeks later the Austrian campaign against spies and saboteurs took a more terrifying turn. Another man had been hung at the castle overnight. A spy, it was said, who had escaped to Italy and then come back to undermine the

Austro-Hungarian forces and disrupt their efforts to keep Trento subdued. Frau Merz heard about it at the market and went to see for herself. It was Signor Benedetti, and as she told them through her sobs, she was able to look at his face for only an instant before she had to turn away. But that was more than enough for her to be certain it was him.

In the Tunnels

The black mouth in the mountainside was the entrance to a network of tunnels. Once complete, the tunnels would lead to open-sided chambers from which artillery could rain shells down upon the Italian forces if they attempted to advance through the pass. The terrain was so inhospitable, so steep and ice-bound, Carlo had difficulty imagining the Italians selecting such a route, yet as Oberleutnant Haas pointed out, they might do so for precisely that reason: They wouldn't expect it to be blocked.

"This will be cold, difficult work," Alexi growled. "But better cold than hot. In Bosnia the heat in the mines was so extreme, I often felt I was being roasted alive."

Carlo's impression of mining had always been that it was only worthwhile if there was gold or silver to be had. Whereas here they would be doing what could be described as mining for nothing. The removal of stone to create empty space.

"You will have to teach me," he told Alexi.

"There's nothing much to teach. Anyone can do it."

"Surely there are proper methods ..."

Alexi shrugged. "Indeed, but they're quite simple. The most uneducated brute can be a miner. That's the secret of the industry. I'm surprised you don't know that."

"So you admit to being an uneducated brute," Florian said.

"Well, let me put it this way: If you ask a mine owner which is more valuable, his men or his mules and donkeys, he'll look at you as if you're a fool and answer with a bray."

Work began the following morning. The tools were already inside the tunnels, left behind by the previous unit. As Haas explained it, the tunneling here had been started in anticipation of the war, long before it began: "While the politicians lied and bickered, we were getting prepared."

As Alexi predicted, Carlo and Florian had little difficulty learning the job. Hand drills with star-shaped tips were hammered into the rock with mallets. Larger drills followed the smaller ones until cracks appeared and shards began breaking away. When a good amount of rock had piled up at their feet, they shoveled it into wheeled carts to be pushed outside and dumped. They worked by the light of acetylene lamps, ate cold rations while sitting with their backs against the tunnel wall, and pissed and defecated in a bucket, which they carried out at the end of their shift.

"See, it's not so bad," Alexi said.

Eventually they reached a point where no additional rock could be removed by hand. Then it was time for explosives. For this, true skill was required, more than Alexi had originally let on. New holes were drilled and gelignite charges were pushed into the holes and packed tight. The tamping was done with wooden rods so as not to produce a spark. When all was ready, Alexi told them to exit the tunnel so he could place the primer and light the fuse. Carlo and Florian required no urging to follow his instructions. They hurried out into the sunlight and put fifty meters between themselves and the tunnel mouth. A few seconds later, Alexi emerged at a gallop and they heard a deep, earth-shuddering roar. It reminded Carlo of home. Just as those who grow up next to the ocean are made nostalgic by the sound of surf, so in his mind he traveled back to the camp in Colorado whenever he heard an explosion or felt the ground quake beneath his feet.

Along with the sound came smoke and dust, which tumbled out of the tunnel to be blown away by the wind. When the air was clear, they went back in to evaluate the success of the blast and remove the rubble. Then they started over again. After they'd been at work for twelve hours, a new crew replaced them. Twelve hours later, they returned.

For the first few weeks, Carlo found the work exhausting. Florian agreed.

"I'll not be able to keep this up," he said.

Alexi reassured them: "It will get easier. I remember how it was when I first started."

"How old were you?" Carlo asked.

"How old? I think I must have been ten."

It did get easier. Carlo felt his muscles harden and he learned some labor-saving tricks. Routines helped. One man held the drill while another swung the mallet. After one hundred strokes they switched places. In the past when Carlo pictured miners toiling at the rock face, men like the ones who frequented his brothers' saloon, he imagined them joking, arguing, telling stories. But in truth the work was too arduous to allow for much talk or laughter. It required concentration and most of his breath. Hours passed without any of them uttering a word. Nor was there much socializing with any of the other men in the small encampment; nearly all the minutes of the day were taken up with sleep or work.

During their first weeks on the mountainside, they paid attention only to the tunnels, making them deeper every day. Yet as time went on, they began to learn the full extent of the fortifications. Up and down the peaks and all along the stark and forbidding range, bunkers and artillery installations were under construction, steel obstacles and barriers of barbed wire were being placed, and dugouts in which soldiers would be able to seek shelter were being carved or blasted into the obstinate stone.

Before long, Carlo noticed his hands had become calloused like his father's—so much so that he could jab them with the point of a trench knife and feel no pain. He would have gotten calluses on his head as well, but for his helmet, which he was constantly banging on the tunnel roof. At times he had no choice but to work on his knees.

When they reached a certain depth, Alexi informed them that the time had come to brace the ceiling. Carlo had been wondering if that would happen and now felt a rush of relief.

"I once witnessed the collapse of a mine shaft," he said.

Florian frowned. "I thought you knew nothing of mining."

"I was a child, not a miner—although I sometimes explored abandoned mines with my friends. When you grow up in a place like I did, you can't help it. One time we disturbed a hibernating bear."

"A bear?" Florian exclaimed, seeming for once to be genuinely interested rather than filled with disdain.

"It was sleeping," Carlo continued. "We heard it and smelled it before we saw it. And it heard us as well, coming awake with a roar."

"What did you do?" Florian asked.

"Ran like hell and didn't look back until I got home."

Florian laughed loudly, but Carlo felt as if he was so far from Colorado, so far from his brothers and Miss Donovan and his dear departed mother, that his memories were about someone else, a character in a book or a dream. Maybe in the future, when he was back in Colorado, he would tell stories about the war and feel as if they were equally distant and separate from himself.

"Children should not go into mine shafts," Alexi said.

PART III

Fire in the Mountains

In the aftermath of Signor Benedetti's death, they all felt great anger and sorrow but quickly realized there was nothing to be done. They couldn't stop feeding their Austrian tenants. They couldn't leave Trento. They couldn't take up arms and rebel. They were mere cooks and gardeners and stable boys and would continue to be thus. Although Teresa hadn't gotten to know Signor Benedetti very well, Frau Merz said he'd been a generous man. And, it appeared, a brave one as well. They didn't know exactly what he'd done but were certain he had been trying to bring the war to a just and expeditious end.

"We must redouble our efforts to make sure the villa is a welcoming place for the family when they return," said Frau Merz. "They have suffered a terrible blow and will need our help."

Hauptmann Schneider, sensing their dismay, came to the kitchen to offer his condolences and assure them that whatever Signor Benedetti's offenses, no suspicion had fallen on them. After he left the room, Luca said, "He only wants to make sure that the fine accommodations he's secured for himself aren't put at risk."

Thereafter, a hollow feeling descended upon the house. Conditions that had once seemed threatening and strange—the curfew, the distant blasts, the mass of soldiers roaming the streets, even the stories Rosa brought home from the hospital about maimed and ravaged men—began to feel almost normal. Instead of breathlessly saying, "Did you hear what happened?" they said, "It's cloudy today. I think we may get rain."

Teresa knew they were lucky to have food and shelter and be in a place that wasn't under fire. Sometimes she even felt guilty about it. Elsewhere, ordinary people like herself were being subjected to terrible suffering, while in the villa their biggest problem was that sugar had become nearly impossible to obtain. Still, it was obvious that conditions could change at any moment, and when they did, it would be for the worse. It was frightening to think that Signor Benedetti's death might be just the start.

Naturally, she worried about her mother while also clinging to the idea that no one would care about Ulfano. She wondered if there was a way she could visit her, perhaps by sneaking through the fences that enclosed Trento and staying off the main roads. However, she couldn't ignore Frau Merz's warnings about what soldiers might do to a girl traveling alone. She'd risk it only if she had proof her mother was in trouble and needed her help.

According to Luca, the horse was improving. He described the condition as a "splint," a swelling on the inner and lower part of the knee, and said, "It's a severe case—it will take a long time to heal."

"Are you still applying the poultice?" she asked.

"Yes. But pitch wasn't working, so now I'm trying boiled comfrey. Mixed with vinegar and castor oil."

Teresa asked where he was obtaining fodder, given that

the military had confiscated all available supplies. "It's better you don't know," Luca said.

There were still no signs the Austrians in the villa were suspicious of Luca or the stable. They had more important concerns. Now that Trento had been turned into a fortress, they were struggling to keep a corridor open between the city and the front.

One of Hauptmann Schneider's men appeared to have developed an interest in Rosa. Teresa noticed how he gazed at her each time she crossed the room. She was beginning to think Rosa might be spending nights in his bed. If so, Teresa didn't care. She was neither Rosa's employer nor her guardian, and given the circumstances, the existence of such a relationship would be no surprise. It was probably happening all over Trento. Then again, she might be mistaken. She certainly hadn't caught them in the act.

Teresa continued to assume everyone else understood the war better than she did. The trip to Rome had given her a glimpse of the wider world, but it had also confirmed how much more there was to know. Even Rosa, whom she considered as uneducated as herself, was bringing news back from the hospital nearly every day. She said the war wouldn't last long—despite the fact that the numbers of wounded being brought to Trento continued to rise.

"What makes you say that?" Teresa asked.

"The Imperial Army is driving toward Italy. On the Western Front, the French are running out of ammunition. The English are becoming frustrated and may soon give up and go home."

"You've become quite an expert."

"Young men are eager to talk to a girl who treats them with kindness. Besides, they're stuck in bed, so what else are they to do?"

Teresa didn't believe it was that simple, or that Rosa's information was entirely accurate. Still, she was envious of her and hadn't gotten over being told she was too untrustworthy to care for wounded soldiers. Again, she considered returning to the hospital, finding the doctor, and pleading her case. *Do I look like a spy?* she'd say.

Frau Merz was of the opinion that the Italians would never shell Trento because they considered it an Italian city and expected to reclaim it should they win the war. But on a rainy afternoon Luca came home with alarming news. The Austro-Hungarian forces occupying the city had placed a circle of mines around the Dante statue. In the event of a siege, they intended to blow the statue to pieces and use the bronze to make more cannons. On the one hand, it was only a statue, and destroying it would be a merely symbolic act. Yet setting mines in the middle of town was frightening no matter what they intended to destroy.

"If they harm Dante, I will take up arms against them," Rodolfo said. To Teresa's knowledge, Rodolfo had no arms to take up, except perhaps a pruning hook. Still, his passion was inspiring and came, Teresa could tell, directly from the heart.

"I'll be happy if the Italians try to liberate the city," Teresa replied. "But I hope they find a way to do it peacefully. I'm afraid of what could happen during an attack."

"The Austrians have better things to do than blow up statues," Frau Merz said. "It's all a ruse meant to keep us afraid."

Rodolfo snorted. "Don't be so sure."

"I am anything but sure," she replied. "None of us knows what will happen or when. And I'd wager our lodgers don't either." She looked at the kitchen doors, the one leading upstairs and the one leading outside. It appeared she was checking to make sure no one was listening. Then she went to a cupboard, opened it, and came back with a newspaper, one of the ones printed in Rome that had been banned since the Austrians arrived.

"Listen," she said and began to read: "Although the Austro-Hungarian army has been unable to penetrate beyond the Isonzo River, the Italian forces have been likewise unable to advance. Field Marshal Cadorna has pledged to break through the enemy lines when he has been given adequate artillery and an increased number of men." She read a few more sentences and looked up.

"So you see there is a stalemate. And since Marshal Cadorna is not to be trusted, it is a stalemate compounded by who knows how many lies. Elsewhere in this same paper it says losses have been in the thousands. *In the thousands.* Seven thousand or seventy thousand? I fear they use those words because the number is too terrible to reveal."

They all looked at Frau Merz in astonishment. Who knew she was hiding newspapers? What other secrets did she have?

She returned the paper to the cupboard. Until now they hadn't spoken about the war in quite this way. Spoken about it as a great catastrophe swirling around them, a catastrophe that might swallow them up, rather than as something abstract and remote. Most striking was how Frau Merz had said *in the thousands.* It brought to mind a corpse-filled field running all the way to the horizon, so many bodies and no one left to put them in the ground.

"Has anyone heard anything about Gaetano?" Teresa asked.

They turned and stared at her as one.

"You know, the fellow who was friends with the Benedetti children . . ."

"We know who you're talking about," Frau Merz said. "And we're certainly not keeping anything from you. I'll put him in my prayers."

For a moment Teresa thought she was being mocked, but no, it was too serious a matter for that. "I wish I could write to him," she said.

Rosa, who until now hadn't been paying much attention, looked up. "Even if the mail resumes, they won't deliver a letter to an Italian soldier. Why not write to one of our fellows instead?"

"An Austrian?"

"It's the patriotic thing to do."

As they returned to their various chores, Teresa continued thinking about the letters she couldn't send. If she were able to write to her mother, she would inquire about her health and apologize for not being there to help with this year's harvest. She would tell her about Rosa and the Austrians and, since this was an imaginary letter no one could intercept, about Luca and the horse. She would describe what had happened to the statue of Dante and ask her to give Allucio a bone on her behalf.

She never considered writing to her father. It wasn't only that he, too, lived in Italian territory and the letter wouldn't be delivered. There was simply nothing she wished to say. She didn't care if he knew about her job in the kitchen, didn't care if he knew about the people she worked with or how Trento had been transformed. To write a letter was to assume the recipient would be interested in you and your thoughts. If that had been true of him, he wouldn't have left her and her mother alone. And then it came to her: She no longer cared if she ever saw her father again. Since the day he left, she'd been forcing herself to think of him as a mere miscreant, a man of poor judgment, someone whose bad qualities had gotten the better of his good ones. That was too charitable. In her eyes he couldn't be redeemed.

At night from her window she could see fire in the

mountains. There were little flares that she assumed came from the muzzles of cannons. There were larger flashes that were probably from the shells when they exploded. There were lines of flame—the treetops on fire. And there were glowing columns of purple for which she had no explanation. They seemed to be made of smoke, illuminated by the conflagration below.

A Citadel in the Sky

When they first arrived at their current position, there had been the occasional afternoon of brilliant autumn sun. At such times, they stood against the rocks and absorbed the warmth, as if it could be stored for later use. But soon winter blew in, quickly and with such force, it was a relief to go into the tunnels to dig. Then one day they blasted an opening in the side of a large passageway to create a recessed platform on which some large piece of artillery was to be placed. After that, winds coursed through as if the very purpose of the tunnel was to channel the frigid air.

Carlo consoled himself with the thought that men had been working underground for thousands of years. It wasn't an activity that happened only during war. All over the world there were mines; all over the world there were tunnels. Thinking about it that way made him feel less imposed upon, less as if he had been singled out for this arduous life.

When they weren't working, they were in their bedrolls, inside their tents. Sometimes they played cards and sometimes they just stared at the canvas overhead. Again, Carlo wished he had the book Miss Donovan gave him. Perhaps one of the brothers had placed it in the school library. He liked to imagine a curious boy picking it up and, even if he couldn't read English, enjoying the pictures of trees.

Near the end of November an artillery unit arrived. They brought with them not only a cannon to be mounted in the tunnel (according to Florian, a Feldhaubitze M. 15) but other guns, mobile as well as fixed. The artillery unit was followed by a platoon of snipers who were to be deployed along the rocky heights. The newcomers seemed bewildered, gazing about wide-eyed at the frozen place they'd been sent. One good thing: They brought with them additional supplies, including better food. Carlo had been in uniform for only a few days when he realized that among soldiers, food was an obsession. They talked constantly about what they ate yesterday, what they hoped to eat today, and, especially, what their mothers made for them back home. He had almost no memory of his mother's cooking. He thought she'd made a kind of cake, yellow in color, but couldn't remember the taste.

In January, a blizzard descended and lasted for days. The wind roared and threatened to lift their tents into the sky. During the worst of it, word arrived that Italian forces were moving in their direction. Carlo and the other miners looked at each other in astonishment. Why had the Italians waited until midwinter to advance? The weather was bad and would only get worse. In some places the snow was waist-deep while in others it had been blown away to reveal rock striated with ice. Which condition was more treacherous for men and mules was open to debate.

Of the Italians, Florian said, "Fools. We will cut them down with our guns." At present, they were in their tent.

Alexi, his head propped on an elbow, smoked a gnarled black pipe. "It is said the Italian alpine troops know the mountains better than anyone," he mused. "Who knows, maybe they prefer to fight in the snow."

Florian said, "Who knows, maybe you should put out that stinking pipe."

Carlo had heard about the Alpini before. They were recruited from Trentino and may well include men from Ulfano. It occurred to him that if he'd stayed home with his father instead of going off to school, he might be serving with the Alpini instead.

That very night the Italians began shooting at them with their largest guns. The sky lit up as shells were fired all along the peaks. Soon so many were raining down from so many different directions, it was as if they were inside a globe of fire. For a time they waited and hoped it would stop. Then a round exploded just above the camp. "To the tunnels, my friends," Alexi said.

Once inside the mountain they felt safer but still the ground shuddered beneath them, partly from explosions outside and partly from the recoil of their own newly mounted cannon, with its undercarriage secured by bolts sunk deep into the rock.

"They'll attack by way of the valley," said Florian. "If they make it through the pass, we're dead."

Alexi shook his head. "There will be weeks of fighting before there's any possibility of that."

Carlo had no opinion on the matter. While many soldiers, Alexi and Florian included, were more than willing to hold forth on strategy, their conclusions were nothing more than guesses. "I suppose we'll find out soon enough," he said.

Shortly before dawn the bombardment ended. Despite having had no sleep, they went straight back to work. Several days earlier one of the tunnels had penetrated the opposite side of the peak so men could now pass beneath the ridgeline instead of climbing over the top. All day soldiers and supplies streamed through. Their next task was to carve out chambers on either side of the tunnels. These would be used for storage and perhaps even as living quarters. The end result, according to Oberleutnant Haas, was to be a citadel in the sky.

The Italian artillery battered them for weeks. Sometimes they retreated to the tunnels. Sometimes they were so weary, they simply put cotton wool in their ears, pulled their heads down into their bedrolls, and attempted to sleep. One morning a platoon of Alpini was spotted coming toward them, using a jagged wall of rock to conceal their advance. The Austrian snipers ambushed them and returned in triumph—not one of the Italians survived.

"I guess you find this difficult," Alexi said.

"What do you mean?" Carlo asked.

"Well, you are Italian."

"I suppose. More than Austrian. But American more than either of those."

"So you don't care if Italians die . . ."

"I care if anyone dies."

"Ah, a humanitarian."

"Most of all, I care if *I* die," he said, and Alexi laughed.

Little by little the accuracy of the Italian attacks increased. A shell struck a cliff near where a group of men was eating breakfast and three of them were killed, shards of stone and metal slicing through their torsos like the sharpest of knives. Another shell landed at the feet of an officer and all that remained of him was a crimson smear on the snow. After that, everyone's behavior changed. Most of them spoke less and turned inward, but a few became almost giddy, laughing at things that weren't amusing and talking more than they should. They struck their tents and instead built lean-tos against cliffs and beneath upthrust carapaces of rock. Some men chose to burrow deep into the snow and take up residence there. The tents had provided no protection from artillery, and if, as they believed, the Italians had observers in the peaks higher up, they'd been far too easy to spot.

As time passed, they learned to distinguish the sounds of the various types of artillery: the initial report when the gun was fired, the explosion of the round upon impact, and the tonal qualities of the shriek or whistle in between. For the most part it was useless knowledge, acquired without effort, yet it bound them together in fear.

Carlo felt he knew little about death. It was tragic but also mysterious—a life is present in the world and then suddenly it disappears. What is that presence made of, and what does its absence mean? And was there any value at all to knowing you were about to die? The conventional wisdom was that an unexpected and instantaneous death was best, but suppose you could have one more moment, perhaps one without pain, in which to gather your thoughts?

Eventually, news arrived of immense battles being fought to the east, near the Isonzo River, and it occurred to Carlo that he and his comrades were but one part of a great struggle all along the border. As if to confirm that fact, a large column of troops passed their camp the following day. Carlo had been assuming that their present location marked the leading edge of the Austro-Hungarian Front. Yet this new force looked as though they intended to march right into the heart of Italy, maybe all the way to Rome.

Occasionally a messenger arrived, face burned by the sun and wind, and eyes so wild and red, it was as if he were returning from hell. Upon reading one of the dispatches, Haas visibly blanched. "Things are going poorly," he said.

A week later the column of troops returned. Again, they passed without stopping, but this time they were so broken and tattered and stained with blood, it was pitiful to watch.

"Look," said Florian, "half of them don't have rifles anymore. They must have left them behind."

"Who gives a damn about rifles?" Alexi said, removing his fez out of respect. "There are half as many *men* as before. It's their comrades they left behind."

After that, they began sleeping inside the mountain, hoping it would provide protection when the Italians attacked. Because they weren't confined to their bedrolls and had the option of moving about, they stayed up later and talked. One night Alexi told them a story about how, as a small child, he'd been lost in the woods for three days.

"I could hear the wolves howling," he said. "They were circling me, closing in. They were in no hurry. There was no place for me to go."

"First his bear and now your wolves," Florian said. "I prefer not to live in such wild places. Give me a peaceful farm."

"So how did you escape?" Carlo asked.

"An angel. An angel appeared and took me back home."

Florian scoffed. "Did it slay the wolves?"

"It carried me above them. Through the air. The wolves were astonished. I could see them gazing up at me from below."

Carlo liked Alexi's story. He had heard some of the older miners in Colorado talk about their encounters with wolves. Although everyone said they were now gone, hunted nearly to extinction, he once thought he saw one loping across an open field.

"Are there still wolves in Bosnia?" he asked.

"I have no idea," Alexi said.

When they weren't working or sleeping or telling stories, the Austrians, Hungarians, and other soldiers of the empire— at least those who could read and write—filled the time by penning letters and Feldpostkartes to their loved ones in Vienna or Budapest. Apparently the Austro-Hungarian government was quite skilled at keeping mail moving between soldiers and their families back home. However, for Carlo, letters and postcards were pointless because messages couldn't be delivered across enemy lines. Then one night as he was about to fall asleep, it occurred to him that he did know someone in Austro-Hungarian territory to whom he might write—the pigeon girl. He even remembered the name of the household, the Villa Benedetti, where she worked. He would risk nothing by composing a brief message and addressing it to the kitchen maid there.

Dear Signorina, he began. *I suppose you are wondering who is writing to you. Remember the fellow who saw you release the pigeon? Well, I am now in the Austrian army and thought I would send you some words.*

He didn't have much to say and knew there were many things they weren't allowed to say, yet it felt good to be writing letters like the other men. Maybe she would be kind enough to reply. *As you know, my Italian is poor but I'll do my best to be clear and try not to make mistakes. I wonder what Trento is like now that Italy has entered the war. I hope the fighting is far away from you. There is some happening where I am. However, I am employed as a miner and have yet to shoot a gun.*

Since you work in a kitchen, I'll tell you about the food soldiers are given. Today we had mush and mush and mush with a little meat. You may judge from that.

He followed with a couple of sentences about the weather and then decided to conclude: *Even if this does not reach you, please reply (I'm making a joke). Truly the saddest fellow in camp is the one who never gets mail.*

At the last minute he crossed out "release the pigeon" and replaced it with "met you on Via Calepina." He didn't want her to get in trouble if the letter fell into the wrong hands. He had to ask another man where on the paper to put the name

and number of his unit so that if she did receive his message—
he assumed the chance was small—she'd be able to reply.

Looking for Luca

One day in March, Rodolfo came in from the garden and
asked where Luca was.

"I haven't seen him since yesterday," Teresa said, and Frau
Merz agreed, a look of concern on her face. It wasn't unusual
for him to be gone for several hours at a time but he never
stayed out all night.

Teresa became more alarmed when she visited the stable
and discovered the water trough was almost dry. She looked
at the horse and said, "Where is your caretaker, can you tell
me?" Then she refilled the trough, bucket by bucket, from the
well. The remainder of the day she spent worrying about Luca
while also expecting him to come flying through the door
with news from some distant part of town.

When the Austrians returned and sat down for their
evening meal, Teresa asked Rosa to make an inquiry about
Luca: Had they seen him last night or perhaps on the street
at some point during the day? Rosa spoke to them often and
knew how to pose the question without inviting suspicion. As
Frau Merz regularly reminded them (especially since Signor
Benedetti's death), it was dangerous to have the Austrians take
an interest in their affairs.

Rosa disappeared into the dining room and came back
with a stricken look on her face.

"Hauptmann Schneider says he was probably taken into
the k.u.k.—the regular army."

Teresa glanced at Frau Merz and at Rodolfo. The news made her stomach churn. "What about his limp?"

Rosa lowered her gaze. "The Hauptmann says they've gotten less particular. He'll be given a few weeks of training and sent away to the front."

"How can he perform the duties of a soldier?" Teresa asked. "How will he keep up?"

"He seems to get around town with no difficulty," Rosa replied. And then, seeing the looks of disapproval on their faces, "I'm sorry. I know he's your friend."

"I will find him," Rodolfo said, beginning to move toward the door. He spoke without emotion, as if announcing he was going out to dig a ditch.

Frau Merz stepped away from the table and put down her knife. "Where will you go? It's already dark. Besides, the authorities won't appreciate it if you interfere."

"Wait until tomorrow and I'll come with you," Teresa said. She agreed with Frau Merz—he shouldn't go by himself, certainly not at night.

For a moment Rodolfo looked as if he was going to ignore them both and continue out the door. Then he nodded and returned to his chair.

Teresa excused herself and went out to check on the horse. She was holding out hope Luca would be in the stable, sleeping in the straw. But there was still no sign of him. She doubted they'd be able to find him among the thousands of Austro-Hungarian troops now garrisoned in Trento. And if they did, it would hardly make any difference—he wouldn't be coming back.

She recalled one of the news stories Frau Merz had read. It described how young soldiers were being thrown at each other in great waves. It said much of the fighting was taking place high up in the mountains, above the tree line, where there was only ice and stone. She tried to picture all the poor boys and all the horrors they must be enduring—Luca and maybe Gaetano as well being "thrown" at the enemy as if they were inert matter rather than flesh and blood.

The next morning, she got up before sunrise, tended to the horse, and set out with Rodolfo to search for Luca. A cold tramontana wind was blowing, so she wore a headscarf and pulled her shawl tight.

Rodolfo seldom spoke to her directly; he faced the world with a certain reserve that kept her from knowing him very well. Luca sometimes made gentle fun of how gruff the old gardener was: "I tell him what's in my heart and he says, 'Shut up, I'm trying to work.'"

"The largest encampment is near the train station," Teresa said.

"Yes," replied Rodolfo, "let's go there."

Each time Teresa went out, she became more alarmed by how Trento was changing. Streets had been torn up for no apparent reason. Shops had been broken into and looted. If someone's garden wall was in the way, they knocked it down, and military equipment was everywhere.

Soon they came upon a long line of heavily laden camions, some motorized, some being pulled by mules. It appeared they were preparing to leave Trento for the mountain front. She and Rodolfo walked beside the column, being careful to avoid attracting attention. Teresa hadn't imagined there could be so many vehicles in all of Trento, nor so many mules. Occasionally, they spied a boy who looked a bit like Luca but it was never him. Perhaps he was already at some remote outpost for training. She worried about Luca. Although he was as strong as any other young man, his small stature made him seem vulnerable. Rosa had told them that, according to Hauptmann Schneider, he might be sent to France.

Beyond the train station they turned left and entered a large piazza, covered in military machinery and tents. When Teresa first arrived in Trento, it had been a favorite place for couples of all ages to stroll on summer nights. How the city had changed.

"I want to speak to an officer," Rodolfo said.

"Do you think that's wise? Remember what Frau Merz said; they won't allow us to interfere."

"I want to speak to an officer," he said again.

They stood for a moment and observed: Wagons were being loaded and unloaded, soldiers walked purposefully from place to place, and more tents were being erected in what little space remained. The chill wind was making every task unpleasant; collars were turned up and caps pulled low. Military pennants snapped in the breeze.

"There," Teresa said, pointing at a soldier with a pistol on his hip, "let's try asking him." His posture as well as the insignia on his uniform made her think he was a figure of authority, one who might be able to help.

As they approached, she began speaking in her halting German. He listened patiently until she was finished and then replied in Italian: "No, I'm sorry. There is nothing I can do. Maybe he will write to you. But I wouldn't be too hopeful. The mail is unreliable. The best thing is simply to pray for his safe return."

"He's been gone for only two days," she exclaimed. "This man is his father. He wants to say goodbye." She glanced at Rodolfo, hoping he wouldn't contradict her. She could think of no other way to convince the officer to bend.

The officer waved his hand in a gesture that took in all before them. "Even if I wanted to find him, I couldn't. Once a man is in uniform, there is no going back."

Now it was Rodolfo's turn to try. He gathered himself and

stepped forward, yet before he could utter a single word, the officer turned and ducked into a tent. For a moment Teresa feared Rodolfo would follow. Instead, he stopped, looked off toward the mountains, and sadly shook his head. His entire body seemed to shrink, to lose its dignity and force.

They continued on through the camp, still hoping Luca might appear. Teresa kept expecting to be stopped and questioned about their business or at least directed to leave the area. But the whole of Trento had become a sealed fortress; as long as you remained inside it, you could go more or less where you chose.

At last they abandoned hope and turned toward home. On their way, they passed the long column again. Now it was beginning to move. The lorries revved their engines. The mules surged forward and the harness leathers creaked. Officers shouted orders. The wagon wheels scraped the cobblestones as they began to turn. She pitied Rodolfo. He and Luca had worked together for many years. According to Frau Merz, no members of Rodolfo's family were still living. As she watched him walk along with sagging shoulders and downcast eyes, she thought he must feel very alone.

In the days that followed, Teresa continued caring for the horse, doing as much as possible under cover of darkness. "Buonasera, Coniglio," she said. "I'm sure you'd prefer Luca, but I'll do the best I can." When she was a child, her family owned a horse, which her father taught her to ride. Even though it was only an old plow horse, she loved riding it into the village or just sitting on its broad back as it grazed in the morning sun. Later, when she was older and their horse no longer alive, she would ask anyone who owned a horse if she could ride it. "You don't want it to get fat," she'd say. But Coniglio wasn't ready to be ridden, not until his leg had fully healed. Instead, she haltered him, attached a lead rope, and walked him along the dirt path beneath the towering trees, out of sight of the house. At times she felt as if they'd left the city behind.

One night, snow began to fall. Soon the ground was covered. For some reason there was a pause in the shelling in the mountains and the only sounds were the horse's footsteps and her own, the horse's breathing and her own. Although she knew she should be in bed, she didn't want to go back inside because everything was so lovely, so peaceful, so calm.

Innsbruck

The temperature dropped and dropped and dropped again. The feet of a guard trooper and an artillery officer became so frostbitten, the men cried out in agony. Oberleutnant Haas did his best to comfort them: "When the mule train comes with supplies, you'll be carried back down." But by the time the mule train arrived, one of them had died from sepsis and the other was told he'd lose both feet.

In an effort to keep from suffering a similar fate, Alexi cut the legs off an extra pair of trousers and turned them into boot coverings. Florian followed suit, slicing up a canvas ground cloth that had belonged to one of the deceased.

"I don't like using a dead man's possessions," Florian complained. "But it's all I can find."

"He would applaud you," Alexi said.

Carlo had no such qualms. Pointing at the canvas, he said, "When you're done, I'll take what's left." He'd always assumed soldiers had proper clothing to wear and had been surprised to learn they were given only the barest minimum. Anything else they needed was up to them to find or make.

Despite the weather and continued periods of shelling, the mountain fortress was nearing completion. Several of the large galleries were already occupied by troops that had arrived over the past few weeks. The first cannon, still the largest, boomed nightly, and three smaller ones, recently added, were beginning to join in. When they all fired together, it was like being inside a volcano. Deafening explosions and the smell of brimstone. Flashes of fire. Rock dust hanging in the air.

At last those who had been digging for the longest stretch of time, themselves and seven others, were told they were to be sent down for a period of rest. Each of them was given a six-day leave pass, a travel pass to Innsbruck, and a little money to spend. It took a moment for them to overcome their disbelief; then they were filled with joy.

"Innsbruck!" they exclaimed, as if the word were synonymous with paradise. But in truth none of them knew much about it, not even Florian.

"Don't your schools teach you about your own country?" Alexi asked.

"There is so much to learn about Vienna and Salzburg, they don't bother with Innsbruck," Florian replied. "Vienna alone has more of interest and value than the whole of Bosnia. Until I saw men wearing fezzes and said, 'Who are those buffoons?' I didn't know your country existed."

The three of them had become quite familiar with each other. Remarks that would once have earned a punch in the nose now received only mocking replies.

"Austria, land of the sausage eaters," Alexi said.

Florian threw up his hands in exasperation. "At least it wasn't an Austrian who assassinated the archduke. If not for your countryman, we wouldn't be here at all."

"The assassin was more Serb than Bosnian. But having gone to Austrian schools, you probably don't know the difference. If the history of the Habsburg Empire teaches us anything, it's that the Austrian people are sheep and eagerly do what they're told."

Feeling bested, at least for now, Florian could only snort and shake his head.

The walk down from the mountains seemed remarkably easy. The trail had been improved and they had the energy of schoolboys released for a holiday. When they reached the point where a lorry would carry them onward, Carlo's wish for sleep was granted. The minute the engine started, he collapsed into senseless slumber. As the vehicle jounced over ruts and stones, his limp body sometimes lost all contact with the steel bed, and not even the hard landing that followed was enough to wake him up. It wasn't just him—the truck was filled with exhausted soldiers being hauled out of the mountains like so many sacks of grain.

When Carlo awoke, it was nighttime and they were entering Innsbruck. He looked out and saw gaslights on every corner, gleaming motorcars, and people dressed in fine city clothes. The shops were open and lit from within. He felt such relief, his eyes filled with tears. The night air seemed positively springlike, at least in comparison to the air on the frigid peaks.

"I am never going back," Florian said.

They got a room in a hotel and had a supper of meat that tasted like meat and green vegetables that were still remarkably green. And tall glasses of beer. They'd been told on many occasions that food was being rationed throughout Austria-Hungary and Germany so the army could have enough to eat. That might be true in some places, but not, it appeared, where those with money lived. Carlo was struck by the number of churches and the number of parks and gardens they passed. Everything was well tended and in good repair.

"We're still quite close to the front," he said. "How is it this place remains untouched?"

"It means we are winning the war," Alexi replied, his voice drenched in irony, "but if the Italians ever overrun us, they'll burn it all to the ground."

Florian looked horrified. "Do you really think so?"

"Or if our side breaks through first, we will go to Florence and sack the museums. We'll pound their precious statues to dust."

"I don't think either side is going to overrun the other," Carlo said. "Not if what's happened so far is any measure."

Alexi, puffing on his pipe in a contemplative manner, said, "I predict this war will lead to a proletarian revolution. What's happening in Russia will spread."

"From what I've heard, what's happening in Russia is one war on top of another war," said Florian. "Not only are the Russians fighting the Germans, they're fighting each other."

"It's what they're fighting *for* that matters," said Alexi. "The downtrodden are finally getting their chance. Once the masses see what's possible, they won't allow themselves to be held back."

Despite the confidence with which Alexi spoke, Carlo continued to believe that any utterance about the war or its aftermath was mere speculation. Maybe this will happen, maybe that. And if this happens, what will follow? Every day there were new contingencies, new questions, new possibilities. It was best to live as if everything could be upended and shattered to bits at any time. In Carlo's view, you were less likely to be disappointed if you refused to have expectations about what tomorrow would bring.

"I overheard someone say the Germans are bombing Paris from zeppelins," Florian said.

Alexi and Carlo looked at each other in amazement. "If they can do that, why bother having us dig holes in a mountainside?" Alexi said. "The war will be over in a month."

After they had finished eating, they went to their rooms and slept until halfway through the following day. Carlo awoke feeling as if the tunnels were part of some strange past that had no connection to his real life, a life he had now miraculously reentered. He washed—hot water, such a luxury—dressed, and then went outside and walked up the street. At a haberdashery he stopped and bought a pair of black dress gloves. Although he could scarcely afford it, purchasing an item of clothing seemed the sort of thing a young fellow visiting the city should do. When he clenched his fists, the leather stretched across his knuckles in a satisfying way.

That evening, they encountered some other men on leave and shared stories about the crazy things that had happened to them in the mountains. But only the crazy things, the laughable nonsense, such as when a fat general who'd had too much to drink tripped and rolled down a hill like a pumpkin, or when some unit built an army of snowmen and watched as the Italians shot them to hell. The actual fighting, the violence and death, remained conspicuously undiscussed.

At a certain point, one of them suggested going to find some women. Another said a particular brothel had been recommended, so he led the way. All fourteen of them ambled along the broad sidewalks, shoving each other and laughing until, remembering they were warriors, they became earnest and straightened their spines.

Before they reached the brothel, Alexi said, "My wife wouldn't like this," and veered off. A few steps later, Carlo, Florian, and one other boy, all unnerved by the prospect of losing their virginity to an unknown woman in an unfamiliar place, turned back as well.

"I understand you can be made sick in such establishments," Florian said.

Carlo, not wanting to be a coward yet not wanting to go on without his mates, added, "Well then, some other night."

But the feeling of cowardice was still present the next morning. And when the men who had visited the brothel began mocking those who hadn't, they had no choice; they had to go back. They should have done it the first time. The girl Carlo was offered said not a single word nor did she meet his eyes. Perhaps it was all a necessary demonstration of his manhood, but in the end it felt like a chore.

"That was a mistake," Alexi said, reflecting on the experience afterward. He paused for a moment and then continued. "I would like to take my wife and children and move to America. What do you think of that?"

Carlo frowned. "I don't see what visiting a brothel and going to America have in common."

"It's obvious. I want to leave all this behind."

"There are brothels in America, you know."

"Indeed. I never said there weren't."

"Maybe I'll go to America, too." He paused. "Go *back* to America, I mean." This wasn't the only time he'd considered it. He was certain his father would not be returning to Colorado, and when they'd first arrived, Carlo had assumed the same was true for him. Being among all the Italian boys in the school in Trento had reinforced the idea that he was on his way to becoming an Italian. Yet now that he had been so abruptly wrenched into the military—and the Austrian military at that—he was having second thoughts. He wasn't sure where he belonged.

"When this is over, you can go wherever you want," Alexi said.

Later that day Carlo began another letter to the pigeon girl. She hadn't replied to his first one but that was no surprise. As he wrote, he felt strangely embarrassed, as if she would be able to deduce what he'd done with the prostitute from his handwriting alone, just as a person's misdeeds can sometimes be revealed by the expression on their face. As a result, his words felt awkward and false: *I am now on leave and having a delightful time. Believe it or not, yesterday I slept until noon. In America we say, "I slept like a log." Is that an expression you've heard before?* He wrote three more sentences about the quality of his sleep before moving on to make some remarks about how the blisters on his feet were finally healing. It was all terribly dull.

The day they were to leave Innsbruck, important news arrived: The Emperor of Austria, Franz Joseph, had died.

"Finally," Alexi said.

"He was our father," Florian said, his eyes filling with tears, "for more than sixty years."

Alexi waved his hands. "He annexed Bosnia. For that he can never be forgiven." Then he glanced at Carlo and said, "History is complicated. One man's beloved leader is another man's tyrant. In this instance the facts are on my side."

The Korporal

She liked being with the horse. Sometimes she looked into his eyes and wondered what he was thinking. Did he remember Luca and wish he would return? In tending to the horse, she tried to follow Luca's example. When he felt the poultice had done its work, he'd started treating the leg with liniment and kept it wrapped in cloth. But now she'd run out of liniment and realized she didn't know where to get more. Perhaps Frau Merz could help—she seemed to know how to obtain anything, whether it had to do with the kitchen, the garden, or some other part of the estate.

"I can make you some," she said, her reply coming so quickly, it was almost as if she'd been waiting to be asked.

"You know how to make liniment to treat the leg of a horse?"

"Peppermint leaves and witch hazel steeped in brandy. The result is a potent remedy for sore muscles. It causes the blood to move."

Excellent Frau Merz, who once again reminded her of her mother. Teresa suspected the two of them would be friends were they to become acquainted. After the war she could arrange a meeting. How interesting it would be to listen to them talk. The peppermint and witch hazel solution did seem to help. After only a week, the horse became more eager to go on walks. At times the limp was nearly impossible to detect.

Caring for the horse served as a distraction from the war, which was growing in intensity by the week. She knew from Rosa that more and more men were being brought in with grave wounds—missing limbs, blinded eyes, torsos torn open to reveal their vital organs, which she was not reluctant to describe. "Today there was a man whose intestines were half out of his body," she said. "They looked very much like the pajata you can buy in the butcher shop. And, do you know, the doctor simply shoved them back inside."

Teresa shook her head in dismay. "How do you keep from breaking down?"

"I close my mind to everything except the task at hand."

"Is that possible?"

"It's not just possible, it's the only way."

The shelling in the mountains continued, night after deafening night. Some said they'd gotten used to it but Teresa found that hard to believe. She tried blocking her ears with beeswax; still she could feel the ceaseless hammering, the distant yet always audible roar. Incredibly, the soldiers living in the house said things were even worse in other places and that they might be sent east, to help shore up the defenses where the fiercest fighting was taking place.

This put Rosa in a bad mood. "It can't happen. I would truly miss them," she said.

For a moment Teresa considered saying, "And they you?" but refrained.

Then one night one of the Austrians stopped Teresa in the hallway and said, "I have seen you going out at night. Why is that?" He had the shoulders of a stevedore and positioned himself so her way was entirely blocked.

She studied him for a moment, trying to conceal her alarm. Despite his youth, his dark hair was thinning and his ears stuck out too much. "Sometimes I can't sleep, so I go for a stroll. Is that not allowed?"

"I thought you might be stepping out to see a gentleman friend."

She lowered her eyes. "No, I go by myself." At least he wasn't accusing her of visiting the stables. Of caring for a contraband horse. She was even slightly flattered that he assumed she had a beau.

"Maybe I could accompany you," he said.

"You wouldn't find me very interesting."

"How do you know?"

She shrugged. "Because I'm not."

He laughed and allowed her to pass. "You're very amusing," he said.

As she continued down the corridor, she worried about her response. She'd said very little but perhaps even that was too much. Frau Merz had warned her to keep her distance: "The less you speak to them, the less likely one of them will want to take you to his room."

At the time, she'd said, "Rosa talks to them often."

"I know. She's made a different choice."

"I think the choice was made for her," Teresa replied. Although she didn't necessarily approve of Rosa's actions, Frau Merz didn't know what it was like to be a young woman surrounded by hungry young men.

"However it happened, she seems to be enjoying it," Frau Merz said, a disapproving look on her face.

For the next few days Teresa did her best to avoid the Austrian who'd spoken to her. As long as she was watchful, it wasn't particularly hard. Once, in the dining room, she noticed his eyes fixed on her as she moved around the table. She quickly turned her back, and when she checked again, he was looking down at his plate. But a few days later, he appeared before her in the same location as the first time, blocking her way again.

"Good evening," he said. "How is your friend?"

She looked at him and drew back. "I told you, I have no friend. At least not the kind you're implying."

"Ah, but I think you do."

"I don't know what you're talking about," she said firmly. It took some effort to keep from running away.

"I don't mean to make you uncomfortable," he said, stepping aside. "I've been told I have that effect."

While in her room that evening, she wondered if she was being backed into a trap. Maybe she should follow Rosa's lead and give herself up. If she initiated it, perhaps she could retain some measure of control. According to Frau Merz, the most casual remarks might invite familiarity. Yet, given her role in the house, how could she avoid it? What if he were to follow her out to the stable? What if he were to accost her on some remote path? She wished Gaetano were here. Or Luca. Even her father. Someone to protect her so she wouldn't feel so vulnerable and alone.

When Teresa saw Rosa again, she said, "The short one with dark hair and big ears. What's his name?"

"Korporal Mayr. Do you fancy him?"

"No. The opposite."

Rosa gave her a dubious look. "Well, he seems like a gentleman to me."

Even though it was obvious she'd get no sympathy from Rosa, she continued: "He keeps asking me questions. He wants to go walking with me. What right does he have?"

"Every right. Compared to some other girls I've heard about, we're being treated very well. You're too nervous about that horse. A single useless animal? Why would they even care?"

Snakes

Their days of leave used up, they returned to the mountains. In their absence, Carlo had forgotten how impressive the fortress was. While he remained ambivalent about being a soldier in the army of the Central Powers, he couldn't deny feeling a certain pride in all they had accomplished. It was as though they'd built a castle from the inside out.

He and the other miners now resided inside the tunnels along with scores of additional soldiers, especially artillerymen, who had come there to fight. Mortars and cannons and machine guns stood ready at every portal, leaving no sector of the mountainside beyond their deadly reach. Spotters with binoculars continued to spy cadres of Italians making their way toward the crest. When that happened, artillery officers were notified and they ordered a barrage. As a result, the south-facing slopes had become littered with the bodies of the enemy. Since any men the Italians sent to retrieve the corpses were strafed with as much vigor as the original attackers, they had no choice but to let their dead lie. Then it snowed and the corpses were covered over. "Snow, corpses, snow, corpses," Florian said, "like layers of an apricot torte."

The fortress not only made it easy to repel attackers; it prevented Italian artillery from doing much harm. A direct hit from the largest of their shells sounded like distant thunder and scarcely shook the walls.

One of the men who had recently joined them said, "I like it here. It may be cold, but we're not being ordered to run into enemy fire across an open field."

"If I was told to do that," Carlo said, "I'd turn and go the other way."

"No, you wouldn't," the new fellow replied. "Officers with revolvers are positioned in the rear. Anyone seen retreating is shot."

Carlo pictured the situation being described. So that was how they forced men with no interest in being soldiers to kill other men with no interest in being soldiers. Suddenly, digging holes in solid rock didn't seem so bad.

Then, as expected, some general decided still more chambers and more connecting passages were needed. This would include a second level, to be accessed by ladders bolted to the rock face. Since the fortress was so fully occupied—it was now almost a small town—explosives were ruled out and most of the work would be done by hand.

The digging was as hard as before but it was comforting to return to their previous routine—chiseling away at the stone and loading the waste into a cart for disposal outside. Although mules could often be used, when the tunnels got too small, the cart had to be pushed by hand. It wasn't an easy task. Yet since they now slept and ate in the tunnels and spent nearly all their hours by candlelight, they'd started coveting the opportunity to feel the wind and sun. "I'll take this load," said Alexi. "Anything to get me outside."

Working in windowless vaults also meant they got confused about the passage of time. Was it morning or afternoon? Or halfway through the night? Sometimes Carlo arrived at the tunnel entrance only to find he was faced not with blue skies as he'd expected but darkness and blowing snow.

One evening Oberleutnant Haas came to them and said he had received intelligence suggesting the Italians were attempting to break into the fortress from the west side, tunneling inward and then up from below. It seemed unbelievable, the kind of thing some officer would dream up to make sure they remained alert. "Before that happens," Alexi said, "the war will be over and I'll be home with my wife."

"A patrol is being sent out to see if it's true," the oberleutnant explained. "If it is, we'll launch a counterattack to stop them. The three of you will plant a charge and blast them to bits."

As soon as Haas was gone, they all swore vigorously. "He can go fuck himself," Florian said. "I don't intend to blow up a tunnel that doesn't exist."

Suddenly, Carlo felt uneasy. He'd been telling himself that one advantage of his current job was he might never have to come close enough to the enemy to see their faces, to look them in the eye. But now it seemed the Italians might overrun their position. He pictured fighting them with picks and shovels inside the mountain fortress. The image was disturbing. To make matters worse, although he was mostly American, he was more Italian than Austrian. It would be easier if they were sworn enemies, if he'd hated Italians his entire life.

Two weeks passed and they heard nothing more about the Italian tunnel. It was possible the patrol had been unable to find it. Or it had been located and destroyed but the oberleutnant considered the three of them too insignificant to be informed. Then, as they were broadening a large vault so it could better serve as a barracks, Carlo noticed an unfamiliar noise.

"Quiet," he said, raising a hand to get their attention. "Do you hear that?"

It sounded like the clink of hammers striking chisels. Throughout the fortress there were men performing maintenance on artillery pieces and unloading provisions and doing any number of other tasks, so perhaps it was only that. Alexi said, "It's nothing," but Carlo decided it was worth reporting to Haas.

He found him in the makeshift office that had been created in an alcove off one of the larger passageways. At present, he was talking to a junior officer, so Carlo stood back to wait. When at last he was invited to speak, Haas was unsurprised. Others had already heard the same noises, and members of the reconnaissance patrol, although unable to locate the Italians' tunnel, had seen mining tools being carried up the mountain, including a gas-powered drill.

"Let them dig," Haas said. "We'll be waiting when they break through."

"Why not intercept their tunnel with one of our own?" suggested the junior officer, a Magyar whose hair stuck out like straw from beneath his field cap.

Haas pushed out his lips and nodded to show he was giving the idea some thought. "Yes, that could work. I'll consider it. But I'm not ready to take action yet."

When Carlo returned to Alexi and Florian and told them what had happened, they berated him for meddling. "Another tunnel. Thank you for that," Florian groaned.

"He might decide against it," Carlo said defensively. "He doesn't seem to be in a hurry. Maybe he'll forget."

However, the following day Haas issued the order: They were to begin another tunnel, aimed, to the best of their ability, in the direction of the troubling sounds. Before Florian and Alexi could say anything, Carlo apologized. "I know, I know, I should have kept my mouth shut."

This new work felt different from what they'd done thus far. Instead of building a stronghold to protect themselves from the enemy, they were now driving toward him, picturing the moment they'd break into his tunnel and could rush inside. No doubt the Italians were having similar thoughts. Did it really matter who broke through first?

"We have become burrowing animals," said Alexi. "Living in the dark like moles."

"Are there any animals who do battle underground?" Florian asked. "If not, your comparison doesn't hold."

Carlo stopped hammering and pondered the matter. "Maybe some variety of snake."

Naturally, they now discussed snakes, those found in Bosnia, in Austria, in Colorado, and their personal knowledge of each kind.

"Poskok zmija, the horned viper," Alexi said. "The most terrible of all the creatures on this earth. Their venom is always deadly. I once saw an entirely black one moving through the grass like a line of smoke."

"The diamondback rattler," Carlo countered. "Just the sound they make—*chchshshsh*—is enough to stop your heart."

"Silence," hissed Florian. "I can hear the Italians now."

Carlo and Alexi joined him in listening, holding themselves still, save for their eyes, which darted about. Of the three of them, Florian's hearing was the most acute, and he was right. Now more clunk than clink, the Italians were getting closer. It was only a matter of days.

The Korporal's Trousers

When Teresa encountered the korporal again, he didn't mention her late-night walks or accuse her of harboring secrets. No, he asked if she knew how to sew.

"The trousers they gave me are too long. Would you help me shorten them? I would pay you for your work."

Her eyebrows went up as she registered his request. "I suppose so," she replied, "provided you won't be annoyed by a crooked stitch."

"I'm certain you'll do an excellent job. I'll bring them to you on Friday." Then, looking suddenly bashful, he hurried up the stairs.

As she continued down the hall, she passed Rodolfo's room and noticed light coming from under the door. Poor Rodolfo. These days, instead of working industriously in the garden, he sat on a bench and stared. And after supper went straight to bed. Back when she'd first arrived at the house, it had been immediately clear to her that Frau Merz, Rodolfo, and Luca had worked there for many years. They could communicate almost wordlessly, with a gesture, a murmur, a glance. But the war had disrupted the old relationships. Signor Benedetti was no more, the family was gone, the Austrians had moved in, and Luca had been taken away. No doubt the same kind of change was happening all across Trento, across Trentino and South Tyrol, across the whole of Europe, from Russia to the Irish Sea.

She wished she knew a bit more about what was happening beyond Trento. The Austrian authorities now governing the city told them only what served their purposes, and the information coming from the Italian side wasn't necessarily more reliable. Just yesterday, Frau Merz retrieved the most recent copy of *Corriere della Sera* from its hiding place and set it before Teresa. "Put down that rolling pin," she said, "and read to me while I work."

Teresa scanned the front page. "This looks interesting—a report from the front."

On Thursday night, in the midst of a violent snowstorm, enemy forces entered one of our advanced positions on the southern slopes of Cimi de Booche. They were driven out by a counterattack.

There were the usual artillery duels yesterday. We shelled the station at Santa Lucia di Tolmino and enemy lines in the Castagnavilla sector with good results.

Also, on the Julian Alps front, there were lively skirmishes. Some of our detachments, after having made gaps in the enemy's barbed wire, attacked by surprise. The defenders were made prisoners.

"It does me good to hear about such success," Frau Merz said.

Teresa looked up from the paper. "The Austro-Hungarians are taking prisoners as well. Rosa says she's seen large groups being brought into town. There's a new camp near the river to contain them, with tall fences and guards all around."

"The Austro-Hungarians cannot be taking as many prisoners as the Italians," Frau Merz replied firmly.

"How do you know?"

"I never read about it in the newspaper."

Teresa laughed. "That's because this is an Italian paper. They report only news favorable to the Italian side." As she spoke, she realized her relationship with Frau Merz was becoming quite familiar. Not as familiar as the one Frau Merz had with Luca and Rodolfo, but they were now able to speak to each other honestly and have no fear of misunderstanding. Teresa could even tease her—something which, when she'd first come to the villa, she'd never imagined she'd be able to do.

It took her two long evenings, staying up late, to finish the korporal's trousers—he'd given her three pairs. She delivered them to him and observed as he inspected her work.

"Thank you," he said. "At last I can stop looking like a fool."

"You didn't look like a fool before. But now you won't trip over them."

"When the war is over, you should find a position in a dress shop or with a tailor."

"Frau Merz says I should open a trattoria."

"Not a bad idea. You have many skills."

"After the war, I expect I'll return to my village. I'm afraid neither a trattoria nor a seamstress is needed there."

He looked at her with interest. "You say that now, but I predict after the war, things will be different. Your village may have changed."

"What do you mean? Do you know something about my village?"

"No, no. Calm yourself. I am only saying that the Austro-Hungarian Empire will be larger and more prosperous than ever before. Even a humble seamstress will be able to have a good life."

After he was gone, she decided she was no longer afraid of him. That didn't mean she'd let him kiss her. Better to save herself for Gaetano. She wondered what he was doing right now, this very minute. She entertained fantasies of him entering Trento on horseback, a liberator of the city. She would be standing by the road, and upon seeing her nod, he'd smile in return. And yes, she would offer herself to him, whether it was sinful or not.

Her reverie was interrupted by Rosa. "Sewing up a man's

trousers. Not a bad strategy, although I could tell you a more direct path."

"You enjoy playing the tart, don't you?"

Rosa smirked, taking up the challenge as Teresa knew she would. "And you enjoy playing the good girl from the village who can do no wrong."

The remark stung. There was some truth in it. "I might surprise you."

"With the korporal? Or are you pining about that fellow who's no longer here? Well, let me tell you, it's easier to have a love affair with someone who's hundreds of kilometers away than with one who keeps inviting you to his bed."

Before Teresa could think how to reply, Rosa turned and left the room.

Later that night, as she was stealthily exercising the horse, it occurred to her that she'd rather be a groomsman like Luca than a seamstress in some shop. Who wouldn't prefer to spend time with a horse instead of a pair of trousers? Then again, the job of groomsman might not be open to a girl—unless the korporal was right and things changed after the war.

In the weeks that followed, the korporal still spoke to her from time to time, but on the whole, his interest in her seemed to have waned. Frau Merz approved. She said, "It's probably because you wouldn't give him what he wanted."

"All he wanted was to have his trousers altered," Teresa replied. "We're required by circumstance to live here together, so why not be congenial?"

"Congenial," Frau Merz snorted and walked off shaking her head.

Rosa was another matter. She informed Teresa that she now fully expected to marry her Austrian, possibly quite soon: "Why wait? Who knows when this will end? If he gets sent elsewhere, I won't have to worry about him forgetting me. I'll feel more secure."

"I agree, sooner would be better," Teresa said.

"Really? I'm surprised to hear you say that."

"Yes, sooner. Before he gets you in a family way."

"What do you know about such things?" she snapped but then looked secretly pleased. If nothing else, Teresa thought, Rosa seemed confident about what she wanted and why. That certainly wasn't something she could say about herself. Maybe when the war ended and Gaetano returned, she could think about her future more clearly. Right now both events seemed a long way off.

With the gradual arrival of spring, Teresa began spending even more time at the stable. If she had a free hour, that was where she went. She liked being outdoors, liked seeing the world turn green. One afternoon she found an old chair in the tack room and placed it in the doorway so she could watch the sun go down. It was very pleasant, very serene. She couldn't be seen from the house and no one ever walked through these woods. Or so she thought. One afternoon, as she was beginning to nod off, she heard footsteps approaching from behind. Turning, she saw Korporal Mayr standing only a few meters away.

"Oh my," she said with a gasp.

"It's just me. Don't be afraid."

Was there a lie she could tell about why she was there? She couldn't think of one. "You've discovered my secret," she said.

"I've known for some time."

"The horse is lame. Or at least it was. It's almost better now."

"I've seen you at night. I don't sleep very well." His voice was in no way threatening but still she felt some fear. What if he'd been hiding his true self and now intended to take advantage of her?

She said, "There used to be a groomsman—maybe you remember him. This isn't really my job."

"You seem to like animals."

"I suppose I do."

"I once cared for an injured fox." He glanced at her expectantly, almost as though seeking approval.

"Did it recover?"

"Yes. I considered keeping it as a pet. But as soon as I let it out of the house, it vanished into the woods."

"You must have been disappointed. You cared for it and then it left."

"I never thought about it that way. It wasn't my place to tell it how to live."

"It was lucky to find you," Teresa said. "Most men would have slit its throat, skinned it, and sold the pelt."

The korporal nodded and glanced in the direction of the villa. "I should get back," he said. "Don't worry, I won't say anything about the horse."

"Thank you," she replied, suddenly aware of how tense she'd been, how prepared to be assaulted—or at least to have Coniglio snatched away into service. But surely it was unfair to think of him that way. He'd done nothing except talk. As she watched, the korporal disappeared into the long shadows cast by the trees.

A Rumbling

When it seemed they were close to breaking through the barrier of stone separating themselves from the Italians, members of the regular infantry were sent to join them. Now, a dozen or more were present at all times, playing cards in the candlelight, cleaning their rifles, smoking as they lounged against the wall. Digging and excavating continued around the clock. Occasionally, someone suggested it might be best if they stopped and let the Italians come to them, but the oberleutnant was getting impatient and ordered them to redouble their efforts. After a period of worry, Carlo stopped thinking about the Italians. All that mattered was making it through the next shift.

Florian had become still more disagreeable, complaining about everything from the food to the temperature in the tunnels. When it was his turn to push the tailing-filled cart outside, he said, "Why don't they give us a mule? I'm tired of breaking my back."

"The passage is too narrow for a mule to turn around," Alexi said. "If you don't want to do it, I will. Or Carlo, perhaps you'd like to see the sun."

"Yes," he said, leaping at the chance. "I'll happily be the mule."

"Be my guest," Florian said. Alexi and Carlo glanced at each other in recognition of the young Austrian's willingness to act against his own interests. As often as not, petulance ruled his brain.

Carlo leaned into the cart and set it rumbling along the planks that led back toward the tunnel's entrance, back toward the consoling sky. As he emerged from the dark passage, he paused and took a breath. The plateau before him, once only a small encampment, was now a fully operational staging area, with rows of tents, crates of food and clothing, and all the tools and equipment being used in the construction of the fortress. Great spools of barbed wire, a material which had turned out to be nearly as effective in halting the enemy's advance as bullets and bombs, lay ready to be uncoiled.

He emptied the cart and then stood in the sun, enjoying

how it seemed to warm the very marrow of this bones. He was hungry and was reminded of one of Florian's complaints, a legitimate one, about how their meals seemed to contain less and less meat. While in the midst of this thought, he heard a rumbling deep in the earth. The ground began to shudder and he turned to look at the tunnel mouth. Suddenly, there was a tremendous roar as the entire mountainside rose up, exploded, shattered, and broke apart. The concussion threw him to the ground and he covered his head with his arms as a storm of stones fell from the sky. A second blast followed and more debris rained down. A piece of rock hit him below the ear, the one place his arms weren't protecting. Another struck him even harder in the back. His vision went black and his mouth filled with blood.

For a time he was afraid to move, afraid to open his eyes. A strange chill coursed through his body and he thought he might be dying. Eventually, rolling onto his side, he looked upward. An enormous column of black smoke was rising into the blue of the alpine sky. Ash fluttered down like snow. Somewhere in the distance he heard screams, though his ears were ringing and it was difficult to be sure what he was actually hearing. The tunnel entrance had been replaced by rubble, the roof having entirely collapsed. He tried to sit up, but as he did so, a sharp pain made him gasp. A fragment of rock had penetrated his shoulder and blood was streaming from his sleeve. With great effort he was able to reach across himself to remove the shard and hold the wound shut. His mouth tasted of copper and he spat a stream of red across the snow.

A few yards away he saw what appeared to be a man's back, barely visible beneath a mound of broken stone. Crawling to him, he began digging, clawing, scraping, using his uninjured arm to clear the debris. But there was nothing to be done. The man's skull had been crushed by falling rock. Farther off, a wounded horse struggled to stand before collapsing into a heap.

Now he was sure he could hear panicked voices, but where they were coming from remained unclear. Glancing upward, he saw for the first time that a large portion of the mountaintop had been blown off and a few survivors were clambering out through the opening made by the blast. Until then he hadn't understood what happened, but all at once it came to him. The Italians had never intended to gain entrance to the fortress. They dug a tunnel beneath it so they could plant an enormous charge and blow it all to hell.

Instinctively, he went toward the survivors, hoping he could help. But in his condition, it was difficult to climb. Before he'd made it a third of the way up, he'd been passed by a handful of men making their way down. Some were weeping. Some had blank expressions and looked through him, as though he didn't exist. All were covered in dust and ash. One gunnery sergeant stopped and raved at him, a few unintelligible sentences, before stumbling on. Given the enormity of the blast, it was heartening to see so many still alive. But as soon as this hopeful thought formed in his mind, the flow of men ceased. Of the hundreds inside, only a few dozen had emerged.

Eventually he reached the jagged summit and looked down. It appeared the top of the fortress had exploded upward and then collapsed in on itself, leaving a vast rubble-filled bowl. Here and there timbers jutted out, along with steel girders like the ones to which the larger guns had been anchored. Also, smaller items such as cooking pots and munitions boxes, helmets, mess kits, and tools. And newspapers, which, although they were heavily censored and arrived weeks late, the men—the ones who could read at any rate—eagerly devoured. Amid all the debris, human bodies were difficult to discern; yet after he spotted two or three, he began to see more, the blue-gray of their uniforms visible beneath the dust and ash. Then, to his horror, he realized he was stepping on parts: a blood-soaked torso, a severed arm, a gray gobbet he feared was some man's brain.

He had encountered neither Alexi nor Florian on his way up. Everything was so chaotic, it was possible they'd passed him without his noticing or descended by a different route. As he made his way down into the ruins, he came upon a man crouched on all fours, shaking his head like a disoriented dog. Seeing Carlo, he began to speak. In German? In Italian? Or was it Czech? No, it wasn't a language at all, merely unintelligible moans. The man gazed at him imploringly, as though, in his own mind, he was making perfect sense. Before Carlo could respond, the poor fellow shivered, collapsed, and expelled his final breath. Nearby was an officer who had been impaled on a broken timber. No need to worry about him.

Carlo wasn't the only one trying to help. Others were making their way across the desolation and attempting to determine who was alive. One of those assisting was a medic, and when Carlo discovered an officer whose leg was bent sideways with a bloody bone protruding, the medic came over and gave him an injection to dull the pain. He handed Carlo a bandage for his shoulder but told him he had more serious injuries to treat so he'd have to put it on himself. A short time later Carlo came upon a man whose pelvis had been crushed. He was crying softly and waving his arms about. Blood. So much blood. Carlo knelt beside him until he, too, was dead.

As the wounded were being treated, some men began to dig. Given the enormous amount of rock, it was difficult to imagine anyone not on the surface remaining alive. Still, it seemed inhumane not to try. Perhaps some of the tunnels hadn't fully collapsed. Carlo listened for cries of help. All he could hear were artillery in the distance and the steady sound of the wind. He continued searching until dark and then made his way back down.

Gipeto Barbato

The soldiers' presence in the villa had been teaching her some things about the nature of the military. Orders were given and dutifully carried out, but no one went looking for tasks on their own. Therefore, as long as there was no explicit command issued about the removal of remaining livestock, the horse would remain safe. At least that was her hope.

Then one morning Rodolfo entered the kitchen looking ill. His face was ashen, his shoulders sagged, his eyes were rimmed with red.

"My pigeons are gone," he said.

Immediately, Teresa thought of the korporal. She shouldn't have hemmed his trousers. She should have listened to Frau Merz and kept him at arm's length.

"Those bastards," Frau Merz said.

Rosa said, "You're fortunate they didn't accuse you of sending messages to the enemy. Losing your birds is not nearly so bad as losing your head."

"How do you think they found out?" Teresa asked, throwing a look of disgust in Rosa's direction.

Rodolfo turned up his palms and wagged his head. "I thought I'd hidden them well enough."

"It wasn't me if that's what you're suggesting," Rosa said to Teresa. "I care nothing about pigeons." And then to Rodolfo, "I'm sorry for your loss."

Korporal Mayr had already left for the day, but when he

returned, Teresa confronted him. "What did you do with the pigeons?" Her hands were shaking.

"What pigeons?"

"Don't lie to me. The ones hidden in the glade beyond the trees. You took them."

"Me?"

"You've explored the grounds. You must have seen where they were hidden."

"I promise you, I know nothing about any pigeons. Surely you're aware they are forbidden ..."

"They belonged to the gardener. They were his pets and nothing more."

"I'm quite serious," he replied, clearly taken aback by her tone. "Suppose a member of the Feldgendarmerie were to discover an Italian citizen was hiding a means of sending messages. They might very well shoot him. At the very least they'd beat him senseless and lock him up."

"Are you suggesting such a harmless old man is a spy?"

"No. I'm merely alerting you to the dangers that exist. And I'm offended you'd think otherwise. I had assumed we were friends."

Friends? She wasn't expecting that. "I'm aware of the dangers. If you didn't take the pigeons, who did?"

He shook his head. "None of the men in this house have any interest in your animals. Most likely someone was passing through the woods, stumbled upon the pigeons, and took them home to eat."

She wanted to believe him. After considering the matter for a moment, she decided she did. "Yes," she said. "You're probably right. I apologize for suspecting you."

He looked relieved. "Thank you. If I hear any talk about pigeons, I promise to tell you at once."

The following day, Teresa helped Rodolfo conduct a

search. They asked the groundskeeper of an adjacent estate and an old woman who sometimes walked across the property on her way to visit her sister. Both denied knowing anything about the pigeons—although the groundskeeper said, "Of course, I wouldn't tell you if I did."

Frau Merz thought it must have been the same Austrian authorities as the ones that took the other animals. Just because they gave notice previously didn't mean they would every time. Her opinion was bolstered by the fact that new edicts had recently been issued by General Dankl, the officer in charge of what was now referred to as the Trento Fortress Zone: All cheese belonged to the military, fishing in the river was prohibited, and silkworms, which had been propagated there for centuries, were being seized because the war effort needed the silk. When Teresa read the new regulations to Rodolfo, he said, "Next they will want our flies and ants." The edict also stated that the punishment for those who broke the rules had gotten more severe. Execution was a requirement, not an option, no matter how trifling the case.

Eventually they gave up on the pigeons and the household returned to the way it had been before. They continued to wonder what was happening beyond Trento, across the wider war. Even with Frau Merz's newspapers, it was difficult to know for sure. Some people said the Central Powers were having success on all fronts while others claimed the Russians were defeating the Germans in the East. About the West, however, there was general agreement: unremitting carnage, many thousands of French and English and Germans dying in the mud.

On the rare occasions when Teresa was sent on errands, she saw men coming out of the mountains looking utterly shattered. Scores of wounded arrived daily, as did prisoners, most wearing the uniform of Italy with a few English and

French mixed in. Although many of them looked like farm boys, their haggard, damaged appearance made her think they'd never work in the fields again. She heard the latest scourge was something called mustard gas, which could burn a man inside and out.

Nevertheless, their Austrian boarders continued going off to work each morning, as if they were bankers or government clerks. And each night they returned and sat down to a supper prepared by Teresa and Rosa and Frau Merz. The house where Rosa used to work had recently been commandeered by another group of Austrians. Perhaps because it had been deserted when they moved in, they were being less well mannered than the ones living in the Villa Benedetti. Evenings, a group of about a dozen men sat outside drinking and singing boisterous songs—after which Teresa often heard breaking glass and the occasional gunshot coming from inside the house.

"You should have stayed behind to care for your employers' property," Frau Merz told Rosa.

"You must be joking," she replied.

"Of course I'm joking. I wouldn't go near that place."

Rosa and her paramour had remained discreet about their liaisons. Amiable, with crooked teeth and straw-blond hair, her soldier didn't want to get reprimanded. But on two occasions Teresa walked into a room assuming it was vacant, only to find them half-undressed, the bed clothes in disarray.

The first time, Rosa said, "Is it so difficult to knock?"

"Am I to knock at every door I enter throughout the day?"

"You could at least make your footsteps more obvious as you approach."

"From now on I shall stomp," she said, putting her foot down loudly to demonstrate.

The second time it happened, Rosa, on her back with her knees in the air, said only, "Shut the fucking door."

As for the korporal, he'd spoken to Teresa sparingly since their discussion about the pigeons. She supposed she ought to be relieved, yet his remoteness hurt her feelings. She wanted his attention but on her own terms.

One morning Frau Merz returned from the market and said, "Everyone is talking. The Germans are on their way."

Rodolfo was sitting at the end of the long table on which they did much of their work. When he looked up, his face had lost its color.

Frau Merz continued. "They intend to break the backs of the Italians. To defeat them in the mountains and push all the way to Rome. At least that's what's being said."

Any mention of the Germans had the effect of producing fear. As Teresa understood it, fighting the Austrians and Hungarians and Bosnians and Serbs was akin to fighting one's cousins. The clash might have its vicious elements, but you wouldn't do to a family member what you didn't want done to you. Whereas the Germans had a reputation for descending upon their enemies with a kind of fury at once inexorable and systematic. People spoke darkly of atrocities, the murder of women and children, the burning of the Belgian city of Louvain.

"What shall we do?" Teresa asked. She had often wondered if there would come a day when Frau Merz would say it was time to leave the villa and Trento. Perhaps this was that day. But no. "Do? There's nothing we can do," Frau Merz said.

Rosa had entered the kitchen and now stood in the doorway listening and twisting her apron in red-knuckled hands. She looked almost as alarmed as Rodolfo. Teresa could read her mind: It was one thing to befriend the Austrians; the

Germans were something else entirely. Before she could say anything, Rodolfo began to speak.

"The Germans are like the gipeto barbato," he said.

They all looked at him. Teresa, coming from the mountains, knew of this terrifying bird but suspected the others may not.

"They kill their prey by carrying it to a great height before dropping it onto the rocks below," Rodolfo continued. "Then, instead of consuming only the meat, they eat everything, even the bones. I have seen one take a lamb. I have heard of one taking a child."

Rosa's eyes were wide and her mouth had become a speechless O.

"A terrible thing," Frau Merz agreed. "Yet how are such harpies similar to the Germans?"

Rodolfo's expression suggested the answer was self-evident, but he explained nonetheless: "They devour everything. They take no prisoners and leave behind only death."

The Aftermath

As darkness fell, the survivors gathered amid the rubble and ruin. An officer who had escaped with nothing but bruises was first to speak.

"I expect they're coming for us now," he said. "Maybe they will attack tonight, although that will be difficult, given the terrain. If not, then at first light."

The idea of being overrun by the Italian forces was terrifying. In preparation they ransacked the armory for weapons and took inventory of the arms and ammunition individual soldiers still had on their person or in their tents. They also relieved the dead of their guns and bayonets, an action which, while necessary, felt unseemly.

"We have the advantage of altitude," the officer said. "One sniper with a Mannlicher hiding high in the rocks can defeat twenty attacking from below."

At that moment Carlo felt a hand on his shoulder. It was Florian. His head was bandaged and he had on only a waistcoat despite the bitter cold. Without saying a word, they embraced.

"Have you seen Alexi?" Carlo asked.

"Not yet. I fear he didn't survive."

"What makes you say that?"

"When I first heard the explosion, I shouted at everyone to run," Florian explained. "But Alexi was a few steps behind me. As the walls crumbled, I reached a machine gun portal and dove through. Luckily, the ground wasn't far below."

"What happened to your head?"

He laughed ruefully. "I honestly don't remember. It's just a small gash."

"Alexi had more experience underground than anyone," said Carlo, trying to be optimistic. "Chances are he escaped."

Florian shook his head. "We can keep looking tomorrow. I hold out little hope. I saw the oberleutnant. What was left of him anyway. I knew him only by the color of his hair."

That night no one slept. Instead, they continued their preparations to fight the Italians as best they could. They built crude parapets out of rubble and the single undamaged machine gun was placed on the highest point of what remained of the peak.

A few minutes before sunrise, as the stars began to fade, the officer who had escaped injury woke Florian and asked him to go for help: "Gebirgsinfanterie-Regiment IV is camped east of here," he explained, "not more than fifteen kilometers away. I expect the Italians are now closing in from all sides, so you'll have to run like hell."

"Why me?" he moaned.

"Don't be a fool," Carlo said. "This is your chance to escape."

Carlo knew how to speak to Florian, how to play upon his impulses. He also knew what was good for him. Half an hour later Florian was gone.

Once the sun was up, their lookouts began scanning the slopes and valleys below. Scouts were sent out in different directions to determine if they were going to be attacked from the flank or from behind, but they returned with no useful news. When, in the middle of the afternoon, an Italian patrol was spotted, they opened fire. The patrol seemed unprepared. Some were killed and the remainder hastily retreated. Carlo was puzzled. Was that to be the extent of the attack? Maybe the Italians thought blowing up the mountain had been sufficient. Maybe they were right.

He continued to search for Alexi. At what was once the entrance to the fortress, he cupped his ear and listened. Hearing nothing, he climbed as high as possible and surveyed the rubble below. Others were searching as well, but after the first day, only three additional survivors had been found. Despondent, he descended and spent some time fashioning a more permanent sling for his arm.

The following afternoon a courier arrived with a message telling them to withdraw. It included a map showing how to travel safely from their present position to the encampment of Gebirgsinfanterie-Regiment IV. Florian had done his job well.

They spent one more frigid night on the mountain and in the morning prepared to depart. But first they lined up so a final assessment could be made: who was present and able to walk, who was present yet would need to be carried in the few conveyances they had at their disposal, and who was absent, now and forever, buried under tons of rock. Alexi was nowhere to be seen. Carlo thought they should make one final attempt to search for those still missing. In this he wasn't alone, but the officer now in charge said, "We must accept that no one else survived. We will follow orders and leave without delay."

For a moment Carlo considered sneaking off and remaining behind to continue looking for his friend. Then he pictured himself alone on the mountainside in the middle of the night, engulfed in blowing snow, and decided he lacked the fortitude to follow through. If he was honest, he couldn't imagine finding Alexi alive.

Their progress down the mountain was remarkably fast, not only because they were going downhill but because each step took them farther from the enemy. Around midday they encountered several mule-drawn ambulances that had been dispatched to meet them, and those with the worst wounds were loaded up and carried away.

They continued on as darkness began to fall. Just when they were about to stop walking and spend yet another night on a windblown ridge, they located the camp of Gebirgsinfanterie-Regiment IV and presented themselves to the officer in charge. Some of them were taken to a casualty clearing station for immediate treatment; the rest, Carlo included, collapsed onto cots or open patches of ground and went straight to sleep.

The next morning Carlo learned his arm was badly broken. A medic set the break, rebandaged the open wound, and immobilized the arm with a splint. He also cleaned and bandaged the wound behind his ear. Carlo had forgotten it even existed. Although his injuries seemed insignificant compared to those sustained by other survivors, he was directed to a nearby field hospital, where he remained for two days. While he was there, he made a few inquiries about

Florian. No one knew anything about him. He appreciated the opportunity to sleep but couldn't stand the moaning and the putrid odors, half vomit and half rotting flesh. Without notifying anyone, he left the hospital, located a senior officer, and asked about his next post.

"It appears you have a broken arm," the officer said.

"It's not bad. I can still work. Isn't there something I can do?" He wasn't sure why he was making the request. Most men would rather put up with the sounds and smells of the hospital than return to the front. He certainly had no deep commitment to the profession of soldiering, nor to the Austro-Hungarian cause. The real problem was that time passed too slowly if all he did was lie in bed. He wanted to get moving, to go on to something else. During the past several weeks he'd become accustomed to working in the tunnels with Florian and Alexi. Now he felt disoriented. He was anxious to find out what he'd be doing next.

"What job did you have before?"

"Maybe you heard of the explosion at—"

He didn't need to complete the sentence. "All that work for nothing," the officer said. "Such a terrible waste."

The next day, to his surprise—the army seldom moved so quickly—he was given orders to go to Klagenfurt to work as an engineer. How remarkable: In the beginning he'd been only a fellow who knew a bit about mining from helping his father. Then he was called a miner, and now suddenly, through no effort of his own, he'd become an engineer. He pictured Alexi, and for the first time since he'd been in uniform, for the first time since leaving America, he wept. Given the chaos caused by the war, the changing borders, and the distance from their present location to Alexi's home in Bosnia, it was likely to be weeks or even months before Alexi's wife and children learned he wouldn't be coming home. Until then they'd be sending tender thoughts to him, thoughts he could no longer receive.

By noon, Carlo was packed and ready to depart. He knew nothing of Klagenfurt except that it was in Austria and to the east. Surely it would be better than an icebound camp in the mountains where stones rained down from the sky.

A Cannon in the Trees

Weeks passed and the Germans had yet to arrive. Teresa pictured them as an enormous thunderstorm moving down from the north. She pictured them overtopping the mountains and blocking out the sun. Then again, the rumors about the Germans might be inaccurate. If there was one thing she had learned, it was that in times of war, nothing was true until it happened. She would believe the Germans were coming only when she saw with her own eyes a wall of gray uniforms marching up the road.

The horse was now fully recovered, so one evening she decided to take him for a ride. She wouldn't put any demands on his leg—all they would do is walk. She checked his hooves for stones, bridled him, and glanced back at the house. He actually seemed pleased to have a saddle on his back. Perhaps he took it as a sign that things were returning to normal. Animals, she believed, wanted to feel they were doing what was expected of them. Like most humans, they appreciated predictability and routine.

Going for a ride was a small matter, not some great act of rebellion, yet it pleased her to be doing it by choice, not because Frau Merz or the Austrians told her to. She planned to ride beneath the trees, where no one could see them. As they set out, the horse's ears went up and his muscles rippled. This was what he'd been bred to do.

Luca had always described the horse as well mannered and so he was. Signor Benedetti's favorite. But after getting the new yellow motorcar, he hadn't ridden him as much.

Emerging from the wood, they crossed a field as the moon came up in the east. Although the horse wanted to go faster, she restrained him. She could smell the pines and recently cut hay, and from the way the horse snorted and tossed his head, she thought he, too, must be relishing the scent. The night air, the feeling of freedom, and the pleasure the horse seemed to take in it—all contributed to her enjoyment of the ride.

Upon reaching the hedge that separated the Benedetti land from the common pasture beyond, she turned back. As the house came into view, she saw that only two of its windows were lit. One was Rodolfo's room and the other was the room occupied by Rosa's lover. No doubt Rosa was with him and no doubt they were in his bed—doing things Teresa was at once offended by and madly curious about.

As she returned the horse to his stall, she began thinking about her father. Perhaps this was because when they still had a plow horse, he was the one who'd put her on its back. Or because picturing Rosa and her Austrian brought to mind her father's adulterous behavior. It wasn't easy to reconcile the fact that he was both things—the father of her childhood, who, while not the best father, seemed to like being with her and was attentive to her needs—and the absent father, the one she now despised for abandoning her and her mother and for failing to even try to explain why he did it.

After that night, she began riding often, two or three times a week. She rehearsed what she'd tell the authorities if they found out: *When you first gathered up all the riding stock, this animal was lame. I've nursed him back to health. Remove him if you must.*

Eventually she decided to risk riding beyond the boundaries of the estate. She couldn't help herself. The air was coolly invigorating, the moon full, and she had convinced herself that ranging a bit farther wouldn't greatly increase her chances of being caught.

Most of her experience riding had been with elderly horses, horses exhausted from work, or those that had been climbed on by children so often, a slow plod was their only gait. This one was different. Every movement was remarkably smooth; she could feel the power in his body even if she wasn't putting it to use. She'd never ridden such a responsive animal, one so deserving of her respect.

As usual, she rode the horse through the trees, but this time she continued on and joined a trail that veered away from the nearby houses, passing between a neglected vineyard and an uncultivated field. If it had been possible, she'd have ridden away from Trento entirely, up into the mountains to Ulfano or even south, away from the fighting, toward Rovereto, toward Lago di Garda and beyond. But she knew that eventually she'd reach a fence, a series of trenches, and a stone fortification— barriers that had been erected to allow Trento to withstand the most vigorous attack. As the Austro-Hungarians knew, one reason Italy had entered the war was to reclaim Trento and Trieste. So long as those two cities remained Austrian, they had the upper hand.

She rode for a while longer, following a narrow path. There was some shelling in the mountains, although not as much as there had been a month ago. Perhaps the battle had moved elsewhere. Or the two sides were simply preparing for the next attack.

When she was about to return to the stable, she looked

down into a bowl-like depression between two hills and saw in the moonlight an enormous cannon half hidden in a copse of trees. Never had she seen or even heard of a weapon so immense. Upon closer inspection, she concluded it was sitting on railroad tracks, tracks that must have been laid for the sole purpose of moving it into this hiding place. She knew nothing of cannons, yet it wasn't difficult to imagine how much damage this one could do. And if the Austro-Hungarians had such a war machine, might not the Italians have something comparable, aimed at Trento? It was a terrifying thought.

Back at the stable, she removed the saddle and bridle and set about currying the horse. It was late, or rather early—by the time she finished, the stars would be fading with the coming dawn. As she worked, she tried to remember Gaetano but found it difficult to picture his face. She wasn't surprised. You had to know someone for a long time before their image became unforgettable. Suddenly, she remembered him bounding into the kitchen in search of a piece of cake. Handsome Gaetano, usually serious but, on that occasion, offering her a smile. It was a relief to know she could still call him to mind.

When Frau Merz saw Teresa the next morning, she said, "You don't look well. Are you sick?"

"I didn't get much sleep last night."

"Is something worrying you?"

"The war. Suppose Trento is attacked."

Frau Merz offered her customary dismissal: "Of all the human emotions, worry is the most wasteful. It changes nothing."

"This will sound foolish but I worry about the animals. The horses and mules, even the dogs and cats. If an attack comes, at least we'll know why it's happening. They won't understand."

"That makes no sense," Frau Merz replied. "If someone shoots me with a gun, does understanding why it happened mean I'll feel any less pain or lose any less blood?"

To Klagenfurt

When Carlo asked where to find the vehicle that would take him to Klagenfurt, he was told none was available and he should just walk. He didn't bother complaining because he knew it wouldn't do any good. At least he had a companion, an Austrian artillery sergeant nearly twice his age. Together, they set out on foot. They were advised to walk until they reached the Drava River, then follow it east. Doing so would keep them away from where the worst fighting was taking place.

The Austrian was taciturn in the extreme, so hours passed in silence. Their only conversations focused on which route to take. "Into the trees or through the field?" Carlo asked. "Field," grunted his companion in reply. On their way they passed numerous villages but avoided going into them because it was never obvious which side of the front they were on. Suppose they stumbled into an Italian garrison? What if they were taken for spies? For food, they relied on small farmsteads, approaching them with caution. In most instances, only women and children remained. Although they had little to offer, they didn't hesitate to share. And after being fed, he and his companion were almost always told they could sleep in the barn.

At a certain point Carlo decided his arm was healed, so he tore off the bandage and removed the splint. Unfortunately, his actions were premature. From then on, he had to hold the arm against his chest to suppress the pain. There were moments when it washed over him with such intensity, he thought he might pass out.

Walking in constant silence gave him time to think. He wondered what had become of his friend from school, Vitale, who had gone off to join the cavalry before the war. Vitale had been impressed by the fact that Carlo knew the names of the actors who appeared in American films. "Charles Chaplin," he would say with awe. "Perhaps the two of you have met?"

He wondered what his life would be like after the war. He was used to having his father tell him what to do, but now that he was no longer a boy, that would change. He'd make his own decisions. He felt like he'd been displaced, displaced again, and then once more. That made it difficult to know himself. He kept having to put his feet on the ground in new locations, none of which he'd chosen. Maybe he'd return to Colorado. There was certainly something appealing about going home. That was all most of the men he'd been serving with could talk about. Then again, nearly all of them were from towns and villages in Austria, so home wasn't far away.

After five days of travel, Carlo and his companion came over a series of hills and saw Klagenfurt spread out below, the sun shining on its tile roofs. He had mixed feelings about ending the journey—although he was very tired, he had enjoyed spending a few days walking across green meadows and through groves of trees. How pleasant it had been to have no responsibilities except to walk.

They approached the town's perimeter cautiously, so as to avoid being shot. After they'd been identified and allowed to enter, they prepared to go their separate ways.

"Well," Carlo said, "we didn't starve or get captured. We didn't get lost. We didn't quarrel with each other."

"No," the Austrian replied, "we did not." Then he walked up the street alone.

Klagenfurt, owing to its proximity to the front, looked less like a market town than a center of operations. Walls of sandbags protected the fronts of buildings and windows were boarded up. Everyone Carlo saw was in uniform and only military vehicles were using the city's streets. He was surprised to find an open café and entered it merely for the experience of doing something ordinary, something separate from the war. But as he sat sipping coffee, he began to sweat, his vision blurred, and he collapsed sideways out of his chair and onto the floor.

He awoke on a pallet amid other men on pallets. The room was large with tall windows along one side, once a ballroom or gallery, serving as a hospital now. From the light outside, he guessed it was morning or perhaps early afternoon. His uniform had been removed but not his underclothes and his arm had been rebandaged and splinted once again. The last thing he could remember was sitting down to have coffee.

A nurse passed by and he asked her to stop.

"I just woke up," he said. "What happened to me?"

"Someone brought you in yesterday. You were out of your head. The wound in your shoulder is badly infected. Another day or two without treatment and you'd have been dead."

"Thank you," he said and then before she could get away, "I'm hungry. Will I get something to eat?"

"It's too early for supper. Let me see what I can find."

Knowing the severity of his injury didn't help. The possibility of dying hadn't occurred to him—after all, it was only his arm. Now, the pain was radiating up through his shoulder and into his chest. The more he thought about it, the worse he felt.

Soon the nurse returned with a bowl of porridge. She helped him sit up and set the bowl on his lap so he could eat with one hand. Although ravenous, he forced himself to consume the porridge slowly, lifting each spoonful to his mouth with care. Through the window he could see a church steeple, tall and tapered, with what looked like several mushrooms of descending sizes on top. The porridge was perfectly bland, neither sweet nor savory, and so paste-like in consistency, if he'd inverted the bowl, none would have fallen out.

That night he slept poorly. There was a good deal of activity nearby, ghostly figures in the lamplight tending to those in pain. He tried covering his head, then felt as if he was suffocating and threw the blanket off. He dreamed he was in his brothers' saloon and that Alexi was there working behind the bar, and then that he was in a tunnel and couldn't find his way out. In the morning the sky was gray and the windows were streaked with droplets. By early evening his own pain had become so intense, he called for the nurse. She gave him something that put him to sleep until the following day.

When he awoke, he asked for writing materials and began a letter to the pigeon girl. She hadn't answered either of the ones he'd sent so far, but she was still the only person he knew in Austro-Hungarian territory; if he wanted to write a letter, it would have to go to her.

My Dear Friend,

I wish when we met I'd asked for your name. I hope you're safe and that your pigeons are safe, too. I've heard Trento is entirely surrounded by Allied forces—mostly Italian. Also some English and French. If they overrun the city, speak to them in Italian so they treat you well.

I was injured in an explosion and am now in hospital in the town of Klagenfurt. Don't worry, it's only my arm. My one complaint is that the food isn't very good. As usual, the most common dish is a kind of mush made from oats. They call it haferbrei and although filling enough, it has no taste at all. (I seem to complain about the food every time I write.)

Today I have been thinking about my dear mother. She died when I was a child, but I remember a few things about her. I would like to go back to Colorado and see her grave again. The cemetery there is peaceful, on a hillside, but I'm afraid that if the town goes bust (as I've heard it might), no one will take care of it. I don't want her to be lying in a dusty place that no one bothers to look after.

Sorry to be so gloomy. If you feel moved to write to me, maybe you can tell me something about your family. Please address any letters to my unit. I'm told the Austrian army will go to great lengths to deliver mail. I'm sending this to Villa Benedetti, as I did the ones before. I suppose you are either there or somewhere else. (Another of my foolish jokes.)

Kindest regards,
Carlo Coltura

PART IV

Gaetano

There came a long period of rain. Days upon days, without respite. It was too wet to ride, too wet to help Rodolfo in the garden, while in the kitchen it was so dark, they had to burn lamps to work even in midafternoon. Not that there was much work to be done. The rationing of food had imposed limits on what they could prepare. Everything they obtained went on the plate, even if it lacked appeal. The Austrians wondered aloud if Frau Merz was keeping the best back and selling it on the black market, but she put an end to their suspicions by inviting them to search her kitchen. From then on, they channeled their frustration into bitter jokes:

"Tomorrow we should like a roast of lamb," they told Rosa.

"As you wish," she said. "And Frau Merz will make a chocolate torte for dessert."

The worst part was the mud the Austrians tracked in. It wasn't really their fault—with mud everywhere a certain amount was bound to enter the house no matter how much care they took. Cleaning fell to Teresa and sometimes Rodolfo, the poor old fellow getting on his knees with a bucket and rag despite her insistence that she could do the job. Rosa was spending additional time at the hospital and managed to avoid such drudgery.

The Austrians seemed more agitated than usual, more on edge. Perhaps the rumors about German reinforcements had been wishful thinking. The banned newspapers Frau Merz read said the Italians were having some success over on the plains—also that the Russians were advancing and the Central Powers were in retreat. Korporal Mayr told Teresa that he and his comrades might be sent to the Eastern Front. It was the first time she'd spoken with him in weeks.

"I don't want to leave," he said. "The overriding purpose of my life is to avoid being shot at."

"I hope you stay here. You treat us fairly."

"It never occurred to me to do otherwise."

"Your parents must have raised you well."

"I suppose so, but they were glad to see me go."

Although it was the kind of remark that invited further elaboration, she didn't press him. Instead, she said, "Tonight we're serving venison for supper. Frau Merz is very proud of herself. It wasn't easy to obtain."

"Venison?"

"With polenta and a sauce I'll be making from onions and brandy."

"Oh my! That sounds delicious. Someday you'll be an excellent wife." The instant the words left his mouth, he looked as though he wanted to snatch them back. "Is that too familiar?" he asked nervously. "I never know what to say."

"You don't need to apologize. To be honest, I couldn't do it on my own. I chop the onions. Frau Merz does the rest."

There followed an awkward silence. Teresa wished he was easier to speak with. Yet there was something appealing about his shyness—better that than annoyingly brash.

"Well then," he said, preparing to depart. Before he could turn, she spoke again. "I'm thinking of going to visit my mother. It's been much too long. But I've heard all the exits have been sealed. Do you think I'll be allowed to leave?"

"I'm afraid not. Only members of the military are being

let out and then only if they have written orders. Even if they gave you permission, I'd advise against it. It's not safe."

The next morning, when she entered the kitchen, Frau Merz stopped what she was doing and said, "I need to speak with you. My dear girl."

As Teresa approached, she could see Frau Merz had been crying. "What is it?"

"The young man you've been asking about, Gaetano Russo. He was killed in battle and won't be coming back."

"How do you know? Who told you?"

"I saw a woman who once worked for his family on the street yesterday. She said it happened at Caporetto, amidst the chaos of that terrible defeat. I didn't want to tell you—I thought it could wait. Then last night after you went to bed, I decided I had no choice. I know how much you care about him."

Teresa fell into Frau Merz's arms and began to sob. But her tears felt false. Although she worried about Gaetano every day, in truth she hardly knew him. Except for a few kisses beneath the trees, any intimacy between them, any evidence of deep affection, had been strictly in her head. And yet, what if he had survived? What if he had returned? What if he had feelings for her like the ones she had for him? It was unlikely anything would have come of it, but suppose it had?

She tried to explain what she was thinking to Frau Merz. However, the more she spoke, the more ridiculous she sounded: "I don't have any reason to cry over him, I mean I do, I care for him like I would for anyone. There was nothing between us, nothing except all the thoughts I've had about him since he left . . ."

"What's wrong with crying for him?" Frau Merz said. "If he could see you, he'd be touched."

"How did your friend find out? I thought information about Italian casualties was unavailable."

"Some members of his unit were captured and brought to Trento. Several of them grew up here and have made contact with people they know."

Teresa sighed sadly, heavily. The report of his death was undoubtedly accurate and there was nothing to be done.

"One piece of good news," Frau Merz added. "That fool General Cadorna, who has been sending young men to their deaths by the thousands, has been removed from his command."

Not surprisingly, Rosa was of a different mind about Teresa's tears. When she heard what had happened and saw Teresa's red eyes and blotchy face, she said, "I pity you, though not because you lost your love. I pity you because you convinced yourself there was some chance he'd care about you. Although I never met him, it sounds like he was just a friendly young man who liked to flirt. A wealthy young man. You should cry for him, but only because you should cry for them all."

That evening, Teresa walked out to the stable in the rain and shared her feelings with the horse. Animals listened without passing judgment. She pressed her face against his soft, powerful neck and said, "What am I going to do now?" and then, "The same as I was doing yesterday and the day before." Although some would say the horse couldn't understand, it seemed to her Coniglio did comprehend in some fashion her feelings if not her actual words. Even if that wasn't true, his company was consoling. After a while she spread a blanket on a heap of straw, lay down, and fell asleep. When she awoke, it was the middle of the night and she had to creep carefully up the stairs to her room to avoid waking the others.

Before getting into bed, she lit a candle and took out the

newspaper article she'd saved about the Englishman and the donkeys in Naples. While many humans were busy killing each other, this fellow Hawksley was trying to reduce the suffering visited upon helpless beasts. She found reading the article a comfort, almost like saying a prayer.

More Letters

After a week of discomfort and wakefulness and peculiar dreams and drugged sleep, Carlo began to feel better. A doctor, the first one he'd spoken with, informed him he'd almost had to amputate and that he might never have full use of his arm again. Fortunately, it was the left one, so he could continue writing letters, as he did the following afternoon:

Dear Signorina,

There are many reasons I regret being taken into the army, but the most important one is that it prevented me from seeing you again.

I am getting better and expect to be out of the hospital soon. Then I guess I'll go wherever the Austrian Army sends me. Do you think this war is ever going to end? It seems like it's gone on for an awfully long time.

The boy in the bed next to me can sing like a bird. I wish you could hear him—it's all in German but the melodies are beautiful no matter the tongue. He doesn't seem to care if anyone is listening and sings only to please himself. He has a bandage over his eyes. We don't talk much. I've heard the nurse call him Horst. Too bad I'm a terrible singer or I'd offer to join in.

Do you have any brothers or sisters? I have two older brothers back in America. They are called Joe and Sal. They own a "saloon" where miners come to drink. I miss them very much. Now that the Americans are entering the war, I wonder if they'll be drafted. Probably not Sal as he has a bad knee from an injury he got while working in a mine.

I hope you'll be interested in writing back to me. If you don't, I won't hold it against you. But if I did get a letter from you, I'd be very happy. I do wish I knew your name.

Very truly yours,
Carlo Coltura

Since he was feeling better, he was allowed to get up and walk about the ward and even go outside. Not far from the hospital there was a garden where he could sit in the sun. For the most part the garden was frequented by old people who gathered there in midmorning to gossip and read the newspaper and exchange goods in a sort of makeshift market—some sugar for a pair of shoes. Occasionally, one of them would acknowledge his presence and thank him for his service—his German had gotten good enough to comprehend that much. He'd never seen a garden as well tended as this one in America, or buildings so handsome, or streets so picturesque. The mining camp where he'd grown up was unkempt and ragged, at the edge of a wilderness that went on for miles and miles. He remembered a day when he and two other boys had gone in search of a place to go fishing. They'd heard about a lake high up in the mountains that was said to be so full of trout, you could pull one out with every cast. It took them half a day to get there, following a creek that flowed down from the lake. As they walked, they pictured themselves as old-time explorers, trappers or mountain men, and talked about what it would be like to build a cabin and live off the land.

Klagenfurt and the surrounding countryside felt to him like the exact opposite of Colorado. Yes, there were mountains here—he'd experienced them in all their fierce grandeur—yet at the foot of every peak, instead of some rough settlement where the houses were made from scraps of sheet metal and scavenged wood, sat a pretty village. And if you walked through the forest in search of a place to fish, you'd encounter farmers and herders and the occasional cottage and then another village only a few miles away.

Once again, he mused about what he'd do after the war. Perhaps he should settle in a town like this. Why not be a shopkeeper or a schoolteacher or buy a few acres for a farm? He used to dream about having great adventures, about sea voyages, and yes, even war. The books Miss Donovan read to them encouraged this. But couldn't he be happy with small things? A small house, a small job, and he might not need a family but would be satisfied to live alone. Although there were times when he was homesick and wanted nothing more than to return to Colorado, perhaps that was foolish. He could just stay here. Of course, the location of "here" was another question. In Italy? In Austria? In some still unknown country he might visit after the war?

Back at the hospital he inquired, not for the first time, about when he'd be released and what he was supposed to do after that. Was he to consider himself permanently disabled or should he expect to return to duty when he'd fully healed? And where might he locate the company of engineers he'd been sent to join? The answers, provided by an especially peevish orderly, were "In a few days," "You'll definitely return to duty," and "Why are you asking me? That's not my job."

To help pass the time he wrote yet another letter to the pigeon girl. He was running out of things to tell her about his life in Colorado, so he settled on the subject of Alexi. He would describe his friend and explain why he was so admirable—and therefore have no shortage of things to write.

Dear Signorina,
In this letter I will tell you about a man I served with who

will not be going home. He was a Bosnian, his name was Alexi, and he was a good friend.

He described how they met, Alexi's wry sense of humor, and how he had become a sort of father to an annoying fellow named Florian. He told her about Alexi's love for his family, his knowledge of mining (aware that the censors might black that part out), and the card game he taught them, adding, *I can teach it to you.*

As he reached the end of the letter, he wrote, *I didn't know him for very long, but he made a strong impression on me. Maybe that was because we were together in wartime. I don't want you to think it was the war that made him good. On the contrary, he was good in spite of this war. A war that takes the meaning out of everything and pounds it into dust.*

By the time he was finished, he was in tears.

Into the Night

The rain finally ended. The mud disappeared and for several weeks the sky was cloudless. Yet Teresa scarcely noticed. All she could think about was Gaetano. She wanted to know more about how he died and wondered if Cristian and Lia had been informed. Although she resented Rosa's harsh words, she nonetheless attempted to do as she'd suggested, mourning him not as her lover but as one of the thousands killed. At times she tried to think about the meaning of life and death. In that she had little success. She wasn't the kind of person who could consider such matters philosophically, who could look beyond daily existence into the mysteries beyond.

One morning, as she was folding the table linen, Rodolfo appeared at her side like a specter and motioned for her to follow him outside.

"I received a message from Luca," he said. "It came this morning."

"From Luca? Is he well? Is he coming home?" She was delighted to hear the news but something about Rodolfo's demeanor suggested—astonishingly—that this wasn't the first time he'd heard from his young friend.

"He needs my help," Rodolfo said.

"I don't understand. What kind of help? Where is he? Has he been wounded?" She thought back to the day they went looking for Luca. Had Rodolfo known more about where he'd gone than he'd revealed? If so, his performance suggesting otherwise had been masterful.

Rodolfo lowered his voice. "I must tell you something. He was not taken away by the Austrians. He went to help the Italians. It was he who took my pigeons. He's been using them to send messages to me."

She was without words. She'd suspected nothing of the kind. Although they were currently shielded from the house by a hedge, she glanced about to make sure they were alone.

"Messages? What do you do with them?"

"I pass them to a certain Signor Esposito, who passes them to someone else. The pigeons I hide away."

"But now something has gone wrong?"

"Sì. When I went to deliver the message last night, Esposito was gone."

"What became of him?" she asked. He didn't respond, so she tried a different question. "What will you do now?"

"I would like to do as the message instructs. However, I cannot."

"I don't understand. What does it say?"

He looked at her for a moment. She could sense he was deciding how much more to tell her. At last he continued: "The message asks that a particular unit of the Italian forces be advised to avoid a particular village. I would carry it to them myself but I am too old."

"Isn't there someone else?"

"Look around you. All the able-bodied men in this city are Austrian soldiers. The only supporters of Italy here are women and old men."

That was true. "Why do they need to avoid the village?" she asked.

"Perhaps it's full of enemy soldiers. Or the local population has been infiltrated by saboteurs. That's not for me to know."

The solution to the problem was obvious to Teresa. "I can do it," she said.

But Rodolfo disagreed. While he was willing to admit to being too infirm to make the journey into the mountains, he didn't think a girl should take his place.

"It's very far," he said. "More than a day's walk there and an equal amount back."

"I can walk as fast as a man."

He shook his head.

"So you'd have Italian boys march into an ambush rather than send me? Where is this village? What's it called?"

Like a schoolboy telling a secret, he whispered the name in her ear.

"I know it," she exclaimed. "It's near where I was raised but farther north. Wouldn't it be best to send someone who's familiar with the area—the roads and trails and the nature of the terrain?" They continued arguing back and forth until at last he relented. Yet he still had some concerns:

"The Austrians living here will realize you are gone. They pay no attention to me; you they notice. Three days is too long."

"We can invent a story, a reason for my absence."

"I suppose. Or you could ride the horse." The instant he spoke, she realized it was what he'd had in mind all along.

"That's true, I could." They were both silent now. She didn't know what he was thinking, but she was already picturing herself getting the horse ready to ride. At last she said, "I have one more question. Does Frau Merz know about Luca?"

"Some things but not everything. You let me deal with her."

Late in the afternoon they met in the shed where Rodolfo kept his tools. Using his workbench as a desk, he sketched a map and showed her where to find the battalion in question. "This valley—it's familiar to you?" he said.

"Every part. I've been through it a hundred times."

"And this one?"

"Not as much as the other. I'm sure I can find my way."

"You can't carry a map. If you were stopped, it would reveal everything."

She was becoming impatient with him. He still didn't trust that she could do the job. "I don't need a map. I know where you want me to go."

He looked at her for a moment, then tore the map to shreds.

"What about the message?" she said.

"I'll give it to you when it's time."

As she waited for nightfall, she thought about how naive she'd been. She was aware that some of Trento's citizens had been engaging in passive resistance, but it appeared Rodolfo and Luca were doing far more than that. She wished she'd known about this earlier. Now that the opportunity had presented itself, she'd do her best to help.

She considered telling Rosa she was feeling ill so she could leave before supper, but that would attract attention and Rosa would be suspicious. Instead, when her evening chores had been completed, she simply told Frau Merz she was going to her room. An hour later she slipped outside.

Rodolfo was waiting at the stable. He looked anxious, as if he'd been having second thoughts.

"You don't need to worry," Teresa said.

"I've been thinking. I could ride—"

"I want to do this," she said, her tone making it clear she wasn't changing her mind.

"You're sure you know the route?"

"Yes. It's time for me to go."

She slid the bridle over Coniglio's head and handed the reins to Rodolfo so he could steady the horse while she secured the saddle. When that was done, she climbed up, settled into the seat, and tested the stirrups to make sure they were the proper length. She wore a heavy sweater that had been knitted by her mother, a pair of gloves Luca had left in the stable, and a fur-lined hat that belonged to Rodolfo. As she ascended into the mountains, the temperature would drop.

She looked down at Rodolfo. "The message?"

"There is nothing on paper. That would be too dangerous. Only the words themselves."

"And who exactly am I to meet?"

"You don't need to know that either. When you arrive at the place I showed you on the map, they will make themselves known."

She nodded and he continued: "The message is this: The Austrian Tenth under General Rohr has crossed the line of October twenty-four and set a trap in a valley northeast of Toliera. Therefore, all Italian forces are to avoid the village and the valleys to the north at all costs. Now repeat it back to me."

"The Austrian Tenth under General Rohr has crossed the October twenty-four line and set a trap. In a valley northeast of Toliera. The Italians must stay south of the village no matter what."

"Good. Say it back to me two more times."

When she had done so, he said, "Tell them Isaac Venturi sent you."

"Who is Isaac Venturi?"

"It's the name I go by for these purposes."

She turned the horse toward their direction of travel. "Arrivederci," she said, and they stepped forward into the night.

Without Precedent

Unfortunately, the infection in Carlo's arm returned a second time, so it was weeks before he was released. During most of that period he was too feverish and infirm to go to the garden or write letters or even, for a few days, lift a spoon to his mouth. It got so bad, he feared they'd given up on him. Although the doctors and nurses were undeniably compassionate and hardworking, it was common knowledge that some patients were deemed lost causes and left to meet their wretched ends.

"Is my infection spreading?" he asked one terrible night, when he'd begun to doubt he'd make it until morning. He'd been shivering for what seemed like hours and, no matter how many blankets they put on him, couldn't stop.

The answer provided was equivocal—"It doesn't seem to be. It's not always easy to tell." But the look on the nurse's face suggested otherwise and he started to expect the worst. Then, suddenly, his condition changed. In a single night, he went from miserable to almost fit. He stood up, went outside, and shook himself like a dog. Even though his feet were bare, he walked up the road and nearly broke into a run. He took several deep breaths and felt as if there was something restorative in the air.

Two days later a doctor, one he hadn't seen before, visited his bedside. "I'm afraid you must return to service," he said.

"You're joking."

"No. I wish I was. In the first years of the war, they'd have sent you away for rehabilitation. That's a luxury we no longer have. To be honest, it's now die or lace up your boots—there's no in-between."

Carlo wanted to go back to sleep but the doctor continued to peer at him, as if expecting some kind of response.

"All right then," Carlo said.

"Yes, all right. I admire your attitude."

"I have no attitude. What else am I supposed to say?"

The doctor laughed. "You'll be issued a new uniform. When you're dressed, there's a warrant officer sitting at a desk on the terrace. Give him your name and he'll tell you what to do next."

As he watched the doctor walk away, it came to him that he'd stopped wondering about when the war would end. This was now his life and it was natural to follow orders, to go wherever they sent him. He no longer expected to understand. He no longer had an urge to resist.

He donned his new uniform (more poorly made than the previous one) and obtained his orders from the warrant officer, along with instructions on where to sleep. He spent the evening drinking in a makeshift tavern in the basement of a church. Food was hard to get but not wine and beer. The beer seemed stronger these days, causing one to become drunk more quickly. When he'd had enough, he found his assigned billet and fell onto a cot without bothering to undress.

The next morning, he went to the headquarters of an engineering unit, as instructed. There, he was told to sit on a bench and wait with three other men. One was sleeping, one had his legs spread and stared at the ground between them, and a third was picking his teeth with the tip of a very large knife.

"Do any of you know where they're sending us?" asked the man with the knife.

Carlo shook his head. The one staring at the ground said, "I thought I was to stay here." The sleeping man opened his eyes, scratched his scalp vigorously with both hands, and said, "To the grave, most likely," and went back to sleep.

They smoked, they drowsed. Carlo's head ached from the night before. He, too, had expected to be working in Klagenfurt but maybe he misunderstood. Since the explosion, his mind hadn't always been right. He was still having difficulty sleeping. Or if he did sleep, when he awoke, he had to remind himself where he was. He'd had dizzy spells. And there were times when he wanted to speak but couldn't quite find the words.

At last a kapitan and a leutnant appeared. After a few preliminary remarks about how fortunate they all were to be engineers instead of members of the infantry, the leutnant told them they were being sent to the Karst Plateau. They'd all heard about the Karst Plateau. It was there that the First Battle of the Isonzo had been fought and the Second Battle of the Isonzo, and the Third and Fourth and Fifth, one after the other with thousands of casualties and little advancement or success on either side. According to reports, it was no less than an enormous blood-soaked butcher shop and Carlo noticed that as soon as the leutnant uttered the word *Isonzo*, he became unable to meet their eyes.

"Fuck me," said the man on his right. "Fuck us all," said the one on his left. While a good deal of the German language still lay beyond Carlo's understanding, their profanity was well within his grasp.

"What are we to do there?" the third man asked.

"Well, this is where it gets interesting," said the kapitan. "You are to assist with the construction of something that will break the backs of the Italians. Something important and large and without precedent, although exactly what it is must remain secret until you reach your appointed destination and the work begins. You'll leave tomorrow at first light."

When the officers were gone, the four men looked at each other with stunned expressions, unable to rise from their chairs. Then they began to speak, each one offering a different theory about what they'd be asked to build.

"A bridge across the Isonzo."

"Or a tunnel beneath it."

"An airfield. To prepare for a final assault."

"He said it was large. Without—what was the word?—precedent. How can you say that about a bridge?"

"Perhaps they want us to build a fortress that can move about."

They all narrowed their eyes and trained them on the man who spoke. "Like a tank?" Carlo asked.

"Much larger. Something men could live in for days."

They scoffed. A fortress on wheels? A ridiculous idea. Then again, the commanders and politicians seemed to possess an endless ability to come up with outrageous schemes.

"It's because the Americans have arrived," one of them said. "We'll need something special to counter them."

To Carlo, they seemed like sturdy fellows, responsible fellows, yet he did not intend to become friends with any of them. Losing friends was too painful. He would keep to himself and simply do his job.

They departed the following day in three motorcars and

a lorry. To their group had been added several infantry whose job was to keep them safe. Some of the engineers considered that amusing—how could a handful of men with rifles protect them from machine guns and aerial strafing and the fearsome Americans? Others took it as a mark of the importance of the mysterious thing they were expected to build: a tunnel, a bridge, or some previously unimagined engine of war, with cannons and armor and, for all they knew, wings of steel to carry it into the sky.

A Clearing in the Forest

Getting out of the city was the first challenge. Teresa rode to the far end of the estate, through a break in the wall, into the woodlot, and joined a path paralleling the river road. The moon was bright, two-thirds full, and despite a few clouds, she could see the way ahead.

Before long she passed a disused cistern and, having been this way before, knew the guard station was coming up. She and Rodolfo had discussed what she should do there. As it would be too dangerous to stop and allow herself to be interrogated, she'd find a way around. She had heard it said that despite the Austrians' efforts to close the city, an individual with determination could easily make it through their lines. This she was about to test.

She guided the horse into the trees and up a steep slope. Rodolfo had told her she would eventually encounter a fence, which she did, yet the gate he'd described was nowhere to be found. After following the fence line for several minutes, she reversed direction and went back the opposite way. At last she saw it, four vertical slats overgrown with vines and obviously no longer in use. She slid down from the saddle and, with some difficulty, opened it and led Coniglio through.

So she'd done it—she had left Trento behind. Now she needed to locate the road leading toward Ulfano and follow it into the mountains. Given her knowledge of the area, that wouldn't be a difficult task. Every so often she recited the message to herself—what a disaster it would be if she made it to her destination but forgot what she was supposed to say.

She wondered briefly if there might be a less exposed, less well-traveled route for her to follow. This, after all, was still contested territory and she might cross paths with soldiers from either side. But there wasn't a better way, certainly not one that wouldn't take her hours more than she'd planned. It was nearly midnight and with luck she could travel for some distance without encountering another soul. If she did meet anyone, she planned to say she was on her way to visit her mother. She ought to be able to sound convincing about that.

She could not have asked for a better horse. Coniglio covered ground so quickly and with so little apparent effort, she thought they might get back to Trento earlier than expected. She concentrated on moving with the horse, on allowing her body to relax.

Suddenly, just as she was beginning to feel at ease in the saddle, three soldiers emerged from the trees, stepped into the middle of the road, and ordered her to halt. For a moment she thought they were the enemy; however, their speech and the cut of their uniforms, at least what she could see of them in the moonlight, showed them to be Italian. That wouldn't necessarily make things easier—they'd have no more reason to believe her, no more reason to let her pass than the Austrians. To either side she was a civilian making an unauthorized journey in the middle of the night.

"Awfully late to be out," one of them said. They had rifles slung over their shoulders but didn't bother to remove them. A second said, "Where are you going? You're only a girl."

"I'm on my way to see my mother," she replied. "I meant to get an earlier start."

"Please dismount," said the first one. "I want to take a look at you."

They sounded as if they'd been drinking. "My mother's waiting up for me," she said, remaining in the saddle. She knew what could happen to a woman who was unfortunate enough to be met by drunken soldiers on a dark road at night. Was that one reaching for a pistol? She wouldn't wait to find out. Putting her heels to the horse, she said *Pronto* and cracked the reins. Coniglio responded as she'd hoped, bolting straight at them. Surprised and befuddled, they lurched to the side. As she passed, she could see them attempting to unsling their rifles but after that she didn't look back. Urging the horse onward, she waited to be shot.

A single round was fired. She'd expected a barrage. Perhaps their guns hadn't been loaded. Or the darkness had made her too difficult to see. Or they'd been drunker than she thought.

She kept the horse at a gallop until she was certain she'd left them behind. Then she returned him to a trot. Although breathless with fear, she was pleased at how she and the horse had responded. Neither she nor Coniglio had panicked and she hadn't been thrown off.

She continued on, meeting no one, the horse still moving as if this were what he'd been wanting to do for months. An hour passed, another hour, and at last they came to the place where she was to leave the main road. In her travels between Ulfano and Trento, she'd noticed this other path before but had never followed it. She'd assumed it was merely a goat trail, scarcely wide enough to allow the passage of a person on foot, let alone a horse. From that point on, the route would be unfamiliar. She hoped she'd understood Rodolfo's instructions. In her mind she pictured the map. A line on paper. Before her, a dark doorway into the trees.

Soon, branches were slashing her arms and she had to raise a hand to protect her face. There were moments when the moonlight shone through the canopy of trees overhead and others when it was as if they were in the darkest of caves. But Coniglio, like all horses, had good night vision and so he continued without hesitating. She heard a sound, a sort of scrabbling in the undergrowth, and felt a rush of fear. But it was probably only a fox or a badger or a wild boar. Such creatures were native to these parts and far less dangerous than the ones in uniform who'd been brought here by the war.

A little farther on, she began having misgivings about the trail. Something didn't seem right. Maybe she had misunderstood the map, or Rodolfo had drawn it poorly. After all, he was an old man and she knew these mountains as well as he did, perhaps even better. She pulled on the reins, weighed her options, and then turned the horse and went back to the main road.

For a time she searched for a different route, another trail angling off the main road that matched what the map had shown. But there was none. She began to get angry at Rodolfo for misdrawing the map and at herself for not asking more questions before she left. She was falling behind schedule, using up valuable time. At least she'd met no more soldiers. At least the horse was doing well. Filled with anxiety, she went back to the original fork. Again, they pushed their way through the undergrowth. She told herself she would ride until she could deliver the message or until daylight. If the sun came up, she'd return to Trento and tell Rodolfo she'd failed.

Finally, the forest began to thin and she sensed she was coming up on some sort of pasture or field. Here and there she could see spots of light, lanterns or campfires, but they were still some distance ahead. Rodolfo hadn't been clear about what would happen when she reached her destination. She assumed she'd be meeting one man, maybe two or three, yet it appeared there were dozens scattered across a sparsely wooded expanse.

She slowed the horse and told herself to remain calm. The last thing she wanted to do was startle their sentries and cause them to open fire. While she was having these thoughts, a voice called out from the darkness.

"Stop where you are and dismount."

Suddenly, she could make out several shadowy figures, at least five, six. She began to do as ordered. There was a seriousness in this voice, unlike the drunks she'd encountered earlier. It was clear she had no choice. From somewhere a lantern appeared, its reflector aimed at her eyes. Before she knew it, the reins were taken from her and she was pinioned between two men, each of them grasping an arm. As she was escorted briskly forward, her feet nearly left the ground.

"I've come with a message," she said.

"Silenzio," was the reply.

L'isola del tesoro

They traveled southwest, moving as rapidly as possible while taking pains to remain in friendly territory. As when Carlo had made the journey to Klagenfurt, it was sometimes difficult to determine which side of the front they were on. Great stretches appeared to be less front than frontier, either too rocky and wooded to guard effectively or simply abandoned because there weren't enough men and armaments to occupy every mile.

Much of the time Carlo slept. He was accustomed to rough roads, hard seats, and abrupt starts and stops. He didn't care what they were assigned to build and didn't think the others cared either. None of them were new to the absurdities of the military or the travails of this endless war. He wondered what his father would think of him now. Carlo guessed he still considered him a boy and would be stunned to see the soldier he had become, a soldier so experienced and weary, nothing surprised him, nothing impressed him, nothing could get him to respond with more than a shrug.

He also found himself wondering what his father thought about his *own* life and choices. Did he have any regrets about returning to Italy? Did he ever have second thoughts about forcing his youngest son to accompany him? Did he ever contemplate why he felt the need to impress people with his money? What were his most cherished memories of his late wife? Interesting questions, but Carlo had the feeling that if he posed them to his father, he'd be told to shut his big mouth and go away.

After three days of travel, they reached a large encampment. In most ways it resembled all the others he'd seen except for one important difference: It wasn't high in the mountains, wasn't surrounded by peaks, and wasn't covered with snow. Thus he considered it a paradise. They still hadn't been told what they were expected to do. He'd seen no clues—no telltale machinery, no raw materials stacked and waiting to be used.

Once they'd settled in, the commanders struggled to keep them busy. They assigned them to move things about that didn't need moving and dig long trenches for new latrines. He didn't mind digging new latrines—they weren't yet filled with shit. A crate of books arrived from somewhere and they all combed through them in hopes of finding something diverting to read. He had low expectations because nearly all the books were in German. But near the bottom he discovered one in Italian, and better yet, it was *Treasure Island*, a book

Miss Donovan had read to them in school. "*L'isola del tesoro*," he whispered and began sounding the words. For the next few days he found real comfort in its pages. In some respects he was similar to the main character, Jim Hawkins—gone away from his home on an arduous journey to the other side of the world.

When he had finished the book, he decided to write to the pigeon girl again. He still hadn't received a reply to any of his letters and had stopped hoping he would. In a way that made the writing easier—he could ramble on about whatever interested him without regard to what might interest her. This time, with *Treasure Island* having brought to mind sea voyages, he described his trip across the Atlantic: *At night the stars went from one edge of the ocean to the other. I could lie down on the deck and look up at them for hours.* He also told her the plot of *Treasure Island*, at least the most exciting parts, and said he intended to keep the book so she could read it, too. While writing those words, he realized that, with each letter, he'd expressed more certainty about seeing her again. What if she was receiving his letters and not replying because she considered them presumptuous? Well, if she felt that way, he was placing no great burden on her. She could just toss them into the fire.

One morning, as he made his way toward the mess tent, he detected an almost palpable energy in the air. He got his plate of mush and stood in the sunlight with a few other fellows, their mouths too full to talk. Eventually one of the men who'd traveled with him from Klagenfurt walked over and stood beside him. He had hooded eyes, a downturned mouth, and a voice that, no matter the subject, seemed filled with despair. Indeed, he was nearly as morose as Florian but lacked Florian's wit.

"I suppose you heard," he said.

Carlo stopped eating and glanced up from his plate. "I did not."

"We aren't continuing on toward the Karst Plateau."

"Where are we being sent?"

This glum compatriot lifted his spoon and pointed toward the mountains. Toward the snow-covered peaks. Toward the very place Carlo had spent more than a year building a fortress in solid rock.

"My god," he said.

"Yes," replied the man with the spoon. "I agree."

He couldn't believe it was happening. He didn't want to be cold again. That's what it really came down to. He wasn't opposed to hard work, nor was he afraid to return to the front. It was the frozen fingers and toes and frigid nights that would finally do him in. He remembered shivering so hard, he feared he'd break his teeth. He remembered the terrible pain when his frozen extremities thawed.

"And what is it we're expected to accomplish there? Or hasn't that been revealed?"

"Well, there is a rumor."

Carlo nodded, took a bite, and waited for the man to speak.

"They are sending us to build an aerial railway."

"An aerial railway?"

"That's what some are saying. A railway attached to cables. It will cross the mountains without ever touching the ground."

All Carlo could do was shake his head.

When first conscripted, he'd thought about running away. Then he decided that was foolish—if captured, he would be shot. But now he considered it again. Maybe he could get back to Trento and ask the pigeon girl to hide him. She worked in a big house. Perhaps it had an attic where he could sit out the rest of the war. Or he could go into the woods and live like some sort of hermit. Neither sounded realistic. Why would the pigeon girl endanger herself and those she worked with on his account? And alone in the woods he'd surely starve. He'd seen some men try to harm themselves so as to be discharged but no one was fooled by that anymore. An aerial railway. He pictured himself climbing trestles, stringing cable, hanging off cliffs, buffeted by freezing wind and blowing snow. And doing it all with only one good arm.

Through the remainder of the day, he heard the same story from other men. Not everyone had spent time high in the mountains. Those who hadn't asked him what it was like. Should he tell them the truth or protect them? He decided to protect them. They'd learn the truth soon enough.

"It's cold up there," he said, "but the work is like any work, the food is like the food we're getting here, and we'll be building things rather than being forced to run straight into machine gun fire—unlike those poor souls in the infantry who, if you ask me, have been sacrificed by the thousands so men with money and power can live as they choose." As he spoke, he realized he sounded like Alexi. The three fellows standing before him, all younger than himself, looked on with respect in their innocent eyes.

Then he heard a familiar voice behind him: "Don't listen to a word he says." Carlo knew at once it was Florian. Turning, he spread his arms and they embraced.

A Partisan

Gradually, the men around her came into focus. By their black capes and hats adorned with the feathers of ravens, Teresa knew them to be Bersaglieri, a unit of the Italian military everyone feared. Luca once told her you couldn't join, you had to be chosen. He said they fought like banshees and had never been defeated in battle. Now she was in their midst.

Her escorts led her forward and soon she was surrounded by light, by fires burning within circles of stones and lanterns suspended from trees. It was obviously a camp of some sort but a temporary one with no structures, not even tents, only packs and bedrolls in heaps on the ground. She was greatly relieved to be there. How close she'd come to abandoning her quest.

Beneath a pair of lanterns was a makeshift table with a man sitting behind it, the brim of his hat pulled low.

"She says she has a message," one of her escorts explained.

The man behind the table removed his hat and set it before him. Now she could see his face—narrow, pockmarked, frighteningly severe. He said, "Welcome to the temporary headquarters of the Sixth Bersaglieri," and then, as though speaking to himself, "I didn't expect a girl." Another man laughed but, upon realizing he was alone in doing so, abruptly stopped.

"It's not written down," she said.

"Of course not. Would you like some water? Perhaps something to eat?"

"No, grazie. I don't have time to spare."

He nodded. "Then get on with it. What have you come to say?"

She took a breath, reviewed the message in her mind, and began: "Isaac Venturi sent me. The Austrian Tenth under General Rohr has crossed the line of October twenty-four and intends to set a trap. It will be in a valley northeast of Toliera. Stay to the south no matter what."

To her surprise, he appeared disconcerted. She hadn't expected him to show any emotion, certainly not to her.

"You're sure? Northeast of Toliera? That isn't possible.

How can they have come so far?" He looked over his shoulder toward someone in the shadows and spoke again: "This is not customary. A girl on horseback who says she knows Isaac Venturi. Is she to be believed?" A third man now joined in the discussion, saying something about the location of enemy forces, but they were using unfamiliar terms and place names and she had difficulty understanding. All of them sounded alarmed.

"She's just a peasant, a contadina," said the man in the shadows. "We should keep her here until we know her information is sound."

She considered protesting, telling them they had no right. But that might make them suspicious. "Detain me if you must," she said.

The man behind the table spoke once more: "You'd only be in the way. Isaac Venturi? He told you this?"

She weighed how much to reveal. Not Rodolfo's name. Not the house where she worked. "The message came to Trento by pigeon. I know these mountains well, so I offered to deliver it to you."

"Have you any idea what this means?"

"None at all."

He studied her for a long moment. "Be on your way," he said.

She was led back into the darkness beneath the trees where the horse was waiting. A soldier held the reins, his other hand resting lightly on the animal's broad neck.

"Where did you get such an exceptional creature?" he asked.

She didn't know how to answer. What if they took him away? It was clear from everyone's demeanor that bringing them a message, even one of importance, didn't grant her special status. They'd do what they thought necessary for their own purposes, to protect themselves and further their cause.

"He doesn't belong to me. I've been taking care of him since his owner's unfortunate death."

"His owner?"

"A man of influence. Is there water for the horse?"

"I've done that already," he said.

The way back was easier. Her only worry was that the sun would be coming up by the time she reached Trento. It would be much better if she could complete the journey in the dark. Again, a wave of relief washed over her. She had delivered the message. Coniglio, seeming to respond to her mood, stepped with vigor, showing no evidence of his previous injury. She was proud to have played a part in helping him heal.

Suddenly, it occurred to her that she could visit her mother. She'd been unable to leave Trento and hadn't seen her for months. So as not to worry Rodolfo, she would stop for only an hour or two, but it would be worth the risk.

She located a trail she was familiar with, one that ran along the side of the valley and was used by sheepherders in the spring. Its well-trod surface made the going easy, and even without her urging, the horse increased his pace. She began imagining what her mother would do when she arrived in the middle of the night. At first she would look alarmed; next, she'd kiss her and laugh. Naturally, she'd insist on fixing her something to eat.

Then, in a moonlit clearing, something caught Teresa's eye. It appeared to be a mound of stones, but its shape was rather odd. Leaving the trail to get a better look, she began to see it was actually a mound of uniforms. Of uniforms on bodies, perhaps ten men, tumbled together, limbs entangled, as if they'd been herded together and shot at close range. After making Coniglio stop, she sat for a moment, unable to move.

Now she could make out dark stains of blood, gaping wounds in the backs of heads. Although there was no movement, she dismounted to look for signs of life. Her hands were shaking as she reached out to touch one and then another, jostling each man a bit as if to wake him from sleep. All were lifeless and cold. Still, she felt the need to continue and began moving the topmost bodies in an effort to detect any movement or sound or warmth beneath. When she felt she'd done the best she could, she stopped. They were so heavy and she was exhausted and it seemed impossible that even one was still alive. Their uniforms were like those worn by the men to whom she'd delivered the message. A few of their feathered hats lay scattered nearby.

Now she could see what this war was about. She'd been naive, ensconced as she was in the villa, far from the fighting, far from the deadly front. She'd seen the men in the hospital but that was different, they were being cared for, and she had been able to tell herself they'd recover, that many would survive. Yet the newspapers said there were thousands and so this was how it must be, all throughout the mountains and across the plains. Dead men in sunlit hay fields, dead men along the roads, dead men floating in rivers, this was what the word *war* would mean to her from now on.

Not yet ready to leave, she remained kneeling beside the bodies, thinking she might say a brief prayer. But before she could form any words, she noticed something and gasped. One of the men seemed to be breathing; his chest rose and fell. Crawling to him, she placed the side of her face against him and made herself still. No, nothing. It must have been a settling of the lungs or spasm of the muscles. But when she pulled away, his eyes were open and he was looking at her.

"Poverino," she said tenderly. "I'm going to go for help." She didn't know exactly how, but it was all she could think to say. When he didn't reply, she said, "Can you tell me your name?" His eyes shifted but he didn't speak.

If she'd been allowed to work in the hospital like Rosa, she might know what to do. She didn't know how she could possibly lift him onto the horse. The best thing would be to get to Rodolfo as quickly as she could. She would tell him about the man and he would send help. Although it might be futile, she felt she had to try. She had some water with her and gave the man a drink. Then she rolled up a dead man's cape, placed it under his head, and covered him with a second cape. She hated to leave him but what other choice did she have? Meeting his eyes once more, she said, "Someone will be back soon." A moment later she was on the horse, riding back toward Trento, back the way she'd come.

By the time she reached the main road, the stars were beginning to dim. She urged the horse onward, as if they were being pursued. Seeing the murdered soldiers caused her to feel both numbness and fury. She wanted to wipe their image from her mind while at the same time wanting revenge. As a child she'd been taught to feel allegiance only to the valley they lived in and to the mountains above it and to Trentino as an ancestral idea. Yet now it appeared she had become a partisan. Perhaps that was how it worked—in any conflict, if it went on long enough, you were forced to choose a side. Rodolfo would know where a doctor could be found, she could guide him back to the clearing, and with luck, the man would survive.

But then, for the third time that night, soldiers blocked her path and ordered her to dismount. This time they were Austrians. Two men with pistols drawn, military police, the ones everyone said to avoid.

Before her feet touched the ground, she was explaining herself, using words she'd rehearsed. However, these soldiers weren't filled with wine or brandy, they were filled with irritability, the kind caused by rising too early to work at a job you dislike. When she was done speaking, it was clear they were unconvinced.

"This area is off-limits to civilians."

"I didn't know."

"How could you not know? There are fences. There are signs."

For a moment she thought of telling them about the man in the clearing. But they would ask her what uniform he was wearing and what was to stop them from going back to finish the job?

Once again she was separated from Coniglio. This time she felt certain she'd never see him again.

As the horse was being led away, she was taken to a motorcar where two more policemen shoved her roughly inside. When the doors were closed, the man next to her said, "You're not crying. The girls usually cry."

She knew if she tried to speak, she'd prove him right. Instead, she looked away, made her hands into fists, and kept her mouth tightly shut. It was now morning. At the Villa Benedetti, Frau Merz would be stoking the fire, and Rodolfo—Isaac Venturi—would be awaiting her return. In the clearing in the forest, the man she'd left behind was also awaiting her return.

Men Will Die

"Look at us," Carlo told Florian, "together once again."

"It's not surprising. We've both been brought here because they are sending the most excellent engineers to do the impossible. As I understand it, to build a railway in the sky."

Carlo laughed. Florian hadn't lost his knack for the

sardonic. "I'd hoped you'd gotten away and made it back home."

"There's no escaping. The war is everywhere, even inside my head."

Carlo was genuinely pleased to have been reunited with Florian. All his criticism of him, all his reservations about his personality and character, now seemed petty. Although he'd vowed to stop caring about anyone but himself, he'd make an exception for his friend.

Florian looked happy to see him as well. He put his arm around Carlo and said to those observing their reunion, "We've been comrades since the beginning of the war." Then he described, with some embellishment, their adventures, particularly those in Innsbruck. It was all lighthearted nonsense. But later, when the two of them were alone, Florian's expression changed.

"I must ask you about Alexi," he said. "When I was sent away to get help, it seemed—"

"He didn't survive. He'll lie forever within that pile of rock."

"I knew it. I'm sorry I asked."

That night, the two of them ate supper together, choosing a spot where they could speak without interruption.

"Tell me what happened after you left us," Carlo said.

"I ran like a gazelle until I reached the sector command. I thought my heart would burst. But when I told the adjutant what had happened, he looked at me as if I was an imbecile. He said, 'An entire mountaintop blown to bits? I think maybe you've been up in the thin air too long.' It took a while to convince him I was telling the truth."

"And after that?"

"To be honest, I considered deserting. I suppose we all do from time to time. They're the courageous ones—the ones who strip off their uniforms and set out for home. Since I had no such courage, I was sent to the Asiago Plateau, where I was put in charge of a platoon rebuilding a small bridge. It was a minor thing, planks lashed to oil drums. But me in charge, imagine that."

"Deserting sounds attractive. If we ever encounter the Americans, I might go over to their side."

"You'll have to take me with you. I'm tired of this army and would like to try a new one."

Carlo told Florian about his injuries and his experiences in Klagenfurt. "I almost died. Still, it was nice to get some rest. I wrote letters. I sat in the garden."

"I'd have made love to the nurses."

"They didn't seem interested in romance. They're too busy emptying bedpans and draining pus from infections. If you were lucky enough to get one in bed, I expect she'd fall straight to sleep."

For a while they reminisced about Alexi. "He had a magnificent heart," said Florian. "But I don't miss his foul-smelling pipe."

When, a few days later, they were ordered to leave for the mountains, Carlo had a sudden premonition he wouldn't make it back. He'd never experienced such fear. It took all his self-control to keep from weeping. He thought of his brothers and suddenly felt certain he'd never see them again. If he died in the mountains, how would they know what had become of him? The Austrian army wouldn't send a telegram to Colorado. As he filled his haversack, his hands shook and his mouth went dry. He had a little brandy he'd been saving and drank it now, all in one burning quaff. Then he went searching for Florian, thinking it might help to talk, but he was busy playing cards with some men he'd just met. Florian was a good card player and would probably take their money. And mock them afterward for how easy it had been.

Returning to his cot, Carlo hoped he'd fall asleep; instead he spent the entire night following his agitated mind as it leaped wildly from thought to thought. One minute he was thinking about working in the tunnel, the next about his illicit half hour with the prostitute in Innsbruck, and the next about a man he saw buried in rubble whose head had been cleaved in half. Then suddenly he began to sweat and felt short of breath. He went outside and looked up at the sky. It seemed empty, huge and dark. After a while he felt more himself and returned to bed.

In the morning they set off. They had yet to be given any clear instructions about their mission, or any description of this thing, this aerial railway, they were expected to build. He pictured the snow, the ice, the sheer faces of rock. No doubt some general came up with this idea without having visited the place, without knowing much about building materials, without an understanding of logistics. Because of such arrogance, many men would die.

He and Florian walked together. Although Florian could still be quite acerbic, he seemed to have softened somewhat. This made his company more tolerable than before.

"Maybe we'll be platoon leaders, by virtue of our experience," Florian said. "Then we can send our underlings to do the more difficult tasks."

"Is that how things worked when you were on the Asiago Plateau?"

"To a certain extent. I didn't mind toiling alongside my men because the work wasn't especially difficult. But up there—" He pointed toward the peaks, the tops of which were covered in clouds. "Up there I intend to do what's necessary to save myself. As should everyone else, if they're in their right minds."

"I wouldn't want to be a platoon leader," said Carlo. "I don't like telling others what to do."

"A reasonable opinion," Florian replied.

From then on, they were silent, lost in the introverted rhythm, both physical and mental, required to carry a heavy pack uphill for hours at a time. One of Carlo's methods for making the time pass was to think back to the mining camp, to his brothers and, especially, his mother. She had been a small woman with dark hair, dark eyes, and an expressive mouth. His memories were those of a four-year-old, vivid pictures without words: *It's a fall day, the leaves on the cottonwoods a buttery yellow and the tall grass turning brown. He comes in from playing outside and there she is, there she is, waiting for him, waiting for him, waiting for him on the doorstep as he runs up the dirt path toward the house.*

He should have asked his brothers to tell him more about her. But they were always busy and it never seemed urgent. If he ever saw Joe and Sal again, he'd insist they sit down and share what they remembered. Now he had only a few fragments, flickering images he returned to again and again.

How Things Worked

The guards took Teresa to a gray stone building near the center of town. She had the feeling they'd watched her leave last night but instead of pursuing her had simply awaited her return. One said, "She doesn't seem like the type," and another, "Yes she does. The little bitch." What did they know about her? Would they be saying such things if her only offense was riding on restricted land? She felt guilty for failing to get help for the man in the clearing and wondered if he was still alive. And she felt guilty about the horse—she should have said more, done more, to prevent them from taking him away. Such a fine animal was likely to end up with a senior officer, well cared for and kept in conditions as good as the ones he was accustomed to. But knowing that provided little solace. Poor Coniglio. He had served her well and she'd failed to protect him, to keep him in her care.

She was taken through a back entrance, up three flights of stairs, and into a small room. With no further comment they left and shut the door. Then came the click of the lock being set. There was nothing in the room except for a chair and a small table on which sat a pitcher of water and a teacup. No bed. What meaning should she take from that? She looked out the window. It wasn't barred, but she was too high up to jump.

She'd heard of women being shot or garroted for activities not unlike the one she'd been involved in. Passing messages, assisting in escapes. *Aiding the enemy* was the usual term. She knew there were people so devoted to the cause, they willingly risked their lives, but that wasn't her, at least not when she'd started out. She had carried the message to the Bersaglieri to help Rodolfo. It had happened so quickly—one day she'd been working in the kitchen and the next riding through the night.

Her fear began to grow. They would take her before some tribunal, present their evidence, and drag her away to become one more insignificant casualty of this terrible war. Her mother would be left alone in the world. She sat down and put her face in her hands. Gaetano. How she wished she'd been able to see him again. A priest would tell her she could meet him in heaven. She didn't believe that, not at all. She always suspected her mother didn't believe in heaven either, at least not as it was described inside the church. It made things too easy. All you had to do was confess your sins and you got carried up to a place of eternal peace. That couldn't be how it worked.

No, the war had made faith meaningless. Faith in what? Better to just survive—if even that was possible. She rested her head on the table and for a time her mind went blank. Perhaps she slept a bit, perhaps not. When she looked up, it was getting dark.

Back at the Benedetti house, they must be wondering what had become of her. Before long, Rodolfo would conclude she was dead. And blame himself for not trying harder to keep her from going. Then again, he might consider her death a price that had to be paid. He wasn't merely an affable old gardener. There was an underlying fierceness to him she'd only recently begun to perceive. Frau Merz, however, was no doubt beside herself with distress. Teresa knew the stern but generous cook had come to like her, to think of her almost as a daughter. Unlike Rodolfo, Frau Merz had no idea where she'd gone. As for Rosa, if she discovered Teresa had been assisting the enemy, she'd say, "I always knew she was a traitor. And a fool."

Her thoughts now turned to Luca. If she understood Rodolfo correctly, it was his actions that had triggered everything. He had taken the pigeons and had been sending them back with secret messages, the most recent of which warned that the Bersaglieri were about to be attacked. Little Luca with his limp moving through the forest, a master spy.

The door opened and a guard handed her a chamber pot. She was happy to see it. Over the course of the afternoon and evening, she'd emptied the pitcher of water, cup by cup.

"Will I get something to eat?" she asked.

"In the morning."

"And if I'm to be here all night, what about a bed?"

"A bed? Is this an invitation? You're not a bad little piece.

Maybe I'll pay you a visit later tonight," he said and closed the door.

She began to tremble. It was now fully dark and the street below was deserted. What time was it? Ten o'clock? Midnight? Later still? Sinking to the floor, she curled up, back against the wall. If the guard returned, there'd be no point in resisting. At the thought of him placing his hands on her, she began to gasp and felt she might pass out. Then, forcing herself to breathe more slowly, she tried to turn her mind into a gray void. It worked for a short time but eventually images of the men she'd found lying in the forest reappeared. She recalled what it felt like to touch their skin. And especially to look into the eyes of the one who was alive. She should have stayed and tried to help him—although what such help might have consisted of, she had no idea. Still, anything would have been better than the nothing she could do for him now. Finally, exhausted, she fell asleep.

She awoke to the sound of a delivery wagon. The morning sky was veiled in clouds and threatening rain. The guard, thank God, hadn't returned. She now wished they'd bring her more water, some to drink and some to wash her face. Her back ached. Before she was fully alert, the door opened. It was a pair of guards, different from yesterday's, and again she began to tremble with fear. They pulled her to her feet, and as they escorted her down the stairs, her mind was reeling—was she about to be taken into some walled courtyard and shot? Her knees were beginning to buckle as they opened the door and shoved her out onto the street.

"Go home," one of them barked. "Don't ride horses where you shouldn't."

And the other, "You're a lucky girl."

She walked away in a daze. Before she got very far, she heard a familiar voice: "Let me accompany you."

It was Korporal Mayr, of the too-long trousers. Astonished, she said, "You? What did you do? You convinced them to release me."

"They didn't want trouble. I told them they were inconveniencing my superior—that you're needed at the house. Were you mistreated?"

"No." Never had she felt such relief. "I was so afraid."

"You were right to be. Men like that do as they please."

They walked on in silence until they were a good distance from the building where she'd been held.

"All I did was pass through the wrong gate," she said.

He raised an eyebrow. "Oh, I think you did more than that."

Back at the Benedetti house, she went directly to Rodolfo and told him how she had stumbled upon the site of an ambush and that at least one man might still be alive. He said, "I'm sorry you had to see that."

"But now you'll send someone there to help . . ."

"No, I'm afraid not," he said. "Who would do it? What horse would he ride? It's too dangerous and too late."

He spoke with authority and Teresa understood. Going back to help the wounded soldier wasn't possible. He was probably already dead. It wasn't even worth asking if there might be a way to reclaim Coniglio. Rodolfo was fond of animals, his pigeons especially, but there were limits. He would tell her to be happy the horse's leg had healed and happy he had been useful but now it was time to put him out of her mind.

The others in the house pretended nothing had happened. They knew she'd been gone but not where or why. At some point she might tell them; it seemed risky to do so now.

As she no longer needed to care for the horse, she spent the first evening and several that followed with Frau Merz and Rosa in the kitchen chatting, sometimes about matters of little significance, sometimes about the progress of the war. She felt she should do something for the korporal to show her gratitude. Not what Rosa would have her do. Korporal Mayr seemed too much the gentleman to expect that. No, some kind of sincere thank-you expressed in more than words. She decided to bake him a cake. It was the only gift she could think of, the only one she was capable of providing.

Frau Merz had some chestnut flour she'd been saving for a special occasion. When Teresa asked if she could use it, she agreed without insisting on being told why. But as Teresa was mixing the batter, Rosa appeared before her with an unsettled look on her face.

"I'm sorry to tell you that Korporal Mayr has been sent away."

"When? He was at supper last night."

"He left this morning. Early, before everyone else was awake."

"Did it have something to do with me?" Teresa asked.

Rosa shrugged. "I don't know the reason."

"Where was he sent?"

"I don't know that either. Why does it matter?" There was a starkness in Rosa's voice. Teresa couldn't tell if it was because Rosa blamed her for the korporal's departure or because she simply didn't care. Then, her tone softening, she said, "I'll see if I can find out where he went and you can send him a letter. But not a cake. By the time it reached him, it would be stale."

A Change of Plans

The trip into the mountains was as arduous as expected. "It's worse when you know what's coming," he told Florian. "You feel the cold twice, first in anticipation and again when it arrives."

"I don't feel cold because I'm heated by my burning hatred of the idiots who command us," Florian replied.

"The artillery is louder than it was last night. We seem to be moving toward it."

Florian listened, held up a finger. "Did you hear that? A Mörser 98."

"I'm going to die this time," Carlo said, surprised to be putting such feelings into words.

Florian snorted. "We both are. It can't happen soon enough."

Carlo laughed. No matter how dark his views got, Florian's were darker. In that way he was a useful friend to have.

By the third day of their travels, they were well into the mountains. A new officer, one they'd never seen before, had assumed command. He spoke grandly of how they'd string cables from peak to peak and send troops into Italian territory in metal cars. Maybe they'd use them to drop bombs on the Italian forces below. "They'll shoot us out of the sky," said one fellow, so loudly everyone could hear. This enraged the commander. "Who said that?" he barked. No one replied. "So be it. You have all lost your ration of brandy for tomorrow and the day after that."

But the punishment was never imposed. Instead, they were given a double ration when, the following day, a courier arrived to inform them that the war was over. An armistice had been declared. The Central Powers had surrendered, the Allies were the victors, and it was time to lay down arms.

They looked at each other in stunned incredulity. Then everyone began to cheer. It didn't matter that their side had been defeated. It was over and that was enough. They certainly hadn't expected it. Perhaps there had been rumors, foreshadowings, in other places, among other units, those closer to centers of command, but up here, it was a complete surprise.

"My god," Florian said. "I thought this day would never come."

Carlo put his face in his hands. He'd truly expected to die. He felt weak and his mind went blank, as though the importance of what was happening was too vast for him to comprehend. A man he had met only yesterday ran over and embraced him as if they'd been friends for years.

For the rest of the evening they all consumed whatever food they could lay their hands on, along with the remaining brandy, wine, and beer. The quartermaster said, "Have at it. Telling men how much bread they can eat is no longer my job."

Unfortunately, there wasn't much bread or anything else. The usual practice was for men who were going on long marches to take only what they'd needed for the duration of the march and have a supply caravan follow. But would the caravan come if the war was over? Surely not. Still, that was a small price to pay for the opportunity to be safe at last and in charge of their own lives.

"Look what I found," Florian said, holding aloft a tin of potted meat and a handful of cigarettes.

Carlo raised his eyebrows in surprise and approval. "Where did you get all that?"

"Over there." He motioned toward a clutch of men gathered around a tent. "They broke into the officers' provisions. There's going to be a fistfight before long, so I grabbed what I could and ran."

Florian opened the tin and he and Carlo sat side by side scooping up the moist brown stuff with their fingers and noisily sucking it in.

"What makes it so good?" Florian asked.

"It's officers' food. It's what all food will taste like from now on."

"I think it's the salt."

Nearby, two men had gotten their hands on a flamethrower and were shooting a plume of fire into the air, while farther off, someone shouted *Zivila Austrija!*—the Austrian battle cry. Carlo laughed ruefully and Florian shook his head. "I wonder if he knows that the Austro-Hungarian Empire is no more."

That night Carlo slept better than he had in months. He awoke only when Florian nudged him with the toe of his boot.

"People are leaving," he said. "They're packing up and heading home."

"Already?" He'd been anticipating further orders, additional instructions about what to do next. Without such direction, he felt a bit lost and unsettled.

"What do you expect? Who would want to stay here?"

"And you? Are you leaving?"

"Yes," Florian said, "I'm on my way now."

Carlo squirmed out of his bedroll and got to his feet. "Wait," he said, "I'm going, too," and began gathering his kit.

Outside, the camp was already half-empty. It appeared that many men, instead of waiting until daylight, had departed during the night. As they set off down the trail, Carlo cast a last look back at the cold peaks. His relief was beyond his ability to express it. Although he was still carrying his heavy haversack—they'd be sleeping out for a few more nights—he had the urge to run.

"I suppose you'll go straight home," Carlo said.

Florian was silent. Perhaps he hadn't heard the question, so Carlo asked again. "Your parents will be happy to see you."

"I have no parents. Nor any home to go to."

"What?" Carlo remembered all the times Florian told

him and Alexi that he couldn't wait to return to his family. "Did something happen?"

Florian shook his head. "I've been an orphan since I was fourteen. My parents both died of consumption. My mother in 1910 and my father in 1912."

"I see," Carlo said and nothing more.

Carlo had no interest in admonishing him for lying. He knew a little about being an orphan—he was half of one—and could understand how Florian might think it easier to pretend to have a family so as to avoid the need to explain. Especially in the army, where a common way of passing time was to reminisce about home.

"I have three older sisters. They are all married and have lives of their own. They aren't interested in me."

"You must have friends, your classmates from school . . ."

He grimaced to show his indifference. "Someday I'll go back. But not now."

Carlo felt that in this brief exchange he'd learned more about Florian and who he truly was than in all the months before.

They walked on, occasionally passing another man or two resting beside the trail. Each time, they paused and spent a few minutes sharing their amazement, their joy about the armistice. One who was sitting on a boulder, boots off, inspecting his blistered feet, said, "Maybe Austria will become part of Italy. Or France."

"It would serve them right," Florian replied. Was he referring to Austria or to Italy and France? Carlo didn't bother to inquire.

Later in the day he again asked Florian about his plans. He'd been trying to restrain himself but his curiosity won out: "If you aren't going home, what will you do?"

"Perhaps I'll reenlist."

"You will not!" Carlo said, laughing in disbelief.

Florian shrugged. "That's assuming there is still an army for me to serve in. I think I might join the Italians. As your own experience has shown, it's not difficult for a man from one country to serve in the armed forces of another. You simply don the uniform and do as you're told."

The Armistice and After

Everyone would remember that day. In Trento, it was clear and cold, with a breeze blowing down from the mountains. Teresa had gone out to pick the last surviving greens from the garden; when she came back inside, Rosa was announcing that the Italians had taken Rovereto, less than thirty kilometers to the south.

"Now comes the siege," Rodolfo said. "They will surround the city and cut off all supplies."

"What supplies?" said Frau Merz. "There's been nothing in the shops for months."

Teresa said, "We'll be bombed. That's what I fear most."

But no preparations for a siege were made. On the contrary, by early afternoon great numbers of Austrian soldiers had begun to depart. The ones who'd been living in the Benedetti house were upstairs packing now.

Rosa disappeared for a while, probably, Teresa thought, to say her goodbyes. Yet when she returned, she said, "I'm going with them."

"They won't allow it," Frau Merz said.

"Who's going to stop me?" she replied and began to leave the kitchen, only to turn back. "You have been so good to me," she said. "May the Blessed Virgin look down with fondness upon you and your loved ones." She embraced them all and ran away in tears.

For the rest of the afternoon, they waited, wondering what would happen next. Surely the Austrians weren't simply abandoning Trento—from the beginning it had been considered a keystone in their plans as well as an emblem of the Austro-Hungarian Empire's expansive reach. But that was precisely what happened. As dusk descended upon the city, the streets were filled with troops, all of them leaving as quickly as they could.

Teresa was watching their own Austrians depart when Rosa approached and said, "Thank you for inviting me to supper all those weeks ago." She motioned in the direction of the house across the road. "I don't know what would have become of me if I'd stayed over there."

"I hope you and your soldier will have a happy life."

"To be honest, I'm not sure I'll stay with him. I found out today he expects me to live with his parents and work on their farm."

Teresa almost laughed but managed to contain herself. "Well, good luck whatever you decide." Then they exchanged another tearful embrace.

Teresa shed no tears for the Austrians. Nor did Rodolfo or Frau Merz. Except for Korporal Mayr, they'd been tenants, nothing more.

The next day the Allied forces arrived and everyone rushed outside to watch. It was thrilling, not only the sights and sounds but what they meant. Trento returning to Italy. Trieste returning to Italy. Italian flags everywhere. So many changes were happening so quickly, Teresa didn't know what to think. Bells rang in the church towers for hours and hours. An enormous number of Italian soldiers, as well as some British, and even, rumor had it, a few Americans, were entering the city on horseback, on foot, and in every kind of motor vehicle. Would a group of Americans now occupy the

216

villa and make their own demands? Had the war really ended or might it recommence? Would the now fatherless Benedetti family return?

For a moment she wondered about Coniglio. Perhaps now she could find him and bring him home. She shared this thought with Rodolfo, who shook his head. "The Austrians used every available horse and mule to evacuate. If Signor Benedetti's horse was still in the city, he isn't any longer. Some officer is riding him toward Vienna as fast as he can." She disliked hearing it but didn't doubt he was right.

The second-floor veranda had been unused since the beginning of the war, but that night Teresa unlocked the doors and went out to look across the city. All at once Trento had become a city of lights—motorcar headlamps and gaslights on the streets and houses with curtains open, illuminated by electricity from within. It wasn't as if things had gone back to the way they were before—they'd never been like this—rather it was as if one outcome of the war, a reward for enduring years of strife, was a proliferation of light in all its forms and a banishment of the oppressive darkness.

A few days later, Rodolfo came to Teresa and said, "I know you like caring for animals. I heard of an Englishman who is here in Trento trying to help horses and mules injured during the fighting. Maybe you should offer to assist. Such work might help you feel less downhearted about the loss of the horse you nursed back to health."

An Englishman. She knew at once it must be the man in the newspaper article, the one who had protested against the mistreatment of donkeys in Naples. It made sense that he would now direct his attention to animals hurt in the war. The horses and mules returning from the front—and a great many did not—had every sort of injury. While walking the streets of Trento, one could see them—starving or lame, with open wounds from shrapnel or gunfire, or lungs ravaged by gas. For a significant number, the only solution was to finish the cruel job begun by the fighting with a bullet to the head. But surely some could be saved.

The next day, she followed Rodolfo's directions to the site of an abandoned market. As she approached, she began to see pens filled with horses and mules, nearly all of them in dreadful condition. Gaunt with discernable wounds. Heads bowed and swaying slowly, suffering in silence, as though waiting for the end. Eyes lifeless, coats thin and coarse, some with harness galls on their shoulders and others with starkly visible ribs. "My god," she whispered and stood for a moment, wondering if she had the fortitude to stay.

She decided she did not. It would be too much to endure. She turned and went back the way she'd come. Caring for a single horse with an injured leg was a simple matter, especially when you were confident the leg would heal. Many of the animals she'd just seen wouldn't recover. Their suffering should have been ended without delay.

That night she had difficulty putting the damaged horses and mules out of her mind. When she closed her eyes, she could see them. She told herself not to be so weak. She should set her distress aside and offer to help.

The next morning she returned to the market. She recalled how she'd been turned away from the hospital because she spoke the wrong language. Now that the war was over, she spoke the right language. Of course the beliefs underlying such judgments were ridiculous. The horses certainly wouldn't care.

She found the Englishman by walking among the pens and listening for someone speaking Italian with an English accent. He was tall and slender, with a mustache and thinning brown hair. After introducing herself, she said, "Are you Signor Hawksley? I've read about your work."

He looked at her for a moment, no doubt surprised to have a kitchen maid approach him like this. "Yes, that's me," he said.

Her suspicion confirmed, she continued. "May I ask what you're doing here? Did the army send you?" She knew she was being bold, but now that she'd started talking, she might as well continue.

"No, not the army, I've come of my own accord. As for what I'm doing, not long after the war started, it became clear that such an enormous number of animals would be hurt in the fighting that I needed to find ways to help."

Teresa motioned toward a horse nearby. "Most of these seem . . . quite damaged."

"Yes, but they're not the worst, not by any means. A large number go straight to the slaughterhouse. Or if their pain appears to be too great, we dispose of them on the spot. The only ones we try to save are those with an honest chance."

She could tell he was anxious to get back to work, so she turned to the question she'd come there to ask. Now her boldness was replaced by hesitation. "I wonder, could I help . . . in some way?"

He looked surprised. "Help? Here? I suppose so. It's not easy. But if you mean it, you can talk to that fellow standing by the gate. He'll give you something to do."

The man he sent her to, Nico, looked at her as skeptically as Hawksley had, perhaps even more so. But he didn't hesitate to put her to work. He explained that over thirty horses and mules were presently under their care, with more arriving each day. The mucking out alone was a sizable job. Their efforts were funded entirely by donations, mostly from England, and Hawksley was able to employ only two men. So yes, they'd be pleased to have additional help, even from a girl. Nico liked that she'd come from the country, for she willingly took up a pitchfork. By the time she went home, she was filthy and exhausted. After washing at the pump in the villa's garden, she went up to her room.

In the days that followed, she returned as often as she could. If nothing else, the work with the horses was a change from her kitchen chores. And with the Austrians gone and the Benedettis yet to come home, there was little to be done around the house. Frau Merz knew where she was spending her time but seemed uninterested, except to remark that no matter how carefully Teresa cleaned her shoes, she'd rather they be left outside.

Although Nico had plenty of menial tasks for her to do—shoveling and raking and cleaning and carrying—it wasn't long before she was being called upon to assist in the treatment of the horses and mules. It was mostly a matter of following instructions. If there was one thing she'd learned from Frau Merz, it was how to do as she was told.

Each animal was different. One would be so afraid, it had to be well secured with ropes before it could be touched. The next one would be so grateful for their care, it would rub the side of its face against her, eyes filled with relief. She often thought about Coniglio and hoped he was somewhere safe.

She found herself paying close attention to Leonard Hawksley. He had a remarkable way with animals, which included the ability to approach the most agitated horse without fear. He had a scar on his face that ran from his hairline to the corner of his mouth. Nico told her Hawksley had been attacked by thugs in Naples who'd been angry at him for trying to prevent animal cruelty there. They sliced his face with a stiletto to teach him that an Englishman had no business interfering in Neapolitan affairs.

"Caring for God's creatures is his calling," Nico said. "And not just horses—any animal, from the smallest and most insignificant to those that are so great and powerful, they could kill you if they wished. Although that seldom happens. It's we who kill them."

"Too bad there's only one Signor Hawksley," Teresa said. "The need is so great."

"True. But he does the work of ten men. He's leaving tonight to open another hospital in Udine."

Learning to Fish

Carlo and Florian made their way down out of the mountains and into the foothills. They estimated that they were somewhere between Gorizia and Maniago. The farther they went, the fewer men they encountered. Now that the war was over, most of the demobilized soldiers from this sector were headed north toward Austria and Hungary, going home. One afternoon they came upon a field so pockmarked with shell holes, not a single tree or bush remained. As they made their way across, they saw fragments of wood and angular pieces of metal, the remains of wrecked caissons and escort wagons and supply wagons, half-buried, as though they'd been pounded into the soil. There were broken rifles and disintegrating boots and many, many pieces of paper—until you saw it like this, it was easy to forget how much paper was used in war.

Later, when they were getting ready to stop for the night, they found themselves at the edge of a broad valley across which had been strung strand after strand of barbed wire.

"It's rather beautiful," Florian said. "The zinc is what makes it shine."

Carlo had no interest in the beauty of barbed wire. "We'll have to go all the way around," he sighed.

On their third day walking, they came upon an abandoned field kitchen. It had already been looted, but beneath a heap of empty crates they discovered a bit of food—potatoes, two tins of beans, some dried plums. They ate with gusto, saving none for later, and went on their way.

Carlo kept expecting Florian to say a final farewell and set off alone. Yet the next morning as he was putting on his boots, he looked up at Carlo and said, "Where will you go from here?"

"To Trento, I suppose. Then on to the village where my father lives. Without a car it will take a while, but what else am I going to do?"

"Do you mind if I come along?"

Carlo blinked, as if this version of Florian were a strange apparition and the true Florian had disappeared.

"If you like. But why would you? Haven't you somewhere better to go?"

"As I told you, I have no family. I'll accompany you for a while. I can always change my mind."

Carlo was relieved to learn he'd have a companion. And by now he and Florian had no difficulty getting along.

So they continued. It was late November and winter was coming soon. Not the kind of winter they'd have had to endure among the high peaks, but winter nonetheless. As long as they didn't get caught in a blizzard, they'd probably be all right.

The first few days passed quickly. Carlo felt lighthearted, spirited. He hadn't realized how completely he'd been keeping his feelings contained. On the fourth afternoon they happened upon what was left of an Austrian artillery unit. At first, the ordered ranks of large gray guns looked forbidding. Then it occurred to him: Nothing was now more useless than a cannon. They were only assemblages of cold scrap metal, their barrels pointed at the sky. Six or seven men remained with the guns, held there as if by magnetic force. After they exchanged greetings, Carlo said, "Have you anything to eat?"

"Actually, quite a lot," said one of the artillerymen. "This was a resupply point for operations to the east." He gestured toward a lorry. "You're welcome to take what you need."

"What luck," said Florian as they began to stuff their haversacks full. But before they could take very much, a wild-eyed fellow came running at them, waving his arms in the air.

"What do you think you're doing?" he shouted. "Who authorized you? Show me your orders or I'll have you put in the stockade."

"He has a pistol," Carlo whispered. "Pick up your pack and let's go."

They hurried off, stopping in a grove of beech trees to glance back.

"Is he coming?" Carlo asked.

"No. Perhaps the one who told us we could take what we wanted didn't have permission to do so."

"I suspect the giving of permission is a relic of the past."

They walked on, often uncertain of the route. Nearly every day there came a point when they decided they were on the wrong road, on the right road but headed in the wrong direction, or entirely lost. An even greater problem was lack of food. They stopped at a farmhouse and found it utterly stripped clean. The cabinets were empty and the root cellar, which looked promising at first, contained only an earthenware jar of spoiled cabbage with black mold on top. They stopped at another farmhouse where a woman with three small children lived. Before Florian could open his mouth, all four of them were on their knees begging for something to eat. Carlo and Florian had no choice—they gave the family the entire contents of their packs.

The next day Florian suggested they forage for mushrooms.

He said, "Although it's a bit late in the year, there could be a few *steinpilz* left." However, when they discovered some pushing up beneath a layer of pine needles deep in the woods, Carlo couldn't bring himself to touch them.

"What's wrong?" Florian asked.

"My mother died from eating mushrooms."

Florian's eyebrows rose in astonishment. "From mushrooms? I had assumed it was from a disease."

"It might as well have been. Once she ate them, there was nothing to be done."

"Do you think these are dangerous?"

"I don't know. I'm so hungry. But I refuse to put them in my mouth."

"No mushrooms then," Florian said, and they went back toward the trail. Carlo appreciated Florian's support. He could just as well have stuffed himself with mushrooms while Carlo watched.

For a time they walked single-file, separated by several meters, each immersed in his own thoughts. Fortunately, the weather had been holding and at night when they made their beds, it was beneath clear, starlit skies. Neither of them suffered from insomnia. If there was anything soldiering had taught them, it was how to sleep rough.

One morning, having seen a few small trout in a stream, they decided to try catching them with their hands. Florian thrust his arm into the water and came up with nothing. Carlo did likewise with no better result.

"Maybe we should use stealth," Florian said. "I remember watching . . ." His voice trailed off as he reclined on the bank and dangled his fingers in the current. "Fishes, I summon thee," he sang. Suddenly, Carlo was swept back to memories of his brother Joe. This was exactly the sort of thing the two of them often did. He wondered if Joe and Sal were among the

Americans who had crossed the ocean to fight. He had no idea how he'd go about finding them. Everything and everyone—himself included—had been scattered. Even with Florian by his side, he sometimes felt like a solitary wanderer, adrift and alone.

In the end they dammed the stream with stones and flushed a few fish into the pool they'd created. This allowed them to catch five. They built a fire, skewered the fish on willow sticks to cook them, and then realized they'd expended over half the day on a modest breakfast.

Carlo said, "At this rate we'll reach Trento in three months."

Florian motioned toward the well-cleaned skeletons of the fish they'd eaten, none of them longer than six inches in length. "At this rate we'll starve to death," he said.

PART V

A Letter from the Past

One day Teresa arrived home from working with Hawksley to find that she had received a letter. To her great surprise, it was from the American, the one she'd met on the street in Trento before the war began. At first she thought he might be writing to tell her something about Gaetano's death and almost stopped reading. But that made no sense. It appeared from the letter that he was serving in the Austrian army, so how could he know about the death of some Italian soldier? No, he was simply reaching out to her in a friendly manner because, he as much as said, there was no one else he could write to. As she studied the envelope markings, she noticed the date and realized it had been written nearly two years ago—how odd to receive a letter from the past written by a soldier whose fate was unknown to her. With luck he'd been discharged and was on his way home. If he was still alive.

Dear Signorina, it began. *I suppose you are wondering who is writing to you. Remember the fellow who saw you release the pigeon? Well, I am now in the Austrian army and thought I would send you a few words.*

He described what it was like to be in uniform and asked her some questions: How was she faring and what changes had Trento undergone as a result of the war? He apologized for his poor Italian but his meaning carried through. Reading the letter took her back to the beginning of the conflict. Trento had changed in every way.

She read on. One line, *Today we had mush and mush and mush with a little meat*, made her laugh. Another, *Truly the saddest fellow in camp is the one who never gets mail*, brought a tear to her eye. It ended, as she assumed all such letters did, with the hope that she'd write back.

She was about to take the letter to her room when, with her all-seeing eye, Frau Merz noticed it protruding from her apron pocket. "Who is it from?" she asked.

"A boy I met before the war began. It came today. He sent it ages ago."

Frau Merz frowned. "A boy? Other than poor Gaetano?"

"An Austrian soldier. I only spoke to him once. He had a peculiar accent and told me he was from America. He wrote to me because he was lonely. You can't fault him for that."

"May I see it?" Frau Merz asked. When she was done scanning the first page, she said, "This letter must have been sitting in some mailbag for months. That it reached you is a miracle." She read a bit more and spoke again: "He writes here that he was taken from the cathedral school. I remember that day. Everyone was shocked about the murder of the teacher. We hadn't imagined such a thing could happen." And finally, she, too, laughed about the mush.

As Frau Merz returned the letter to Teresa, her expression became somber. "It's likely he's dead. He wrote one letter to you and then got shot."

"Likely? You shouldn't say that. You have no idea."

"But I do. It's simple mathematics. If nine out of ten rabbits have been slaughtered, what's the chance that the one you intended to keep as a pet remains alive?"

Teresa frowned. "I don't like the way you put things," she said.

She went to her room and, despite the probable uselessness of doing so, sat down with pen and paper and began a reply.

It was a way for her to counter Frau Merz's grim analysis. Or perhaps it had something to do with the fact that she'd never been able to write to Gaetano. No, it was merely the fulfilling of an obligation—when you receive a letter, you're supposed to write one in return.

Dear Signor Coltura,

I was pleased to receive your letter. It took more than a year to reach me. So much has happened since you left that it will be difficult to explain but I'll do my best.

It must have been unpleasant to be taken away on such short notice. I know I would dislike it. One day you're a student and the next you're placed in uniform and thrown into the war. Now that the armistice has been signed, is it possible you're free to go home?

I'm sorry to hear the food in the army isn't good. Here in Trento even potatoes have been hard to get. But as my superior Frau Merz says, anything can be used to make soup.

If you could see Trento now, you'd be surprised. It was taken over by the Austrians and turned into a fortress. They knocked down buildings and destroyed bridges and took whatever they wanted. Now it is being turned back into an ordinary city again. The Austrians threatened to blow up the statue of Dante. But still he stands in defiance, looking north.

Many of the residents who were Italian citizens went into exile when the fighting started. This includes my employer, the Benedetti family. Unfortunately, Signor Benedetti was executed by the Austrians. Then some Austrian officers moved into the house. You may be comforted by the fact that their ability to speak Italian was worse than yours. Now we wonder if the Benedettis are ever coming back.

She continued in a similar vein for another page. She mentioned caring for Signor Benedetti's horse but said nothing about her ride into the mountains. She wrote that the pigeons were doing well but didn't say what they'd been used for. Although the war was over, she was still afraid to disclose too much. She had developed habits regarding what could be said and who it could be said to that would take some time to break.

In closing, she wrote, *I hope you are still alive.* Then, lacking any idea of where to send the letter—she knew from Frau Merz's newspapers that the armies of Austria and Hungary had fallen into disarray—she folded the pages and tucked them beneath the mattress of her bed.

The next morning she got up early and went to work at Leonard Hawksley's hospital. Frau Merz continued to tolerate her absence. Since the Austrians had departed, taking Rosa with them, Frau Merz, Teresa, and Rodolfo were alone in the enormous house. They'd cleaned all the rooms, closed up most of them, and cooked only for themselves.

Overnight, a little cart horse had been brought to Hawksley's hospital. Though her compact yet powerful body was sound, she had been blinded when she became entangled in barbed wire, raking the strands across her face as she struggled to break free. The gashes on her head would heal, but she would never see again.

Nico showed Teresa how to clean the wounds and left her to finish the job. Using the tip of a knife and sometimes a needle, she patiently removed any foreign matter. There was a good deal of grit and gravel, as it appeared the horse had rubbed her face on the ground in an effort to diminish the pain.

When she was done, she found Nico and he gave her a vial of what he called Dakin's Solution. He said, "Put this on the wounds and massage it in, as thoroughly as the animal will permit. Don't tell anyone we're using it. I'm not sure where

230

Hawksley gets it but it's the newest thing, and there's scarcely enough to treat all the injured men."

"Suppose the wounds heal. Who will want a blind horse?"

"A question for which I have no answer," Nico said.

At the Villa Benedetti that evening, two more letters from the American were waiting. Like the first one, these were months old, but she read them with interest. It was fascinating to follow the progression of a single soldier's experiences. One letter had been heavily censored, nearly half the words blacked out, while the other had not. Perhaps as the war had gone on, the censors had given up.

Once again she decided to respond. In her last letter she'd written about Trento during wartime, the many things that happened and how it had changed. This time she described the people in the villa, Frau Merz, Rodolfo, Rosa, Luca, and even sour Silvia before she quit and went away. As she wrote, she became more open about certain facts, the kind she'd have been reluctant to mention if the war were still underway. For example, Frau Merz's secret cache of newspapers, and the disappearance of Luca, although not what he did when he was gone.

She found it soothing to write to the American. It was a way to reflect on the events of the past few years, slowly and in her own way. Still, it felt strange not knowing what had become of him. It was possible she was writing to a ghost.

A week later yet another letter arrived. She began to wonder how many there would be. It appeared this one had been written from a hospital. He said he'd been wounded, yet it was unclear how. While he had a sense of humor, he continued to apologize for his Italian. A good number of lines were spent describing his previous life in America. Just as she had with the first three, Teresa went to her room and wrote a reply.

A Way to Die

It began to snow. The flakes were large and wet and plummeted straight down. Carlo and Florian were accustomed to walking in such weather but still it seemed unfair. The war was over. Shouldn't the snow be over as well? The worst part was their boots and socks. In no time they were soaked through.

This time of year, darkness arrived earlier every day. By midafternoon they'd begun wondering where to spend the night and were relieved when they came upon a farm. They didn't expect to be offered accommodations in the tiny cottage, but there was a low-slung barn that would do well enough.

It soon became apparent the place was deserted. They pounded on the door to no response. Peering through gaps in the shutters, they saw only black.

"We should force our way in and look for food," Florian said.

Carlo wasn't about to argue. In three days they'd had a few small fish and the last scraps of a loaf of bread. Using a stout branch they pried open a window and climbed in.

Surprisingly, the ashes in the stove were still glowing. "Whoever lives here hasn't been gone for long," Florian said. Carlo lit a piece of kindling and used it as a torch. It was the meanest place imaginable, with a dirt floor and only a few sticks of furniture. A chair and a recently slept-in bed.

"Suppose they come back?"

Florian ignored the question. "You stoke the fire and I'll get some snow to melt. It will be a luxury to wash." Then he took a tin pot and went outside.

After they'd cleaned up, they found some clothing heaped in a corner and changed out of their uniforms—or what was left of them. There were no boots in the cottage, but they did find two pairs of dry socks. Although now they would look like the lowest of peasants, it was better than wearing the garb of the losing side.

As they were making jokes about their appearance, the door burst open and two men rushed in. They were Italian soldiers both holding rifles, which they pointed squarely at Carlo's and Florian's chests.

"Who are you? What are you doing here?" one of the Italians said.

"This is your place? We thought it was empty," said Carlo. Florian, who spoke no Italian, shook his head.

The one with his rifle pointed at Carlo nodded toward their Austrian uniforms, which were strewn across the bed. "You must be deserters," he said. "Unless, of course, you are spies."

Carlo laughed. "Spies? How can we be spies? That might make sense if the war wasn't over. But no, we are on our way home." Then he translated as best he could for Florian: "They seem to believe the war is still being fought."

To Carlo, the Italians looked rather like himself and Florian. One tall and dark, one fair and wiry, both of them about their age. "The war is not over," the tall one said. He shoved the barrel of his rifle into Florian's midsection and Florian's expression became one of anger combined with fear.

"What do you mean? Of course it is," Carlo replied. "An armistice has been declared."

Now, all at once, Florian was asking him to interpret, the tall one was calling him a liar, and the wiry one was saying, *La guerra e finita? La guerra e finita?* in a tone of voice that could mean either he still didn't believe it or this was the first he'd heard.

"If the war isn't over, what are you doing here?" Carlo asked.

"We were separated from our unit," said the wiry one. "We don't know where they've gone."

"They've gone *home*. Just as we—"

Before Carlo could finish his sentence, the tall one said, "Basta! Outside, now," and motioned with his rifle toward the door. Carlo glanced at Florian and did as he was told. When they had left the cottage, the tall Italian ordered them to start walking and the four of them set off across the snow-covered field, toward a distant wall of trees. Behind them, Carlo could hear their captors whispering furiously but couldn't make out the words.

"One of them believes me," he told Florian. "And it shouldn't be hard to convince the other one. He ought to be happy to know the truth."

"Where are they taking us?" Florian asked.

"I don't know."

"Well, I'm not having it," Florian said. And with that, he spun around, grabbed the tall man's rifle, and wrenched it out of his hands. But before he could put it to use, the other Italian shot Florian in the center of his chest. Looking stunned, he took one step back and fell heavily to the ground. For a brief moment, Carlo and the Italians stood gazing down at Florian, at the wound, at the rifle in his hands, and at his face, which, after only a few seconds became blank, pale, and utterly drained of life. Acting on instinct, Carlo turned and ran.

He expected to be shot in the back before he reached the trees but neither of the Italians fired. Once he was surrounded by undergrowth and shadows, he paused briefly and glanced back. The Italians were still standing over Florian. He was sure he'd have been able to convince them that the war was over if Florian's impulsiveness hadn't gotten the best of him. He thought briefly about going back after dark to take revenge.

Instead, he did what Florian would want him to do: disappear into the forest and keep going south.

He soon reached a steep embankment, clambered down, and forded an icy stream. After scrambling up the slope on the other side, he emerged into a clearing. Instead of crossing it, he veered to the right and continued along the tree line, so he'd be less visible. He was sure the Italians weren't following him but it was best not to take any risks.

Eventually, he came upon a small shed without a door. Too exhausted and numb to go any farther, he went inside. By then, everything he was wearing had become sodden. He'd had nothing to eat for two days. His haversack was back with the Italians who'd killed Florian, so he no longer had a blanket or tarp. Crouching in the corner of the shed, he wrapped his arms around his knees and, despite being terribly uncomfortable, soon tipped over and fell asleep.

In the middle of the night he awoke, shivering uncontrollably. For a moment, he didn't know where he was. At last it came to him—he was lost in the mountains, cold and hungry, and worst of all, his friend was dead. He thought he heard voices and, fearing it was the two Italians, held his breath. But it was only the wind. He had once considered Florian unworthy of his friendship. Then his mind had been changed and he'd begun to feel a real fondness for him. He tried to think if there was some way he could have saved him. Maybe a forceful warning: "Don't take any chances, at least not yet." But knowing Florian, that wouldn't have been enough to keep him from grabbing the gun.

If Carlo had learned one thing, it was that there was no good way to die. Yes, some ways were more painful and some quicker, but there was no such thing as a heroic death. Eat bad mushrooms like his mother or be shot down in the snow, it was all the same. He wept in the darkness for the loss of his friend.

Allucio

It wasn't only the lights that made Trento a new city. Those who'd left at the beginning of the war, civilians and soldiers alike, were returning by the hundreds. During the day the streets were filled with motorcars and at night with revelers who sang celebratory songs, drank whatever they could find, and set off fireworks. Workers were repairing the damaged roads, and shops that had been closed for months were beginning to open their doors.

Every day Frau Merz wondered aloud about the Benedetti family. Why hadn't they returned or at least sent word about their plans? "I hope no harm has come to them," she said.

Teresa tried to reassure her: "I expect they'll be here soon."

Now they could read the Italian papers without fear: *Amistizio! The War Is Over! Complete Victory!* the headlines said. Throughout the country a terrible weight was being lifted. In its place was a combination of chaos, anxiety about the future, and pure joy. Teresa wrote to her mother, inquiring about her well-being. A reply came back in two days. Her mother explained that there had been very little food for the past year and still there were shortages, but all that mattered was that her daughter was safe. She wrote, "When you're unable to reach a loved one, you fear the worst."

A few days later the Benedetti family returned—all five of them at once, with no advance warning of their arrival. Frau Merz nearly fainted. Although they had tried to keep the house in order while the owners were gone, it suddenly seemed as if there were a hundred things to do and not enough people to do them. Frau Merz gave Teresa and Rodolfo each a long list of tasks and an exhortation to work as quickly as they could.

"They are a family without a father," Frau Merz said. "We must do our best to make them feel at home."

One of the first things Teresa noticed was that Cristian and Lia had changed from schoolchildren into adults. Cristian wore his military uniform. Frau Merz said he had served as an aid to General Montuori.

Teresa asked how they should express their condolences about Signor Benedetti.

Frau Merz said. "I will offer them on behalf of the entire staff." And then she made a small gesture to show that "entire" might not be the right word since only three of them remained.

"I suppose they've heard the bad news about Gaetano," Teresa said.

"I expect so. But you shouldn't say anything. It isn't your place."

Unfortunately, it would now become more difficult for Teresa to take time away to help with the injured horses and mules. She might even have to stop entirely since Frau Merz would need her at the house.

Despite the additional work, it was good to have the family back. Except for the Signora, they were all young people, so it wasn't long before lively chatter began erupting during meals and bits of laughter could be heard on the upper floors. Teresa scarcely recognized the two younger children, they'd grown so tall.

Signora Benedetti, encountering Teresa alone in the dining room, spoke to her directly: "I'm pleased you stayed. It must have been difficult to have the house filled with soldiers."

"I think ours were better behaved than most."

"We can comfort ourselves with the knowledge that such things will never happen again."

Frau Merz acted quickly to hire more help—two girls to assist in the kitchen and another to clean upstairs. She chose not to replace Luca. They all held out hope he'd return.

"I suppose it can now be disclosed that Luca wasn't taken into the Austrian army," Frau Merz told Teresa. "He went away to fight secretly for—"

"I know, and have for some time," Teresa said, pleased for once to be as knowledgeable as Frau Merz.

"I fear he was captured," said Rodolfo, and Teresa could tell he meant, but was refraining from saying, "captured *or killed.*"

Like Teresa, all three new girls were from the countryside. Young people from the mountains were pouring into Trento. It was as if the end of the war had released a new energy that was being expressed in part by an urge to come to the city, where there were cinemas and bars and jobs that paid better than farming or chopping wood. Frau Merz seemed to enjoy instructing her new charges, and they responded well. At the same time, Teresa felt herself becoming less interested in the kitchen work. Much more of her mind was occupied by Hawksley's mules than by the preparation of meals.

As there were now additional hands in the house to do the work, Teresa told Frau Merz she wanted to visit her mother again. "I don't know what you've been waiting for," Frau Merz said.

This time she didn't need to leave the city under cover of darkness or fear for her life. All the checkpoints and guards had disappeared. Nonetheless, she was a little nervous because she was carrying a good deal of money—the many months of wages she'd been unable to send home. She'd heard it said that one aftereffect of the war would be men with little regard for the rules of society roaming about.

She caught a ride in an empty lorry on its way to pick up

a load of wool from shepherds who, the driver informed her, had been sheering their sheep and hiding the wool all through the war, in anticipation of the day the textile mills reopened. The driver said, "The army would have confiscated it if they'd known." When he had no more to say about wool, he began flirting with her. "Tell me about your boyfriends. I'll bet you have more than one." Though he was as old as Rodolfo and seemed harmless enough, she was glad when he finally let her off.

She approached the village with trepidation. During the war she'd heard many stories of destruction. Individual houses bulldozed, fields poisoned so nothing could grow, whole towns flattened by artillery shells and bombs. But as she came around the last bend in the road, she was filled with relief. Nothing had changed. Being a village of no importance appeared to have some value—the war had passed Ulfano by.

Upon reaching her mother's house, she stood in the road and conducted an inspection. Just to be sure. It, too, seemed unscathed: The garden was being tended, the wood pile was as large as it ought to be, and nothing was in obvious disrepair. Yet perhaps she was being too optimistic. There was no cow grazing in the field, nor any chickens pecking in the yard.

Anxious to see her mother, she ran the last few steps and burst inside.

"*Mamma mia*, where did you come from?" her mother exclaimed. She was pouring water from a pitcher and nearly lost her grip as she turned.

Teresa began to cry. She hadn't anticipated how touched she'd be to see her mother's face. Many were the nights she'd lain in bed worrying about her and now here she stood, her hair grayer, her face more lined, yet still looking quite well. They embraced, stepped back, and embraced again.

"I was so worried about you," her mother said. "I wanted to write but Trento was closed up tight."

"I'm sure I was more worried than you."

Her mother held her daughter's hands and inspected her.

"I'm no different than before," Teresa said.

"Well, I doubt that . . ."

"I apologize for not sending you money. Here's all I owe." She held out a packet filled with bills and coins.

"Owe? Why do you say owe?"

"You know what I mean."

Her mother pushed her toward a chair and said, "You must tell me everything that happened since I saw you last. It's been a very long time."

"I'm looking forward to it. But first I must see my dear Allucio."

Her mother's expression changed from warmth to sorrow. "I'm very sorry. He's no longer with us. I should have put it in my letter but I wanted to tell you to your face."

Maybe she only meant he'd run away. If so, he'd come back. Or some passing soldiers had confiscated him, although why would they take an elderly dog? Even as she had such thoughts, she could tell by her mother's expression that the worst thing possible had occurred.

"A great convoy came down the road one morning. Such things didn't happen often, so it was a surprise. Poor Allucio was frightened. He went out barking, thinking he could stop them. Of course they stopped for nothing. I tried to call him back but he was caught beneath the wheels."

Again, Teresa began to cry. These weren't tears of relief, they were deep, brokenhearted sobs. It had never occurred to her that she wouldn't see her beloved Allucio again.

"Forgive me," her mother said. "There was nothing I could do."

Teresa took a breath. "It's not your fault."

"I buried him in the woods. I can show you where."

She gazed at the floor. When she was able to speak again, she said, "You must miss him."

"Yes, very much. I shared my thoughts with him daily, whether or not he understood."

Teresa knew how to interpret her mother's reserve. On this occasion it meant she, too, had a broken heart. Allucio had come to them when their family seemed incomplete and helped to make it whole again. If someone were to challenge her and say, "How was a common dog capable of that?" her reply would be, "He was not a common dog."

"If he suffered, it was only briefly," her mother added. "By the time I reached him, he was gone."

"You're not just preserving my feelings . . ."

"Have you known me to do that before?"

Well, Teresa thought, *perhaps it wouldn't hurt if you tried.* But rather than dwell on her emotions, she dried her eyes and stuck to the facts. "Which side, which army did the convoy belong to? You didn't say."

"What difference does it make?"

She'd now had enough of her mother's bluntness and decided it would be good if they talked about something else. First she told her about the new girls at the villa and then about working with Leonard Hawksley.

"I've been helping an Englishman care for some horses and mules injured in the war."

"Don't take too much time away from your duties in the kitchen," her mother said. "Now that those new girls have been hired, you could find yourself without a job."

241

An Unpleasant Meal

For several days after Florian's death, Carlo wandered through the mountains, uncertain of where he was. He continued to come upon scenes of great devastation. A once-grand villa reduced to rubble, a blackened, crater-filled pasture where a dozen horses lay decomposing in the sun. He was becoming accustomed to it all. This was what war left behind. When he saw other people, he did his best to avoid them rather than ask for directions or food. He caught a few more fish and found some unharvested vegetables, root crops left in the ground in a forgotten furrow. When he devoured too many carrots and turnips, they didn't sit well on his empty stomach. Nevertheless, he stuffed more turnips into his pockets for later and walked on.

He fell into an extended reverie about his brothers. Ever since the Americans had entered the war, he'd wondered if Sal and Joe had gotten drafted. Suppose they'd served somewhere in Italy, even in the north? What a coincidence that would be. As soon as he was back in Trento, he'd write them a letter and see what he could find out. He also thought about Sal's new wife. He hoped she would like him and that they'd become friends.

When he last saw his father, before he left to attend school in Trento, he'd gotten the impression that, from that point on, his father would have little interest in what he did with his life and wouldn't care if he returned to Colorado. But maybe he'd misunderstood. He could imagine his father saying, "What do you mean, you're going back? After all the trouble I took to bring you here?" If that happened, how would he respond?

One afternoon he encountered the enticing scent of meat being roasted. Following the smell, he moved through the trees until he could see four men standing around an open fire.

All of them were wearing pieces of military garb combined with other clothing, indicating that they, like Carlo, had been demobilized and were on their way home. That was a relief—at least they knew the war had ended. But since the pieces of their uniforms that remained were Italian, he wondered if they'd want to punish him for serving on the other side.

Crouching in the shadows and taking care to be silent, he observed the gathering and smelled the meat. If he revealed himself, he wanted to do so on his own terms. What they were roasting was long and slender, perhaps the leg of a cow or horse, perhaps an entire hare. His mouth watered.

"Buongiorno," he said, stepping forward while remaining ready to run.

All four heads turned toward the sound of his voice, and one of them, a wall-eyed fellow with white-blond hair, said, "Buongiorno. Who are you and where are you from?"

It had been a long time since Carlo had told his story but he decided to do so now. They might find it amusing and offer him a bite of their meat.

"My name is Carlo Coltura and I started out in America. When I was sixteen years old, I crossed the ocean and went to live in a village in Trentino called Ulfano—have you heard of it? —nothing would please me more than to learn it's nearby." Having thus begun, he went on to tell them about his time in Trento, his conscription into the army of Austria-Hungary, his travails in the high mountains, and his journeys thereafter. Although he no longer wore his uniform, he was honest about his service. Being caught in a lie seemed more dangerous than telling the truth.

When he was finally done, the one with the roaming eye said, "That was much more than I cared to know." Then he offered Carlo a large knife and told him to cut himself a piece of meat.

Carlo was surprised to be handed the knife—either he looked trustworthy or they assumed they could shoot him before he could turn the knife on them.

Stepping forward, he began to see the roasting flesh more clearly. It was neither hoofed animal nor hare but some large bird—he could tell by the wings—with head and feet removed. There wasn't much left and he didn't hesitate. Sawing along a bone, he managed to remove a thin slice. The taste, he discovered, had little relation to the tantalizing smell. It was so greasy and bitter, he wondered if it had been rotting before they put it on the fire.

"What is this?" he asked, trying not to allow his expression to show how repellent he found it.

"A gipeto. The giant bird that eats bones," said one of the others, a boy of not more than fifteen. "I bet you never ate one before."

"A gipeto?" Carlo asked.

"A lammergeier," said the wall-eyed man. "That's the Austrian word."

He remembered hearing of such a creature, possibly from Alexi, possibly from someone else, but he hadn't really believed it to be more than a myth. He wasn't sure he could swallow. Then again it was only a bird, no different in its way than a chicken or a grouse.

"It eats carrion," said the boy. "Whatever carcasses it can find. Even the bones. Nothing gets left behind."

"Which means," said a third fellow, "that the last few years were good for it. I'm sure it dined on a few Austrians. Some of our countrymen as well." Upon seeing the look on Carlo's face, they all laughed loud and long.

"Do you have any food with you?" asked the wall-eyed man.

Carlo pointed to his bulging pockets. "A couple of turnips..."

He shook his head. "No turnips. What about something warm to wear? As payment for the meat."

He should have expected this, if only because there were four of them and one of him.

"I could give you my socks. I found them in a farmhouse. If you make me give up my boots, I might as well lie down and die right here."

"The socks then. We'll draw lots to see who gets them."

Carlo sat down, removed his boots, stripped off his socks, and handed them over.

"Have another piece," the wall-eyed man said. "In case you're wondering, we're reasonable and won't ask for anything else."

His hunger was more powerful than either the disgusting taste or the idea that what they were consuming might be human flesh transformed. Indeed, it was all he could do to keep from taking the entire bird in his hands and gnawing the bones clean.

When he'd finished his second helping, he said, "Thank you. Now I'll be on my way."

"You're welcome to sleep here..."

"No, I want to get back to Ulfano. My father's waiting for me." Despite their reassurances, he didn't trust them. There was no way to predict what they might take or do.

"Ulfano," said the wall-eyed man. "There are so many villages in these mountains. I'd like to help you but I've never heard of it. As for us, we're headed east."

After he left the men behind, Carlo stopped from time to time and listened to make sure he wasn't being followed. He thought about the gipeto and began to regret having eaten its flesh. He also thought about the blisters he was bound to get from wearing boots over bare feet.

That night he found a haystack in a field and burrowed inside. To his surprise he slept better than he had for days, with no nightmares jolting him awake. He was so warm and comfortable, he didn't want to get up. When at last he poked his head out, the sun struck him square in the eyes. Though he still didn't know where he was, he felt hopeful. The previous evening, before bedding down, he'd gotten some water from a spring; now he returned there to wash and have a good long drink. Then, thinking Trento and Ulfano must be toward the southwest, he set off at a brisk pace.

The Thoughtlessness of Humans

Teresa continued telling her mother about everything that had happened in Trento. When she mentioned the letters from the American boy, her mother said, "An American? How did you meet him?"

"On the street in Trento."

"You're meeting boys on the street?"

"He asked me a question. It was nothing bad."

"An American in Trento?"

"Yes. Then he went off to war and wrote me some letters."

"Does he have family in Trento? What's his name?"

"Carlo. Carlo Coltura."

Her mother appeared puzzled. Then a look of recognition fell across her face. "Coltura? That explains it. His father lives here."

"Here? In Ulfano?"

"Yes. His father's name is Angelo. He grew up here and then went to America. He took his wife with him and I guess she died over there. He came back with a good deal of money."

She paused as if to sort out the various parts of the story in her mind. "I heard he sent his son to school in Trento, but I never thought you'd meet him." She went on to explain that Angelo Coltura had purchased a house and some new furniture and didn't hesitate to flaunt his wealth.

"So you know him? The father, I mean."

"Enough to say hello if I pass him on the street. I went to school with him when I was a girl."

Carlo had never mentioned Ulfano in his letters, but why would he? What an interesting coincidence this was. They'd certainly have things to talk about if he returned.

"Where is he now?" her mother asked. "Angelo Coltura's son?"

"I don't know. Dead perhaps. The letters I received were written a long time ago—halfway through the war." She gestured over her shoulder as if the past were physically behind her.

"If he's alive, maybe he'll come back here. And when his father dies, he'll get his money ..."

Teresa was accustomed to her mother's habit of twisting conversations toward matters that interested her, whether or not such matters were of interest to anyone else. She had a feeling she knew where this conversation was going.

"He wouldn't get all the money," Teresa said. "He has two brothers."

"This is something he wrote to you?"

"Yes. But suppose he was the only one, what are you suggesting?"

"That if he's been writing to you, he must want to see you again. And if such a thing happens, who knows where it will lead? Money isn't the worst reason to get married."

"Married?" Teresa exclaimed. "That's ridiculous! I barely

know him!" Then she muttered, "Don't talk nonsense," and went outside.

That night in bed she thought about Allucio. Death seemed to have bypassed Ulfano except for one poor dog who was sacrificed when the war's unrelenting machinery roared through. Like the horses and mules under Leonard Hawksley's care, Allucio had suffered because of the thoughtlessness of humans and their inability to resolve their differences without bloodshed. She pictured Allucio's face, his moist eyes, his black nose, which she used to tell him looked like it was made out of India rubber. And then she realized she could no longer say whoever loves me must love my dog.

She fell asleep, only to awaken halfway through the night with her heart pounding and her hands clawing at the bed. It was a nightmare about the men who'd been shot and heaped together in that field. About the one who had looked her in the eye.

"Wake up," her mother said. "You're having a bad dream."

She gazed around the room and untangled the bedclothes from her legs. "Thank you. I'm better now."

"What was it?" her mother asked.

Not wishing to explain, she said, "I'm not sure. Something dark and frightening but unclear."

Teresa didn't stay in Ulfano long. She was eager to return to the Benedetti villa and even more eager to get back to her work with Leonard Hawksley. Before she left, she put her arms around her mother and said, "You and I have been very lucky. Terrible things happened during the war."

Something about her remark made her mother angry: "You think I don't know that? There's a village not far from here where everyone was turned out of their homes. The men were shot, the women raped, and the houses burned to the ground. Do you think I've been sleeping? Don't tell me about luck." She said a few more words under her breath and her expression softened. "I'm sorry. It's difficult to stop being afraid. I'm so happy to see you again."

"I'll be back in a few weeks," Teresa said. Overcome by the knowledge that her mother was alone and might always be alone, she added, "Do you think you would want another dog?"

"There will never be one like Allucio," her mother replied and sadly shook her head.

Back in Trento, life in the Benedetti household continued to return to its prewar state. Cristian now considered himself head of the family and was becoming involved in what people were calling "the New Trento," by which they meant the Italian Trento. For most of the nineteenth century, the city had been under the rule of the Habsburgs; it would now be part of a united Italy. There was optimism in the air and politicians could barely contain their excitement. She heard Cristian say, "My father dreamed about this and now it will come to pass."

The changes caused Teresa to wonder about her own future. Helping care for the house in the Benedettis' absence had felt like a duty, but now she wasn't sure she wanted to devote her life to preparing food for others to eat.

She continued to work with the horses and mules as often as she could, several hours a week and sometimes more. She hated seeing how many had to be sent away for slaughter, although as Hawksley hastened to say, when an animal is in constant pain and clearly won't recover, there's no greater gift. She knew he was right but was relieved she wasn't the one who had to make the final decision nor the one who had to perform the act.

Among Hawksley's obsessions was hygiene. He said, "Nothing is more important than cleanliness—of the water the horses drink, the food they eat, the stalls and paddocks where they spend their days. Cleanliness can prevent pneumonia, pleurisy, pink eye, the infection of cutaneous injuries, any number of maladies. Whatever the condition of the animals, we must, above all, keep from making things worse."

She took his counsel to heart, but the harder she worked to keep things clean, the dirtier she herself became. At the end of the day she went home so filthy and exhausted, she wondered what those she passed on the street were thinking. For the most part, they glanced at her and shifted their eyes away. Then one day she caught sight of a tall young man who wasn't averting his gaze. It took her a moment to place him: It was the American, Carlo, the author of the letters. He'd made it through the war alive.

He recognized her as well and crossed the road. "It's you!" he said. "I can't believe it! I've only been back for a few days. I walked all the way from the front."

He was terribly thin, like a man made of sticks, but his expression was eager and bright.

"Please disregard my appearance," she said, embarrassed. "I've been helping care for some animals. I'm on my way home to wash."

"I trust your pigeons are doing well."

"They're . . ." She didn't know what to say. "As they always are." And then, "What do you mean, you walked all the way from the front?"

"I was far away to the northeast, beyond the border, when the armistice was declared. Without a map or compass and hardly any food, I set off for home with a friend." He paused and she noticed a change in his eyes. "I got lost more times than I can count. Some nights I slept in haystacks. I walked for days and days."

Teresa could tell he needed someone to talk to. His words were pouring out. She said, "I received your letters. I wrote back a few times but never mailed them. I didn't know where they should be sent."

"How many did you get?"

"Four."

"Oh, there were more than that."

She took a breath and composed herself. "You must be hungry. If you come home with me, I can give you something to eat." As she spoke, she realized it was the same invitation she'd made when she first met Rosa. If you worked in a kitchen, it was the natural thing to do.

"That would be wonderful. It's been difficult to find food."

As they fell into step beside each other, she commented on things he'd written: "What you experienced in the mountains was terrifying. How did you manage to survive?"

"I'll be happy to tell you all about it. But first can you remind me of your name?"

She glanced at him and wasn't surprised to see him blushing. "Teresa Miori," she said.

"Teresa," he repeated and smiled.

At the house, she washed as quickly as she could and then took him to the kitchen, where she set out as much of yesterday's polenta and stew as could be spared. The new girls looked on with interest. "He just returned from the front," Teresa explained.

"So this is the one who wrote to you," Frau Merz said. "I would think an Austrian soldier would be afraid to show his face in this city."

He blanched and furrowed his brow. "I had no choice. They came to the school and—"

"Don't be so serious. I'm joking," Frau Merz said.

While the new girls laughed, Teresa could sense in them feelings of resentment. Who could blame them? The girls were Italian and there was no way of knowing what sort of suffering they or their families had experienced at the hands of enemy forces during the years of the war.

Minos the Judge

The moment Carlo spotted the pigeon girl on the street, he felt better. Revived. He'd been preparing himself to be disappointed, but this was the opposite. Such expressive eyes. And the tendrils of brown hair not contained by her scarf. He was very glad he'd sent the letters. Despite their tardy arrival, they seemed to have meant something to her.

Although meeting those she worked with was a little overwhelming, he ate heartily and thanked them all for the food. When only he and Teresa remained at the table, it was time to talk. Her first words were a surprise.

"Did you know I'm from the village of Ulfano?"

She said it in an almost offhand way, but Carlo was astonished. He asked her to repeat it, and when she did, he said, "Truly? My father was born there. He lives there now. Who would have thought?"

"My mother told me. She lives there, too."

"Incredible," he said, wishing he could think of a more precise word. He had come across the ocean and fought in a war and it had all seemed meaningless but maybe it wasn't. He had seen her toss the pigeon in the air. Her family and his came from the same tiny place, a place hardly anyone else had heard of. *Destino*, that was the word, but he didn't say it aloud. Perhaps she would say it first.

"Have you been to Ulfano since you returned?" she asked.

"No, but I plan to go soon."

Teresa cleared his dishes and they went outside. There, she introduced him to the gardener, an old fellow who eagerly extended his hand.

"Where did you serve?" the gardener asked.

Once again he had to decide how honest to be. Once again he decided it was safest to tell the truth.

"In the mountains, with the Austrian—" he began, at which point the gardener's eyes flashed and he turned and walked away.

"I'm sorry," Teresa whispered. "He's not willing to forgive."

They fell silent, until Carlo spoke again: "Earlier today, you told me you were caring for animals. Which animals? Do they belong to the owners of this house?"

"No, horses and mules injured in the fighting. Animals used in the war."

"Ah, I see." He waited for her to elaborate. When she didn't, he chose not to press. He'd seen firsthand what had happened to living creatures in the mountains and on the field of battle. It would be unpleasant to discuss.

"Where will you stay tonight?" she asked.

He shrugged. "Men like me, those with no place to go, are being allowed to sleep in the square where the statue of Dante stands. They've set up tents. There are more of us than you might expect."

"They don't care what army you served in?"

"So it seems. Although as you can tell from your gardener's reaction, not everyone agrees."

"What about the mines around the statue?" she asked.

"I'm told they never actually existed. The whole thing was a ruse."

She said, "We were terrified. The Austrian bastards." Then she smiled. "I wasn't speaking of you."

Once more they fell silent. Finally, Teresa said, "I ought to go back inside. Come here tomorrow at the same time and I'll give you another meal."

He walked away thinking the opportunity to see her

again couldn't come soon enough—although perhaps his feelings were being influenced by how long it had been since he'd spoken to a girl and by the hardships he'd experienced. No, it was more than that. He'd thought about her often while he was in the mountains. Each time he wrote a letter, he imagined himself sitting across from her, looking into her eyes. Teresa Miori. She was pretty and intelligent. And from the very village that was his father's home, his ancestral home. He glanced back at the villa and shook his head.

He hadn't gone far when he came upon a taverna and decided to go in. It was packed with ex-soldiers, in many different uniforms, as well as some like himself who wore civilian clothes. When he reached the bar and tried to order, he was told there was no food and nothing to drink. So it wasn't really a taverna, not at present, just a gathering place for men with nowhere to go. That's why there wasn't much shouting or laughter. No one was getting drunk.

Suddenly, he caught a glimpse of red fez and his heart leaped. How could this be? As he pushed through the crowd, he began feeling more and more hopeful. When he was only steps away, the man turned. Of course not. He looked ten years younger than Alexi. Upon seeing Carlo, he put his hands up and said, "Please don't attack me. I haven't the strength."

"Forgive me. I thought you might be someone I knew."

The man lowered his hands. "A Bosnian?"

"Yes. But I was sure it wasn't possible. The fellow I'm speaking of is dead."

"What was his name? We're a small country. We might be cousins. I might owe him money."

To Carlo's surprise, he couldn't remember Alexi's surname. Perhaps it would come to him. Then it did: "Alexi Dzeko."

The Bosnian shook his head. "I'm afraid not. But if he was a friend of yours, I'm sorry he's dead." His voice and expression became reflective as he continued: "I'm sorry he's dead even if he *wasn't* a friend of yours. Even if you hated him. I'm sorry for all the deaths, every wretched one."

"We were together in an engineering unit."

"So you are Austrian?"

"No," he said and then told the story of his service, condensing it somewhat so he wouldn't be mocked like the last time he told it, to the men eating the hideous bird.

"What did you do in the war?" Carlo asked.

"I was a grave digger."

Carlo's mouth fell open and the Bosnian guffawed. "I'm joking." He leaned forward and whispered in Carlo's ear. "Actually, I was a sniper. Instead of digging graves, I filled them. But we're in Italian territory now, so I don't speak of that. Another matter I don't speak about is that it was a Bosnian who assassinated the archduke and started this absurd war."

Carlo remembered Alexi saying the same thing when they first met.

They agreed then to go together to find a place, if such a place existed, that had something left to drink. Carlo wondered if all Bosnians were so companionable. Based on his experience with Alexi and now this fellow, it was a province not of assassins but of good-hearted people wearing fezzes and making ironic jokes.

His new friend's name was Ismail. "What will you do now that the war is over?" Carlo asked as they ambled up the street.

"I'd like to go home but it's a long way. I haven't much money. Were you given any money when you left military service?"

"No. We were told to expect separation pay. I never saw it."

"I suppose we shouldn't be surprised," Ismail said. "The Habsburg Empire is no more."

They passed another establishment, its shelves as bare as the previous one. A third had given up and locked its doors. In the end they went to the camp at the Dante statue to claim a bed for the night.

Before retiring, they spent a moment gazing up at Dante, who cradled a book in one hand and reached out with the other. Beneath him, at various levels on the monument, were additional figures, posed for dramatic effect. The one that interested Carlo most was near the bottom. It was a man seated on a dragon, a snake wrapped around his naked torso and a look of deliberation on his face.

"Who do you suppose that is?" he asked.

"Minos, the judge," replied Ismail. "As souls arrive in Hades, he determines where each one will be sent." He paused and recited: "'Through me the way into the suffering city, through me the way to eternal pain.'"

Songbirds

The following day a woman came to the horse hospital with a dog. It had short legs, was entirely black, and appeared to be starving, so weak, it could scarcely walk.

"I see that you care for horses," the woman said. "But this dog served honorably as a courier during the war."

Teresa told the woman to wait a moment while she sought out Nico and asked what to do. Though Nico shook his head disapprovingly, when she went back to tell the woman no dogs were allowed, she couldn't bring herself to turn the poor creature away. She thought that was what Leonard Hawksley, who was presently in Udine, would want. This dog bore little physical resemblance to Allucio but reminded Teresa of him nonetheless. Maybe it was how his eyes shifted from wariness to warmth when she spoke. Since it was she who had offered the dog a place in the hospital, she'd take responsibility for his care.

That evening when Carlo came for supper, she mentioned the dog. "The hospital is for horses and mules," she said, "but I found something to feed him and locked him in a stall for the night. I probably shouldn't have allowed him to stay."

"Dogs were used for many purposes," Carlo replied. "I saw them serve as sentries, to warn of intruders. Although I never witnessed it myself, I heard they sometimes helped find wounded men on the battlefield."

Frau Merz gestured at Teresa and said, "Her dog—her mother's dog—was run over by some thoughtless soldiers."

"Allucio," Teresa said. When everyone kept looking at her, as though expecting her to continue, she said, "While I'm happy to discuss other dogs, I'd rather not talk about him."

Changing the subject, the new girls began asking Carlo about America. At first they played the role of students, as if they truly wished to learn. Then, unable to control themselves, a bout of shameless flirting began.

"Are all the men there so tall?" asked one. "I like your accent," said another.

When supper was over, Teresa and Carlo went walking in the garden. She suspected he might want to kiss her and was inclined to allow it, as long as he was respectful. Before the war, she'd have been more restrained. Now things were different. Not only was she older but what counted as proper behavior seemed to have changed.

"I've decided to go to Ulfano tomorrow," Carlo said. "Would you like to come along?"

"Thank you for the invitation but I was just there. Besides, the villa has gotten very busy and I'm not sure I can be spared." That was only part of the reason; she was also reluctant to leave the horses and mules—and now the dog. "I'm sure your father will be happy to see you," she said.

He didn't look convinced. "I suppose he will."

She and Carlo were learning to talk to each other. To encourage him to be less shy, she said, "I'm glad we met again."

He took her hand. "Yes, and we're lucky it happened so soon. I thought it would take weeks to find you—if I ever did."

"There were times I worried you'd been killed in battle."

Carlo laughed. "There were times I almost was."

He kept hold of her hand as they strolled through the garden. He told her about a taverna he'd visited that had nothing left to serve, and about a good-natured Bosnian he'd met. When they were in the shadows beneath the trees, she let him kiss her. He was very earnest and she forgave him his clumsiness—she was just as awkward. It was the first time she'd been kissed since Gaetano, before the war.

Carlo said, "I don't plan to stay in Ulfano for more than a day or two." He paused. "To be honest, it feels strange to have the freedom to do as I please. It makes me uneasy. Service in the military put me in the habit of being told what to do."

"Doing as you please is a burden?" she teased. "I'm sure you'll get used to it before long."

He put his arms around her and kissed her again. This time she felt slightly sinful, although not enough to send him away. If she were caught acting like this in Ulfano, her reputation would be damaged. Girls in mountain villages were brought up with the understanding that the smallest indiscretion could lead to their ruin. She said, "This has been very nice but that's enough for now."

"I understand," he said. Then they told each other goodbye and she watched him walk away.

Back inside, everyone had a question. When she tried to ignore them and go up to her room, Frau Merz said, "Please tell them what happened out there. They'll keep pestering you until you do."

So she admitted he'd kissed her but didn't say how many times. In response, one of the girls said, "Che meraviglia!" and another, "I've done more than that."

The following day at the hospital, she went straight to see the dog. The instant she opened the door, his delight in seeing her was obvious. As his black body swirled around her legs, he greeted her with joyful yips.

Shortly after she was done feeding the dog, she discovered Leonard Hawksley had returned. She found him with Nico, who was asking if his trip had been a success.

"Yes, I believe so. I've arranged to open a facility in Udine. It has the endorsement of General Scutari. This is the first time we've gotten help from the army. The general saw how important animals were in the war effort and wishes to honor them." After Teresa and Nico expressed their approval, Hawksley added, "Then again, maybe it's only nostalgia. Scutari knows machines have taken the place of horses and simply wishes life could be as it was before."

Whenever Hawksley spoke, Teresa listened intently. He had a certain charisma, the result of being committed to doing good works in an uncompromising manner. He seemed confident that if he labored hard enough, things would improve. Nico once told her Hawksley wrote a leaflet about the proper care of horses that was printed and distributed to thousands of Italian soldiers. When did the man have time to sleep?

Later that day, when it was almost time for her to hurry back to the Benedetti house, she took Hawksley to see the dog.

"I know we treat horses and mules only. But I felt I had no choice."

"How could you have done otherwise?" he said. "Let me tell you something. I have recently spoken to some elected officials about writing a law to prevent the blinding of captive songbirds. It's a barbaric practice, done so the poor creatures won't know day from night and therefore sing without rest. Compared to a horse, a small bird may seem insignificant. But we must help them if we can."

"I Thought It Would Last Longer."

That night Carlo dreamed about Alexi. "Where are you going?" Alexi asked. Even within the dream, he knew it was a question that could be either meaningless or prophetic. Nor was he entirely sure Alexi said "you." He might have said, "Where are *we* going?" a sentence Alexi had uttered daily as they made their way through the mountains, following some self-important officer on horseback who hadn't bothered to tell them their destination or what they'd be doing when they arrived.

After he awoke and left the dream behind, Carlo set off beneath a cloudy sky. He didn't try to flag down a ride. He'd become such a strong walker, he could easily cover great distances twice as rapidly as before the war.

He had obtained some different clothes, better than the ill-fitting ones he and Florian had stolen from the farmhouse. Yet even if he were still in uniform, he didn't think anyone would take offense. Maybe that would happen in Rome or Naples, where, according to the newspapers, there had been reprisals against those who fought for the enemy; here in the north it seemed people wanted to leave it all behind. It wasn't that they were especially forgiving, just too exhausted to care.

As he walked, he thought about his first trip along this path, on the day he and his father arrived. He hadn't known what to expect. Everything after leaving the mining camp in Colorado had been new and surprising. The endless fields and forests he saw on the train across America, the vast ocean he saw from the ship, the colorful and crowded port city of Genoa, and the walk to the village, which, while home to more people than the mining camp, seemed smaller, more insular, more enclosed by mountains and sky.

Today as he reached Ulfano, it began to rain. He left the main road and found his way to the narrow passage and went up the stone steps to the blue door. It was all as he remembered. He pushed on the door. It was latched, so he had to knock. No one answered so he knocked again. The door opened to reveal the housekeeper, Signora Sala. She looked at him in amazement.

"It's Carlo," he said, "back from the war."

She crossed herself, muttered an invocation, and to his surprise, began to sob. "I must take you to your papa," she said.

Although the bedroom was only dimly lit, he was able to see his father seated in a stout chair, a red-and-brown coperta across his lap.

"I'm back," Carlo said plainly, abruptly, and went to the window to part the curtains. As it was still raining, the light was gray and filtered, but now he could better make out his father's face. He looked a good deal older than the last time Carlo saw him. That was to be expected. It had been more than four years. Signora Sala looked older, too.

"Why did it take you so long to come see me?" his father asked. "The war's been over for many weeks."

"I had to walk home. I was three hundred kilometers away."

"Were you wounded?"

"I'm fine," he said, choosing not to mention his arm. "What about you? Why are you sitting here in the dark?"

Instead of answering the question, he looked at Signora Sala and said, "I want to be alone with my son."

When she was gone, Carlo sat down on the edge of the bed. "What did you want to say?"

"While you were away, something bad happened. I need to explain."

"Something bad? Are you sick? You look healthy enough to me." The truth was he looked rather pale. Although perhaps it was only the lack of light in the room.

"No, that's not it. What I want to tell you is that I've used up all the money we came with. All that's left is this house."

"I don't understand. What happened to the money? You bought horses and a carriage. New clothing and an expensive watch . . ."

"The soldiers came and took the horses and carriage. Also, a beautiful hunting rifle I purchased after you left. I lost everything else playing cards and almost had to sell the house." His father shook his head sadly. "I thought it would last longer. I suppose I'll go back to work. You'll have to find a job, too."

Carlo was both furious and confused. How could he have used it all up? His father sometimes played cards for money at his brothers' saloon, but he'd never known him to do it to excess. There had been so much—at least that was what he'd been led to believe. It wasn't that he felt he had some right to the money; it was that he felt he'd been deceived. His father had gone to America, made his fortune, and come back here, bringing his youngest son. It had always seemed as if those three things were connected—leaving America, the money, and insisting Carlo come along. And not merely insisting he come along but promising him a wonderful life after they arrived. Once, while they were on the ship looking out across the water, his father had said, "Aren't you glad I made enough money to bring us home?" He said he supposed he was, but he should have said, "The answer to that question depends on what happens in the months and years to come."

As for his "home," Carlo was no longer certain—never had been, really—where it was. Here in Ulfano? In Trento? Back in Colorado with his brothers? Or someplace he had yet to find? It seemed every soldier talked about home as if it was beautiful and inviolable and easy to locate on a map. But maybe that was only talk. In the end, Florian had revealed there was no place he wanted to return to. And if Carlo really thought about it, Alexi's description of his family and life in Bosnia sounded too good to be true. It seemed possible that the idea of home was a fraud, more dream and ideal than fact.

"I don't need you to tell me to find a job," Carlo said, his voice turning bitter. "Of course I'll find a job. I never imagined I wouldn't need one. I also never imagined you'd spend the war going broke."

An Unexpected Visitor

Now that Carlo had gone to Ulfano, she tried to avoid thinking about him. Nothing was more common in wartime than brief love affairs, romances cut short. If he never came back, her feelings wouldn't be badly hurt. Or so she told herself. But that didn't mean she was losing interest in him or hoped he wouldn't return. Her mother would certainly be pleased if she ended up with a man who wasn't from the village. And an American at that.

In his absence she had the black dog to distract her, and he was doing well. Every day it was a bit more difficult to feel his ribs and spine. And now there were others: The hospital had become home to an Alsatian with shrapnel wounds, a mastiff with a broken leg, even a goat that had been shot in the hindquarters. The goat was brought to them by a softhearted ambulance driver who couldn't bear to do as his friends recommended and roast it over a fire.

It soon became obvious that the Alsatian was too far gone and needed to be put down. It was the first mercy killing she witnessed. Dogs couldn't be sent to the slaughterhouse, and upon seeing what Hawksley was about to do, she decided it would be cowardly to turn away. As a child, she'd seen pigs slaughtered but this seemed different, although she couldn't say exactly why. They were all dumb animals and lived or died according to the whims of men.

He took the Alsatian into a stall, grabbed it by the scruff, removed a pistol from his coat pocket, and shot it in the head. It was done before she could even close the door. She shut her eyes to keep the tears in. When she opened them again, Hawksley said, "If we had more money, we could use chloroform, which I would prefer."

"I can see that caring for animals is costly," she said. And thought to herself, *Even killing them isn't cheap.*

"I spend half my time writing letters soliciting donations," he continued. "Most of them I send to England, where there are some wealthy people I can usually convince to send a few pounds. But it's never enough."

Hawksley left carrying the body of the dog and Teresa went off to feed the horses and mules. She wondered if she could learn to be as unsentimental as Hawksley—if she could do what was required and not let her emotions interfere. Hawksley had a rule that none of the animals could be given names. Now she understood why.

Along with the dogs, she had discovered she was particularly partial to mules. They seemed both indestructible and wise. She liked the sound they made when they were hungry or excited, half horse and half donkey, a whinny rising to an insistent and amusing and sometimes outrageous bray. Other times they were so stolid, it could be difficult to tell what ailed them. Nico showed her how to use her hands to check for hidden damage. One enormous sorrel mule stood motionless for nearly half an hour while she examined him. He had sores on his fetlocks that could easily be treated but also a large shrapnel wound on his flank. Nico instructed her to clean it with salt water and cotton wool.

When she was finished, he inspected. "Well done. This one should be all right. We'll keep him stalled for the next few days. If you see any swelling or inflammation around the wound, let me know. We don't want it to become infected."

As Teresa led the mule to an open stall, it occurred to her that if something were to happen to her, she'd be missed by the mules and dogs more than by the Benedetti family. They'd replace her without a second thought. Of course, Frau Merz and Rodolfo would be sorry to see her go, but to be honest, the work in the kitchen seemed increasingly tedious. The Signora wanted things to be orderly. She wanted things to be predictable and well planned. Such expectations were not surprising, especially after the upheaval they'd all experienced. Yet when Teresa pictured order, when she pictured predictability across the months and years ahead, they didn't look very appealing.

Late one evening, when the dishes had been washed and put away and they were about to go up to bed, something quite *un*predictable happened: Luca returned. He entered without announcing himself, and for a brief moment no one noticed him standing there. Suddenly, Frau Merz shrieked, the new girls, thinking him an intruder, clutched each other in fright, and Rodolfo, hearing Frau Merz, hobbled in from outside. After staring at Luca for a moment, Teresa, Frau Merz, and Rodolfo fell upon him and kissed his face.

He looked older and harder. His skin was windburned, his lips were cracked, and his hair, which hung over his ears and collar, looked as though it had been chopped with a dull knife.

Teresa said, "I didn't think I'd ever see you again," and Frau Merz, "I prayed for you." Rodolfo could only sob.

They made him sit at the table, surrounded him with food, and watched him eat, as if seeing him do something so ordinary was evidence he had truly returned.

After he was done, he sat back and patted his belly but they wouldn't let him be.

"Now tell us," Frau Merz said. "Where have you been?"

"Many different places. More than I can count. Most recently in Pieve di Cadore and before that near the Brenner Pass. Wherever I was needed. Now I'm finished and glad of it."

Frau Merz said, "I'm sure you have many stories. Suppose you tell us one."

"He's only just arrived," Teresa said, "and you want him to perform."

Frau Merz waved her off. "Talking doesn't take much effort. Besides, it's not like I'm asking him to give a speech. Only a brief tale before we go to bed. Something that happened or something interesting you saw."

"I've never been able to refuse her," Luca said, and everyone laughed. Then he sat up, squared his shoulders, and began: "One day I was walking along a road when I heard behind me the sound of an aeroplane. To my surprise, it flew right over me and landed on the road a short distance ahead. I could see it was British, so I wasn't afraid to approach. When I looked inside, the pilot was badly injured, shot through both arms."

All of them gasped, including the new girls, one of whom looked so upset, Teresa thought she might faint. "What did you do?" Frau Merz asked.

"I told him I would assist him in getting out and help however I could. But we were a long way from any hospital and he didn't think he could walk. He said, 'If you get into the cockpit with me, I will tell you how to operate the controls. We can fly to a hospital instead.' I agreed—what else could I do? He told me to crank the propeller so he could restart the engine and then climb inside. For once my size was an advantage—a larger man wouldn't have fit."

They stared at him in amazement. He'd obviously lived through it or he wouldn't be here today; yet that didn't diminish the suspense.

"I sat in front of him—on his lap, so to speak, and he told me what to do, what pedals to push and what levers to pull. We sped along the road until we left the ground—you can't believe what it feels like to fly—and landed successfully near a field hospital only a few kilometers away."

As he concluded, they all made sounds of approval, two of the new girls even applauding. Then Luca gave a sort of shrug and said, "I'm afraid the pilot had lost too much blood to survive."

Frau Merz urged him to tell another story, but Teresa had heard enough about the war. She said good night and went up to bed.

The House Across the Road

Carlo decided to leave Ulfano and come back down the mountain after just one night. Seeing Teresa would make him feel better. Upon arriving in Trento, he went directly to the Benedetti house, and when she stepped outside to meet him, he took her in his arms. They kissed as if they were accustomed to doing so, as if they'd done it many times.

"How is your father?" she asked.

"He's doing well." It was a lie but he didn't feel like telling her he'd thrown away all his money. He wasn't ready for her to know what kind of man his father was.

"You were right to go see him. It's your responsibility as his son."

"I know. But I'd rather be here with you."

That evening he ate supper at the Benedetti house, at the servants' table in the kitchen as before. There were eight of them present: he and Teresa; Frau Merz, who ran the kitchen; the gruff old gardener; three recently hired girls; and a young man called Luca, who had just returned from the war. Apparently he'd spent years in the mountains, placing himself in great danger, serving as a messenger and a spy. And done it all voluntarily, unlike Carlo, whose service had been entirely against his will.

Much of the talk was about the future—how Trento was changing, what it would mean for the city to be part of Italy, and what working in the house would be like now that the Benedetti family had returned. After a while, the girls began encouraging Luca to tell them more about his exploits. He was something of a hero, after all.

"I'm not the only one," he said. For a moment, Carlo thought Luca was going to direct their attention to him. That would have been awkward—how could he have been heroic when he fought for the enemy? But what Luca said was, "You should ask Teresa and Rodolfo what they did."

Everyone looked surprised. "Yes, please tell us," said Frau Merz.

Carlo watched Teresa and the old gardener with interest. When the gardener shook his head, it was left to Teresa to respond. "I suppose you're talking about the time I rode into the mountains. I did it for Rodolfo, to tell—"

Before she could continue, Luca interrupted. Apparently

he was having second thoughts about his request: "The details aren't important. Without their assistance, many men would have died. That's all that needs to be said."

For a moment, everyone, especially the new girls, looked confused. But none of them insisted they be told more and so the conversation moved on.

After the meal, Teresa was called upstairs by the lady of the house. Before she left, she glanced at Carlo, a look of disappointment on her face. "I was hoping we could talk," she said.

"Don't worry. I'll come back later tonight and wait in the garden."

He left the villa and walked through Trento with no purpose other than to fill the minutes until he could see Teresa again. The sky looked like a sheet of blue-gray steel—a condition he knew portended snow. As he wandered, a decision began to form in his mind: He would marry Teresa and return to Colorado. The money they'd need for the crossing was no obstacle—he could earn it in a matter of weeks. He thought briefly about his father. Carlo had never really expected to get any of his father's money. They'd been poor for all of his childhood, then for a brief time they had some money, and now it was gone. Thus, he wasn't surprised he'd have to pay his own way.

Walking faster, he began humming a tune. He felt transformed. From the day his father first said they were leaving Colorado, he'd been doing what others ordered him to do. Now he would make his own decisions and have Teresa by his side. He passed a brightly lit *osteria* and considered going in for a glass of wine but decided to continue walking and breathing the fresh night air.

By the time he got back to the Benedetti villa, snow had begun to fall. He stood in the garden waiting for her to appear, hoping she hadn't forgotten and gone up to bed. An unlikely possibility, but he knew better than to be too confident, better than to assume her feelings about him were as strong as his were about her.

At last the door opened and she slipped outside. Once again into his arms.

"Is there somewhere we can go?" he whispered.

"I thought about the stables, but Luca has started sleeping there again. I guess he likes having things as they were before."

"There are some establishments near the center of town …"

"The house across the road is abandoned. Some soldiers lived there for a while but now they're gone." She made a tentative gesture in its direction.

How resourceful she was! He was still getting to know her and would add this to the list of things he admired. She went through the gate and he followed. He wouldn't say anything about how they might have a future together, not yet. There was no hurry. They could continue to enjoy each other's company for a few weeks or even months; then, when the time was right, he'd reveal his plan.

The house was even larger than the Benedettis', although in much worse repair. The shrubbery had grown up to obscure the ground-floor windows and refuse was piled on the front terrace, heaps of broken furniture, empty food tins, and what appeared to be parts of a dismantled motorcar engine blocking the door. It didn't look promising, but around the back was another door with a cracked window. He decided it wasn't vandalism to finish breaking it out.

Once inside, they shook off the snow and began removing their outer garments, then thought better of it. The air was frigid, even colder than outside. From a pocket in her apron, she produced a candle and lit it with a match. Again, he was impressed by her careful planning. "You're well prepared," he said.

They spent the next several minutes going from room to room. While it had once been a very fine residence, the soldiers had destroyed it. There were holes in the walls, and the floors were warped as though there'd been a flood.

"Do you know who owns it?" he asked.

"I did once. I've forgotten the name. Whoever it is, I hate to imagine them coming back to this."

They decided not to go up to the second floor. It seemed likely it would only be more of the same. They sat on the stairs and he put his arm around her—his good arm, the other one could no longer be raised that high.

"I have something for you," she said, reaching into her pocket once more. This time she held up a packet of papers. "Each time I received a letter from you, I wrote a reply." As she offered them to him, she said, "But after the armistice, there was no way to reach an Austrian soldier. I almost threw them away."

There appeared to be four. He started to open one but she stopped him. "Not now, not while I'm here. Take them with you. They're not very good but I thought you might like to read them. I wrote mostly for myself."

"I'm glad you saved them." After a moment of silence, he said, "Tell me about the event you mentioned at supper. I didn't know you took part in the war."

"It was a small thing. I delivered a message to a group of soldiers in the mountains. The military police took me into custody when I returned. But with the help of a kind Austrian korporal, I was released. Because of him, I was detained for only one night."

"Even so it must have been frightening," he said and let

the matter drop, though he was intrigued by her response. He sensed she was holding something back.

They kissed and remained quiet for a time. The house made its sounds and through the window they could see the falling snow.

"I'm going to find a job," he said. "And a place to live."

"That's good. What kind of work will you look for?"

"While I was in the tunnels, I learned how to do things with stone. There's lots of rebuilding going on, so I expect I can get hired." He'd vowed not to do that kind of work again, but this time he'd be doing it to earn money for something that was important to him.

"You speak better than when I first met you."

"I've also learned some German. I had no choice."

They kissed once more. He wondered if there was a bed upstairs and how he might go look. But it was too soon for that. "You're still caring for the horses?"

"As often as I can. The kitchen has gotten busy since the family returned."

"I suppose you could quit if you wanted to."

"Then I'd have nothing to live on."

"I meant quit the horses."

"Oh, I see," she said, acknowledging her misunderstanding. "No, I'd rather not."

They talked for at least an hour, maybe more. He told her about his schooling in Colorado, including Miss Donovan, and she told him about her meager schooling with Don Tomasi, the annoying village priest. He told her about his brothers and she said she'd have had five or six brothers and sisters if given the choice. At last she said it was time for her to go home and they continued to talk as he walked her back. It was the longest conversation with a woman he'd ever had.

PART VI

The Mule

Now that Teresa and Carlo had spent some time together, she had decided he was a nice boy, somewhat clumsy, with passable Italian and a sincere heart. Nonetheless, she intended to be cautious with him as with any man who showed interest in her. It was her father's fault. By abandoning her mother, he had caused Teresa to question the trustworthiness of all men.

She found herself wishing Rosa had remained in Trento so she could get some advice. Since that wasn't possible, she asked the three new girls if they'd ever been courted and, if so, what it had been like. At first they all blushed and went mute. Then the eldest said, "I might know a few things," and the short one with dark hair, "I hope you're not asking how to commit a mortal sin."

She and Carlo returned to the house across the road a few days later and then a third time and a fourth. The more they were together, the more at ease she felt, and she could tell it was the same for him. Eventually, she might let him do what she assumed he wanted to do. Unlike the new girl with dark hair, she didn't believe going to bed with a man you weren't married to would send you to hell. She didn't think Rosa was going to hell and certainly didn't think her mother would go to hell if she happened to meet another man. She suspected many others felt the same way—possibly because the horrors of war had changed their ideas about hell. Rather than a place you could be sent to after death, it was present here on Earth and could be experienced by anyone, without regard to the severity of their sins.

When she was with the horses and mules, she sometimes wondered what they thought about the terrible things they'd been forced to endure. Did they believe they'd walked through hell? Did they have nightmares of a sky filled with fire and shells falling all around? More importantly, did they understand that such events were in the past and now they could rest easy because the people caring for them would do their best to keep them from harm? To put it more generally, what was the nature of animal thought? It was a question that puzzled her and she didn't think philosophy or science had answered it. She gathered her courage and asked Leonard Hawksley: What, in his opinion, could animals remember and how much did they know?

He was kneeling on the ground, peering into the box of oils and powders he referred to as his medicine chest. Upon hearing her question, he looked up, his expression surprised and a bit pained.

"I'm sorry," Teresa said. "I didn't mean to distract you."

"It's all right. To be honest, I have little interest in the details of animal thought."

"But you must wonder. You're with them every day."

"Of course. I also wonder what's in the minds of many humans I meet and they seldom choose to inform me. If I ask them directly, they tell me only what suits their purpose— the humans, I mean." He paused and said, "I know animals experience suffering and that's enough."

She'd assumed he was done speaking; he'd closed the box and risen to leave. Yet suddenly he turned back, his voice filled with barely suppressed rage: "And let me tell you, even those that escaped being killed or wounded by enemy fire have suffered. I've seen horses driven insane by the constant shelling, made so wild they had to be put down. I've seen artillery mules that spent weeks in harness left with great festering sores. Not a single animal used in this war chose to be part of it and all of them bear its scars." He shook his head. "I'm sorry. My anger isn't directed at you."

Suffer. Such a terrible word. And the animals kept coming and coming. In the past two days, nine horses and a dozen mules had been brought in and only half of them could be saved. The giant mule, the one with the shrapnel wound, seemed to have been improving, but then Teresa located a second wound, high up on the inside of its right rear leg. It was an upsetting discovery. How could she have missed it? She went looking for Nico and ran into Hawksley, who accompanied her back to the mule.

"It's small but very deep," Teresa said, as Hawksley positioned himself to examine it.

"I don't think this one is from shrapnel. Nor from a bullet," he said. "It may have come from a lance. Look here. You can tell by the triangular shape. That type of wound is difficult to clean. I'm trying to picture how it happened. A line of cavalry advancing with lances outthrust looks formidable until they are torn to shreds by machine guns. I thought they'd been abandoned early in the war." The point of his musing seemed to be that, as with most of their patients, the mule had a distressing story it would never be able to tell.

Teresa did her best to treat the newly discovered wound, but as Hawksley suggested, its location and depth made doing so a challenge. As always, she applied the special salve.

In the days that followed, she studied the mule for changes. No matter what she did, it simply stood, a great inscrutable statue, maybe improving, maybe not. She hadn't seen it drink much water, but she wasn't always present, so it was difficult to tell.

She decided to ask Luca if he had any advice. She'd been trying not to bother him, partly because he had his own work to do now that the Benedettis were back, and partly because he often seemed distant, immersed in his own thoughts.

"I'd have to see it," he said.

"It won't take long. I only want your opinion. I can do the rest."

"Tomorrow then."

When they got to the hospital the next day, she introduced Luca to Leonard Hawksley and showed him the stalls, the paddock, the makeshift barn. She explained how animals in need were located and treated and the steps taken to find places for those deemed to have recovered. She expected Luca, of all people, to be enthusiastic about Hawksley's work, but he continued to show scant emotion and spoke only when necessary.

The mule looked the same as it had for days. Luca examined it carefully, from head to tail, spending a surprising amount of time on its eyes and mouth before studying the wound itself.

"I should have found it earlier," Teresa said.

When Luca was finished, he stepped away from the mule. "It's infected," he said, "very badly," with a finality that made her stomach churn.

"I've been using something—sodium hypo . . . I can't remember the name."

"Well, it didn't work. Nothing would have worked. This mule has lockjaw and doesn't have long to live. Send it to the killer as quick as you can."

She'd learned to contain herself when there was bad news about an animal. Yet this time was especially difficult. Rosa, regarding the men she cared for, once said, "When one dies, you move on to the next. You don't cry. You turn your attention to whoever still has a chance." Luca looked upset, too, perhaps even more than Teresa. She probably shouldn't have asked him to help. He seemed so troubled these days. People talked about men coming back with "disturbances of the nervous system." She feared he was one of those.

As it happened, the mule wasn't sent to the killer—it died that night, and by the time she arrived the following morning, Hawksley was overseeing the process of its removal. A chain with links as thick as her thumb had been wrapped around its great body and two equally large mules were dragging it away.

When she saw Carlo again, she told him all about it: "I should have watched him more closely. I should have stayed with him through the night. He wasn't taking water. He'd stopped eating. He was dying before my eyes."

In response, some men would have offered hollow pronouncements: "It was only a mule," or "Death comes to us all," or worse yet, "You did the best you could." But to his credit, he said only, "I'm so sorry," and left it at that.

A Message from Ulfano

Carlo read the letters Teresa gave him. They provided a clear picture of what her life had been like across all the months of the conflict, when he'd been in the mountains wondering how she was faring. She described her work and the people she lived with and the house itself. Also, the Austrians who occupied it for a time. When she wrote about the horse, he could sense her fondness for it, and it was obvious how much she missed her dog. In the last letter she shared a reflection he found especially meaningful: *I once thought I'd live my whole life in the village of my birth. I'd work hard and have a family and travel no farther than the fields and forests outside my door. Now that has changed. Whether or not the change is for the better, I can't yet tell.*

When Carlo went looking for a job, he had little difficulty finding one. Rebuilding what had been destroyed in Trento was going to take months or years and hundreds of workers; after that there would be new projects, launched with the optimism of a country that could count itself among the victors. He was hired to help repair a bridge and found himself marveling at how pleasant it was to go to work and not have to worry about being shelled.

Locating a place to live wasn't as easy, what with so many soldiers returning home. The first trainload of Italian prisoners of war, released from German and Austrian camps, had arrived just last week. After several days of looking, Carlo found a place in a rooming house near the Piazza di Centa. While he was pleased to have a bed to sleep on, he had to admit that his new lodgings bore a strong resemblance to an army barracks—a dozen men to a room, at least half of whom were snoring or belching or passing gas at any given time.

He took meals at the Benedetti villa four or five times a week. Fortunately, nothing caused him to think he was overstaying his welcome. He enjoyed the food and the conversation but most of all he enjoyed what happened afterward, when Teresa would slip away with him and they'd go to the abandoned house across the road. The first few times they only kissed as he held her in his arms; then they discovered a miraculously unsullied straw mattress in an otherwise empty room on the third floor. When Teresa saw it, she surprised him with her matter-of-factness: "Look, it's been here waiting for us all this time."

"We ought not to make it wait any longer."

"So it seems we agree."

While in the army, he'd heard a great deal of talk about what it was like to do it with a maiden, a girl who had yet to be tried. It was better, it was worse, it was painful, it was glorious, it required special techniques that were written down in a book. But again she seemed remarkably calm and mature about the entire matter. They lit a fire, got undressed, and caressed each other attentively.

"I don't want to become—" she said.

"I know. In the army we were given these." He wasn't sure what she'd think. After a brief pause, she said, "I was told you might be prepared." He wanted to say, "Who told you?" but kept his mouth shut. Being silent was the best way to avoid appearing that he didn't know what to do.

The act itself, the embracing and the instinctive motions and the stillness at the end, was much more pleasant than what he experienced at the brothel in Innsbruck. After it was over, he said, "How do you feel?"

"I'm well."

A long, slightly awkward silence followed. "I wish we could sleep here," Carlo said.

"Like logs?"

It took him a moment to realize she was teasing him, quoting from one of his letters. "If not logs, then what?" he replied.

"One way I've heard it said is, 'I slept like un ghiro,' a dormouse."

He laughed. "That's much better. You are my ghiro," and pulled her body against his.

For a time they were quiet. Then she asked a question: "When you hold me like this, does it hurt your arm?"

"No."

"I'm sorry, I didn't mean to make you think about it."

"Honestly, it's all right." That wasn't true. It hurt constantly and in his job he had to work especially hard to compensate for the weakness. However, there were other men who had worse injuries, so it seemed wrong to complain.

In the days that followed, they made love often and would have gone on doing so, but one night they arrived to find the windows had been boarded over, the refuse hauled off, and the locks replaced. They looked at each other and burst into laughter. How devastating to find their love nest closed up tight!

They pretended it didn't matter. Stripping off their clothing and reveling in their bodies was a part but not the whole of their growing love. And surely there was somewhere else they could go—the attic of the Benedetti villa perhaps? Yet when they tried, their efforts were thwarted. Just as they were closing the attic door, they heard the voice of one of the new girls not far behind: "Teresa, Frau Merz is looking for you." A few days later, they concluded that a grove of saplings near where Rodolfo was keeping his new flock of pigeons would suffice. But as soon as their lovemaking had begun, they were interrupted by a pair of boys looking for a missing cow.

"The only solution is for us to have a little house of our own," Carlo said. He hadn't planned on saying anything so forward—the words just came out. She blushed. "That would be nice. But for now let's go deeper into the woods."

The more he was with her, the more he admired her. She would make a fine wife. He was anxious to propose, anxious to move forward with his plan. If she said yes, he'd work until he had enough money to book passage. That wouldn't take long. He'd also have to tell his father he was returning to Colorado. What if he wanted to go with them? Having lost all his money, he might now think returning to Italy had been a mistake.

As it happened, Carlo had to visit his father sooner than expected. One afternoon he returned from work to find a man waiting at the rooming house to give him a message:

His father had taken ill and he needed to come to Ulfano as quickly as he could.

"You know my father?" Carlo asked. The messenger was dressed as though he'd just come in from the fields.

"I know his housekeeper."

"How did you find me?"

"I went to places where soldiers gather and asked if anyone knew an American who spoke poor Italian and had served in the Austrian army. It didn't take long."

Carlo went directly to the Benedetti villa to tell Teresa he'd be returning to Ulfano. "I'm not going to wait until morning. If I leave now, I'll be almost there by the time it gets dark."

"I hope it's not the influenza."

The thought had crossed his mind. He'd first heard about it a few weeks ago and now more and more people seemed to be getting sick. "He's old but very strong. I expect he'll be all right." He paused and then added, "Going away like this, do you think I'll lose my job?"

"These days everyone needs all the workers they can find. You're too valuable to be dismissed."

"I think you overestimate my abilities." He almost told her that he needed the job to earn money not only for room and board but to buy passage for the two of them on a boat to America. Yet once again he concluded it was too soon.

"When you're in Ulfano, would you look in on my mother? I'd go myself but I'm busy caring for the animals. There aren't enough of us to go around."

"Of course," Carlo said. Then they embraced and he walked hurriedly away.

When he reached his father's house that evening, the blue door was open and five people were coming out. One was Signora Sala, one was the village priest, one was a doctor, and the other two were an old woman and her sister who lived nearby. He could tell by the looks on their faces that something terrible had happened, that he was too late. After Signora Sala explained who Carlo was, the doctor told him his father had taken sick a few days earlier and died overnight. The cause of death was a severe fever, one that failed to respond to the usual treatments. Some others in the village were ill as well.

Signora Sala took him upstairs to see the body. The doctor told him not to stay long because it could be dangerous to be in the same room. As Carlo stood beside the bed looking at his father's face, he thought about how the two of them hadn't liked each other very much, especially during the last few years. But the job of a father was to provide for his children, and his father, even without a wife, had done well enough.

As Carlo left the room, he realized he was now, like Florian, without parents. It was a condition that reminded him of being in the mountains when a blizzard descended and suddenly there were no landmarks to guide him and he could see only a few feet ahead.

Bad News

She was beginning to suspect Carlo would ask her to marry him. If that happened, what would she say? Before the war began, there had been a wave of matrimony, boys about to leave for the front wanting to have a girl to return to, and girls enthralled by the prospect of having a brave lad in uniform dreaming about them while far from home. Now, it was occurring even more frequently. Faustina, the prettiest of the new girls, was going to be married next month. She'd known the boy in question only a fortnight. Indeed, scarcely a week went by without news that so-and-so was getting married. Frau Merz said next year there would be so many bambinos on the street, the entire city would look like a nursery.

At the same time, amid all the joy, the number of people falling ill from influenza was rising. It came on quickly, and while many recovered, some did not. Frau Merz said she knew of entire households that had been infected. Teresa hoped Carlo's father had some lesser illness, that he'd be better by the time Carlo reached Ulfano. A stomach ailment perhaps.

She kept comparing Carlo to Gaetano. Gaetano had been more the gentleman, with better manners and a refined way of speaking that made her feel important. Yet there was something quite appealing about Carlo's Americanness. Although he was bashful, he was also less concerned about how others perceived him and therefore more natural, more himself. Not that comparing the two of them was of any value—Gaetano was never coming back.

After Carlo left for Ulfano, she went back inside to work. She expected to spend a dull afternoon scrubbing floors, but there in the kitchen, having coffee and a piece of buttered bread, was none other than Rosa. Rosa, who upon running away with her Austrian, had been confident she was on the road to a better life.

"What are you doing here?" Teresa asked.

"What does it look like? I've come back."

"So you have, but why?"

Rosa broke the bread into two pieces and began to elaborate: "I decided to get away before it was too late. Before we were married, I mean. Unfortunately, he put a baby inside me. I'd rather raise it here than on a dismal farmstead, so I snuck off in the middle of the night. You should have seen that place. A world of mud and shit. Some will look down on me for leaving him but I can bear it."

Teresa glanced at Frau Merz, who grunted dismissively and said, "Of course I had to hire her again."

"Don't worry," Rosa added, "there's no danger he'll come after me. He's too lazy to bother."

The new girls studied Rosa from a distance. Teresa could imagine their thoughts: What had it been like when the house was filled with Austrian soldiers? How dangerous and thrilling it must have been. How romantic it must have been. But what a mistake she made!

That evening, after everyone else had gone to bed, Teresa and Rosa washed the last few pots. "I'm told you have a boyfriend," Rosa said. "An American. You're very lucky, but be careful. Look what happened to me."

Teresa pictured the nights she and Carlo had spent together and took a nervous breath. Rosa's situation made the chance of an accident seem more real.

"Has he proposed?" Rosa asked.

She shook her head. "Not yet. But I think he might. So far he's treated me well."

"Maybe he could take you away from here."

"Did I say I want to leave?" Teresa thought it ironic that Rosa would make moving out of the Benedetti house sound desirable when she'd chosen to return.

"Well, it's a good thing you didn't go off with that korporal," Rosa said.

"Because he was Austrian?"

"No, didn't you hear?"

"What? Hear what?"

Rosa lowered her voice. "He was the type who preferred boys to girls. Someone found out and turned him in. So he was sent to the Serbian front."

Teresa was stunned. She'd heard about such men, although always in whispers, as if they lived only in large cities, in places she'd never visit, among people she'd never meet.

"Your fiancé told you that?"

She nodded. "But don't call him my fiancé. Call him that rotten son-of-a-bitch."

That night in her room Teresa thought about the korporal. She wished she could see him again. He was the only one of the Austrians who had treated her like more than a scullery maid. There ought to be some value placed on that. The poor man. The thing he'd feared most was being sent to the front. From what she'd heard, no one came back from Serbia. He'd been serving honorably, following orders. And he had saved her. They should have left him alone.

Two days later Carlo returned. He came to the back entrance and stood there, not knocking but waiting for someone to notice, a peculiar look in his eyes. Teresa knew at once there was bad news. What if it was about her mother? As soon as she opened the door, he spoke: "I'm sorry to say my father has died."

"Oh, Carlo. How awful. When did it happen?"

"Right before I got there. A fever, as you predicted. They said it took him very quickly. I didn't get to say goodbye."

They embraced and she held him tightly, trying to think of what else to say. "I'm so sorry," she murmured. "It must have been a terrible shock."

"Your mother is well," he said. "A few others in the village are sick, but she told me to tell you she's safe and taking good care of herself. She used the money you gave her to buy a new cow."

The Book of Trees

As Carlo described how he learned about his father's death, Teresa started crying. He hadn't cried when he saw his father's body but he did so now.

"When will he be buried?" she asked.

"It's already happened. I told them I was his only family and didn't want to wait. They did it the next day."

"Have you informed your brothers?"

He nodded. "I sent a telegram this morning."

"And you're sure my mother is all right?"

"She seemed so. Yes, I'm certain of it. You don't need to be concerned." He liked how reassuring her made him feel. He wasn't used to being able to put someone's mind at ease.

That night at supper he told the others of his loss. He found himself being unexpectedly forthright: "I should have gone to visit earlier. We didn't always get along but nobody deserves to die without their family present." They all offered their condolences and recounted their own experiences with death. "I was working here when my mother passed," Frau Merz said. "You shouldn't blame yourself. There was no way to know he'd fall ill."

"More people are getting sick every day," said Rosa, whom he'd just met. "I hope it doesn't happen to me."

After the meal ended, he was determined to find a place to be alone with Teresa. He followed her into the pantry and said, "Where can we go?"

"Are you sure? You just lost your father. Maybe you'd rather spend the evening by yourself."

"Nothing would be better for me than to be with you."

"Upstairs then," she said. "The door to my room is unlocked. I'll meet you there."

"You won't get in trouble?" She had once explained to him that allowing a man into her room was the one thing she was certain would lead to her dismissal. Frau Merz had made that clear.

"Go," she said and shoved him out the door.

He made it without being seen—he was careful to scan

the corridor before proceeding—and Teresa arrived seconds later, a look of mischief on her face.

"We'll be very quiet," he said, taking a seat on the narrow bed.

"I'm hoping Frau Merz will be forgiving. She's too clever to be fooled. It may come down to what she thinks of you. Don't be surprised if there's a knock at the door."

They lay back and looked at the ceiling. Gently, Teresa began musing about Ulfano and his father's attachment to the place and how strange it was that the two of them had met in Trento and not there. That she was fonder of the village than he was didn't surprise him. He hadn't spent enough time in Ulfano to get to know it well.

He considered asking her to marry him right then but lacked the nerve. He considered it a second time an hour later, when their passion had ebbed and she was nestled in his arms. Still, he lacked the nerve. He dozed for a brief period and awoke at the sound of her voice:

"It's time for you to leave."

"I know. Although I'd love to stay."

"I wish you could. But we've tested Frau Merz as much as we dare."

He returned to the boardinghouse, slept well, and went off to his job in the morning thinking about the fact that his father had come home to Italy to die. He could imagine the old man saying, "That's just as I intended."

Before Carlo left Ulfano, the housekeeper, Signora Sala, came to him and said, "What are you going to do about this house?"

"I don't know. I haven't given it any thought."

"Could I live here until you decide?"

The request caught him by surprise but he said yes. Then she asked if her son could move in as well. Again, he said yes.

Also perhaps her sister? She probably hoped he'd do like his father—go back to Colorado while keeping possession of the place. And stay a good long time.

That day the work was hard, lots of lifting and carrying and digging and shoveling, but he didn't mind. Afterward, instead of going to the boardinghouse, he decided to visit the cathedral school. He'd left his book about trees there and wanted it back. He also hoped the teachers would know something about his friend Vitale, although he was almost afraid to ask.

His old Latin teacher, Brother Toscano, answered the door. "The American!" he said joyfully as he pulled Carlo inside. It was gratifying to be remembered, even more so to be met with such enthusiasm. He'd half expected whichever brother greeted him to say, "Who are you?"

Brother Toscano led Carlo to a room he hadn't been in before, a sort of parlor behind a door through which students weren't allowed to pass. He made Carlo a cup of tea and said, "You must tell me everything. I'm so pleased you came."

As they sat across from each other, saucers balanced on their knees, Carlo did his best to describe what he'd done and gone through without including things that could be viewed as unseemly or that were too upsetting to relive. He didn't mention his arm but he did talk about the ceaseless cold. "It doesn't matter how cold you are if you can come home to a warm bed. But to be cold every hour of every day and then through the night, for weeks on end . . ." He shuddered and shook his head. Neither of them mentioned the terrible morning when he and the other boys had been taken away, when Brother Leonardo had been murdered in front of them.

"I prayed for all of you," Brother Toscano said.

"Have you heard from Vitale DeMarco? When I was here, he was my closest friend."

"I have not. But I'll give you the address of his family. You can write to them if you wish."

They spoke a bit more about Trento and the future and the unpredictability of life. Then Brother Toscano said, "I'm so very glad to see you. Of all the boys who left here to go to war, I know of just four who survived."

At last Carlo asked about his book. Without hesitation, Brother Toscano stood up and said, "I know right where it is." When he returned, he had not only the book but several papers. "I found these on the floor the day you were taken away," he said, handing him the torn documents showing him to be an American citizen, "and there's also a letter from America, which was delivered here months ago. I hope it's good news. We've had too much of the bad." Carlo stood, tucked the book, papers inside, beneath his arm, and thanked him for being so hospitable—and for remembering him.

From the front steps, Brother Toscano said, "If you see any of the others, tell them to visit." He looked out across the piazza. "Nothing changed at this place for years. Students came and went without any serious mishap or disruption. Then the war began. It didn't destroy the building, for which I'm thankful, but it destroyed everything else."

As Carlo walked away, he looked at the letter. It was from Miss Donovan. He couldn't wait to read it, so he sat down on a stone wall and tore it open. It was dated August 10, 1917, more than a year ago.

Dear Carlo,

I hope you are well. I often wonder about you and pray you're in a place of safety—if such a place exists. I should have written more frequently. I'm afraid I'm a bit of a procrastinator. It's a secret I keep from my students—I don't like them to know my flaws.

For a time I thought I might move to a town that wasn't

quite so small. But some minerals used in the manufacture of weaponry were discovered in this area, so I have more students than ever, almost enough to hire a second teacher. Imagine that!

I guess you know your brother Joe is in England. Sal says he wasn't involved in the fighting and should be coming home soon. You must be proud to be an uncle. I saw little Elsie only yesterday. She is delightful and her father dotes on her, as indeed he should.

Did you hear that the state of Colorado has outlawed the sale of liquor? Your brothers' saloon has now become a diner and Sal is learning to cook.

He looked up from the page. So Joe was in the service. It was strange to know that he had crossed the ocean but might already be on his way back home. They would have a lot to talk about when he saw him again. If he'd known this earlier, he might have tried to get to England to see him.

And he had a niece! Such a great deal had changed without him knowing. The saloon had become a diner! His niece's name was Elsie! Suddenly, all he wanted to do was return to Colorado. Teresa would go with him and he would no longer feel as if the last four years had been without meaning. The purpose of his time here had been to meet her and marry her and take her home.

Seven Years

When she was next at the horse hospital, Hawksley told her he was planning to move all operations to Udine. He said, "Our new facility there will be better equipped. It's going to have dipping vats to treat the horses for mange. It will have space for more animals, and my ambition is to have a hydraulic operating table like one I saw in France."

She didn't want him to leave. When she'd started

working there, she hadn't been sure she could tolerate being in the company of so many helpless creatures in distress. But now that she had seen the amount of good she could do, she wanted to continue. She was learning a great deal and took pride in her ability to work with the mules. They were sometimes considered less valuable than horses—viewed as machines rather than living creatures. And yet the war had proven them to be the noblest of beings. They had tolerated extreme weather, carried huge loads, and walked into torrents of enemy gunfire without wavering, without bolting or refusing to proceed. Her current favorite was one the color of chocolate whose lips twitched with pleasure whenever she scratched its neck.

"Will there come a day when places like this aren't needed?" Teresa asked.

Hawksley scoffed. "Look around you. It's true there are fewer life-threatening wounds than before. But we're still seeing lameness, parasites, infected harness galls, gas-damaged lungs." He paused to survey the hospital grounds and Teresa followed his gaze. "Many are simply starving when they come to us. That won't end anytime soon."

"The stable hand at the house where I work might know how to get more fodder," Teresa said.

"The fellow who diagnosed the case of lockjaw?"

"Yes."

"Please ask him. He seemed like a good man."

This time when she went to see Luca, he appeared slightly less forlorn. He said he knew a farmer who had hay for sale, and that although the asking price would be twice what it had been before the war, he'd get the best deal he could. "There's not much for me to do here," he added, motioning to the empty Benedetti stables, "so I might as well help. The

Signora won't be wanting any more horses. They belonged to her husband. She'll buy another motorcar instead."

Their business concluded, Teresa started to leave, then turned back. "I have a question. That night, after I delivered the message, I came upon a place in the forest where there were a dozen or more dead men, all in a bloody pile, most of them shot in the head." She continued, telling him about the man who was still alive and how she was detained by the police until it was too late to send help. Finally, she said, "My question is this: Who were those men and what happened to them? I asked Rodolfo but he refused to say. It's as if the part of him that was Isaac Venturi no longer exists."

For a time Luca remained silent and she thought he might be gauging how much to reveal. Then he spoke: "It was a terrible thing. That unit, the one you delivered the message to, didn't know how far the enemy had advanced. They also didn't know about the ambush being set for them. So a small patrol was sent ahead, as was customary. All the members of that patrol were captured and executed. But you arrived in time to warn the remaining force. If not for you, the entire unit would have been massacred."

"Luca, I was late. I didn't go the way I was supposed to. The ones who were killed, what you call a small patrol, must have left just before I arrived. Don't I bear some responsibility for their deaths? At least for the man I couldn't help." These thoughts had been in the back of her mind since the night she'd ridden into the mountains. Now, for the first time, she was putting them into words.

He took her hands in his. "No. You're not responsible. You didn't know what would happen. How could you have known?" He grimaced. "The war was responsible. The men who made the war."

She tried again to convince him of her guilt. "I should

have taken the route Rodolfo told me to. He said to follow his instructions exactly. My mother always says I'm headstrong, that I insist on doing things my own way."

"It was no mistake. You did what you thought best."

"I also lost Coniglio," she said. "You should at least blame me for that."

Luca shook his head. His expression seemed to say, *You know so little about the events of which you speak.* "When I left Coniglio, I knew you'd care for him. You used him to complete an important mission. He was stolen by men who'd have been happy to kill you if you'd given them a reason. None of it was your fault." He paused for a moment. "What you're feeling is a common thing. You want an explanation for something that can't be explained. I saw four hundred men buried by a single avalanche. Maybe I should have been able to stop it. Maybe I should have told them to take a safer trail. But I did not."

That night when Carlo visited, she told him she was tired and preferred to stay in by herself. He looked a bit hurt but she promised they could be together the following day. Then she went up to her little room, stood at the window, and watched the sky go dark. She understood what Luca had said; it was the way of war that such things occurred. One decision leads to another and outcomes can't be predicted. However, did that mean no one was ever to blame? Even if they agreed that the politicians and generals, the ones who started it all, were most at fault, she believed, as her mother had taught her, she should acknowledge her own mistakes.

The next day, as she began feeding and watering the horses and mules, she did her best to put everything out of her mind except the work at hand. When Leonard Hawksley came around, she told him Luca would help get more hay. "He knows of a farmer with some to sell. He says it will be expensive . . ."

"We have no choice. Enough food is among the best remedies we can offer. If we don't have that, we might as well give up."

A while later, as she was continuing her work, she noticed a man standing some distance away. He was staring at her as though he knew her or wanted to ask a question. The dog Teresa was caring for had come to think of himself as the hospital guard and now stood beside her barking. "Hush," she said as the man approached. Suddenly, she realized who it was—her father, dressed in the unmatched clothes of a demobilized soldier, his hands hanging at his sides.

"What are you doing here?" she asked incredulously.

"I've come to see you. It took me a while to find you but now here I am."

He looked very different from how she remembered him. He was thinner, almost emaciated. His cheeks were hollow and his hair had gone gray. "Where have you been?" she asked.

"Many different places. Have you heard of the fighting at the Isonzo River? I was there. What about the Battle of Mount Ortigara? I was there, too. Before that—well, I can tell you over a glass of wine. I've been gone for—"

"Seven years."

"Yes, I guess that's right."

"I don't want a glass of wine." She was thinking, *What is it that made you care to find me? Was it the war or something else? And do you think I'm suddenly pleased to see you? No, I am not.*

"I'm on my way to visit your mother. You should come home with me."

"I'm too busy here. And I will tell you, she won't want to see you either."

"How do you know?"

"I know."

It was clear he was taken aback by her outspokenness.

He'd expected her to welcome him or at least obey him and follow him home.

"What is it you're doing here?" He gestured at the horses and mules, the stables and paddock beyond.

"Caring for animals wounded in the war."

He scratched his head and muttered, "I see. But why?"

The question didn't deserve an answer. "I told you, I'm busy."

Still, he didn't leave. "How much are they paying you? I could use a little money if you have any to spare."

"I'm sorry you had to be part of the fighting. I'm sure it was dreadful. But I can't talk anymore."

"I think you owe it to your father to be a good girl and do as I ask."

This time she chose only to shake her head. How strange it was to see him like this. He might as well have died and come back to haunt her. After observing her for a moment longer, he shrugged and walked away.

A Bright Picture

Miss Donovan's letter had confirmed that there were good things waiting for him at home. He would write to his brothers and ask to be made a partner in the saloon. Or rather the diner. He was confident they'd agree. Now that his father had died, there was nothing to keep him here. To keep him and Teresa here. Miss Donovan said Sal was learning to cook. Who better than Teresa to teach him?

He washed up and combed his hair. A few days ago he had purchased a new shirt from a shop that had just reopened. He'd wear it tonight. Maneuvering his injured arm into a sleeve was becoming easier with time. One of the other fellows at the boardinghouse saw him getting ready and offered him some bay rum. "Put this on your face," he said. "It will cause her to lift her skirts and—"

"Shut your mouth," Carlo said. "She's going to be my wife."

When he was dressed, he checked himself in the mirror and then walked across town to the Benedetti house. He thought a straightforward approach would be best. "I would like to marry you," or "I've come to ask you to be my wife." He planned to begin speaking as soon as he saw her. Otherwise he might lose his nerve.

Along the way he noticed that every trace of the Habsburg military was gone. Now all the vehicles were civilian, save for a few belonging to the Italian and British armies. The signs on businesses and those showing the names of streets were being changed back to Italian. There was still plenty of cleaning and repair work to be done, but Trento was no longer a fortress zone. He'd hardly noticed it happening.

At the same time, the influenza was spreading. One of the buildings that had been converted to a hospital at the beginning of the war remained a hospital. Some of the tents that had been erected to accommodate the wounded still stood. Ambulances were coming and going and medical personnel could be seen moving about.

Before he approached the Benedetti villa, he paused to collect himself. It was a perfect evening for a walk in the garden, so he'd ask her to join him there. When he reached the entrance, Rodolfo was about to go inside. Carlo said, "Would you please tell Teresa her friend is waiting?" As expected, Rodolfo threw him a look of disgust but Carlo was confident he'd deliver the message, for Teresa if not for him.

He felt intensely conscious of his body, of how he was standing and what he was doing with his hands. Teresa had said she liked how tall he was, so lately, instead of slouching, he'd been attempting to stand up straight. He watched the house, waiting for her to emerge. She would know something out of the ordinary was about to happen. She'd see it on his face.

Suddenly, there she was, coming out the door, down the stairs, and into the garden, wearing her apron and brushing flour from her hands. "What are you doing out here?" she said, laughing, "You know, if you knock, we'll let you in."

"I have a question for you." He waited until she was standing before him to continue. She still looked amused; something humorous must have been happening inside the house. He took a breath and spoke: "Would you go to America with me? As my wife?"

Her expression changed and he knew at once he'd made a mistake. He'd been too abrupt. For the first time since he'd known her, she was unable to look him in the eye. He did his best to recover because he had no choice: "Of course you'll need time to consider it. I promise I can make a good living there if that's what you're worried about."

As he tried to think of what else to say, it occurred to him she might not want to leave her mother. His own father's death had released him. It was a harsh way of putting it, but it was true. Maybe he should offer to take her mother with them—no, not yet, that could come out wrong. There were times one should simply stop talking.

She met his gaze. "I will consider it," she said. "I'll have an answer for you soon. I promise not to make you wait."

"If there's something holding you back, please tell me. We'll overcome any obstacles. We can . . ." Again he stopped himself. He felt awkward. He should have rehearsed more.

"You know I haven't a dowry. Nothing at all."

"Dowry? In America, girls don't need dowries. You can forget about that."

"Allow me a few days," she said, her voice measured. "Don't take it as a bad sign. Take it as a sign of my respect. Now let's go inside." She leaned forward and kissed him, which somehow made him sad.

Throughout the meal and afterward, Teresa kept herself busy and at a distance from him. The one named Luca, ordinarily reticent, talked about how Italy was being treated in the peace talks in Paris—according to him, the Allies were breaking many of the promises they'd made during the war. Frau Merz said, "The Americans are running things now," and threw Carlo a disapproving glance, as if it were somehow his fault. He didn't argue with them. He'd never cared about politics and didn't know enough to question their opinions. They all sounded well informed. Perhaps you paid more attention when the destiny of your own country was in another country's hands.

Again tonight Teresa whispered to him that she wanted to be alone. But this time there was a good reason. She had an important decision to make. Carlo couldn't bring himself to believe she'd say no. He'd come to feel he and Teresa were meant to be together. Now that he had asked the question, she would realize how much he cared for her and consider the advantages of moving to America. With such a bright picture in her mind of their new life together, she would willingly agree.

On his way back to the boardinghouse, he encountered Ismail, the Bosnian he'd met when he first returned to town. Carlo could tell he was drunk by the meandering way he walked.

"I know you," Ismail said. "The American. The engineer. What the hell have you been doing with yourself?"

Carlo didn't want to stop, but Ismail was blocking the way. One never knew about a man in his condition. He might punch you in the nose or share some strongly held opinion or throw his arms around you and say you'd be friends for life.

"I've just been to visit my girl," Carlo said.

"Your girl? I wish I had one. The Italian girls are pretty, don't you think?"

"Yes. Yes I do."

"Come with me, I'll buy you a drink. Wait, I don't feel so good." He crumpled slowly to the cobblestones and became a motionless heap. In memory and in honor of Alexi, and ignoring the pain in his arm, Carlo hoisted the Bosnian onto his back and carried him to a greensward beneath a chestnut tree. As he laid him on the grass, he said, "Sleep well, my friend."

Ti Amo

So he had done it, he had asked. The idea of starting over appealed to her. She began to visualize all the parts of such a transformation: the wedding ceremony, the packing of her things, the painful farewell to her mother, and the trip to Venice, or perhaps Genoa, to board a ship. She had never seen the ocean. Then across America to Colorado, which Carlo said was ten times farther than Trento to Rome and possibly more. Other people had made the journey, so why not her?

Although leaving her mother would be difficult, she'd understand. Actually, more than that; she'd encourage it. Teresa could hear her voice: "Go. Don't worry about me. You're fortunate to have met such a man. Everyone wants to go to America. You could do much worse."

Later that evening she began to feel poorly. She had been working hard at the horse hospital and equally hard in the kitchen, so maybe it was only fatigue. Unless it was the influenza. Everyone seemed to know someone who'd had it. She'd even heard of a family where two children died. Not that she considered herself in danger. She'd fallen ill and recovered without difficulty many times before. However, in the middle of the night she began sweating and shivering, and by morning her body ached so badly, she was unable to get out of bed.

Having noticed her absence, Frau Merz came to her room. "I'm sorry, I'm not feeling well," Teresa explained.

"You poor child," she said and went to get her some soup. But Teresa couldn't eat the soup. She could scarcely lift her head. She slept and dreamed about the mules. They ran in circles, seemingly trapped in that motion and unable to break away. Beyond the mules a building was on fire and people were calling for help. When she awoke, it took her a moment to figure out where she was.

Frau Merz came again and then Luca and Rodolfo and finally Carlo, who sat attentively beside her on a straight-backed chair. She smiled weakly and was embarrassed about her appearance. "Don't look at me," she said, and later, "Thank you for coming, now please go away." As he started to get up, she said, "No, stay. I don't know what I'm saying." Then she went back to sleep.

The next time she opened her eyes, Luca had replaced Carlo. "Please go see Signor Hawksley and explain why I've been absent," she said. "Tell him I'll be back as soon as I can."

When Frau Merz returned, she informed Teresa that Rosa had fallen ill as well, and that the Benedetti family had gone to a house in the country, intending to stay there until the contagion passed. "So it's just us again," she said.

Suddenly, Teresa felt it necessary to tell her about Carlo's proposal.

"I'm not surprised," Frau Merz said. "Has he met your mother?"

"Briefly. But now we'll go see her together. I won't do anything unless she approves."

"What about your father? Can you find him? A girl should not get married without her father's consent."

She hadn't told Frau Merz about her father's recent visit. There would be too many questions. As a woman of her generation, Frau Merz might even urge her to give her father a second chance.

"My father has nothing to do with this," Teresa said.

Frau Merz leaned forward, as if to share a confidence. "You know, I'm not married and haven't suffered from the lack. Girls think their lives are over if they can't capture a man."

"I didn't capture him," she said. Feeling faint, she closed her eyes and turned away.

She should have asked Luca to inquire about the black dog. Surely Nico would think to feed him.

The next day Carlo was seated beside her again. She felt a little better. The fever seemed to have broken.

"How long have you been here?" she asked.

"Since yesterday. I came after work."

"You were here all night?"

"Except when I went to the kitchen to get something to eat." He took her hand. "What can I do to help?"

"I'm finally getting hungry . . ."

He disappeared and returned with some of Frau Merz's soup. This time she devoured it. He disappeared a second time and returned with a cool cloth to place on her forehead.

They sat for a while in silence. Teresa liked having him there. He didn't need to talk; his presence alone was enough. Finally, he said, "I have to go back to work."

"You'll be exhausted."

"I'm used to it. In the army I never got a full night's sleep."

He took her hand again, pressed it to his lips, and said, "I expect you'll be on your feet again soon."

Not long after Carlo left, Teresa heard something happening down the hall—doors opening and shutting and the muffled voices of Frau Merz, one of the new girls, and even Rodolfo. A few minutes later, when Frau Merz looked in on her, Teresa asked for an explanation.

"Rosa isn't doing well," Frau Merz said. "I hope she doesn't lose her baby."

Teresa wanted to get up and help but Frau Merz said it wasn't necessary; she ought to stay in bed. After that, she had difficulty resting but eventually she fell asleep. The next morning Frau Merz came with tragic news: Rosa and her unborn child had died.

Teresa wept for Rosa and the child and thought about how brave Rosa had been to go away with her soldier and even more brave to come back of her own accord. They hadn't always agreed about everything, but there was much about Rosa to admire. She had strong beliefs and wasn't afraid to defend them. She never avoided hard work.

Rosa was to be buried the following day. As with Carlo's father, it seemed to happen very quickly, and Teresa wondered if that was because of the influenza, this rush to put the body in the ground. Since Rosa had no status in the parish, the service was to be a simple graveside ceremony. Teresa wanted to attend but Frau Merz insisted she stay home and rest. So she mourned Rosa from her bed.

When she was finally strong enough, Teresa returned to the horse hospital, greeting the black dog as soon as she arrived. Upon seeing her, Leonard Hawksley said, "I was hoping you'd come back. Your friend told me you had recovered, but I didn't know if you'd want to keep working here."

"Of course I will. Nothing has changed. I was ill. Now I'm feeling much better—almost as good as before."

He explained he was about to go away, to move some horses from Castelfranco to Udine, and added, "It will be a great help to have you here while I'm gone." She was surprised and pleased to hear him express such confidence in her. Their conversation over, she was beginning to consider which stall to clean first when an idea came to her.

"Suppose I were to leave the villa and only work here. Could you pay me anything? I wouldn't need much. An allowance for food perhaps."

She was surprised to hear herself make such a proposal. It wasn't something she'd planned. She hoped she wasn't embarrassing herself. What if she was overestimating the value Hawksley placed on her work?

He looked perplexed, then pleased. "That would be very useful. It's not easy work but you know that. The pay would be irregular, as it depends on donations. I wouldn't let you go hungry."

She was overcome, unexpectedly so, by a feeling of relief. From her first day working with Hawksley, she'd felt useful and at home. And she didn't doubt that he would make sure she was fed, just as the animals were fed, and that would be enough.

She cleaned a stall and helped Nico treat a case of thrush. She still felt a little weak from the illness. It would be another day or two before she was fully herself.

But what about Carlo? He wanted her to go to America with him. If she chose to work with Hawksley, that couldn't happen. She supposed she could tell him she'd marry him if he was willing to remain in Italy, but she knew how much he wanted to go home. If he stayed here, she would always feel that she really had "captured" him and kept him from doing as he wished. He ought to return to Colorado and find a wife there. She wasn't exceptional, someone he couldn't replace.

Until then she'd assumed that, after some anxious hours of deliberation, she'd end up accepting Carlo's proposal. What changed was that she'd taken the mules into consideration. Many people would say, "How ridiculous," but that didn't prevent it from being true. It had begun to occur to her that working with Hawksley was part of a larger idea. On several occasions, the korporal had said that the world would be *different* after the war. Although she'd never been precisely sure what he meant, she thought that working with Hawksley and the animals could, for her at least, mark the beginning of a life unlike the one she'd always thought was awaiting her. A different kind of life within a different kind of world.

When she was finished with the horses, she told Nico she was leaving early and went to find Carlo. It was time to give him an answer. She'd made him wait long enough.

He had shown her where he was living—the exterior, not the interior, which he said was rather squalid, filled as it was with young men. Determined but also fearful, she approached the door and knocked. Beside the entrance was a lavender bush that seemed slightly out of place.

When a boy answered, she said, "Excuse me, I'm looking for someone who lives here. Carlo Coltura." The boy, who was younger than Carlo, studied her briefly, then nodded and ran back inside. A moment later Carlo appeared.

"You look well," he said. "Much better."

"Thanks to you. Every time I opened my eyes, you were sitting at my bedside."

He shrugged. "You should also give some credit to Frau Merz's soup."

She could have made a comment about the soup, but

feeling she was losing her nerve, she forced herself to proceed. "I've come to tell you my decision," she said.

Teresa kept her explanation simple. The more details about her thinking she provided, the more likely he'd try to change her mind and say something she didn't want to hear. At some point in the future she could write him a letter and try to explain her decision. For now it was best to say, "I'm sorry but I can't."

"It's because you've been sick," he said. "You're not thinking straight."

"Oh, Carlo. It has nothing to do with being sick. I've thought about it endlessly and I'm sure this is what I must do."

"Your mother could go with us . . ."

She shook her head firmly. "That wouldn't make any difference. I want to continue working for Signor Hawksley. And you want to go home."

He didn't respond. She was afraid he was silent because he was thinking about how to make her change her mind. Finally, he said, "Ti amo." His accent was perfect.

"Oh, Carlo," she said again, and then, "Grazie," which she realized sounded rather cold. He embraced her awkwardly, stepped away, and went back inside.

She returned to the hospital and stayed until well after dark. As the clamor from the streets diminished, she began to hear the animal sounds, the snorting and coughing and shuffling about as they settled down to sleep. During the war there had been weeks upon weeks when the sounds of shelling filled the night. Now, at least in this corner of Trento, the loudest noise came from the heavy breathing of a mule.

The next morning she told Frau Merz about her rejection of Carlo's proposal. Teresa knew she'd give an honest appraisal and not attempt to spare her feelings.

Frau Merz looked up from her work. "You don't want to go to America? Can he really be that bad?"

"But you said—"

"That was different. I'd marry a blind man if he'd take me to America. I'd marry a drunk. Go tell him you made a mistake."

Teresa was taken aback by her vehemence and certainty. Should she have accepted Carlo's proposal? He definitely wasn't blind or drunk.

Frau Merz continued: "Is there any chance he'll forgive you if you tell him you changed your mind?"

"Yes, I think he would."

"Then go now. If you don't, you alone will be responsible for ruining both your lives."

Tasting Metal

After Teresa rejected him, he felt empty, worthless, and very tired. He didn't think she'd want him to make any heroic efforts to change her decision. That was all right. He would put her out of his mind. At least he'd try. It might not be so easy. Then again, maybe he should return to the Benedetti villa and offer a better argument. *I will care for you. Think about how well we get along. Ti Amo. Please reconsider.* But when he said the words in his head, they sounded false. He knew what she'd say and didn't want to hear it: "I'm sorry, Carlo, I've given you my answer." *Well*, he thought, *men are rejected by women all the time. Don't make too much of it.* He wished Alexi were there to give him some advice.

The following morning he prepared to leave. It seemed to him that the best way to curb the pain of rejection was to move ahead. Any reservations he'd had about returning to Colorado disappeared, and he couldn't wait to be crossing the ocean. Packing his belongings was easy. In a worn satchel he'd saved from the refuse bin at the rooming house, he stowed a few items of clothing, a comb, a piece of soap, a bottle of water, the book about trees, and the packet of letters Teresa had written to him but never sent. He considered disposing of the letters, but they took up no space and weighed almost nothing. His money he hid in his boot. One of the other men at the rooming house told him he'd be more likely to find a ship in Venice than Genoa, so he began walking east. He thought he had enough money for a ticket. If not, he'd find another job.

It didn't seem fair that he had survived while Florian and Alexi had not. Probably not Vitale either. Yes, he was now part of a bewildered and undeserving minority, those who'd survived without knowing why. What had he done to merit more time on Earth? He'd intended to write to Vitale's father but hadn't done so. This might be an instance when it was better not to know the truth.

It was a pleasant day for walking, cool but not cold, with no sign of rain. However, before he'd gone very far, he began to feel weak. He sat on a stone wall and wiped his brow. He wasn't hungry. His mouth tasted of metal. Although it might be nothing, he had to consider the possibility of influenza. Not only had he spent hours by Teresa's bedside, but one boy at the rooming house had gone off to the hospital and another had become so ill, his uncle had come to take him away.

After a brief rest, he set out again, reminding himself that when he was in the mountains, he'd walked for days on end with a heavy pack on his back.

Early this morning he had been filled with optimism about his journey, about going home. Now, however, what he really wanted to do was lie down in the weeds and sleep. If he hadn't watched Teresa during her illness, hadn't seen how crowded the hospital in Trento had become—crowded to overflowing—he wouldn't worry. But what if he got too sick to continue on?

Suddenly thirsty, he removed his water from the satchel and took a drink. He was a long way from Venice, and if he turned around, he could be back in Trento by midafternoon. Then he could find a bed somewhere, sleep until he was feeling stronger, and start again. Although his place in the rooming house might already have been claimed by someone new, Brother Toscano would surely allow him to stay at the school.

So he began to retrace his steps. As he walked, he thought about Teresa. He couldn't help himself. Even though she had refused to marry him, he was glad he'd cared for her when she was sick. So much of what he'd done during the war had seemed meaningless. When his friends had died, there'd been no way he could help them. He certainly hadn't saved Teresa's life, but sitting beside her through hours of fever and restless sleep, getting her water to drink and soup to eat, making comforting remarks while holding a cold compress on her head, had made him think his actions, his words, his very presence, could be of use. He liked knowing that he could help someone and that he could do it because he wanted to, not because he'd been ordered to or because circumstances left him no choice.

For a time he felt better and considered the possibility that turning back had been a mistake. Then all at once the weakness returned. He was becoming feverish as well and congratulated himself on making the right decision, even as he was annoyed about getting sick. He'd been so ready to go home.

When he reached Trento, he decided to go directly to the cathedral school. Once again it was Brother Toscano who answered the door. At first his face lit up. "Why, it's my friend from Colorado! Did you forget another book?" But his expression quickly changed. "Is something wrong? You don't look well."

Inside, a few boys coming down the stairs stopped halfway and stared. They were obviously new students, and to Carlo, they looked like mere children. Brother Toscano waved them back up the stairs, then took him by the elbow and guided him into the room where they'd had tea only a few days before.

When Carlo was seated, he said, "I'm sorry to bother you again. I was wondering if I could stay here for a few nights. I'm about to leave for America but I'm not quite ready yet."

"Of course. You'll always be welcome here. Although perhaps you ought to see a doctor first. You're very pale. Would you like something to drink? You really don't look well."

Before Carlo could reply, another teacher, one he didn't remember, entered, nodded at Carlo, and whispered something in Brother Toscano's ear.

"I'll be back shortly," Brother Toscano said and followed the other teacher out the door.

Something about Brother Toscano's manner made Carlo think that he'd rather he didn't stay. Who could blame him? He had new students to deal with, and if it was influenza, it wouldn't make sense to allow someone to bring it into the school. He kept tasting metal. Not wanting to be an inconvenience, he picked up his satchel and slipped back outside. For a moment he stood and looked across the piazza toward the duomo, remembering the first time he'd seen it, how awestruck he'd been, and then the day he'd noticed a girl releasing a bird into the sky.

He was feeling very weak, very tired. And it was beginning to get colder. Although he didn't know how to go about seeing a doctor, he did know where the hospital was, the one where Austrian soldiers had been treated that was now being used for patients with influenza. It seemed the logical place to go.

He was having a little trouble breathing. His lungs felt like they were full of wool.

They put him in a room with a dozen other patients. The army barracks, the rooming house, and now this—it seemed he was destined to spend his life in such crowded quarters. He wasn't worried about being sick. He knew he'd recover. After all his time in the army, he was strong, his brothers were waiting for him in Colorado, he would see Miss Donovan again, he would talk to Joe about his time in England, and he would meet Sal's wife and his niece. Yet, as he was picturing his family and friends, such pleasant images, something in his mind turned and he thought about the death of his father, about the death of Rosa and her unborn baby, and he began to feel afraid.

"Only Family Members"

Teresa didn't take Frau Merz's advice. She'd made her decision and had no plans to speak to Carlo again. If Hawksley hadn't invited her to work with him, she might have given the matter more thought, but now she couldn't get the horses and mules out of her mind. She hadn't told Frau Merz she was leaving—another difficult conversation—but intended to do it soon.

Then Luca came to her and said, "I saw your American."

She wasn't sure why he was telling her this. "Did you talk to him?"

"No, it was from a distance. He was on one of the benches outside the hospital, waiting to go inside."

So Luca was, once again roaming the streets, noticing creatures in need of help.

"What do you think is wrong with him?" she asked. "Has he been injured? Could you tell?"

"It was at the place where influenza patients are being cared for. I suppose he's come down with that."

Teresa's stomach began to churn. It had been only two days since she'd given him her answer. After that, she'd assumed he would work a little longer in Trento, then go somewhere to find a boat that would carry him back to America. If one thing had been clear when they parted, it was that he wanted to make his way home.

"I ought to go see him." She said it aloud to make it a commitment. "I'm his closest friend in Trento."

Speaking to him again wouldn't be easy but failing to do so when he was ill—if, in fact, Luca was correct—would be heartless. She could simply pay him a visit as one would any sick friend. It even seemed possible that doing so could make their parting seem less harsh, less abrupt.

The next morning she went to the hospital and searched the benches outside for Carlo, in case he was still there. She'd heard it said they were so busy, it was sometimes days before patients were brought inside. Although she should have expected it, what surprised her was that many of those waiting were women and that there was a wide range of ages, from babes in arms to some who looked older than Rodolfo. There'd been reports that the disease was most virulent in those about her own age. Rosa's age. Carlo's age. Fortunately, most survived.

The last time she was at this place, she was told she spoke the language of the enemy and was dismissed and sent home. Now she took some satisfaction in knowing that she was still speaking the same language and those who objected were gone.

Joining the queue extending out from the door marked "Visitors," she tried to decide what she'd say to Carlo and wondered how she would be received. He would be within his rights to tell her to go away.

The woman in front of her said, "I'm here to see my brother, what about you?"

For an instant she didn't know what to call him. Feeling a bit awkward, she said, "A friend. A soldier. I'm actually not sure he's here."

"I expect they can tell you when you get inside."

"I was sick with it already. The man I'm going to visit helped take care of me, so I want to do what I can for him." It was the first time she'd thought about it that way. She could say something similar when she saw Carlo. "You were kind to me, so when I heard you were in the hospital, I wanted to repay you."

The woman ahead of her said, "My oldest brother was killed at Gorizia. If Enzo dies, I don't know what I'll do."

At last Teresa reached the door and told the attendant Carlo's name.

"What is your relation to him?" the attendant asked.

"A friend," she said again. What else could she call him?

"I'm sorry. Only family members are allowed in."

She thought for a moment. "But there's no one to visit him. His father recently died and the other members of his family live far away."

The attendant studied her, made a note in his book, and let her enter. She was struck by how much things had changed since the end of the war. Military rules of order, always so unbending, had gone away.

She passed two large wards that appeared to be filled with women before coming to the one for men. And there was Carlo, at the end of the row nearest the door.

He was sleeping. Peacefully, it appeared. As there were no chairs, she copied some others who, based on their clothing, seemed to be visitors and perched on the edge of the bed. Nearby, a doctor was speaking to an orderly in a voice too low for her to hear.

She was increasingly nervous. What would she say when he opened his eyes? What would he say in return? Looking around the room, she was thankful that when she'd been ill, she'd been allowed to stay at the villa instead of being sent to a place like this.

Eventually, Carlo began to stir. She turned slightly and placed a hand on his arm so he'd realize she was present. "Carlo," she said, "how are you? Luca told me you might be here."

He lifted his head from the pillow and looked at her. "Oh, it's you. I'm glad you came." Now that he was facing her, she could see how pale he was. Beneath his eyes the skin was almost blue.

"I'm very sorry," Teresa said. "I think I might have given this to you."

He shook his head. "Everyone's getting sick. It isn't a matter of how a person gets it. It's whether they recover or not. I'm sure I'll be better soon."

There was something about his expression that made Teresa think he didn't entirely believe his own words.

"I was on my way to Venice to find a ship that could take me to America," he continued. "But then I started feeling poorly, so I turned around and came back." He smiled as if to imply he'd been the victim of some kind of joke.

"Terrible luck," she said, smiling as well to show she understood.

"I *hope* I get better. Just before you arrived, they took some fellow out of here. I suppose you can never be sure."

Uncertain of how to respond, she spent a minute

straightening the light blanket covering him and helped him adjust his pillow.

"How are the mules?" he asked. She could see he was working at being cheerful.

"Oh, most of them are doing well." She didn't tell him Signor Hawksley was moving to Udine and that she planned to go with him. There was no reason to do so.

Seeing him like this was confusing. Maybe Frau Merz was right and she should accept his proposal. Perhaps she'd said no to him because she lacked courage. Going to America wouldn't be easy. Following Signor Hawksley wouldn't be easy either, but it didn't involve crossing the ocean and leaving her mother and all she knew behind.

She sat for a while as Carlo dozed. Then a nurse came by and told her it was time to go.

Coming awake, Carlo said, "I'd like her to stay," but when the nurse shook her head, he didn't argue. "I understand. Teresa, thank you for coming. When I opened my eyes, I was surprised to see you sitting here."

"I promise to come back tomorrow. We can talk more then."

Once outside, she realized how warm it had been in the ward. She wished she could speak to her mother. She always gave her good advice. Was it really a lack of bravery that had prevented her from agreeing to marry him? Maybe the brave thing was to do what she really wanted to do, not what others thought she ought to do. On the other hand, she could make several people happy—Carlo, Frau Merz, and yes, her mother—if she went to America with Carlo. So why was it so difficult to decide?

She returned to the villa, helped Frau Merz for the rest of the afternoon and evening, and then went up to her room. Four days ago, she'd been satisfied with her choice, but now, here she was, filled with uncertainty. She hoped she could fall asleep.

When she reached the hospital the next day and said Carlo's name, she was told to step aside and wait. She wondered if the attendant was going to change his mind about admitting her. But soon a doctor approached and led her to an alcove a few steps down the hall.

Before Teresa could understand what was happening, the doctor began talking about hemorrhages, hemorrhages of the lungs, multiple hemorrhages that couldn't be stopped occurring halfway through the night. He said, "I'm terribly sorry. With this illness, a patient's condition can deteriorate quickly. When it happens, there's little we can do."

For a moment she couldn't speak. Then, with tears streaming down her face, she said, "Now he'll never get home."

The doctor didn't ask her to explain. He stood with her for a bit longer, but he had already begun to step away and she knew he had work to do. When she asked if she could see Carlo, the doctor said his body had been moved to the morgue and she could find it there.

A Name and a Story

Carlo could have been buried in Trento but Teresa knew at once he ought to lie beside his father. That he and his father hadn't gotten on well mattered less than that he shouldn't be alone. Frau Merz knew whom to contact to get the body released to Teresa's custody, Rodolfo would make a casket, and Luca knew someone with a lorry who could take the body and casket to Ulfano. Teresa could ride along. She never would have imagined she'd end up as Carlo's closest relation, the one responsible for making sure he was cared for after he died.

Since Teresa had taken responsibility for Carlo's burial,

she also received his personal effects. There was a book in English with beautiful illustrations of trees, the letters she'd written to him, some letters from his brothers and the teacher he'd revered, and the tattered documents that showed him to have been an American citizen, as well as those that showed him to have been a soldier in the Austrian army—documents, that is, that traced the strange path he'd followed. She would wrap it all up and go to the post office to ask how it could be sent to Colorado. She almost removed the letters she'd written because she was a little embarrassed by them. But they belonged to Carlo, so she would send them on.

In Ulfano, Don Tomasi said a funeral mass in the small church. In addition to Teresa and her mother, there were a dozen others in attendance, most of them because they'd known Carlo's father. When the mass was over, they all climbed the path up to the cemetery that was cut into the mountainside some distance above the village. It was an inconvenient location, but in places like Ulfano it wasn't easy to find flat ground. The steepness of the trail meant that the pallbearers were always the parish's strongest men.

The day before, when Teresa arrived in Ulfano and told her mother about Carlo's death, she thought she might have to remind her who he was. After all, the last time they'd discussed him, he hadn't even returned to Trento from the war. But without a moment's pause, her mother said, "So first Angelo Coltura dies and now his son. Such a tragedy. They probably should have stayed in America. They'd have been safer there."

Teresa also asked about her father: "Did Papa come to see you?"

"Yes. He said he spoke with you. He told me you thought I should take him back."

"That's not true, I didn't . . ." She was preparing to be

indignant but the look on her mother's face told her not to bother.

"I know. You wouldn't say such a thing. Although I'm sure he hoped you would and went to see you for that reason." Her mother's eyes narrowed briefly and Teresa guessed she was considering what other schemes her husband might have hoped to employ. "I told him I didn't believe him and never wanted to see him again."

"What happened then?"

"He said he didn't like the work you're doing. With the horses. He said, 'Who does she think she is, St. Francis?'"

"What did you say?"

"I should have said, 'Better a saint than a sinner,' but my mind didn't work that fast. Instead, I told him to shut his stupid mouth and get out."

"That's all it took?" She wished she'd been there. It would have been satisfying to watch.

"That's all. I'd have used a pitchfork if I had to. He called me a few choice names and wandered up the street."

"Is he still in the village?"

"I think he stayed for a couple of days. Someone told me he got drunk. Then he disappeared. Maybe he's gone back to Rome."

Now, as Don Tomasi spoke, Teresa shivered in the icy wind and found herself thinking about the cemetery in Colorado where Carlo's mother was buried. When he'd described it to her, she had thought it sounded like the very place she was now standing. Both bleak and beautiful, on a high point overlooking the village—or camp, as Carlo called it.

Since Carlo's death, Teresa had experienced many different emotions. She blamed herself for giving him the disease and she wished she'd tried harder to stay with him at the hospital, even through the night. She wished she could have said she'd accompany him to Colorado without it being a lie. She almost wished Signor Hawksley had rejected her offer to work with the horses and mules. Then she could have said yes to Carlo. And even though it made no sense, the thought passed through her mind that if she'd accepted Carlo's proposal, he wouldn't have gotten sick.

After the ceremony was over and they were making their way back down to the village, her mother whispered, "It might sound disrespectful, but putting people in the ground is one thing Tomasi does well."

That evening, as Teresa ate some of her mother's stew, she decided it was now time to reveal her intention to go to Udine to work with Leonard Hawksley.

"Do you remember the Englishman I told you about? Signor Hawksley?"

"Yes. I hope working for him hasn't put you on the bad side of Frau Merz."

"Don't worry, I'm not on her bad side," she said. And then, "He's opened another hospital for injured animals in Udine."

Her mother frowned. "Why are you telling me this?"

"Because Signor Hawksley wants me to go there to help."

"So you're following some Englishman to Udine?"

"I wouldn't say following him. I'm going because he's offered me a job."

"Has this Englishman asked you to marry him?"

"No, Mama. You're not listening. Signor Hawksley cares only about his work. I'm learning to treat animals that have been hurt by shrapnel and bullets and barbed wire. I'm learning how to keep diseases from spreading."

Her mother nodded and sighed. The sigh alone was almost enough to make her change her plans.

"Well then, you must write me letters," her mother said. "I was sad when they stopped the mail."

Later, when her mother was dressing for bed, Teresa went outside, walked into the forest, and stood alone in the darkness. One thing she missed when she was in Trento was the smell of the mountains, of larch and spruce and pine, and of the snow fields higher up. Wishing Carlo were with her now, she began to cry.

She stayed in the forest for a long time, mourning Carlo and thinking about what might have been. When she went back inside, the lamp had been extinguished and her mother was asleep. After she moved to Udine, she would return to Ulfano to see her mother as often as she could. When she did, she would go up the trail to the cemetery and visit Carlo there.

In the morning she left for Trento on foot. As she was walking along, she came upon two men headed in the opposite direction. One had a bandage over his eyes and the other was guiding him, though he, too, was damaged, supporting himself with a crutch. Such men were now common and she no longer averted her gaze. Just as she was about to pass them, the sighted one threw out his crutch to block her way.

"You work at the horse hospital, do you not?" he said. "I've seen you with the Englishman."

Teresa nodded. "I'm on my way there now."

"Is it true you welcome all animals? Any kind, of any origin?"

"Yes, all animals, as long as they are injured or ill."

"Even if the horse is German? Even if it was used by the enemy?" He motioned to his friend's bandage and to his leg, conveying the rest of his question without words: And even if that enemy did this?

She replied in the way she'd heard Leonard Hawksley reply to similar questions in the past: "The animals we treat have no nationality. They never chose to fight." Then she stepped around the crutch and walked on.

Tomorrow she would collect the black dog and depart for Udine. She had decided to violate Leonard Hawksley's rule and give the dog a name. It would be a secret one, like the names Luca gave to the horses. Perhaps something amusing like Dormouse. No, that wasn't right for this dog. She would choose another saint. The good thing about saints was they came with a story. Consider Saint Allucio. He was a shepherd in Tuscany. He built shelters for travelers on mountain passes and, if memory served, a bridge over the Arno. He gave money to the poor and performed certain miracles, although she couldn't recall the priest saying what those were. Maybe miracles weren't necessary, simply good works. He liberated captives. He healed the infirm and brought an end to a war between two city-states.